REDEEMED

RACHAEL DUNCAN

Redeemed
Rachael Duncan

CKN Christian Publishing
An Imprint of Wolfpack Publishing
6032 Wheat Penny Avenue
Las Vegas, NV 89122

Paperback Edition

Library of Congress Control Number: 2018964380

REDEEMED

Chapter 1

ASHAMED

The night air was warm, deliciously fresh, carrying the tantalizing scent of freshly baked bread, vine-ripened grapes, plump, juicy figs, and lustrous Mediterranean olives, as well as a vast array of other desirable fruits, vegetables, and fine delicacies of which the ancient land of Moab could boast. It was quite a wedding feast indeed – a presumptuous display of wealth and lack of want, enough to turn most of the Moabite women present slightly green with suppressed envy, enough for the young men to murmur brief remarks of admiration for the bride's successful father, and enough for the older biddies to utter whispered gossip about such frivolous waste and the vain, pompous show of wealth. Despite such thoughts, everyone attending this glorious wedding feast wore their brightest smiles and very best faces.

Gathered around a large, raging bonfire, the guests danced and sang, shifted and swayed to the joyous beat of the tambourines, the lyres, the harps, and the drums. Many of the young women danced gracefully and skillfully, smiling coyly beneath tilted lashes as their men watched them with admiring eyes. The low rumble of many deep voices conversing, along with the roar of the bonfire and the mesmerizing beat of the drums was enchanting, awe-inspiring.

One beautiful young woman seemed particularly lost in the magic of it all, seated quietly on a silken cushion before the blazing flames, which cast mysterious shadows that danced across her slender frame. Her dark eyes were bright with interest and maybe even passion, as she watched the women dance and the men clap in perfect time, as little children giggled and bumped into the swirling skirts and busy legs of their young mothers, as the older men chuckled and the older women watched with disapproving scowls. Clothed in rich scarlet and purple cloth and golden thread, this young woman looked as though she were made for grand times such as these. Her features were exotic and quite striking, with slim, dark brows that arched gracefully above deep, inquisitive brown eyes, thick, lusty black lashes, rose-colored lips that framed a stunning smile, and soft ivory skin that was coveted and rare due to the brutal, unforgiving Middle Eastern sun. There was a soft glow, a radiant purity, about this woman, for the kind of beauty she possessed came not from countless hours of primping or self-improvement– as was the case with many Moabite women – but instead from the burning intensity of a beautiful, quiet spirit within. She did not seem aware of her striking appearance at all, which made her all the more innocent, sweet, attractive.

Such grace, such ease with which they move and spin, the woman thought to herself, basking in the wonder of the starlit night. She couldn't help but notice the sheer joy in the eyes of the other young women as they caught the gaze of their husbands among the crowd of onlookers. They seemed so happy, so enraptured by the love and admiration of their men.

I wonder what it must be like, she thought wistfully. *To be truly loved, and to love in return.* She dismissed the thought just as quickly as it had occurred to her. It did one no good to wish or daydream. No, one must instead accept their present circumstance and simply make the best of it.

That is what she had determined to do the day her parents explained to her that she was to marry a man – a man she did not know or love. "For a woman, love comes *after* marriage," her gentle mother had explained at the time, reading the terror in her fourteen-year-old daughter's eyes. "Don't worry, my daughter. All will work out in the end. The man has offered your father a fine bride price. And you get along so well with his mother! That in and of itself is a rare blessing!"

Ah, his mother. Sweet, sweet Naomi! Ruth couldn't help but smile when she thought about her. Her mother-in-law truly was a jewel. She knew very few women who had a decent relationship with their husbands' mothers. But there was just something different about Naomi... She was so unlike any woman that Ruth had ever met. Gentle and kind, with an unexpectedly feisty spirit and a heart of pure gold! Naomi and her husband had traveled far from their own land – an ancient land of many mysterious legends and customs called Bethlehem – and settled in Moab to escape a severe famine. There, in Moab, they had raised their two young sons and quickly adapted to the drastically different lifestyle of a land and a people not their own.

Rather, Naomi's husband Elimelech had adapted quite nicely. Though Naomi stood by her husband and accepted the culture and customs of the Moabites, she still spoke of her homeland with great fondness and the deepest longing.

Oh, how Ruth loved to hear the stories of Naomi's land and of her people! Many a night she had found herself enraptured by the miraculous tales of the Promised Land and the mighty God Who had guided Naomi's ancestors safely home – leading them from the strange and pagan land of Egypt with a pillar of cloud by day and a blazing pillar of fire by night. Though Elimelech and his two sons had eagerly conformed to the ways and customs of a people who had absolutely no regard for their own righteous ways, all these years Naomi had somehow managed to hold herself a safe distance away from such reform. She continued to observe the laws and regulations of her God – at least as much as was possible in a place such as Moab. She continued to pray faithfully to the God that she had served all her life, and continued to recount her beloved tales of His awesome might and power. Though she had been rudely transplanted from the quiet life she had always known and cherished, she had somehow managed to keep the ways and the laws and the customs alive in her heart. Ruth had always admired that about her. Naomi was not afraid to be different. And she wasn't different in the abrasive, radical way of the headstrong, the careless, or the rebellious. She carried her differences with grace and ease, and never once cast judgment upon those who thought differently than she.

Ruth's quiet thoughts were interrupted by the shrill, grating voice of her sister-in-law, Orpah, and she was suddenly reminded that, though her mind and thoughts were elsewhere, she was still there in the presence of many guests at the wedding feast. "Ruth! For heaven's sake, you're missing out on all the fun!"

Ruth laughed as Orpah swooped down and grabbed her by the arm, jerking her to her feet and pulling her towards the circle of dancing women. "Orpah! You know I don't dance..."

"You don't do *a lot* of things! When are you going to start to *live*?" Orpah was still pulling her toward the dancers.

Ruth paused and gazed at the swirling mass of colors – women clad in robes of every hue – rich shades of purple and orange and yellow and green and scarlet. Something within her stirred, a deep longing to belong, to be free... and yet, she held back. She knew she had a place in this world, and as much as she enjoyed the starlit ambiance of this pleasant evening, she knew this was not it.

Orpah continued to tug. "Well? What are you waiting for? Come!"

Ruth shook her head. "You go. I prefer to watch."

"Oh, come on!"

"No, you go."

"Oh, *come*, Ruth! Just try it. Just this once. You'll see what you're missing and scold yourself for cowering behind the others all these years!"

"I'd rather not."

Orpah sighed loudly through her nose. She had never been the graceful one. Though also quite attractive, Orpah's loud mouth, brash nature, and frequent complaints often blinded one to that fact.

"Go on – enjoy yourself and dance to your heart's content," Ruth said kindly. She smiled as she pushed Orpah back in line with the dancers, then returned to her silken cushion, relieved to have escaped the presence of her spoiled and demanding sister-in-law.

"Will you never learn to dance, Ruth?"

Ruth glanced over her shoulder to see her husband Mahlon seated with his back against a tall post, his long legs crossed at the ankles and a golden goblet of wine teetering in one frail hand.

Ruth felt her high spirits failing fast, as they always did in Mahlon's presence. She forced a smile and tried to face him cheerfully. "Perhaps; perhaps not. Certainly not tonight!"

There was an exasperated sigh. "Then I shall ask another question: will you ever cease to disappoint me, Ruth?"

Ruth fought to keep her composure, but her shoulders slumped instinctively and her eyes filled with hurt. "Have I disappointed you, Mahlon?"

Mahlon took a loud swig of wine before tossing the golden goblet aside as carelessly as if it were an old, worn-out sandal. He was obviously intoxicated. Again.

"Have I?" Ruth repeated, trying with all her strength to muster up even the slightest bit of feeling for this man – this man to whom she had been married for nearly ten years! And ten long, weary, disappointing years they had been!

"Don't play games with me, woman!" Mahlon raised his voice shrilly, and several bystanders turned to look upon the scene with scornful eyes.

Ruth felt her cheeks burning crimson with shame and embarrassment. *Not again. Not tonight. Please, not again...*

"What are you looking at? Why are you looking at me?!" Mahlon was nearly shouting now, his eyes blackening in a drunken rage, his words rough and slurred.

Ruth knew better than to try to calm him down when he was intoxicated. She had tried it many times before. All she could do was take the brutal accusations that he would mercilessly fling her way, staggeringly help him find the way home, and, after enduring several hours of slander and ugly shouting, drift off to sleep even as the hot, silent tears stung her face still flushed from the awful humiliation.

How did this ever happen? How did I ever end up in this dreadful situation? Ruth wondered as she rose slowly to her feet and braced herself for yet another embarrassing episode with her irresponsible husband on a night that should have been joyous but instead would turn out to be devastating. Gathering her courage, she walked over to Mahlon and gently offered her hand. "Shall we go home?"

"I DO NOT WISH TO RETURN HOME!" It was much more than a shout this time.

Many of the guests milling about nearby began to look uncomfortable and disturbed. Despite the awkwardness of the moment, Ruth's eyes sparkled. "Perhaps *you* do not wish to return home, but I think the guests might prefer it."

Mahlon took her hand this time. He then jerked her arm forward with much more force than his frail body appeared capable of.

Ruth yelped in shock and pain. Mahlon's face was only inches from hers. She could smell the unpleasant stench of his breath, feel the heat of it on her face. Setting her jaw firmly, she turned her head and looked the other way.

Mahlon gave her arm another violent shake, growling words of protest too slurred for her to understand. Though he could drink himself into oblivion, then lash out and scream and threaten for many unendurable hours and somehow completely forget that it had happened the next day, Ruth could not forget. She would not forget. She would not allow herself to be deceived into trusting someone who, clearly, could never be trusted.

"You let her go, you filthy pig!"

Before Ruth could pull away from Mahlon's angry, grasping fingers – before she could even realize what was happening – she heard a rustling of fabric behind her and a very angry Orpah had knocked Mahlon upside the head with her own golden goblet. Mahlon's eyes went instantly blank, and his lanky body slumped over, unconscious.

Ruth's eyes grew wide with horror as she looked back and forth from her unconscious husband to her overly zealous sister-in-law. "Orpah, how could you..."

Orpah held up a hand. "No need to thank me, Ruth!"

Ruth shook her head emphatically. "But, Orpah, he's..."

"An idiot? Yes, I know."

"Orpah! But what will he do when he wakes up and..."

"Don't worry, Ruth, he won't remember a thing about this in the morning. He never does! Far be it from me to stand by and watch him abuse you like that. Far be it from me!" With one hand on her hip, Orpah *harrumphed* her firm disapproval and, tossing aside her golden weapon, beckoned towards the limp body on the ground. "Let's lift him into a wagon or something and get him home. Chilion can help."

Ruth was still incredulous. "Surely Chilion would not approve of his own wife striking his brother senseless!"

Orpah shrugged. "He was *already* senseless."

Ruth stared at her, silent. She couldn't argue that point. But, *still*! What would Naomi say? She would be horrified, utterly horrified!

Although she would be every bit as horrified by her son's dreadful behavior, Ruth thought sadly as Orpah went to track down her own husband – Mahlon's older brother Chilion – to bring him back to assist in the tricky relocation of his brother.

Ruth sank to the ground beside her husband, trying to avoid the critical stares of prying eyes. She looked intently into the face of the man who claimed to love her. *If only you could be like your mother,* Ruth thought for the millionth time. How could the son of such a wonderful woman turn out to be so irresponsible, so cruel? How could he have so easily forsaken the principles of kindness, of gentleness and responsibility and honor that were so dear to the heart of the woman who had raised him? How could he constantly break the heart of such a gentle woman so callously, so easily, with so little regret? Had he no heart of his own? No conscience? No sense of morality or justice?

Ruth sighed and shook her head. How could he? Being raised up in a place like this, by a father who had turned his back on all that was good, all that was right? In a place where drunkenness and prostitution and crooked dealings were glorified, where unmentionable, illicit acts and rituals were performed and eagerly observed by evil-hungry people every single day, where frightened, innocent children were offered up as sacrifices to satisfy the wicked cravings of false gods and their morbid followers? How could *anyone* expect to grow up in a place like this and not become twisted, immoral, demented?

Ruth knew that she was the exception rather than the rule. For as long as she could remember, she had known that she hadn't belonged here, that something was wrong – terribly wrong – about the ways of the world around her. She had been born with a strong sense of justice, a desire to do right, and a desperation to escape the evil traps and snares that so easily entangled those around her. And so she had spent the first fourteen years of her life stumbling about in a dark and dangerous world, clinging to her own innocence with every ounce of strength that she possessed, hopelessly confused and desperate for someone – *anyone* – to explain to her the conflict raging within her heart, mind, and soul. What was truly *right*? What was truly *wrong*?

Could she trust the fierce instincts that screamed against the dark deeds her young eyes witnessed each and every day? For if the gods her people worshipped were true, then she was hopelessly lost and her conscience was desperately wrong. But something deep, deep down within her innermost being whispered to her that she was safe, that there *was* an answer to be found, that one day her uneasy mind could finally rest knowing that she had discovered the truth.

Then, she met Naomi. Dear, sweet Naomi! Naomi – so unlike the other women of her time. While the rest of the married, middle-aged women spent their spare time engaged in vicious gossip or frequenting the dwellings of greedy male prostitutes or money-hungry fortune-tellers, Naomi immersed herself in the ancient Scriptures of her God, set aside time daily to spend in sweet communion with Him, and devoted herself to being the very best wife and mother she could be. She worked harder than anyone Ruth had ever known – keeping her family clothed, warm, and fed, feeding the animals, minding the endless household chores that most of the Moabite women had long-since abandoned. Ruth had been instantly drawn to Naomi's quiet strength and cheerful work ethic. Like a breath of fresh air permeating a dark, dank, suffocating prison of gloom, Naomi's character shone brighter than the brightest beacon of hope that Ruth's eager eyes had ever seen.

With every spare moment Ruth could find, she would beg her dear mother-in-law to read aloud her sacred writings, to explain their meanings, or to retell one of the exciting stories of old in which her faithful God would once again step in and save His people from complete and utter disaster.

"Do you know what I like most about this God that you serve so faithfully, Naomi?" Ruth had whispered one night, after Naomi had enthusiastically read from an aged, weathered scroll the famous Ten Commandments written by the very Finger of her God so many years before. "That to your God, there is right and there is wrong, and it does not waver or change. His laws are firm and they are for everyone to obey. Here in Moab, everyone does what he or she sees fit – rather, they do what they wish, regardless of whom it may hurt. But your God is not like that. His yes means *yes*, and His no means *no*. And you can depend on Him to remain the same."

"Both yesterday and today and forever!" Naomi had agreed, her eyes shining brightly with the intensity of one who believes in something with all her heart and soul.

It had not taken long for Ruth to realize that Naomi possessed all the wisdom and knowledge that her hungry soul had craved...

Again, Ruth's thoughts were disrupted by shrill cries from the boisterous Orpah. "He's right over here! For heaven's sake, *do* hurry, Chilion!"

Ruth rose slowly to her feet, feeling slightly dizzy from the heavy smoke of the bonfire, the uproarious chattering and laughter of countless wedding guests ringing in her ears, and the disturbing trauma of the evening. She turned to face Orpah and Chilion who were both bounding towards her, her eyes stinging with tears, clasping her hands tightly together to still their anxious trembling.

"Chilion! Thank you for coming, we need your help."

Chilion nodded slightly and stared in disgust at the fallen form of his insolent brother. He was a tall man, much sturdier than his brother Mahlon, and a bit more level-headed. Though he enjoyed the pagan pleasures of Moab every bit as much as his brother did, he had no desire to make a fool of himself in public.

"We have no idea what happened, Chilion," Orpah wailed dramatically, "but when we found him lying here on the ground, we knew that *you* would know what to do!"

Chilion shot Orpah a very skeptical glance, then turned back to Ruth. "What did she do to him?"

Ruth bit her lower lip and nervously averted her gaze, cornered. Chilion knew his wife very well! Too well, in fact. "Um…"

"Never mind that. We'll load him up in the wagon and take him home." Chilion turned and disappeared into the crowd.

"Where is he going?" Ruth asked Orpah, fearful that he would not return.

"He's going to bring the wagon over here," Orpah responded carelessly, adjusting her sheer head-covering and smoothing down her dark hair. "I told him we were going to need it, but he didn't believe me at first when I told him that Mahlon was, um, incapacitated."

Ruth nodded in shame and lowered her eyes.

Orpah noticed Ruth's discomfort and touched her shoulder – an unusual gesture of kindness. "Oh, don't look so discouraged, Ruth. All men have their vices."

Ruth forced a smile. "We all do, I suppose."

Orpah elbowed her in the side and grinned playfully. "Although I must say… of the two brothers, I think *I* got the better end of the deal!"

Ruth smiled again, and this time it was genuine. *That* sounded more like the real Orpah.

Chilion returned a moment later, guiding their underfed gray donkey by the bridle and receiving irritated glances from the guests who were forced to make way for the animal and the broad wagon to which it was harnessed.

Chilion brought the beast to a halt a few feet away from

the young man sprawled out on the dusty ground. He looked to Ruth. "I'll grab him by the shoulders. Ruth, you take his feet."

As Ruth bent to take hold of Mahlon's scrawny ankles, she heard Chilion address Orpah under his breath, "We will talk about this at home."

Orpah cringed.

Chilion knelt behind Mahlon's head, steadying a hand behind each of his brother's bony shoulders. He looked to Ruth, who was already grasping Mahlon's ankles. "You ready?"

Ruth nodded, feeling flushed and mortified as nearby guests snickered and nodded in their direction. How could Mahlon bear to exhibit such shameful conduct time after time, week after week, day after day?

"Alright. One, two, three, lift!"

Ruth lifted with all her might, yet she could barely lift her husband's ankles from the dust. She wondered how on earth she was going to be of any help heaving him into the wagon.

Orpah stood behind their splintering old wagon, bracing herself against the wooden siding as if she were capable of keep the thing from shifting beneath the added weight of its unconscious cargo.

"Higher, Ruth!" Chilion grunted with clenched teeth as he lifted Mahlon's head and shoulders in the direction of the vehicle.

Ruth gave it her best effort and managed to swing Mahlon's feet into the wagon as Chilion simultaneously eased his upper body in. Unfortunately, Mahlon's midsection was sagging and, with his ankles in Ruth's shaking hands and his shoulders in Chilion's, his body dangled like an awkwardly-shaped letter *V* in midair, and his rear slammed into the side of the wagon with a loud *THWUMP!*

Orpah crumpled over in a fit of uproarious laughter as Ruth desperately overcorrected and re-swung her husband's lower half towards the wagon, with the same result.

"In the name of the gods, Ruth, what are you *doing*?" Chilion roughly pushed her aside and shoved his brother's legs into the bed of the wagon. "And *you*!" he shoved an angry finger in Orpah's face, who was still laughing hysterically, tears streaming down her flushed cheeks, "I've heard quite enough from you!"

Orpah cleared her throat and quickly fell silent, but the corners of her eyes were still crinkled with mirth and utter delight.

Ruth knew she would never hear the end of this one.

"Well, it's a good thing he was unconscious for all that!" Orpah stated, her green eyes gleaming with mischief. "When he comes to his senses he's going to wonder why his backside is ten shades of black and blue!"

"Orpah!" Chilion's eyes were clouded over with disgust. "I said *that's enough*. Let us be on our way home."

Chapter 2

A DECISION

Naomi was a lovely lady, though her age was beginning to show. Her hair, once every bit as sleek and black as a raven, was now streaked with gray and often pulled tightly away from her weathered face. With soft eyes that often glowed bright with the sincerest kind of love and affection, a warm, inviting smile, and a very small, feminine stature, she had been blessed with the gift of aging gracefully, despite the pain of being uprooted from her beloved home and, several years later, the agony she must have endured upon the death of her husband, Elimelech. The strain and devastation of such unfavorable circumstances had robbed many a woman of the joys and simple pleasures of life, burying them instead beneath a crushing load of bitterness and distress. But not so for Naomi. Somehow, Naomi had borne such burdens with a grace and a humility that had spoken volumes to young Ruth.

Now, as Ruth sat in silence beside her dear mother-in-law before the glowering, smoldering remains of the fire just outside their humble dwelling, she could hardly bear to see the tear that trickled slowly down Naomi's pale cheek.

The night was still clear, and the stars still glittered magnificently in the inky darkness of the midnight sky. But sadly, the evening had lost every trace of the magic it had once possessed.

Inside the rough-shod, sunbaked mud-and-stone-constructed structure that Ruth and her husband, her brother-in-law, sister-in-law, and Naomi called home, Ruth could hear Chilion and Orpah bickering loudly, along with Mahlon snoring off the immense amount of alcohol he had ingested that evening at the wedding feast. Her spirits had sunk so very low that she feared she would not have the strength to hoist them back up again. With every angry sneer from Chilion, and every desperate, wailing plea from Orpah, and every groggy, inebriated snore from Mahlon that met her sensitive ears, she felt the doom closing in on her, deep, dark, suffocating, threatening to crush her very soul, to squeeze the last bit of vibrant, hopeful life right out of her. Day after day she had battled such mental and emotional assaults, clinging tightly to the hope that one day it would all make sense. Sighing wistfully, Ruth closed her eyes and tried to remind herself of the promises in which she had placed her trust.

"My God is powerful, Ruth, and He has a plan for each of our lives," Naomi had once said. "He has a plan for you, too, my daughter. Trust in Him, and He will not abandon you."

"But, Naomi," Ruth had answered, her soft eyes filled with anxious concern, "how could your God have a plan for *me*? I am not one of His chosen people like you read about in the Holy Scriptures – not an Israelite, as you are." Why, the Israelites even had a label for those who were not included among the chosen few – Gentiles. Ruth had brought this to Naomi's attention as well. And Naomi had merely smiled and readily replied, "And has not my God also demonstrated time and time again that He is full of love and tender mercies? He has indeed! His love is far too great and strong and wide and deep to rest upon a mere few! His love is for *you* too, my dear. This I know, and I can assure you of its truth with the *highest* of confidence!"

For years Ruth had clung to those life-giving words of hope, listening intently to the sacred Scriptures that Naomi read every night before the flickering flames of the fire. Once, the circle around the fire had been very full – with Naomi reading aloud to her entire family. Slowly but surely, however, Mahlon, Chilion, and Orpah had found weak and pathetic excuses to dismiss themselves from the daily obligation of listening to the Words of the Lord, but Ruth would not have missed it for anything in the world. How she longed to know the mighty God of which those precious verses spoke! How she longed for the assurance of knowing that she belonged to Him – that she truly was His child and that she was safe beneath the shadow of His wings.

Now, as she and Naomi sat alone before the fire – the ever faithful pair – and as the tears continued to drop from Naomi's full gray eyes, Ruth wondered if she had the strength to press on. If Naomi – so strong, so immovable, so completely reliant upon the Lord – was starting to despair, how could Ruth ever hope to stand?

Reaching to take Naomi's small, frail hand, Ruth leaned in close to the grieving woman and managed a very weak smile. "Naomi, why do you cry? What a beautiful night to read our dear Scriptures and bask in the glory of the evening! Shall I find the scroll, Naomi?"

Naomi smiled through her tears and squeezed the small

hand resting gently in her own. "Not tonight, my dear. I fear I haven't the strength to read aloud this evening."

Ruth was near despair. How could Naomi refuse her beloved Scriptures at a time as lonely and terrible as this? Ruth knew that she could derive the strength and peace she would need to get through this night and, heaven forbid, many more like it if that was the burden she was meant to carry.

"Come now, Naomi, you know the Scriptures will do both of us much good!" Ruth tried again, her eyes large and hopeful.

Naomi turned to look her daughter-in-law in the face, and actually chuckled. "Oh, child. You remind me of my dear sons when they were but innocent children, pleading for a bedtime story as I rocked them to sleep each night."

Ruth couldn't help but smile at that. "I suppose I feel somewhat as they did, Naomi! Please, may we read again tonight? Even if only a few verses?"

"Oh, my daughter."

"Please?"

Naomi looked slightly peeved, but with one more look at Ruth's desperate, innocent eyes and longing expression, her features softened and her face broke into her usual, kindly smile. Her voice sounded weary, but earnest. "Well, what are you waiting for? Fetch me the scroll!"

Ruth grinned and was instantly on her feet. Naomi watched her as she disappeared into their home, returning a moment later with the dear scroll clenched tightly between trembling fingers.

Naomi reached for the scroll, but Ruth good-naturedly seemed to ignore the gesture. She settled down comfortably across the fire from Naomi, legs tucked up beneath her, and began to unroll the delicate papyrus scroll.

"Well?" Naomi asked curiously. "Aren't you going to pass it to me, dear?"

Ruth's soft features shone radiantly in the gentle light of the smoldering stones as she responded, "Many a night you have strengthened me by reading these powerful words. Tonight, it is my turn to strengthen *you*."

Ruth's words were like a soothing balm to the aching woman's soul. Her eyes glistened as she settled back and pulled her cloak tighter around her small shoulders, shivering slightly in the crisp night air. "I thought that teaching my daughter-in-law to read would be a blessing to *you*, dear, when in fact, it has turned out to be a blessing to this weary old woman's soul," she said fondly.

Ruth met Naomi's compliment with yet another genuine smile. It was quite a shocking rarity to encounter a woman in the Middle East who was not completely illiterate. Naomi's late husband Elimelech had tired of reading the Scriptures to his wife each evening, so he had hastily taught her how to sound out the words and syllables for herself. Naomi had said that she felt hurt, disappointed, at first when he had refused to continue reading to her. But now she could see how – even all those years earlier – the Lord had been looking after her and used even the unbelieving Elimelech to accomplish His purposes. If Naomi had not learned to read herself, upon her husband's death she would no longer have had access to the words of the Lord.

The blessing had been multiplied when eager, young Ruth had shown an interest in learning to decipher the sacred texts, and Naomi had secretly taught Ruth how to read as well. Ruth had proven an astute, ready learner and she had quickly mastered the art of reading.

Ruth's voice was soft and melodic, filled with wonder and vivid expression as she read aloud such exciting tales of the ancient Israelites burdened beneath their yoke of slavery and cruel oppression. She read of devastating plagues and mighty miracles performed by Almighty God to set His people free. She read of the great hero Moses – a man whom God had used to do incredible things. She read of the ruthless Pharaoh and the evil magicians who would stop at nothing to keep God's chosen people enslaved in their own pagan land.

As the words leapt to life from the worn, faded page of Naomi's scroll, Ruth could feel her resolve gradually restored, feel the strength returning to her poor, broken spirit, feel the fire beginning to burn in her weary heart yet again. These words were ever faithful to administer strength, courage, and peace to the weariest and loneliest of souls. Ruth wondered how such power and might could be harnessed and contained in these writings of old, but she had grown to trust and believe in the utter truth of the passages.

She couldn't help but compare her own small world to that of the Israelite people, in terrible bondage in a cruel, pagan land, at the mercy of godless, unkind people. Though her story was quite different from theirs, she too was at the mercy of a man and a people who did not belong to the Lord and did not understand His ways. She, too, was unable to escape her sad circumstances on her own, and she knew that only an act of God – a miracle, as had happened in the case of the Hebrew slaves – could change the unfair lot that had been dealt to her. She wondered if it was too bold, too daring, too presumptuous, to hope that the powerful God of the Israelites could perform a mighty work in *her* life as well.

Ruth continued to read, completely lost in the depth and the drama of the story. Now the Israelites had finally followed their courageous leader Moses into the wilderness, where they came upon the vast Red Sea. Though Ruth had heard the story countless times, she never tired of the way the Lord stepped in and devoured the army of the hard-hearted Pharaoh and the Egyptians, despite the faithless doubt of the Israelites and the incredible odds against them.

"*And when Pharaoh drew near,*" Ruth continued, completely unaware of the time or the place or anything but the incredible magnitude of the story, "*the children of Israel lifted their eyes, and behold, the Egyptians marched after them. So they were very afraid, and the children of Israel cried out to the Lord. Then they said to Moses, 'Because there were no graves in Egypt, have you taken us away to die in the wilderness? Why have you so dealt with us, to bring us up out of Egypt? Is this not the word that we told you in Egypt saying, Let us alone that we may serve the Egyptians? For it would have been better for us to serve the Egyptians than that we should die in the wilderness.' And Moses said to the people, 'Do not be afraid. Stand still, and see the salvation of the Lord, which He will accomplish for you today. For the Egyptians whom you see today, you shall see again no more forever. The Lord will fight for you, and you shall hold your peace.'*" Ruth became aware of the warm tears that were trickling slowly down both cheeks. She was overcome, but in the very best way. It was as if those words had willed themselves to life and leapt into her own heart to comfort, to console, to protect, to promise. Lowering the scroll, Ruth looked to Naomi and saw that she, too, was crying softly.

Ruth reached for Naomi's hand and searched her eyes knowingly, repeating the tender words that had touched her very soul. "*Do not be afraid. Stand still, and see the salvation of the Lord...*"

Naomi shut her eyes tightly and began to pray softly. "Show us Your salvation, Lord..."

Ruth gave her hand an extra hard squeeze. "*For the Lord will fight for you, and you shall hold your peace.*"

Naomi remained very silent and very still for some time. Ruth knew better than to interrupt such a sacred moment between her mother-in-law and her Creator. She, too, remained still and, lowering her eyes respectfully, she waited.

After what seemed like a very, very long time, Naomi lifted her face heavenward and smiled through her tears. "Praise our God, Ruth. He is so good. Again, He has been faithful to comfort the sore heart of this forgetful old woman."

Ruth looked up and managed a smile of her own. "I am glad to hear you say that, Naomi."

"And He has used *you*, my dear, to administer such comfort. Thank you, Ruth, for being His willing vessel. You have been so faithful."

Ruth nodded slowly. What had Naomi said? *Praise* our *God?* Our *God?* Could such a blessed statement be true? Could He truly be *her* God as well as Naomi's? Ruth's mind was a muddle of swirling questions, questions that desperately needed answers. But was now the time to ask? And could anyone but this good and mighty God Himself answer such questions?

"Naomi," Ruth began very slowly, "you speak the truth. This God Whom you serve *is* good. Very good. But, Naomi, I fear to hope..."

Naomi's gentle eyes grew very serious. "What is it that you fear, my child?"

"I fear..." Ruth bit her lip, hesitant to express the concerns buried deep within her heart, as if voicing them aloud might actually confirm their awful reality.

"Yes, child?"

"I fear that, as much as I long for the God of which you speak, He would not want me in return." There, she had said it. After all these years of wondering, hoping, doubting, fearing, longing, praying... she had finally broached the frightening subject with the one person she truly trusted on this earth. Naomi would be honest with her – regardless of how difficult the truth might be. At least now she could know. Even if she was afraid to know, she *must* know.

"Oh, Ruth!" Before she even knew what was happening, Ruth was enveloped in the soft, loving arms of her mother-in-law. "Of course He wants you! Have you not seen, my child, the way He has been reaching for you, calling to you, inviting you to come to Him? He longs for you to give yourself fully to Him, and then, as He did for all His children in ages past, He will perform a mighty work for you and through you!"

Ruth pulled gently away from Naomi's arms, which were by now trembling with passion, and searched her face with the deepest of longing. How she wished those words could be true!

But Naomi wasn't finished yet. She continued in the deepest earnest, "Do you not remember what the valiant warrior Joshua once said after God's people had reached the Promised Land? He said, *'Choose for yourselves this day whom you will serve, whether the gods which your fathers served that were on the other side of the River, or the gods of the Amorites, in whose land you dwell. But as for me and my house, we will serve the Lord.'* We all have a choice to make, my daughter. Though you dwell in a land of many gods – whom you have seen have no might, no power, but are merely stone and wooden images carved by weak human hands – you have been given the beautiful gift of choice. You must *choose* this day whom you will serve."

Ruth took a moment to ponder the powerful words spoken by Naomi. "I may choose the Lord – *your* Lord – even as a foreigner? Even as a Gentile?"

Naomi took both of Ruth's hands in her fragile own. "My Lord sees past the outside appearance and mere circumstances, Ruth. His all-seeing eyes probe far deeper than what we small, imperfect beings can see."

Naomi paused to study her eager daughter-in-law. She was amazed at how very young Ruth looked – so childlike and innocent and pure. She appeared desperate to accept Naomi's confident assurance, and yet she looked so very hesitant, so very unsure.

Naomi sighed and smiled patiently. "Let me tell you yet another story, my sweet daughter. You see, I knew of a woman long ago. She came not from the tribes of Israel, but rather from a foreign city – from a place called Jericho. She had grown up among a very heathen people with very pagan, inhuman practices. In fact, she herself was a prostitute."

Ruth's hand went to her mouth, and she blushed slightly at the mention of such a degrading trade. "What happened to her?" she whispered.

Naomi smiled. "She met my Savior. When several Israelite men were sent to spy out her city, the Lord led them straight to her house. In fact, she saved their lives when men from Jericho came looking for them. The Lord honored her for her courageous spirit, and when He sent the entire walls of Jericho crumbling and crashing to the ground like dilapidated, old ruins, she and her family were spared."

Ruth was enthralled. "And then what happened?"

"She went to live among the Lord's people, and she became one of us. She married a fine Israelite man, completely forsook the pagan ways she had once known, and dedicated the rest of her life to serving the Lord with all her heart and soul. She had found the one true God, and she determined that *nothing* would keep her from Him."

"Nothing?" Ruth repeated softly, her eyes glistening with tears of joy - warm, liberating tears of complete and utter gratitude and acceptance.

"So you see, my daughter, nothing is impossible with my God. His love reaches across time and space, beyond all understanding, surpassing all human knowledge and wisdom." She paused, then reached out to take Ruth's hand once more. "Choose *this* day, Ruth, whom you will serve. Do not put it off. Do not wait. Choose now."

Ruth bowed her head, the tears flowing freely now. Never before had she felt so light, so free, so very secure and so very loved. Her heart cried out silently to the God that she had feared and reverenced from a distance for so long, and, suddenly, felt her entire body, heart, and soul enveloped in a supernatural peace, a confidence, a sacred assurance that truly *did* surpass any and all understanding.

"Choose this day," Naomi repeated, her voice soft and filled with warmth.

Looking up to meet Naomi's gaze which was now burning with intensity, Ruth nodded her head and smiled ever so deeply. She felt the deepest kind of joy, bubbling over within her and overwhelming her very soul. She now knew beyond any shadow of doubt that, regardless of the trials or tribulations that might be hurled her way, she could pull through. With the mighty God of Naomi's fathers on her side, who could *ever* destroy her? There was not even the slightest hint of doubt in Ruth's tone as she readily replied, "I have already chosen."

"Oh, my child! My dear, sweet child!" And again, Ruth found herself being gathered up into the faithful arms of

Naomi. Naomi was laughing and crying all at once. A moment later she pulled away, and, holding her cherished daughter-in-law at arms' length, Naomi ventured with her eyes full of wonder, "Do you know, Ruth, the most amazing part of it all?"

Ruth shook her head eagerly. "What is it, Naomi?"

Naomi simply smiled. "He chose you first."

Chapter 3

SOON

In a land far from the pagan rites and rituals of the depraved Moabites, a man quite familiar with the story that Naomi had just recounted – the story of God's mighty hand at work through the life of a foreign woman in a distant city – pulled himself upright in bed. He shot a quick glance in the direction of the arched, tile-lined window with its face set toward the rising sun. Of course, he had deliberately placed that lovely window in that specific location in order to showcase the beauty of each Bethlehem sunrise – how wonderful it would be to catch the first glimpse of the gleaming golden sunbeams every single morning, gently slanting across the rugged terrain of the pastoral land he had fallen completely in love with. At least, that's what he had thought years prior, as he patiently designed this home with full intentions of marrying and raising a family of his own here. It was an impressive home indeed – not too showy, not even terribly expensive. But the large stone entryway, the arched windows and doorways, the tile flooring and rooftop, the spacious living quarters, and the blossoming courtyard around which the entire house was built contrasted quite drastically with the other simple homes of the village. He had built this home to last. He had imagined the pitter-patter of tiny feet racing to and fro across the tile entryway. He had envisioned a pretty wife smilingly greeting him and rewarding him with a warm, hearty meal after a long day out in his fields. He had almost heard the laughter, the merrymaking, the sweet sound of family fellowship that would meet his ears upon returning home each evening... Oh, but he was a busy man, and he had found little time for such joyful pursuits as courtship, marriage, and rearing a family– much less time to remain in bed long enough to watch the merry morning sun play peek-a-boo with the graceful hills and white stone dwellings of the villagers.

The dawn was soon in coming – he could smell it, taste it, feel it in the air. After years and years of rising just before the sleeping sun, he had grown quite accustomed to the mild, balmy pre-dawn hours. It was his favorite time of the day, in fact. For, at this early hour, the rest of bustling Bethlehem remained soft and silent in its gentle slumber.

Taking a moment to stretch his strong arms, he smiled slightly at the stiffness he was beginning to feel in his back and shoulders each morning. So the rumors were true. He *was* getting older.

Tall and solidly built, with a firm jawline and deep, observant eyes, he didn't look a day older than thirty. However, his weary muscles were beginning to remind him that – now in his early forties – he wasn't as young as he used to be.

Rising fully from his plush mattress and humming in a low baritone as was a familiar habit of his, he hurriedly splashed his face clean with cold water, trimmed his beard, dressed himself, and belted his richly colored robe and tunic.

Mere moments later, he knelt in the quiet solitude of his garden courtyard, the gentle splashing of a nearby fountain threatening to lull him once more into a gentle slumber. The delicate tile floor was every bit as cool as the refreshing, early morning air. The soft, floral fragrance of exotic blooms and blossoms beyond number filled the air with the sweetness of a woman's perfume. It was nearly intoxicating. Graceful green tendrils climbed and inched their way up tall, arched terraces, budding in a vast array of exquisite shades of pink, powder blue, and lavender. The rich foliage and sheltering palms formed a canopy that seemed almost protective, impenetrable. Here was a safe place, a quiet place. Here was escape from the worries and cares of life beyond the safe, sturdy stone walls of home. Here, the butterflies could hum their tiny wings and the birds could sing their cheery songs without interruption. Here, morning after morning, week after week, year after year, this wealthy, influential man of Bethlehem would bask in the glory and the presence of his Maker.

Folding his hands and placing them firmly on the marble bench before him, he bowed his head and began to speak with the utmost respect to the One whom he owed all his success, all his health, his strength, his mental capabilities. He had found that here, in the stillness and the quiet of this sacred garden courtyard, he could speak more frankly, more openly, with the One Who already knew his heart – his every desire.

"Lord God Almighty," he prayed solemnly, "I thank You for this glorious day, for this beautiful morning, for another blessed day to live and move and breathe to glorify Your holy Name..." and as the sun rose steadily in the balmy

Bethlehem sky, this dedicated man of God lifted up his prayers, his petitions, his requests, to the God of his father and mother, the God of his ancestors, the God of Abraham, Isaac, and Jacob. He remembered by name those who worked in his fields and lifted up their families, their children, the private struggles of those who had dared to confide in him – and many a man found him to be a trustworthy mentor and confidante. He prayed for those less fortunate than he, and begged the Lord to reveal to him how he might best minister to their needs. He prayed for the other villagers – for those he knew, as well as for those who merely passed him by.

Lastly, he humbly presented his personal requests before the Lord, willing to accept whatever reply the Lord saw fit to give to him.

"Righteous Lord," he began, his voice barely audible above the gentle splashing of the fountain, "You have blessed my life beyond measure. You have met my needs and generously provided not only *enough* but plenty – that I might meet the needs of others as well. And with a full heart, I thank You..." he paused, took a breath, pondered over the plea he was about to deliver to the very throne room of Heaven. Clearing his throat, he began in a very hushed tone, "Lord, for many years I asked of You to bring to me a wife. And not just any woman, Lord – the woman that You would choose for me. I asked for a woman of virtue, for a woman whom I could trust to partner with Us in raising our children in Your laws and Your statutes. A woman of such character is of far greater value than the wealth that, by Your power, I have accumulated over these long years. For many years I prayed, and yet, she could not be found. Lord, many years ago I released this burden into Your hands. To be quite frank, Lord, I had given up. But something has been stirring in my heart, Lord. The longing has returned, and doubly so. I wonder is it not my own selfishness that arouses this desire in my soul, Lord? Or could it be..." he paused and took another breath. "Could it be that You are whispering words of hope, of promise, to my heart? Has this hope, this longing, reawakened with such astounding vigor because You have a purpose and a will to fulfill such deferred dreams and aspirations?"

Somewhere high above the courtyard, a dove cooed its gentle response. The wind whispered softly through the tangled vines and lush, low-hanging palm fronds. As if for a brief moment in eternity, the strong man of God felt as if he were the only man on earth. He and the Lord God Almighty. He could literally feel His presence, sense His warm favor, for he was enveloped in a marvelous sense of peace so all-encompassing, so overpowering, that nothing could have interfered. It was simply beautiful, overwhelming.

There, in that moment of unspeakable peace, he felt that he had received an answer. He sensed a gentle, quiet bidding that whispered to his heart even more softly than the wind had just moments before rustled its way through the stunning greenery of the courtyard.

Soon.

Soon? Whatever could it mean? Did the Lord intend to answer his prayers, to fulfill his deepest longings, sometime in the near future? It was almost too much to hope for, too much to ask for!

Soon.

But there was no doubt about it. No doubt in his mind. The Spirit of the Lord had given him an answer. He considered asking for a sign, some type of confirmation that he could carry with him, that he could lean upon, depend on in the weary days ahead as he waited to see the Lord's plans carried out.

But, no. He would not ask. He would not test the holy God Who had already been so kind to him, so very generous, so *loving*.

His flurried thoughts were interrupted by a shrill, almost panicked cry from somewhere in the house beyond.

"Master! Master Boaz! May I approach, please?"

He recognized the voice as that of Ada, his housekeeper. Successful as he was, he owned not a single slave. Being a bachelor, however, he did employ a few very well-paid servants.

Jumping to his feet and brushing the dust from his knees, his alert eyes sought out the arched entryways that led into the house. From which entry was Ada approaching? Surely this must be some rare, possibly life-threatening emergency for her to interrupt his quiet time with the Lord. Every person under his employ knew the rule: *Never* interrupt Master Boaz during his time with God.

His body had instantly swung into action, preparing for the worst, bracing himself for the blow that was surely to come. "Ada! Please, come out wherever you are!"

A red-faced and very breathless Ada stumbled into the courtyard wringing her hands nervously, her apron covered in flour. "Master Boaz! A thousand apologies, sir, but I must speak with you at once!"

Ada was a plump, rosy-faced woman who had waited not only on Boaz but upon his beloved mother as well. She had been a dear friend to his mother as well as a servant. Boaz had always viewed her as somewhat of a mother figure and a beloved friend, insisting that she call him by his first name rather than Master. But with her traditional background and upbringing, she had refused such "nonsense" as she called it, and held tightly to the respected formality.

"What is the emergency, my dear woman?"

The alarm was apparent in Boaz's typically understanding eyes, and Ada immediately held up both floury hands and offered quickly, "No, no! No emergency, Master. As I did say, I apologize a thousand times over for interrupting your quiet time. But... it couldn't wait."

Feeling somewhat peeved that Ada had intruded upon such an intimate moment shared between he and his Maker, Boaz took a deep breath and reminded himself to be patient as his Lord was patient. Clearing his throat, he ventured calmly, "Has something happened?" His eyes gave a slight twinkle as he added, "Do I want to know?"

Ada nodded emphatically. "Oh, yes! Most definitely, sir! You see, I was of a mind to wait until you returned from your daily time with God. That's what I wanted to do, sir. But then the Lord told me... He told me not to wait."

Boaz felt his eyebrows lift in his surprise. His whole body tightened, for he did not take such matters lightly. Ada had loved the Lord all her life. In fact, she had taught his own mother much about their Lord. If anyone was to receive a message, a revelation, from Him, it would be her.

His throat was so constricted that he barely heard himself speak. "What has the Lord told you?"

Again, Ada shook her head. "Not to *me*, sir. To you. The message was for you." She took a deep breath and clasped her hands before her, her large eyes darting nervously about the courtyard. "And this He has spoken to my heart: Surely the Lord is with you, and He has indeed spoken to you this morning. His plans are good and perfect and true. He will bless you, as well as many others."

Boaz felt a lump in his throat as bittersweet emotion

welled up inside of him. He hadn't felt this way in a very long time. Years, perhaps. He felt honored, humbled, anxious.

"I know not what it could mean," Ada continued, her voice thick with emotion. "But, without ceasing, He has been impressing this one word upon my heart, and I believe it is for you."

Nearly stunned to silence, Boaz brought himself to meet her gaze. "My dear woman, what could it be?"

Ada shook her head in nervous disbelief. "Perhaps it will be less of a mystery to you. For the word He has brought to my heart and to my mind, sir, is this: *Soon*."

In Moab, the sun was a glowing sphere of fiery red, soft orange, and golden flames, rising ever-so-steadily in the pale, hazy morning sky. Soft streaks of rosy pink, pale lavender, and the slightest hints of the lightest shades of blue lingered lazily in the cloudless sky, breath-taking in all the glory and majesty of the arriving dawn.

Ruth couldn't help but linger a moment at the crude square-shaped hole cut into the mud-baked brick walls of their dwelling, drinking in the wondrous beauty and splendor of the early morning hours. And she couldn't help but smile as she thought about her loving Creator Who faithfully fashioned each and every sunrise – a rare and beautiful gift He chose to bestow upon His children daily.

He could have made every morning dull and gray and bland, yet He chose to stun us each and every day with something new and beautiful and bright and glorious! Ruth thought to herself, marveling in her spirit at the incredible peace she still felt all these weeks after making the most important decision she would ever make – the decision to follow after the one, true God. Her problems had not disappeared by any stretch of the imagination, but her heart was at peace and she firmly believed that the Lord would take care of her.

For the Lord will fight for you, and you shall hold your peace... she had reminded herself constantly over the last few weeks. This battle called life was not hers – it belonged to the Lord. She had prayed and willingly released her burdens, worries, and fears into the capable hands of her Savior.

Well, I'd better get myself down to the well before the morning rush, Ruth reminded herself, becoming suddenly aware of the heavy clay jar which she was skillfully balancing against her hip. She always tried to visit the well for the day's supply of water before the rest of the women of the town assembled for their daily, early-morning routine of fetching water and chattering in the most carefree manner, all the while exchanging vicious, stinging gossip about anyone who may not have been present. Even before giving her life to the Lord, conscientious Ruth had felt extremely uncomfortable in such a hostile environment. She was careful to make every effort to reach the well before the other women, somehow (most often with the help of the friendly, nearby shepherds) shove the heavy stone covering aside, swiftly and quietly draw water for her family, then, sweating and grimacing at the strain, shove the weighty stone back in place and slip back to the shelter of her home. Even with the help of the young, lanky shepherds, moving that enormous stone covering was quite a daunting task.

Ruth's quiet thoughts were interrupted by a particularly loud snore from Mahlon, who still lay sprawled on their shabby straw mattress in the opposite corner. Ruth turned to observe the limp form of her husband in repose. Ruth had overheard many parents remark about how tranquil and innocent their children looked when sleeping. Not so with her husband. His pale face was worn ragged with the cares and anxieties that weigh down the body, mind, and spirit of one given to alcohol, drunken rage, and one's own sinful desires. He often groaned or cried out in his sleep, startling Ruth awake in the most disconcerting way. He would toss and turn, and many a night she had been roused from a deep sleep by an unpleasant smack in the face from the sleeping Mahlon.

She had long-since accepted the fact that this was the husband chosen for her, and there was nothing on earth she could do to change such circumstances. For many years she had silently loathed his very existence, cringed upon his presence, mentally and emotionally detached herself from the man she knew she could never respect. However, she had never once betrayed such feelings to Mahlon – she had handled her disillusionment and heartbreak with the grace and poise of one who had been given everything she could ever hope for.

Now, after asking Naomi's faithful God to become the Lord of her life, Ruth slowly began to feel her extremely negative emotions toward Mahlon wane ever so slightly. She knew this must be the direct result of God at work in her life, for there was no way on earth she could have conquered such dreadfully bitter feelings of anger and hurt by her own strength. Rather than fierce resentment flashing through her veins with every disdainful word Mahlon sent hurtling her way, Ruth began to feel something else – the deepest kind of sorrow, the strongest sense of pity for a lost soul who had somehow completely missed the overwhelming, boundless love of his Father in Heaven.

Vividly, Ruth recalled the warm summer night many

years before, when, in complete and utter despair, she had thrown herself crying at Naomi's feet, begging her to talk to her son, to find out why he treated her so ruthlessly. "Whatever the reason, I would change it if only I *knew*!" Ruth had sobbed, Mahlon's furious shouts and searing accusations still swirling like mad chaos in her reeling mind.

"Oh, my poor Ruth!" Naomi had whispered, taking the young woman in her arms, who was now being wracked by the violent sobs of the hopelessly heartbroken. "It isn't *you*, my darling! *You* have done nothing wrong. My son Mahlon is terribly confused, Ruth. The ways of the world have held him captive too many years now."

"But there must be *something*," Ruth somehow managed between sobs. "There must be something I can do to make him hate me less."

"There *IS* something you can do," Naomi responded, without missing a beat. "You can *pray* for him, Ruth. My God is powerful beyond compare. He will hear your prayers if you will only cast your cares upon His very capable shoulders."

That night, so many years before, Ruth had not taken to heart the encouraging advice offered up by Naomi. *Now*, however, Ruth had replayed the memory over and over in her mind, and she embraced the hopeful admonitions of her spirited mother-in-law.

I must pray for him, Ruth often thought, *for it is the only hope he has. If he should choose not to accept the Lord and His ways, Mahlon will perish a lost soul held hostage by the filthy pagan ways of this terrible land.*

And pray for him she did. Day after day. Night after night. Week after week. Sabbath after Sabbath. She prayed for him as she scrubbed the dirt-stained floors. She prayed for him as she prepared the midday meals. She prayed for him as she gathered fruit from the vine and baked the day's fresh bread. She prayed for him as she drew water from the well and as she washed the dishes leftover from each meal. She prayed and prayed and prayed and prayed.

Still, even as she prayed, the last part of Naomi's comforting dialogue from that hopeless night plagued her thoughts and her heart. She tried not to dwell on such words, tried to shove them far from her mind. However, those stubborn thoughts refused to budge. Instead, they took root in her heart and soul, mocking her and threatening her with every feeble prayer she offered.

"You must understand, Ruth," Naomi had said, "that no matter how hard you pray for Mahlon, *he* must make the decision to choose the Lord. Our God is all-powerful, and He can speak to Mahlon's heart and demonstrate His mighty power and love, but He will never *force* anyone to love Him. Ultimately, *Mahlon* must make that decision for himself. You cannot *make* him choose the Lord, and the Lord will not force him to do so."

Oh, Mahlon, Ruth thought, setting aside the heavy water jug and kneeling at her cruel husband's bedside. *How long will you reject the only One Who can save you? Will you* ever *accept Him?*

Folding her hands on the rough straw mattress and bowing her head reverently, Ruth uttered one more prayer for this stubborn man before beginning the day's chores.

"Lord God," she breathed, "please save the soul of this man. Stagger him with Your awesome power and bring him straight to his knees, Lord. Help him to recognize his need for You, and welcome him with open arms, Lord."

"What's the matter with you?" Though his voice was still thick with fatigue, Mahlon's tone sounded gruff and insulting. Early in the morning was the only time that his voice actually sounded low like that of the other men. Once he had shaken out the sleepiness, his voice grated on and on with an unusually high-pitched quality for a young man.

Startled by the interruption, Ruth jumped to her feet and tucked the large, earthenware jar beneath her arm once more. "Did I wake you?"

"What do *you* think? Can't a man even sleep without his old nag muttering all sorts of bizarre prayers and incantations over his still body?"

Ruth blanched, but determined not to hurl back an equally-stinging insult. How she longed to fly right at him, pointing out the obvious fact that he so readily denied – that the rest of the men in Moab had long-since been up out of their beds and hard at work, providing for their wives and children, while *he* laid around like a worthless sloth of a man in bed? Even so, Ruth held her tongue and replied calmly, "I was praying for you."

"How pious of you."

Again, Ruth chose to ignore his biting sarcasm. Her eyes twinkled playfully as she replied, "Why, thank you!"

For the first time that morning, Mahlon half-rose from the bed, his blood-shot eyes wide with animalistic rage. "How dare you mock me, you ungrateful shrew of a woman!"

Both appalled and slightly frightened, Ruth bit her lower lip and blinked back tears. She had never intended to mock him – only to playfully lighten the unpleasant conversation. "Mahlon, I would never –"

"Get out of this room and away from my presence!" Mahlon's shrill scream was so painfully ear-splitting that Ruth was sure the entire town must have heard him.

"Mahlon – "

"NOW! Before I remove you from this place myself!!!"

Ruth did not argue. Though she doubted Mahlon would resist his own laziness long enough to physically throw her from the room, she had no desire to stick around as he lashed out at her with a well-rehearsed, wide variety of intimidating verbal abuse. Without another word, she ducked under the low-hanging doorway and hastened to attend to the day's chores.

Chapter 4

ADARA

In what would seem to Ruth a world away, a gentle young woman rose with a start from her loom, the smell of slightly burnt bread meeting her nostrils in the most unwelcome way.

"My bread!" she gasped, dashing to the ancient courtyard just outside her small, comfortable home and kneeling before the faithful clay oven she used each day to supply the daily bread.

A contented sigh of relief escaped her lips as she retrieved the rounded, flat loaves of barley bread and realized that they were nicely browned indeed, but certainly not burnt. She assumed that the careless mistake of burning the day's bread must have fallen upon the unfortunate shoulders of another, as the lingering aroma of a poorly supervised recipe reduced to ashes still lingered in the air.

After all, *her* dome-shaped clay oven was not the only one in the courtyard. She and her husband were not poor by any means, but more along the lines of middle-class. Her husband worked a very important job as the foreman of the field of one of the wealthiest, most influential men in Bethlehem – a generous man who delighted in paying his loyal employees a very decent salary. However, her husband was not an extravagant man, and he was quite content to remain living in the small cluster of homes built by his ancestors in years past. This small grouping of modest houses near the endless, rolling fields of promising crops was built around a common courtyard, where the women of the households – mostly relatives of her husband, Kemuel – attended to the baking, the washing, the gardening, the care and feeding of the animals, and other outdoor tasks that must be accomplished day to day.

Toting her freshly baked bread back into the house with her, the lovely young woman with dark brown tendrils dancing about her fair forehead set the steaming loaves in the windowsill to cool and eagerly went back to her loom.

Adara was a fastidious housekeeper. Yes, she was young, but she was certainly not inexperienced. Her dear mother had taught her everything there was to know about how to run a successful household. That kindly woman had lived and breathed to meet the needs of her family, to minister to her loving husband, to nurture her many children.

Adara had watched her mother with the deepest kind of awe and respect as she had glided gracefully about the house, giving her children gentle admonitions when needed and filling each simple room with warm laughter and cheerful conversation as she worked. The tightly-packed clay floors were always scrubbed clean and glistening, the dishes were always gleaming in neat rows from their orderly places on the kitchen shelf, the summer and winter clothes were always ready and waiting for eager wearers with each passing season, the meals were always warm and freshly prepared when their doting father arrived home each evening, and the animals were always cared for and well-fed.

As a little girl, long before Adara's bright mind had become occupied with thoughts of courtship, marriage, and child-rearing, Adara had resolved to keep her own house with the diligence, care, and responsibility with which her own mother had kept theirs.

And she certainly had. Not only had Adara succeeded in developing a busy daily routine which served to meet the needs and demands brought forth by each and every new day, but she had faithfully carried out each task which that routine had presented. And she tackled the day's chores with such an eager readiness, such a cheerful exuberance, and such consistent results, that the other women of Bethlehem both admired and envied her skill.

Perhaps that small bit of envy was what fueled the vicious gossip and slander that circulated so freely between the women of the village any time Adara was present, or, for that matter, if her name was so much as mentioned in passing. Consumed with jealousy, they had found the soft-spoken, doting housewife to be quite an easy target. And, using her own personal sorrow and misfortune due to circumstances far beyond Adara's control, they had mercilessly preyed upon her from the moment she was given in marriage to the man that most of the young women of the town had set their sights on.

It used to greatly disturb her. Adara's gentle heart had earnestly desired friendship, companionship, among the women who shared her heritage, her great hope as the chosen people of the Most High God. However, she had received nothing from such women save ridicule, disdain, and savage remarks.

For though it was true that Adara was a stellar housekeeper, a devoted wife, and a committed follower of the one, true God, one massive obstacle stood like a leering, looming giant between her and acceptance from those around her.

Adara was unable to bear children.

It was not for lack of trying. She and her husband Kemuel had beseeched the Lord year after year for the blessing of a child. They had prayed, they had wept, and, after six years of marriage they had finally come to accept the cold, hard fact.

Most likely, they would never have children of their own.

The first few years of trying had been dark days indeed for the young, hopeful wife – so very youthful, so beautiful, so full of promise. She could not wait to bless her beloved with the gift of children. She could not wait to see his face reflected in that of the young child they would soon – Lord willing – hold in their arms. She had hoped and prayed for the strength to govern her children with the same graciousness and poise her own mother had demonstrated day after day.

And yet, as the weeks dragged into months, and the months progressed into long, trying years, Adara had sunk into a miry pit of the deepest, darkest kind of despair. The hateful tongue-lashings she constantly received from the women – even from the relatives of her dear husband – plagued her thoughts and whirred loudly in her ears.

To be barren is to be cursed, she was reminded upon every road, every turn. She had been accused of any and all known evils – she had been called a harlot, a hypocrite, a busybody, a slanderer – for everyone sought the proper label for the apparent "sin" that must be preventing her from bearing children. Surely the Lord must be punishing her for some great, hidden iniquity.

In those early years, she had feared to set foot beyond the house. She had wilted beneath the withering gazes of the women who had been blessed with children, and turned crimson beneath the curious stares of the men who wondered why a man as respected as Kemuel had been so disgraced.

In those days of dark disquiet and unrest, she had dreaded the awful fate that was sure to assail her – the inevitable, ultimate dishonor that so often met the eyes of a barren woman. She had waited fearfully, expectantly, for the man that she loved more than life itself to present her with a certificate of divorce. After all, she could not give to him the one thing that every man longed for – a son to carry on his family name, to inherit his land, his property, his wealth, and all that he had worked so hard for throughout his entire lifetime to obtain. Why, without a son, everything that Kemuel would achieve in life would merely be passed on to the highest servant. However, as they did not have a single servant to their name, his entire life's work would be lost.

Sadly, she realized that Kemuel had every reason to dismiss her and to seek a better mate.

Nearly drowning in sorrow and regret, Adara had locked herself in a dark, unrelenting prison of guilt and despair, crying out to God, begging that He bless her womb, that He give her a child, that He remove her bitterness and shame.

And He had indeed answered her prayer – just not in the way that she had expected.

During the darkest season of her young life, Adara had cried out to the Lord yet again, begging, pleading, beseeching. She may have been the best housekeeper in all of Bethlehem, but what good was it if she could not give her husband the children he so desired?

Pitching headfirst upon her cherished loom – the loom given to her by her dear mother, whom she so desperately wished were still living to give hope or counsel to her aching heart – Adara had released the floodgate of bitter tears, allowing them to cascade down both cheeks. She would cry. She would wail in anguish. No one was here to listen. Only God could hear, and only He could answer her broken-hearted plea.

She had been astonished by a puff of air that met her face, now stinging with salty tears. Someone had entered their home. Through her blurred vision she could make out a sturdy frame, broad shoulders, a tall figure with a purposeful gate...

Her sorrow instantly turned to fear, and she rose from her loom, searching through her tears for something – anything – that could be easily snatched up and used for self-defense.

"Adara?"

The voice belonged to her husband. His voice was thick with concern as he hurried to his wife and took her in his strong arms.

How good it felt to be held by the man that she loved! Adara found herself sobbing all the more, realizing how very much she would miss him should he choose to dismiss her. If only she could give him children! He deserved that more than any man she had ever met. *If only...*

"My love, why do you cry?"

Adara shook her head and buried her face in his chest. Surely he knew! Surely he knew the pain she felt upon each new month as she discovered that, yet *again*, she was not with child. Surely he knew how she longed to make him happy, to meet his every desire, to give him a house full of laughing, rampaging, promising children! And surely he shared her pain!

"Come, sit with me, my darling."

Swallowing hard, Adara nodded her gentle consent and allowed him to guide her by the elbow to the stone ledge jutting out beneath the large, arched window that overlooked the busy courtyard beyond. Sunbeams slanted gracefully across the hard clay floor, reminding Adara that there were still chores to be done, that useful hours of daylight were slowly wasting away as she remained shut up indoors, bemoaning circumstances that she could never change.

Though her heart was breaking, she found the pain ebbing ever so slightly as curiosity got the best of her. Why had Kemuel come home at this early hour? Surely he was needed out in the fields! Had something happened? Was he injured? Or perhaps ill? Or maybe he had merely forgotten something and simply returned for it.

Finally discovering her tongue, she swiped her tears across her soft sleeve and asked anxiously, "Why have you returned home so early, my love? Was there trouble out in the fields?"

"Actually, yes."

Adara's luminous brown eyes met his, and she felt the unpleasant knot in her stomach tighten painfully. His own eyes looked ever so solemn, so very serious.

"Yes, there was," he repeated, clearing his throat and running a large, brown hand through his copper-colored hair. "But first," he continued, his hazel eyes never leaving her own, "I want to know why my precious wife has spent the morning alone in our house, sobbing her heart out as though the world were coming to an end."

It may well be for me, she thought pitifully, turning her face from him in shame. *I have behaved childishly, and my own husband is now ashamed of me.* She offered briskly, "I have not spent the entire morning in such a shameful manner. I have already baked the day's bread and scrubbed the – "

Kemuel held up a work-roughened hand to silence her. "I asked not for excuses, my love. I am not ashamed of you. It breaks my heart to see you in such a state."

Touched, Adara felt the tears brimming anew and desperately tried to hold them back. Kemuel longed to connect with her, to understand the inner workings of her heart. She knew that to be married to such a man was an inexplicable privilege, and she took a moment to calm her troubled spirit. She knew she must express her thoughts in a mature and direct manner, and that would be quite impossible in her present state. Choosing her words carefully, she ventured in a voice barely above a whisper, "I weep because you are a good man deserving of every happiness, and yet I cannot give you the greatest blessing which you so richly deserve." Stating her thoughts so frankly, so bluntly, sent her tears flowing yet again, and she bowed her head to hide the glistening drops of water falling into her lap.

"Oh, my love." Taking her hand in a firm grip to ensure that she could not pull away, Kemuel cupped her face with his free hand, forcing her to look at him.

What she saw stilled her heart as well as all the wayward thoughts of gloom that had tumbled about her weary mind, for the kind face of her husband emanated all the genuine love, all the patient understanding and the purest kind of devotion so dear to the heart of a woman. There was not a trace of judgment, nor disdain, nor resentment – all of those negative emotions that she would have expected him to harbor in his heart toward the woman to whom he was legally bound but whom could never meet his deepest need, his greatest desire. Instead, she saw only *love*.

Crying harder now, she tried to look away but he would not allow it. Rather, he leaned in closer. "I love you, Adara," he said, the quiet strength that she so admired in him more evident now than ever before. "Do you know how good our God is?"

Adara blinked away her tears, perplexed at this sudden turn of conversation. Especially at a time such as this, when He had deliberately left their most desperate prayer unanswered. "He is very good..." she managed quietly, although her tone sounded anything but convinced.

"You do not sound sure."

Adara lowered her gaze and repeated feebly, "He *is* very good. He has done many wondrous things."

"*Many* wondrous things," her husband added firmly, a faint smile playing about the corners of his lips. "In fact, He has performed a wondrous deed this very morning."

"He has?" Adara wondered if it had anything to do with the trouble Kemuel had mentioned occurring out in the field.

"He has, indeed. For I had scarcely resumed my work out in the fields when I felt my soul overwhelmed with trouble. As I mentioned earlier."

"Oh no." Adara gripped his hand even more tightly and bit her lower lip to still the trembling.

"And what troubled me, my love, was the very thing that has so disturbed your gentle heart this morning. For the thousandth time, I found myself questioning Almighty God, asking Him *why*? Why keep such a joyous blessing from two people who have loved Him and served Him so faithfully?"

Lowering her gaze, Adara simply nodded. She understood his conflicted thoughts more completely than he could ever know.

"I see what it is doing to *you*, my love. I see the hurt in your eyes each time we go to the marketplace and the other women play their silly little games. I see the shame etched all over your lovely features every time we set foot from the house. And it hurts, my love. It hurts to see you in pain. As I supervised the workers in Boaz's field, I silently lifted up my requests to God. Even more than I begged Him for a child of our own, I beseeched Him to take away the heavy burden that your small shoulders have carried for far too long."

"Oh, Kemuel – "

"And, instantly, with the strength of a thunderbolt, I felt the Lord's presence with me – right there in that field. It was as if all the world around me stood still, frozen in time. Every little breeze that rustled through the tall shoots of grass was magnified like the thundering waters of a hundred waterfalls. And, in that moment, I believe that the Lord spoke to me, Adara."

Adara was mystified, and her eyes were wide with wonder and even a hint of fear. "What did He say?" she breathed.

"As plain as day, I heard these words pounding relentlessly in my head, 'Have you forgotten My servant Sarah?'"

"*Sarah*?"

"Yes."

"What does it mean?"

"Instantly I was reminded of Sarah, the wife of Abraham..."

Adara drew a hand to her mouth at the obvious implications of the question that her husband believed the Lord God Himself had whispered to his heart. Why, Abraham was the father of their people, the Israelites! God had promised Abraham that his wife, Sarah, would bear him a son. But, alas, poor Sarah's womb was barren, and besides that, she was well advanced in years – far past the age of bearing children.

Kemuel's dark eyes glimmered with a light – a fire – that Adara had not seen in a very long time. "I felt desperately ashamed, for I realized that the Lord was calling me out right then and there on my lack of faith. If God could work in the dusty old womb of an aging woman who had been barren all her life, was it too great a task for Him to work a miracle in the womb of my own promising, young wife?"

The fire in Kemuel's eyes was so alive with passion and sheer joy that it was contagious. Adara felt the very presence of God filling their humble home – mighty, all-encompassing, empowering, overwhelming.

Taking both her hands in his own, Kemuel went on forcefully, an unmistakable glow emanating from his every feature, "I have not lost hope, Adara. The Lord has revived my waning faith! As the Lord has said, do we not remember His faithful servant Sarah? Not to mention her dear sisters in the faith – Rachel and Rebekah and Hannah– who were also barren? You are in good company, my love!"

Slowly but surely, Adara felt an undeniable, joyous sensation engulfing her entire being – tingling from the very tips of her small toes to the top of her pretty head. Surely the Lord was with them, for she could feel His presence even now! He cared deeply enough about two average, ordinary people to whisper comfort to their aching hearts.

"And as for me," Kemuel continued, his eyes softening with genuine love and affection, "I want you to know that you have already given me *everything*, Adara. I trust that the Lord is fully able to bless us with children. But even if He does not, He has already given me a gift far more beautiful than I could have ever asked for or even hoped for. That gift is *you*, Adara, for your name – meaning, "noble" – is truly fitting, my dear. You are far nobler than any woman I have ever met. My heart safely trusts you. You work tirelessly to demonstrate your love for me. And that is the greatest gift any man could possibly ask for."

As he had taken her into his arms once more, Adara had silently thanked Almighty God for answering her feeble prayers, for blessing her with a man fully committed to Him, for showering her with unexpected and underserved blessings. And right then and there, in that very moment, she had decided that she would spend the rest of her days simply *praising Him*. She would glory in His splendor and fearful awe and majesty. She would choose to praise Him – whether He ever chose to bless them with children or not. And she resolved to bless her husband in every single way that was in her power to do so. He was a good man, and he deserved all her love, all her devotion, all her respect.

For the first time in many, many months, she was happy. No longer would she worry about what the other women said. No longer would she flinch at the unwelcome glares or the hushed whispers that met her ears as she passed by. Regardless of whatever vicious rumors might be circulating about her out in the streets, in the marketplace, or at the well, she would refuse to release the wondrous, deep-rooted joy that the Lord had planted within her heart.

Adara knew that she would forever carry with her that precious memory she had shared with the Lord and with her husband. She still had not borne a child for Kemuel. The women continued to ridicule and demean her. The men continued to advise Kemuel to put away his barren wife and to find another who could grant him a son to carry on the family name. However, that sense of peace, of boundless joy and sweet anticipation of future plans that the Lord might see fit to carry out in her life, had not been carried away with the daunting circumstances of Adara's present state. That very day, she had made a decision to truly submit to the Lord's will for her life. And she would not turn back.

Now, seating herself behind her beloved loom, Adara set to work at one of the tasks she most enjoyed, smiling as she recalled how the Lord continued to walk beside her and her dear husband with every passing day.

Adara was a master at the loom. Tough, unyielding fibers and dull fabrics became breathtaking garments of rich hues and bold patterns once her cherished loom and skilled fingers got hold of them.

Garment-making was not a simple task by any stretch of the imagination, but hard work had never intimidated Adara. In fact, she welcomed it! Before the wool, goat hair, or flax could be formed into thread, it had to be carefully washed, then picked clean, and slowly but surely pulled straight. After the first three tedious steps of fabric-making were completed, the fibers were then spun, intertwined, and drawn into an even strand. Only then were the spun fibers ready to be stretched out on a loom and transformed into the loveliest of garments.

Today, as Adara's quick feet skillfully worked the pedals of her mother's old loom, she couldn't help but feel a slight twinge of excitement, of eager anticipation. God was at work this morning. Not that He wasn't working every other morning – but she could especially feel His Spirit moving today. She had grown more and more sensitive to the Spirit's subtle movement as she and her husband sought after the Lord and His will for them each morning before he left for the fields, and every evening upon his return.

Have you forgotten My servant Sarah? Thinking upon the

Lord's admonition to Kemuel that momentous day in the field only fueled Adara's high spirits.

Humming cheerily, Adara continued to work, pray, and praise simultaneously. Her blissful state was interrupted by the persistent barking of Tal – a stray watchdog that had "adopted" Adara and Kemuel several months before.

The door was propped open to allow the cool morning breezes to filter through the muggy living quarters, and Tal's pointed ears and elongated snout emerged through the opening as he continued to bark fiercely.

Adara rose from her loom and knelt before the large, yellow dog, stroking the fine, bristling hairs on his neck and back. "Tal! Whatever has gotten into you?"

The dog let out a dramatic whine, his large, perceptive eyes searching hers as if to say, "Surely you understand what I am trying to say!"

Laughing, Adara straightened and brushed the dust from her nearly floor-length tunic, hemmed with unique, flowing criss-crossing patterns of her own creative design.

It was at that moment that Kemuel appeared, ducking through the doorway and already dusty after a few busy hours in the fields.

Tal gave one final whine as if to state that he had made his announcement and – surely enough – a visitor had now reached their door, then he hurried back outside to bask in the sun and enjoy the crisp morning breeze.

Adara's heart skipped a beat. She knew that Kemuel would not come home this early unless something rare and unusual was at hand. In fact, he had not asked permission to leave the fields before his appointed time since that fateful day when the Lord strengthened both their hearts with His message to Kemuel.

"My love! Is everything alright?"

Kemuel appeared somewhat winded, and his face looked flushed. Adara felt a tweak of consternation at his harried appearance, but all anxiety melted away when Kemuel broke into a broad, beaming smile. "The Lord has amazed me yet again!" he declared, taking her by both shoulders with trembling hands.

"What has happened, Kemuel?" she could barely contain her excitement. She had sensed the Lord at work from the moment she had risen from her bed. And her conscience had not fooled her.

"Boaz insisted that I return home long enough to thank the Lord with you, my dear."

"He did?"

"He did!"

"And what are we thanking Him for?"

"As I went about my usual duties, I continued to pray to the Lord for strength, for direction – "

"As you do each day," Adara added, proud of her husband's willingness to seek the Lord in his daily decisions.

"Yes. And though I accept His will regardless of the outcome, I have continued to pray for a child with every passing day."

"As have I."

"I felt a stirring in my heart especially strong this morning, my love. Again, I felt a very real sense of the Lord's presence. And I lifted up my request to Him with an open heart, right there in the field, with workers gleaning all around me singing praises of the Lord's might and power even as they worked!"

Adara could only smile. She silently thanked the Lord for providing her husband with an uplifting environment in which he could work and provide a living for the two of them.

"It was at that moment," Kemuel went on, "that Boaz approached me."

That was nothing unusual. Boaz was a firm believer in the God that they served, and a trusted friend of her husband as well as his employer. Very rarely did a day pass that Boaz did not find time to share hope and encouragement with young Kemuel.

"What did he say?" Adara prodded, her enthusiasm getting the best of her.

"He shared a very personal experience with me," Kemuel replied, reaching for Adara's hands. "Apparently, the Lord has been working mightily in *his* life as well. He said that the Lord had recently made a very strong impression upon his heart, and though he has no doubt that the message was intended for him, he felt the Lord urging him to share the very same message with *me*..."

The Lord's enveloping presence was nearly overwhelming as Adara looked intently into the eyes of her husband and waited for him to repeat the words entrusted to them by another mighty man of God.

"And what message did the Lord ask Boaz to share with you, my husband?"

"As I stood there in the field, glorying in the very presence of God, beseeching Him to grant us a child of our own if His perfect will would allow, Boaz came alongside me and, planting a hand firmly upon my shoulder, he shared with me a story. And these are the words that he believes are meant not only for him, but for you and I as well..." his voice trailed off as he closed his eyes for a brief moment, undoubtedly uttering a silent prayer of thanksgiving to the Lord. "Adara, my love, this is what the Lord has said, and there is no doubt that He does indeed intend to share this message of hope, this promise, with us as well as with Boaz..."

"My love, I have wondered so much that I am nearly beside myself!" Adara exclaimed, breathless. "What is it that the Lord has said?"

Kemuel smiled tenderly, and his gleaming eyes never once left hers. "*Soon.*"

Chapter 5

PLAGUED

The sun burned fierce and bright, high in the steamy mid-afternoon desert sky, its stifling rays beating mercilessly upon the backs of anyone who had not yet retreated to the relief and semi-coolness of their stone dwellings. This was the time of day when the men returned from the fields or their various trades to enjoy the pleasant conversation of their families at home while sharing a decent meal, to refresh themselves with cool, fresh water lovingly drawn by their women, and to relax or even take a quick, rejuvenating nap before returning to the fields for the remainder of the day.

Naomi bustled about the small area designated as the household kitchen, collecting crude serving utensils and clay plates from the various shelves as she chattered with her two daughters-in-law, who were also quite busy helping her prepare the midday meal.

"How is the bread coming along, Ruth my dear?" Naomi inventoried as she reached for the drinking goblets on the highest shelf. She took a moment to glance over the old clay goblets, turning them over in her hands. "Just imagine," she stated solemnly, "these are the very goblets given to Elimelech and I on our wedding day. Ah, I thought they were the loveliest I had ever seen! Why, at the time they were all brightly colored with delicate paints. Look at them now – so old and faded, not a single trace of beauty remains... rather like myself!" She threw back her head and laughed good-naturedly, then she handed the first two down to Orpah, who was already seated comfortably at the mat, eager to indulge her ever-growing appetite.

Orpah took the goblets and set them carelessly down wherever they happened to land. "Oh, *please*, Naomi, you're no spring chicken but you are still gorgeous and you know it."

Ruth, bent over the hot stone oven, was still struggling to fight away the gloom still hanging heavy from her early-morning encounter with Mahlon. Swiping away a few sweaty strands of richly-colored hair from her delicate forehead, she smiled at Noami. "I must agree with Orpah, Naomi, you are still quite beautiful."

Naomi blushed pleasantly, her cheeks deepening in rosy color and one dimple teasing the edge of her smile. "Oh, enough of that, my daughters! Here, Orpah, do be a sweetheart and set these goblets at their proper places as well, will you?" She handed Orpah two more faded goblets.

Ruth peeked in at the bread, which was already smelling tantalizing and delicious to three very hungry stomachs.

"*Please* tell me the bread is almost ready," Orpah whined, reaching for a juicy grape from the rich cluster of fruit arranged on a platter at the center of the mat. "I'm famished!"

"Why, my dear, you know we must wait for the men of the house!" Naomi chided kindly, rearranging the goblets Orpah had artlessly displaced.

"What *men*? I haven't seen any men around here, though I wouldn't mind if any decided to come around..."

"Now, now!" Naomi arched a brow in stern disapproval. "That is no way for a modest – and might I add, *married* – woman of purity to talk."

"Woman of purity?" Orpah echoed incredulously. "I don't see any of *those* around here either – except for maybe Ruth."

Though scandalized by Orpah's careless talk, Ruth managed a half-smile and wiped the smooth flour from her busy hands. "You can relax, Orpah. The bread is piping hot and ready to come out of the oven!"

"Well then? What on earth are you standing there for? Take it out!" Orpah helped herself to several more lustrous grapes, even as Naomi eyed her with obvious disapproval.

Chuckling, Ruth stooped over the oven and carefully retrieved the small, rounded loaves of unleavened bread. Even as she carried the steaming loaves to the mat where she and her family would gather around to enjoy the food and the fellowship of one another, Ruth silently thanked the Lord for the spiritual nourishment He had so faithfully provided for her day after day.

I couldn't live without Your love, Lord, she prayed, her heart overflowing with tender gratitude. *I believe I would rather exist without my daily bread than without Your love.*

"Looking good, Ruth."

Ruth felt a rough tweak on the shoulder and turned to see that Chilion had somehow entered the house unnoticed, his features slightly leering, his eyes cold. She felt her cheeks grow warm at the obvious inappropriateness of his comment.

Orpah's green eyes flashed fiercely. "Chilion!"

"What?" Chilion plopped down upon the plush pillow

beside his wife and jammed a handful of grapes into his mouth. "I was talking about the bread."

Orpah did not look forgiving. "Of course you were."

Naomi appeared embarrassed at her son's brusque misconduct but said nothing. She took her own seat next to Ruth and appeared to be searching for something.

"Is there something wrong, Naomi? Have we forgotten something?"

Naomi crinkled her brows. "Yes! My other son!" She laughed, relieved that the previous conversation had swiftly veered off topic. "Where is Mahlon?" Her eyes met Chilion's questioningly.

"Don't look at me," Chilion snapped. "How am I supposed to know where that no-good, drunken slack-off is?"

Naomi leveled her gray eyes at him. "That is no way to talk about your brother."

Chilion's eyes looked strangely distant as he retorted, "Then tell him to change his personality." He pitched forward slightly, then righted himself.

"It's not like you're any better," Orpah smirked, completely oblivious to her husband's odd behavior.

Ruth, however, noticed right away and reached for the ground to steady herself. She could feel the slow, cold terror beginning to creep ever-so-steadily up her spine, constricting her throat, clouding her thoughts and mind like the deepest, blackest cloud. Something was wrong with Chilion, terribly wrong...

Ruth looked frantically to Naomi, and observed that she, too, had noticed. Her kindly countenance was already growing pale.

Ruth forced herself to direct her attention back to Chilion. His face, lips, and hands appeared strangely ghost-like, rather like the white underbelly of a dead fish. His typically-firm jaw was partially sagging like that of an old man who had recently suffered a stroke. His eyes, once dark and flashing, appeared hollow and vacant. His skin was stretched taut across cheekbones that appeared much more prominent than usual.

Naomi ventured very slowly, very cautiously, "Chilion, are you alright?"

"What kind of question is that?" Chilion's voice rose defensively, strangely slurred.

Orpah's eyes narrowed and she smacked him on the arm. "What's wrong with you? Are you *drunk*?"

Ruth had to admit that he sounded very much like Mahlon often did after his careless drinking binges. Ruth had witnessed Chilion drunk on several occasions as well, but he held his wine better than his scrawny brother. She had never heard him slur that way, even when he had been drinking.

"Can't you women leave a man alone?" Chilion nearly shouted, pitching forward again, this time upsetting the beautifully-arranged platter of fruit.

Orpah was furious. "What in the world? Watch yourself, Chilion!"

Naomi's eyes were wide with fright. Instantly on her feet, she hurried to her son's side. "Chilion, talk to me. What is happening to you?"

As if the scenario could have gotten any more bizarre, Chilion began talking to himself. "They just won't leave us alone, will they? All we want is some peace and quiet! In the name of the gods – " With that, he slammed his fist down – hard – upon the clay bread plate, splitting it down the middle with an ear-splitting *CRACK*!

Orpah screamed and backed away from the lunch

spread, her mouth agape and her eyes wide as saucers. Her veil had slipped off her head and her hair was now billowing wildly about her shoulders.

Throwing himself to his feet, Chilion veered right and left like a drunk, his eyes growing redder and his teeth clenched. Like that of a man who had completely lost his senses, he began swinging his fists two and fro as if boxing viciously with an invisible opponent.

Naomi was beside herself with fear. "Chilion!"

And then, with a final shout of rage and indignation, Chilion pitched head-first to the ground of hard-packed earth, his skull punching a large dent in the dirt with a sickening *thud.*

Ruth's world reeled in a thousand crazy, topsy-turvy directions. Her vision felt strangely blurred, as if she could see only a mad swirl of various shapes and colors. She could hear something – something ear-splitting and nerve-wracking – but she couldn't figure out what it was. Screaming? Yes, one long, endless scream. Was that Orpah? And sobbing. Gut-wrenching, heart-rending sobs. Naomi?

Ruth shook her head hard and begged God for clarity. She realized that, at this point, she was in a state of blind panic and could be of no help to anyone.

Dear Lord God, please help me!

Instantly, the fog cleared and, as she drank in the horrific scene around her, she nearly considered begging God to blur her thoughts and mind all over again.

Chilion lay face-down on the ground, completely motionless. Recalling the terrible fall he had just taken, Ruth knew it would be a wonder if he hadn't broken his nose and shattered every bone in his face – if he even survived.

Orpah was huddled over the fallen form of her

husband, screaming in terror and shaking him furiously by the shoulders. "Get up!" She screamed at the top of her lungs. "You can't do this to me! I won't let you do this to me!"

And Naomi's entire body was being wracked with heavy, violent sobs. She, too, knelt beside her still son. Burying her face in his neck, she wept and wept.

Ruth felt as if her heart were breaking – not for Chilion's sake, but for Naomi. She had already lost her husband. Could her old heart handle the loss of her eldest son as well?

Someone must do something! Ruth thought desperately, her mind racing in a thousand endless directions. Taking a deep breath, she realized that that "someone" must be *her*. Both Naomi and Orpah were far too hysterical to do Chilion a bit of good.

Again, she pled silently for the Lord's help, then, coming gently between Naomi and Orpah, Ruth knelt before the still form of her arrogant brother-in-law.

Naomi lurched toward Ruth and buried her face in her tunic. "Oh, Ruth! What are we going to do, Ruth – "

Ruth took Naomi by the shoulders and replied steadily, "It's going to be alright, Naomi. Let me have a look at him."

Like that of a small, grief-stricken child, Naomi nodded weakly and hesitantly backed away.

Orpah was still shrieking, her voice rising in pitch every couple of seconds. It was eerie. Ruth touched her shoulder as gently as possible and managed, "Orpah, I need you to stay calm if we are going to do your husband any good at all."

Orpah reverted to desperate whimpering rather than shrieking, which Ruth greatly appreciated. "Oh, in the gods' names, Ruth, what is happening? Is he *dead*?"

Ruth gazed levelly at Chilion's back and shoulders for several seconds. "He's breathing."

"Praise God! Praise God!" Naomi broke into a new fit of sobs, the tears flowing freely. "Then he is alright?"

"I am not sure," Ruth responded honestly. *A fall like that is bound to give him some type of brain damage,* Ruth thought skeptically. *Not that he was particularly bright before this happened.* And then it suddenly occurred to her that, should Chilion die from whatever was ailing him, he might very well die without the Lord. Ruth reached for the pressure point tucked beneath Chilion's jawline and felt a very weak pulse. She realized that he could be dying. But what could she do? How could she help? She felt overwhelmed and frightened at a sudden realization – both Naomi's and Orpah's future depended upon her ability to act quickly and save the life of this man.

No, she reminded herself firmly. *Not* my *ability – the Lord's. The future belongs to* Him, *not to me.*

"We must get him away from here," Ruth rose to her feet in a commanding manner. "I need to have a good look at him, and get a cold compress on his head. We can't do that with him lying face-down in the middle of the kitchen floor."

Gulping back pathetic sobs, Orpah nodded and struggled to her feet.

Naomi's eyes widened at the prospect of three small women somehow relocating a 180-pound male even the short distance from the kitchen to a bedchamber. "But, Ruth, how will we do it?"

"By God's strength," Ruth responded without hesitation, rolling back the long, flowing sleeves of her tunic and gripping Chilion's ankles. It seemed like mere days since she had gripped her own senseless husband's ankles in this very position in order to lift his unconscious form into Chilion's wagon, the night of the wedding feast... Then it occurred to her.

"Mahlon!" She cried, dubious that it had taken her this long to remember. "Mahlon can help us carry him!"

"Yes, yes!" Naomi shook her head emphatically. "Get him!"

Ruth's eyes darted across the room. Where in the world was he, anyway? She hadn't seen him since she had prayed for him early that morning and he had threatened to forcefully remove her from the room. Perhaps he had left for one of his drunken, adulterous, ungodly "religious" excursions to one of the pagan temples of Chemosh. If so, he would not return in any state of mind capable of being of any help to them. On the other hand, it wasn't unusual for him to remain idle in bed for several days at a time. There was a good chance that he was still right there in the house with them. Could he have possibly slept through all that chaos?

There was only one way to find out. Purposefully, Ruth dropped Chilion's ankles in the dust and hurried for her own bedroom, praying that Mahlon would still be there.

Ducking through the low-lying, sagging doorway, Ruth swept into the room, pausing long enough to allow her eyes to adjust to the all-encompassing dimness. She could make out the smelly straw mattress in the corner, and the narrow silhouette of her husband still lying in bed, his bare feet sticking out from beneath the rough, woolen sheet.

Ruth felt a surge of hope course through her entire body. He was still here! They would not have to shoulder the burden of such a large man alone.

"Mahlon!" She cried, her voice gaining strength. "Oh, Mahlon!"

She received no response. Ruth felt her relief souring to

utter resentment and frustration. If Mahlon was pretending to sleep through this in order to remain slothfully in bed...

"Mahlon!" Ruth knelt at his bedside and gripped his shoulders. "Wake up, please! We need your help!"

Even in the dim light, Ruth could not miss the eerie paleness of his features, nor the wide eyes that remained open, motionless.

"Mahlon?" repulsed, Ruth recoiled in horror and disgust. Surely he wasn't...

"Mahlon, Mahlon, please!" It took every ounce of courage that she possessed, but Ruth rocked forward on her knees and began to shake her husband's stiff shoulders. "Mahlon, please, say something! Wake up!" Her voice broke, lost in a procession of frightened sobs. "Please!"

Jumping to her feet, she gazed through tear-blurred eyes at the still form of her husband.

He wasn't moving.

Chapter 6

LOST

Mahlon is dead.

The thought echoed endlessly through Ruth's exhausted mind – frightening, haunting, chilling, foreboding.

He is dead. Dead – without the Lord. Dead – without the assurance of God's approval. Dead – without the prospect of salvation. Dead and gone forever – his name would soon fade to a distant memory, and soon after that, his very existence would be remembered no more.

And he died alone. Ruth shuddered at the thought, her back pressed firmly against the wall, hugging her own weak knees close to her chest. She had no warm feelings for the deceased Mahlon, no void in her heart upon his departure. Yet, she couldn't help but ache at the thought of the man gasping and wheezing for breath as death's dark shadow hovered over him, as terror and utter panic must have swept over his entire being and overwhelmed his very soul.

I should have been there. There must have been something I could have done. She did not love the man in the sense that most women "loved" their husbands – she had never once desired him, never longed for his embrace, never missed him when he was away. She knew this was because he was so entrenched in pagan, fleshly evil that to allow her heart to feel such things for him would only drag her down in the mud and the mire of his despicable sins. She had known from the moment she had been given to him in marriage that he was not a safe man – she could never give her heart to him, nor trust him to protect or cherish her. However, upon giving her life to the Lord, she had been flooded with an overwhelming desire to pray for him, to beseech Almighty God on his behalf and plead that Mahlon would somehow forsake his pagan ways and choose to live for the God of his fathers as well.

But now he was dead – gone – and that opportunity to save even the dark soul of her husband was forever lost.

Perhaps I did not pray hard enough. Perhaps, if I had been there as he lay on his deathbed, I could have convinced him to submit to the Lord. If only I had known. If only I could have been there. If only...

Folding her arms over her knees, she buried her face and wept despairingly over the loss of a young man who had chosen to reject the only One Who could have possibly saved him. Such a terrible loss was gut-wrenching, tragic. In that awful moment, her mind was flooded with memories – memories that she had intentionally shoved aside for years and years.

She was reminded of her wedding day. The girls she had grown up with cherished fond memories of their weddings – of that first night with the man they planned to spend the rest of their lives with.

Not so for Ruth. The day she had been given to Mahlon

in marriage was more like a living nightmare than a fairy-tale. She remembered tossing and turning restlessly the night before the wedding, petrified at what was to come the following day. She remembered the tears stinging her cheeks as she begged and pled with her mother to save her from such a fate, to intervene.

"I cannot marry him," she had whispered, the awful reality of what was to come tearing at her very heart. "He is not a good man, Mama. He does not love me."

"You silly girl," her mother had chided, exasperated. "Mahlon would not have sought your hand in marriage had he no feelings for you."

But Ruth had known better. She knew of his reputation. She knew how often he frequented temple prostitutes and sacrificed to the cruel god of the Moabites – Chemosh – the god who was said to have demanded the blood of innocent babies and small, helpless children.

But the idle, simple-minded, self-seeking Mahlon had noticed Ruth – a young, bright-eyed girl of rare beauty, and so full of life – and had decided that he wanted her. And when his kindly mother – still grieving the recent, unexpected death of her husband – had come to negotiate with Ruth's father, Ruth's pitiable fate had been sealed.

She remembered the moment she had been given to her husband. She had been clad in the loveliest of wedding garments, and her mother had cried softly, claiming that she was a stunning vision indeed, an angel of unusual beauty. Mahlon had lifted the veil before her face and recoiled, repulsed by the tear-stained cheeks and puffy red eyes that met his.

Though Ruth had fought to forget the painful memory for ten years now, she was shocked at the vividness with which she could recall that one defining moment. She remembered the sudden surge of hope that had flooded her heart the moment her eyes had locked with her future husband's. She remembered pondering that maybe, just *maybe*, he would reach out in tenderness and reassure her with a promise of commitment and devotion... a promise that might somehow persuade her to rethink her distress.

But, no. It was at that moment that Ruth fully understood and accepted the fact that this man had no kindness in him. His taut features stretched even tighter and he leaned uncomfortably close, sneering. "If I had known you were capable of looking this revolting, I never would have asked you to marry me."

Ruth's heart had thudded wildly as her greatest fears were harshly confirmed.

Gripping her arm tightly and pulling her close to him, he snarled, "I don't care how you do it, but you had better get yourself together and look somewhat appealing before our wedding night. Be thankful you have several hours to pull yourself together, you ungrateful shrew."

Such memories were nothing but a painful stab to the heart. Ruth shook her head in disbelief, dismissing her unpleasant thoughts with a shaky sigh. Ever since she had surrendered her life to the Lord, she had been sure that somehow God would intervene and win her husband to His side. Why else would He have allowed her to endure such horror for the past ten years after becoming Mahlon's wife? There had to be some defining reason, some specific purpose. She had been sure of it. But now Mahlon was gone forever, and he had probably died shaking his angry fist in the face of the God that she had grown to love so much. It all seemed so utterly pointless, so completely, maddeningly meaningless.

Somewhere in the distance, a bird chirped its lonely

song. The sun was setting slowly on yet another disappointing day in Moab. Ruth pressed her back even harder against the crumbling stone wall of their dwelling and shaded her blurry eyes from the sun's final rays. She knew she should be inside, comforting Naomi, or assisting Orpah. The frenzied young woman had spent the day half-heartedly attempting to nurse her unconscious husband back to health.

Oh, poor Orpah.

As if things could get any worse, Chilion was also dying. Ruth knew it, she just refused to voice such a disheartening truth. She was convinced that Orpah knew it as well. Each time their eyes had met as they had busily fetched water for Chilion's parched throat or pressed cold compresses against his sweaty forehead, their eyes had silently shared the awful truth. It was only a matter of time. Even as Mahlon lay dead on the straw mattress of Ruth's bedchamber, the same horrific fate was now overtaking his older brother. Ruth assumed that he would be gone before the sun rose again.

"What troubles you, my daughter?"

Ruth started at Naomi's unexpected presence. She raised her slim brows incredulously and gazed up at her mother-in-law through her tears. What kind of question was that? She shook her head and lowered her gaze, unable to voice her anxious thoughts.

"Oh, my dear Ruth," Naomi lowered herself slowly to the ground beside her young daughter-in-law with great effort. Draping an arm across Ruth's shoulders, and, as if reading Ruth's very thoughts, she said quietly, "There is nothing you could have done, Ruth. There is nothing any of us could have done."

Ruth felt a new, fresh stream of tears at Naomi's gentle assurance. She reached for Naomi's hand and held it firmly for several moments. Naomi had just lost her youngest son, and Heaven knew she was about to lose her oldest as well. She had lost everything – her husband *and* her children. Ruth knew that *she* should be the one comforting Naomi, and yet here she was, crying like a child, while her bereaved, aging mother-in-law administered comfort to *her*. "Oh, Naomi," she wept, "I am so sorry. So terribly sorry..."

"Don't, child! You were faithful to my son to the very end, even unto death. Even as he mocked you, neglected you, mistreated you... you demonstrated our Father's love day after day, and you did so expecting nothing in return."

Ruth looked to Naomi in utter amazement. For the first time, it occurred to Ruth that the sacrifices she had made and the forbearing love she had bestowed upon an unkind and ungrateful husband had not gone unnoticed – at least not in Naomi's eyes. Naomi had indeed noticed, and now her soft eyes filled with tears and with a look that spoke a thousand silent words of complete appreciation and gratitude.

"Ruth," Naomi continued, "Your selfless life spoke to my son more than measly, meaningless words *ever* could. Even though Mahlon made it exceedingly difficult, you chose to reflect the love of our Father in Heaven. There is no greater witness than that, my daughter. No greater witness than that."

"Yes, but to what avail?" Ruth surprised herself with the passion by which she spoke "And for what purpose? Mahlon is dead, and now he will *never* know our Lord, Naomi! It is too late!" Her voice trailed off and she realized that she had no tears left to shed. "It is too late," she repeated softly.

The strength in Naomi's eyes surprised Ruth as she responded, "Perhaps not."

Ruth searched Naomi's gray eyes hopefully. "What are you saying, Naomi?"

Naomi shook her head, her jaw set firmly and her eyes searching the distant hills now tinged pink and golden with the final rays of the setting sun. "I am saying, Ruth, that no one knows what took place those final moments of my son's life. No one knows what exchange might have occurred between my son and his Creator as he realized that he was passing from this life to the next. Perhaps the Lord spoke comfort to his heart. Perhaps Mahlon chose to accept it, chose to offer a feeble cry of repentance to the One Who had been patiently waiting for him all along." Naomi paused, her lip quivering as the cold, hard reality of the death of her child continued to take its terrible toll. "We will never know, but we will always hope."

Ruth squeezed Naomi's hand and somehow managed a smile. "You are right, Naomi. We will never know, but we can put our trust in the Lord and we can choose to hope."

"And," Naomi added, wiping away her tears with the back of her hand, "you ask to what purpose did such things have to happen? And to what avail? It will not offend this old woman to think that surely you must have wished a thousand times that another man had taken you to be his wife. My son left much to be desired, and sadly he treated you – a rare treasure, a precious gem – in a dreadful, unacceptable manner. But, Ruth, there is absolutely no doubt in my mind that the Lord had a very specific purpose in bringing you into my life. There must have been a reason behind my son's decision to choose you."

Ruth looked to Naomi, curious. "For many months I believed that the purpose was to bring Mahlon into a relationship with our God."

Naomi smiled, and shook her head knowingly. "Imagine, Ruth... had you married someone else, *you* may have never met the Lord, never known the one, true God! Had one of these Moabite men taken you to be his wife, surely you would not have heard of the mighty God of Abraham, of Isaac, and of Jacob from him – nor from his family. Though your life as the wife of my son was poor and miserable at best, your eternal fate was sealed for glory when you met the true God of my fathers! Do you see, Ruth, how the Lord had a purpose for you – how He took even an undesirable, unpleasant situation and worked it out for your good?"

Ruth's mind reeled as the pieces all fell into place like that of a complicated puzzle. She was amazed at the precision and detail in which the Lord had purposefully coordinated all the events of her life to make something beautiful. Even the most painful circumstances forced upon her had been skillfully crafted into something wonderful by her Father's hand.

Naomi touched Ruth's shoulder gently and added with an air of finality, "And I am certain that the Lord will continue to work in your life in beautiful ways, Ruth, if you remain faithful to Him."

"Oh, Naomi!" Ruth threw her arms around the aging woman's neck and embraced her warmly. How Naomi's words had comforted her aching heart and tumultuous thoughts! In that one moment, Ruth resolved to never doubt the Lord's will, or His love for her. A God Who had so carefully directed the steps of a young foreign woman – even before she had known Him or given her heart to Him – would surely not forsake her. All along, with every disappointing twist and turn her life had taken, He had been there, guiding her steps, leading her safely by the hand through an unforgiving and unmerciful world. He had proven faithful. She knew that she must prove faithful to Him as well.

It suddenly occurred to Ruth that her work was not over. Within the confining walls of her own home, a lost soul lay dying and in desperate need of his Savior. Ruth felt a twinge of guilt for taking even this precious amount of Naomi's time when her very last family member wasted away in a dark, lonely room.

With a sense of urgency, Ruth rose to her feet and offered Naomi a hand. "We may have little time left, Naomi," she said quickly. "Your words have meant much to me, but now it is time to comfort Chilion in his hour of need. Perhaps it is not too late for him, Naomi!"

Naomi's eyes clouded over with tears as she allowed Ruth to help her rise. "I have tried and tried to talk to him, Ruth. He merely sets his jaw and looks the other way. I have committed my cause to the Lord. I pray that our God will reach him yet. You are right. There is very little time."

Solemnly, the two women entered the dark, foreboding bedchamber. Orpah stood at the opposite end of the room, as far away from her dying husband as possible. Though she felt great obligation to care for him during these last moments of his, she obviously feared that his condition was contagious.

She would be feeding him by means of a ten-foot pole if we had one, Ruth thought in frustration. This was no way to reach a lost soul – no way to convince him that they truly had his best interest at heart and wanted to help him.

Sighing sadly, Ruth touched Orpah's shoulder then pushed past her and knelt at the bedside of the once sturdy, haughty Chilion – now limp and ever so still, his chest rising and falling slowly with every labored breath that he took.

He looked deathly pale and his lips were crusty and dry. Ruth wondered if he was conscious.

After uttering a silent prayer for the soul of this man, Ruth ventured in a very low whisper, "Chilion?"

Slowly, painfully, Chilion turned his head in her direction. Grimacing, his dark eyes – once fierce and flashing – fluttered open. Ruth felt her heart drop at the gaping emptiness in those eyes. He seemed completely resigned to the fate resting before him. He had lost all hope. He had given up.

Ruth's eyes clouded with tears. She could not bear to see another soul perish without the hope of God's love. Silently, she begged God to give her the right words – words that would touch Chilion's very soul and soften his stony heart. She picked up the damp cloth on the small, wooden table at his bedside, dipped it in the basin of cool water, and gently dabbed at his feverish forehead. "This doesn't have to be the end, you know."

Somehow, Chilion managed to stretch his lips into a contorted, rueful grin. "Ah, Ruth," he rasped painfully. "Always the optimist."

Ruth passed over his leering sarcasm and pressed on, her eyes flooded with willful determination. "But it *doesn't*! I can't let you go without the Lord, Chilion. He loves you too much. Don't do this to Naomi, Chilion! Don't do this to your wife! How can they bear losing you if they have no hope of ever seeing you again?"

"Do you even hear yourself, Ruth?" Chilion scoffed, struggling to speak. "You're listening to..."

"To what?" Ruth demanded, fearful of what he might say next.

"*Fairytales*, Ruth! That's all they are," Chilion rasped painfully. "You're listening to my mother's fairytales, and there's not a bit of truth in them. Who ever heard of a God raining bread from the sky like spring showers, just to feed a herd of selfish people who didn't even deserve to breathe? Who ever heard of a God Who actually took the time to look down from His throne in Heaven to notice a stubborn people so small that to Him they must have appeared as mere ants? To interfere with great signs and wonders and miracles – the kind that you so often read about but never actually *see*? Who ever heard of a God like that, Ruth?"

"Not only have I heard of Him, but I *know* a God like that, Chilion. Yes, I know that it sounds too wonderful for you – too good to be true – because the gods you serve are mere idols, fashioned from stone, wood, and clay! Idols created by human hands – then worshipped by the very hands that created them! How could a lifeless chunk of rock or wood perform miracles in the life of the ones who fashioned it? Our God isn't like that, Chilion! *He* fashioned *us* – created each and every one of us with His own mighty hand! We must give to Him the glory which He deserves! We must acknowledge Him as Lord of our lives if there is to be any hope – "

"Oh, please. You sound like my mother," Chilion's eyes were defiant, but the growing weakness in his voice frightened Ruth.

"He loves you, Chilion. He wants to give you good things..." A tear dropped from Ruth's eyes, landing on Chilion's hand. His eyes met hers, and he softened ever so slightly.

"Listen to me, Ruth, I know your heart is in the right place. I know you just want to help. But don't worry about me, alright? My fate has already been decided."

"But it *hasn't*!" Ruth cried, taking his hand in her own. "It hasn't been decided, Chilion. God gave each of us the choice! We can choose whom to serve! Don't you see how the choice is yours, Chilion?"

Chilion's chest began to rise and fall even more rapidly as he struggled for every rasping, excruciating breath. Her eyes pleading, Ruth looked to Naomi, who still stood at the opposite end of the room, cradling the sobbing Orpah in her arms. Gently helping Orpah settle down upon a rough-hewn, wooden stool near the doorway, Naomi crept to Ruth's side and took both her son's hands in her own, stunned at how very limp and lifeless they felt in her own weak hands. "My son," she whispered softly, "indeed Ruth speaks what is true. The choice belongs to you. This is the greatest, most important decision you could ever make, son."

"And most likely the *last*," Chilion managed ruefully.

Naomi looked helplessly to Ruth, her lips quivering, her hands trembling even as she cradled Chilion's in her own. But she pressed on, her voice soft and shaky. "Do you know how much I love you, Chilion?"

Chilion set his jaw firmly and nodded, ever so slightly. Even the slightest bit of motion seemed to take a huge toll on his dying body, and he grimaced in pain.

"Have you ever once doubted my love, my son?"

His whisper was barely audible. "No."

"Do you know, Chilion, that our God loves you even more than I ever could?"

"*Your* God, not mine."

Dabbing gently at Chilion's forehead again, Ruth smiled softly. "But He can be your God as well as ours. Are you ready to make that decision, Chilion?"

The silence that followed was ominous, foreboding. With bated breath, the three women in the room waited to see what Chilion's response would be.

Setting his jaw firmly, Chilion craned his neck and turned his head away from the pleading women who knelt at his bedside. With the firmness and finality of an unexpected blow to the face, he replied, "No."

Then, he was gone.

Chapter 7

ORPAH

Ruth slept fitfully that night, drifting between a dreadful state of wakefulness and haunted slumber, disturbed by the horrible fact that she, Naomi, and Orpah now shared their simple dwelling with two dead bodies – two empty, lifeless shells of men that had once been living, vibrant, beloved.

Ruth had never seen Naomi so distraught. She had managed to hold herself together upon the death of Mahlon, but losing both sons within a matter of hours seemed to be a burden of inexplicable magnitude. Ruth feared for the dear woman's sanity. How could one lose everything – her entire family – within a few short hours and remain sane?

Naomi had wept for hours – mourning, wailing, sometimes screaming her protests, rocking back and forth like a desperate, fear-crazed child, cradling her knees to her chest and burying her tear-streaked face in her knees. "My babies! My poor, poor babies!" she had sobbed, her cries piercing Ruth's soul, chilling her heart to the very core and flooding her mind with haunting images of the difficult life that was sure to follow the three widows now living under that one lonely roof.

And a difficult life it would surely be. Ruth shuddered to think of what the remainder of her life – as well as Orpah's and Naomi's – might turn out to be. With no men to protect or provide, they had very little hope of survival– especially in a land as perverted and sadistic as Moab.

The Lord will take care of us, Ruth reminded herself over and over again as her open eyes searched the inky blackness of their dwelling. She lay stiffly on her back near the stove in the kitchen section of their dwelling upon a makeshift bed of straw. Naomi and Orpah lay several feet away from her, also on temporary beds of scratchy straw. None of them desired to share a bedroom with a corpse. Tonight, the kitchen would be their place of refuge.

Sighing in frustration, Ruth rolled over onto her side, propping herself up on her elbow and searching the thick darkness for Naomi's still form.

Ah, there she was. Ruth could barely make out the small silhouette of her sleeping mother-in-law, just a few feet away. Ruth was thankful that Naomi had finally managed to fall into a fitful slumber. Perhaps sleep would wash away the stark memory of that afternoon's unbearable trauma – at least temporarily, until morning arrived.

For the first time since that fateful night before her wedding day, Ruth actually dreaded the arrival of the dawn.

How will I ever comfort Naomi? How can I bring peace to her aching heart? And what of Orpah? Oh, Lord, I need You more than ever. Have I the strength to pull through? Rising slowly, silently, to her feet, Ruth carefully ducked out of their shabby dwelling place and crept out into the darkness. She needed some time alone with God. Only by His awesome strength could she possibly gather the courage to press on.

Lighting a small fire in the pit before the house, Ruth lowered herself to the ground and gazed into the kindling flames, silently pouring out her soul to her Creator, begging for His mercies, His provision, His guidance and protection.

Precious Lord, I need Your help. I don't know what to do. I know I must do my part to provide for this broken little family of mine. How might I lighten the pain that must be gripping poor Naomi's heart tonight? How might I work to keep us fed and clothed? Please, Lord, show me what to do. Lead me down the path that You have chosen for me, Father. I have seen Your hand upon my life from the very day I was born. I trust that You will not leave me now, even in this dreadful hour of great tragedy. Please show me what to do, Father. Please show me what to do.

Ruth tried to calm her racing mind and focus on the warmth of the fire, the tranquility of the night, the stars shining like tiny gems in the distant sky, dazzling her with their exquisite beauty and magnificence.

Instead, her thoughts ran wild within her aching mind – fearful thoughts, anxious thoughts, indignant thoughts, angry thoughts.

I could remarry, she thought with a fearful shudder. *It may be the only way to provide for Naomi, Orpah, and myself. But to intentionally marry a Moabite man, who bends his knee to the dreadful gods of Moab? I couldn't. I would rather go hungry.* She shook her head in bitter helplessness.

But what of Naomi? Poor, poor Naomi. I cannot let her amble through the rest of her lonely existence in want of food, clothing, shelter. I cannot. I must look out for her. Perhaps there is another way. She sighed loudly, defeated. *But must a woman marry to be secure?* Again, she sighed. *In this world, she must. But perhaps not...I have heard of women who have been quite successful weaving cloth and selling it to the merchants... or making jewelry... or pottery...* Again, she shook her head. She had neither the skills nor experience to attempt such bold business ventures, but perhaps she could learn. *But even if I could learn, how could we afford the materials needed to make such things for sale?* Another dead end. But she refused to give up. She'd think of something. *Well, there are women so desperate that they sell their own bodies...*

Ruth shuddered. *No.* She would *never* stoop to such a level. Even if in dire need, if in complete and utter distress, she would *never* sell the body her Lord had given her. She knew that her strength of body and mind was a gift to be used to glorify and honor Him. Such a terrible practice could not possibly please Him.

But I must provide somehow. Oh, Lord, what must I do?

The answer came to her as clearly and distinctly as though it were being whispered directly into her ear. The voice was still, small, speaking softly to her heart. *Do not be afraid. Stand still, and see the salvation of the Lord, which He will accomplish for you today... The Lord will fight for you, and you shall hold your peace...*

Hiding her face in her hands, Ruth choked back sobs and cried out to the Lord with a joyful heart. "Thank you, God! I know You are with me. I know You will never leave me!" Trembling in awe and the most incredible sense of wonder, Ruth marveled that the God of the universe would take the time to minister to her doubtful heart with the very words He had revealed to her that one sacred night in which she had given her life to Him. The night in which He had stolen her heart.

"What on earth are you doing out here, Ruth? It's the middle of the night, for goodness' sake."

Her joyous thoughts interrupted, Ruth turned to see Orpah emerging from the gaping mouth of the doorway like a dim star escaping from a black hole.

Ruth smiled. "Good morning, Orpah."

"*Morning*? Is it even morning yet, Ruth?"

Ruth gazed up at the stars, twinkling faintly in the distant sky. Sheer, wispy clouds streaked their way across the midnight sky, barely visible, rather like smoke rising horizontally from a hot oven. "If not, it should be here soon," she replied, enjoying the warmth of the flickering fire and the coolness of the wee morning hours. "Would you care to join me?"

Orpah looked around as if she expected her mother to appear out of nowhere and scold her for getting out of bed. "Well… alright," she agreed reluctantly, plopping down on the ground next to her sister-in-law and pulling her shawl tighter around her shivering body. "Is it cold out here or am I still shuddering from the horror of it all?"

Ruth shook her head. "Perhaps both."

Orpah sighed, discouraged. "Perhaps."

Both women sat in silence for what felt like hours. Ruth felt at peace in her heart, and she feared that Orpah might attempt to shatter her blissful state of calm at any moment. Not intentionally, of course. Orpah did not share Ruth's faith, and was quick to admit that she didn't understand it but wanted no part of it. How could she possibly understand this peace that surpassed any and all understanding during a time as trying as this? She *couldn't*, without the help of God Himself.

Finally, after an eternity of silence, Orpah spoke. "Are you afraid?"

Ruth took a moment to ponder the question. Then asked quietly, "Afraid of what, Orpah?"

"Of being alone." Her tone was dark, foreboding.

"Alone?" Ruth repeated.

Orpah nodded.

"Of course not. I'm not alone."

Orpah arched a dark, slender brow. "Yes, you are, Ruth. We both are."

Ruth's eyes twinkled playfully. "How can you say that? I'm right beside you, and you're right here with me. If we're together, then how can we possibly be alone?"

Orpah rolled her eyes dramatically. "Be serious, Ruth. We *are* alone. We've lost both our husbands. Both of them – gone – in one day. Just like that!" She snapped her fingers in a mysterious manner and stared off into the distance, her eyes vague, her lips taut. "What are we going to do? We've lost everything – *everything*! We're widows, Ruth – *widows*! Can you wrap your pretty little head around that fact? Here we are, Ruth – so young and beautiful and so full of potential – and yet we're already *widows*! We might as well have died with our husbands."

"You are right when you say we have lost our husbands, Orpah, but it's not so bad as you say. Naomi was widowed ten years earlier than we, and she has lived a beautiful life even without her Elimelech!"

"Sure, but Naomi was an *old woman* when her husband died! Look at us, Ruth! We're not *old*! We're young! We're beautiful! We have so much to live for, and yet our lives have ended before they ever truly began! It's over, Ruth. It's *over*." Orpah pummeled the ground with an angry fist, emphasizing each bitter word that proceeded from her mouth.

Ruth glanced anxiously over her shoulder, fearful that Orpah's angry outbursts might awaken the sleeping Naomi at any given moment. She couldn't let that happen. Naomi needed her rest. "Orpah – "

"Where are we to go from here, Ruth? We have nothing – absolutely *nothing* – to live for!"

Ruth shook her head solemnly. "That's not true, Orpah."

Orpah looked to Ruth in disgust, her green eyes flashing dangerously. How many times had Ruth seen Orpah shoot Chilion that very look of indignation?

"Alright, Ruth," Orpah responded, her voice low and threatening. "If you know *so* much, then would you be so kind as to explain exactly what it is that I'm missing here? What on earth do we have to live for?"

The One Who created us, Ruth wanted to scream. She wanted to sing and dance and shout it from the rooftops. The answer was so simple, so clear. And it was all so wonderful, so reassuring. In the brief twenty-four years that she had lived on this earth, she had already learned that this life was certainly not about her own comfort, her own pleasure, her own will. There was a greater purpose, a rock-solid reason behind every little occurrence on this sin-saturated planet, and one day her God would work all of it out for good. Why couldn't Mahlon, Chilion, or Orpah see that? Why couldn't they have turned from their selfish ways to find true, everlasting joy, a purpose for living, moving, breathing?

Though the answer was blatantly obvious to Ruth, she knew that childish Orpah would never understand. Orpah – who had been handed everything she had ever wanted from the moment she had uttered her first infant cry. Orpah – who had been born into a wealthy home and lavished with all the worldly pleasures that money could purchase. Orpah – who had been wed to a poor man because she had made up her mind that *he* was the one she wanted, and her parents could refuse her nothing that her hungry little heart desired. Orpah – who had later decided that perhaps marrying a simple man had not been the brightest idea for a woman of refined taste, and had later granted herself the pleasure of any alternative male company her heart might have desired… without her husband's knowledge, of course.

Orpah did not understand what it meant to deny oneself, to surrender one's own will or desires. So surely she would never understand what it meant to live for anyone other than herself.

Still, Ruth would not give up. Perhaps there was some bit of compassion, of mercy or goodwill in Orpah's greedy heart. "You ask me what we have to live for, Orpah? The answer is quite simple. I will live for my God – "

Orpah sighed loudly through her nose. "Well, good for you, Ruth. And what about *me*?"

What about me. Orpah's own words exposed the very intent of her heart. Ruth sighed sadly. *If only we could stop worrying about ourselves and start living for others…* she mused wistfully.

Once again, her silent musings were broken by Orpah's obstinate reproach. "Hello? Ruth? Is anybody home?"

"Oh, I'm sorry, Orpah. I believe I was lost in thought."

"So I gathered."

Ruth smiled and stated plainly, "There is yet another thing that you and I both may live for."

"Please, do tell."

Ruth smiled softly. "Naomi."

The silence was nearly ear-splitting. Orpah stared wide-eyed at her sister-in-law. She took a moment to regain her composure, then burst out impatiently, "You can't be serious, Ruth!"

"Of course I'm serious."

Orpah was instantly on her feet, pacing to and fro before the faint, flickering firelight and gesturing with her hands like a mad woman. "Well, thank you, Ruth! My life is suddenly so full of purpose!" she spat out sarcastically. "I cannot wait to spend the rest of my life looking after a desperate, moody, needy old woman who – by the way – has *also* lost everything and has *nothing* to live for!"

Ruth's eyes followed the pacing form of her furious sister-in-law, and it was almost comical. Silently, Ruth asked God for the strength to minister to this poor, confused woman and hopefully bring her to a full understanding of His perfect love for her.

Orpah was nearly shouting again before Ruth could even open her mouth. "You know everyone is going to be talking about us, right? I'm not even going to be able to go to the well to collect our drinking water without a thousand eyes boring into me, and all the women whispering behind my back about poor, widowed, little Orpah! You know it's true, Ruth!"

A rueful smile played about the corner of Ruth's ruby lips. "You're probably right."

"And you're just going to sit there grinning like an utter fool?"

"Let them say what they will."

"How can you say that?" Orpah demanded. "Don't you care?"

"I care what the Lord thinks of me. The rest can think what they may."

Orpah's nostrils flared. "Do you know what *I* think of you right now?"

"I can imagine."

"And do you care about *that*?"

Ruth's eyes gleamed merrily. "Not at all."

Orpah threw her hands up into the air and groaned. "Oh, you're *impossible*, Ruth! Maybe *you* don't care, but *I* do! How can I live my life when I can't even go to the well to gather water without all the women gossiping behind my back about what a miserable life I have?"

"Then prove them wrong."

"What are you talking about?"

"Prove them wrong. Prove to them that your life is anything but miserable!" Ruth smiled convincingly.

Orpah shook her head, infuriated. "But my life *is* miserable!" She nearly screamed.

Ruth glanced up at her with a playful gleam in her dark eyes. "But it doesn't have to be. Only *you* can decide how you are going to conduct yourself, Orpah – how you will handle the trials that life throws your way."

"You're not making any sense, Ruth. I can't bring Chilion back to life. He's dead. Gone! And – just in case you need me to spell it out for you, Ruth – that makes me a widow! Don't you know the social standing of a widow, Ruth? I'll be a *nobody*! And I'll have to shuffle around town in those drab, dark mourning garments looking like an ugly, old spinster –"

"Well, you will have to remain in seclusion for the designated time of mourning first – " Ruth cut in somewhat playfully, knowing that it would only further infuriate her sister-in-law.

"Exactly! So while I sit here all alone – looking hideous, mind you, in those awful garments of mourning – other young women will be getting on with their happy lives, with their happy husbands and happy families. And I'm just going to rot!" Orpah plopped back onto the ground, a puff of dust seeming to emphasize her distress.

"Go with me, Orpah – before anyone else arrives."

"What?"

"To the well. You are worried for your reputation you say. Well then, if you wish to avoid becoming a public spectacle to all your happy friends with their happy families, then go with me before they arrive!"

Orpah rolled her eyes. "We weren't even talking about the well anymore."

"I think the quiet time before dawn might suit us both. We will arrive long before the rest of the women of the town. And we can quietly go about our business then return home." Ruth grinned. "I could sure use the help pushing aside that heavy stone – "

"But I don't want to go early in the morning before the rest – those women are my friends! I can't lose my husband *and* my friends! I'll die!"

"But you're worried that your friends are going to be gossiping about you, isn't that right, Orpah?"

"*Yes*! Finally, you start to get it, Ruth."

"Then perhaps you should find some nicer friends."

"*Ugh*! Just forget it, Ruth! You'll never understand." Orpah pulled her knees up to her chin and began to rock back and forth like a spoiled little child.

As Ruth gazed upon the defeated form of her bereaved sister-in-law rocking pitifully to and fro, her heart began to throb with pity for the helpless woman. Without God in her life, she had no hope. If only she would accept the help of the One Who could transform her broken life into something beautiful, as He had done for Ruth.

Stretching out her hand, Ruth placed it softly on Orpah's shoulder.

Orpah jerked away and glared at Ruth through tear-blurred eyes. "Maybe I won't have to worry about it. Maybe we'll all be struck dead with the same disease, then we'll all die and be laid to rest, and we won't have a single care in all the world."

"Orpah, don't talk like that."

"Don't tell me what to do, Ruth! Aren't you afraid?"

"Of?"

"Of catching it? The disease, I mean. The one that killed them."

Ruth bit her lower lip. The thought *had* crossed her mind, especially since she had been the sole nurse and caregiver to Orpah's dying husband. But rather than dwell on that disturbing prospect, she had adamantly decided to cast such a care upon the Lord and trust Him to protect her from all pestilence and disease.

"I'm not afraid. My God is faithful. He will protect me," she finally responded.

"Then why did you hesitate?" Orpah snapped.

"Sometimes I know not how to answer you, Orpah. You disagree with everything that I say."

"With good reason!" Orpah snapped again. "You say your God will protect you?"

"I do."

"Just like He protected Naomi?" Orpah hissed.

"What do you mean?"

"Protected her!" Orpah sneered, her eyes cold, her voice hard. "After all that woman's been through, you truly have the gall to say that your God has *protected* her?"

Ruth felt her cheeks flush with righteous indignation. How dare this ignorant young woman speak of the Lord God Almighty – the One Who spoke the earth into existence, the One who parted the roaring waters of the Red Sea and led His chosen people safely home, the One Who held the entire universe in the palm of His hand – with such derision, such disdain?

"You call *that* protection, Ruth? No, thank you. I'll be having none of that."

"Naomi is still here, isn't she? And she still has her health, her sanity, her faith – "

Orpah snorted. "We shall see how long *that* lasts."

Ruth bit her tongue fiercely and forced herself to remain calm. Lashing out in fury would certainly not save Orpah. In fact, that kind of reaction was probably exactly what Orpah was fishing for. Ruth refused to give in.

Help me be strong, Lord, she prayed. *Help me to defend Your holy Name.*

Slowly, steadily, Ruth responded, "I know the Lord, Orpah, and I know Naomi. Both have earned my trust. Naomi may weep for a time, but her faith will not be shaken. Truly, God *has* protected her. She is still here – "

"Well, she might as well *not* be," Orpah concluded with a haughty *harrumph*. "Her life is over."

"Only if she chooses to see it that way." Leaning back, her work-roughened palms planted flat against the cool, dusty ground, Ruth added with a smile, "However, I know her well enough to say that she will not see it as such. Naomi still has much to live for. Her purpose in life has not ended merely because the lives of her sons and husband have."

"You are unbelievable."

"Is that a compliment?" Again, Ruth's dark eyes gleamed playfully.

"*No*," Orpah snapped. "Absolutely not. You're the most unrealistic person I have ever met."

"Perhaps. But may I ask you a question?"

"No."

"Then I will ask it anyway, and beg forgiveness afterwards. You say I am impossible... unbelievable... the most unrealistic person you have ever met..."

"That is *exactly* what I say."

"But between you and I, Orpah, which one of us would you say is the happiest? Which one of us is truly at peace in her heart?"

Orpah's eyes flashed colder than steel. "Because one of us walks around with her head in the clouds playing make-believe all day long – that doesn't mean she's happier than the other. She's simply more gullible than the other."

Ruth hoped that her eyes would not betray the hurt and anger welling up inside of her. She knew that she must remain calm, regardless of the stinging insults Orpah continued to hurl in her direction. *It's truly no different than the way I learned to respond to Mahlon,* she reminded herself silently. Even as the thought crossed her mind, she felt the sharp pang of loss in her gut, an unsettling reminder that her husband was no longer in the land of the living.

Orpah sighed loudly, her features softening ever so slightly. "Look, I know your faith is important to you. And if it can somehow carry you through this awful time, then I shall even be happy for you."

Ruth gave a little half-smile of acknowledgment. "I wish you would be willing to open your heart to this truth," she whispered softly, "for it would carry you through these trying times as well, sister-in-law."

"I do not need a crutch." Orpah shook her head adamantly. "I'd like to think that I'm stronger than that, Ruth. My father taught me well. He knew that religion only distracts people from their true potential. You have to know what you want in life, Ruth, then you have to go after it. Like my father, I'm not going to let some make-believe, feel-good story get in the way of what I want for my life."

"Even if God's plans for your life are far greater than your own?"

"Have you not heard the tales of Chemosh and the gods

my ancestors worshiped? They are not interested in helping *me*. They need *me* to help *them*."

"My God is not like that."

Orpah cupped her face in her hands, several loose tendrils of dark brown hair bouncing about her prominent forehead. "It has been a very long day, Ruth. I have no desire to discuss such things tonight – "

"Orpah – "

"Enough, Ruth!" Orpah turned to look Ruth straight in the face, her slender brows nearly meeting in the middle as her face contorted in restrained fury. "Tomorrow we bury them. It will be yet another day of agony. We should get some rest."

With that, Orpah pushed herself back to her feet and disappeared into the dark shadows of their dilapidated home.

Shutting her eyes tightly – as if that could somehow shut out the troubling thoughts whirling about in her sorely disturbed mind – Ruth uttered a final, silent prayer before retreating for some rest herself.

Lord, I tried my best. Please grant me the courage and the ability to continue to share Your love with her.

Chapter 8

THE BURIAL

Ruth wondered if she had been presumptuous to assume that Naomi would recover from her loss and continue to serve her Lord with the grace and determination with which she had served Him thus far.

Naomi was inconsolable. Ruth had never seen her in such a condition. She appeared to have aged another fifteen years overnight. Her eyes were puffy and bloodshot, appearing completely lifeless and set deep within dark, hollow sockets, as mournful as the blue circles beneath those red-rimmed eyes. Her hair stuck out every which way, completely unkempt, and Ruth would have certainly mistaken her for a mentally deranged beggar woman had she not known better. She had been aroused by the first early rays of golden sunlight, yet their slanting beams of cheerful yellow did little to brighten Naomi's desolate spirit. Ruth had been startled by the shrill cries of sheer grief coming from Naomi's corner of the kitchen. Those cries both chilled and frightened Ruth. Though her wails had eventually subsided, she was obviously drowning in the deepest type of sorrow this world allowed. She moved from room to room slowly, silently, looking much more like a pale, tormented spirit than the spritely, cheery, middle-aged woman that Ruth had grown to love.

After a terribly long night of pitiful tossing and turning, Ruth had risen from her straw pallet shortly after her disheartening conversation with Orpah, long before Naomi had begun to stir, deciding to get a head start on the day's dreadful arrangements.

She had already ventured to the well and drawn water for the day. She had already affectionately fed and watered their thin, aging donkey which grazed in the cramped pen behind the house. She had even baked some flat, unleavened bread and set it out to cool, hoping that Naomi would not refuse to eat but rather would understand the importance of keeping up her strength.

That seemed doubtful now.

But even as Ruth worked, she found herself musing, nearly brooding, completely lost in thought.

Naomi was beside herself. Orpah seemed to be vanishing from the scene more and more frequently these days. It looked like Ruth was going to have to remain the clear-headed one – at least long enough to get the ugly situation in check.

She winced at the first morbid thought that crossed her mind.

What was to be done about the bodies of Naomi's two sons?

Ruth had heard Naomi's stories of the strange burial customs of her native homeland in distant Israel. Would Naomi expect Ruth and Orpah to follow such customs upon the burial of their respective husbands? If so, Ruth would willingly honor Naomi's desires. She had already begged the Lord for the grace to put Naomi's needs above her own throughout the heart-rending ordeal of putting Naomi's two children in the ground.

Carefully laying the fresh bread on the stone ledge surrounding the oven to cool, Ruth reviewed the bits and pieces Naomi had shared with her about Israel's funeral and burial customs. She recalled Naomi mentioning a large funeral procession to be held to honor the deceased. Friends, relatives, and neighbors across the land would gather to follow closely behind the pallbearers as the body was taken to the family sepulcher. Some would play musical instruments. Others would join in the solemn funeral chants. Still others would raise their voices in melancholy moans of anguish and shrill cries of bitter grief. Why, Naomi had even said that the wealthy would often hire "professional mourners" to accompany the funeral procession to liven things up a bit. After all, how would it look if the family members and guests appeared anything other than completely grief-stricken upon the loss of a loved one?

As nice as those time-honored sentiments might have seemed, Ruth couldn't help but wonder if such fanciful customs could possibly be honored in a land such as Moab. She tried to recall the circumstances following the death of Naomi's husband, Elimelech. However, that tragic event had occurred many long years before. In fact, Elimelech had passed even before Ruth's undesirable union with his son, Mahlon. At that point, she had enjoyed her pre-sunrise conversations with Naomi at the well – who had also begun collecting the day's water even before the native women arrived – but Ruth had had no real knowledge concerning Naomi's private life and affairs. She wondered what kind of funeral Elimelech had received.

Ruth's next thought was equally fruitless. If even such a funeral procession was a possibility, how were she and

Orpah to go about making the arrangements? Naomi was certainly in no state of mind to arrange an extravagant ceremony.

Ruth realized that she had little time to plan. She knew that the Israelites buried their dead almost immediately. Today would have to be the day, whether they were prepared or not. It certainly would not do to let the bodies merely sit and decompose in their very home. Poor Naomi would be horrified at the sheer disrespect once she came to her senses.

Ruth decided that she would begin by asking Orpah for help. Perhaps she would know the proper channels by which they must communicate in order to set up such a thing.

Speaking of Orpah... Where was she? Furrowing her brows, Ruth fanned at the hot bread cooling on the shelf and rose slowly, slightly dizzy from the heat. She wondered if she would collapse from sheer exhaustion.

Her questions were answered by a rough knock at the door. Ruth could hear Orpah's brash tone from the other side of the door. "No need to knock, just go in," she was saying impatiently.

Ruth straightened as a tall, sturdy man appeared in the kitchen – a man she did not recognize. But the animalistic grin and the hungry eyes quickly reminded her that – baking alone in her own kitchen – she had neglected to wear her shawl and her long, lush hair was now spilling wildly about her shoulders. In one swift motion she quickly grabbed up her shawl and pulled it over her head, her cheeks burning crimson and her legs feeling rather shaky.

Orpah appeared behind the brusque character a moment later and Ruth quickly shot her a look that demanded an immediate explanation.

"Oh, did we startle you?" Orpah carelessly crossed the kitchen and helped herself to some of the fresh bread.

Ruth felt righteous indignation welling up within her, and she prayed that the Lord would help her hold her tongue and keep her peace.

How could Orpah be so brash, so blatant? To bring a strange man into the home of two young, unmarried women was a terrible disgrace! Why, it was unthinkable!

And not only did Orpah *not* appear even the slightest bit distraught the morning following her husband's death, but she had neglected to wear the traditional widow's clothes of mourning. Heaping insult upon injury, she had even been so brazen as to paint her eyes and lips and apply color to her cheeks. And now she was publicly socializing with another man, whom Ruth guessed was most definitely single and available.

Ruth swallowed the bile rising up in her throat as the dreadful realization hit her: Orpah looked much more like a harlot than a grieving woman bereft of her husband.

The whole ordeal made Ruth feel utterly sick, and she prayed that Naomi would not venture into the kitchen to see Orpah behaving in such a disgraceful manner.

Ruth took another moment to regain her usual poise, then asked calmly, "Orpah, what is going on?"

Orpah was already devouring a second helping of fresh bread. The rough-shod character still stood leering at the entryway, and now shot Orpah a withering look of disdain. Orpah threw back her head and laughed callously. "Oh, silly me. What kind of hostess am I? Refresh yourself with some bread and water, Balak."

The man did not appear at all interested in bread and water. He dared several steps in Ruth's direction. "Who is this? I do believe you failed to introduce us, Orpah. Your *widowed* sister-in-law, perhaps?"

Ruth instinctively retreated to a safe distance away from the stranger, pretending to busy herself by pouring water from a goatskin flask for this uncouth man named Balak. She offered the cup to Orpah, rather fearing to take the water to the stranger herself. She felt as if she were under inspection, and a most unwelcome inspection at that.

"Oh, stop it, Balak," Orpah retorted, shoving the cup of water in his general direction. "Her husband's dead body is still right here in the house, for goodness' sake. She's not available... or interested."

Well, there's the only true statement I have heard proceed from your lips in days, Ruth thought, disgusted. Gathering her courage, she turned to the tall stranger and stated firmly, "Our husbands have very recently passed away. The grieving mother is still present with us in this house. If you are unable to conduct yourself with sincere respect for both the deceased and their mourning mother, then I will have to ask you to leave, sir." Turning to look Orpah straight in the eye, she added, "And that goes for you as well."

Balak straightened and, with his lips curved in a rueful sneer, he replied coolly, "Yes, ma'am."

"Forgive her, Balak," Orpah said curtly, her eyes fierce as she glowered at her sister-in-law. "She speaks in such a degrading manner simply because she thinks she is better than everyone else."

"She surely *looks* better than everyone else," Balak murmured under his breath, taking a long draw from the fresh water Ruth had poured for him.

"Before you say anything else insulting, might I tell you why Balak is here today, Ruth?" Orpah's look was withering.

"I have been wondering about that very thing," Ruth

replied, staunchly holding her ground. She would not allow Orpah to thoughtlessly trample all over Naomi's already-broken heart. She would not hesitate to dismiss both Orpah and Balak if need be.

"First, let me ask you a question. How exactly did you plan to bury the dead, Ruth? Were we simply going to hoist the stiff bodies over our shoulders and tote them down to the outskirts of the city, dumping them in the common grave ourselves?"

Ruth nearly flinched at the callousness with which Orpah spoke. She desperately hoped that Naomi was not within earshot of this conversation. "Don't be absurd," Ruth responded calmly. "I knew that this was something that you and I must discuss." She cast an unwelcome glance in Balak's direction. "Alone."

"Whatever you must say, you may say to both of us," Orpah shot back, her green eyes darkening like two blazing coals.

Both of us? Ruth felt her face flush with stifled frustration. How long had Orpah even known this man? For a couple of hours? Or perhaps a matter of minutes? Ruth certainly hoped that she had not entertained his company prior to her husband's death. Did Orpah have any idea how ridiculous she sounded? How shamefully she was acting? What if her late husband Chilion could see her now? What would he say?

Lowering her eyes and gathering a long breath, Ruth calmed her surging thoughts and asked God for the ability to reason patiently with this difficult woman. Boldly, she leveled her eyes at the perturbed young woman across the room and firmly concluded, "Something must be done about our poor husbands' bodies. They must be laid to rest, and this must be done deferentially. This matter is between you and I and our distraught mother-in-law, who is in no condition to make such arrangements herself. Shall you and I step outside and discuss the matter privately, or shall I go to Naomi and add yet another heavy load to her already-burdened shoulders by sharing the disgraceful behavior that you are exhibiting so shortly after the death of her sons?"

Balak did not give Orpah a chance to respond. "I'll wait outside," he muttered, somewhat daunted by this gentle woman's staunch resolve.

"Ruth! In the name of the gods – what has gotten into you?" Orpah hissed, closing in on her stoic sister-in-law like some savage animal.

Ruth remained where she was, feet firmly planted upon the dusty clay floor. She refused to be intimidated by Orpah's ranting and raving, as Chilion so often had. She knew that she must be strong for Naomi, and she would rather face a thousand angry Orpahs than see Naomi break beneath the weight of such insurmountable trauma and pain. "We must lay our husbands to rest alongside their deceased father. That is how it should be done. I have heard Naomi mention such a custom on numerous occasions. That is what we shall do."

Orpah pursed her lips into a familiar, childish pout. "You said we were to *discuss* this matter, Ruth. You will not tell me what I am to do. I can make my own decisions."

"This is not about you, nor I." Ruth's voice remained low, even. "This is about honoring the memory of two men who are no more, and administering comfort to their grieving mother – a woman who deserves to be carried through this difficult time more than any other woman I know. We will honor her customs and her traditions, and we will not sorrow her spirit further by the way we conduct ourselves throughout the process. Do you understand, Orpah?"

Orpah's lips drew together – an unyielding, slender line. And her scowl spoke more than mere disapproval. But she could not argue with Ruth's logic. She knew that – even in a place as morally depraved and lacking in the social graces as Moab – she must reign in her outrageous behavior... at least until the allotted time of grieving had passed. Crossing her arms, she sighed loudly through her nose. "Fine. Under one condition."

"I am listening."

"Balak has offered to help us bury the bodies. Given the circumstances, I think we should accept his help. We are not equipped to handle such a task on our own. As I recall, Elimelech is buried on a hilltop not far from here. We would be hard-pressed to transport both bodies up that steep hill ourselves."

Ruth looked away, peeved. Orpah *did* have a point. They *would* need help transporting the bodies to their proper resting place, and she didn't know of anyone else whom she could request assistance from. Though she keenly disliked this leery, shady character named Balak, she reluctantly conceded to the request. "I understand, Orpah. And I am grateful for the assistance. However, you must conduct yourself in a manner worthy of a grieving widow in Naomi's presence. You must not insult her dead son's memory by the way you are behaving with this man."

"As you wish, Ruth. However, I demand that you stop treating me as a child. That high-and-mighty, holier-than-thou nonsense does not become you." Orpah's cheeks looked doubly flushed beneath the mounds of makeup she had smeared upon her face.

Ruth managed a smile. "Thank you for taking the time

to discuss this matter privately. We had best get started, should we not?"

"Already?"

"We have wasted enough time as it is. The job will prove tedious, I am sure, and the sun is already beginning to rise high in the sky."

Orpah sighed resignedly. "I suppose you are right."

It was no easy task. And Ruth wondered if there had ever been a more pitiful funeral procession recorded in the fading pages of time.

There had been no grievers, no mourners. No cries of lament or anguish from relatives or friends. No women playing tambourines or lyres or stringed instruments. And certainly no professionals hired to liven up the dreary parade that was every bit as dead and lifeless as the two bodies lying stiffly upon the pallets borne on the shoulders of Ruth, Naomi, Orpah, and Balak.

Ruth and Orpah had worn the expected black garments of grief – which had proven extremely confining and unforgiving beneath the brutal desert sun. Naomi had surprised Ruth when she had emerged from her chambers adorned in traditional sackcloth, the rough material falling in ungraceful folds about her small frame, ashes smeared upon her face and hands.

Ruth's heart – along with her spirits – had plunged at the sight. She knew that sackcloth and ashes was worn only by those who had been plunged into the deepest, darkest depths of despair. She had prayed with a quiet fervor unlike ever before, beseeching Almighty God to shower His perfect peace upon the heart of her despondent mother-in-law.

To Ruth's great relief, Orpah had behaved herself as firmly instructed, though she couldn't help but wonder how long that would last.

Exhausted to her very core, Ruth sank onto the makeshift straw pallet which she had laid across the floor of the dark chamber that she and her husband had once shared. It had been a toilsome, trying day. She was emotionally spent and overwhelmed with both physical and mental fatigue. Attempting to forget the gruesome details of the day, she prayed that sleep would come easily tonight and tried to find a comfortable position upon the scratchy straw pallet.

After half an hour of restless tossing and turning, she decided that perhaps there was a reason why desirous sleep proved so elusive.

It was not easy to drift off into a peaceful state of slumber in the very room in which her husband had departed. In fact, it was downright unsettling.

Drawing herself up to a sitting position, her chin resting lightly upon her knees which she hugged closely to her chest, she pondered the strange circumstances of the day – with the Lord's help, she had tackled and overcome tasks that she had never imagined would fall upon her own reluctant shoulders.

The crumbling clay wall felt cool against her aching back and weary shoulders. She noticed the slanting beams of silver moonlight cast majestically across the dim floor before her.

Even in the midst of all this gloom, in this dark chamber of dread and uncertainty, there is still beauty to be had, she thought with a tender smile aimed at the One Who – even now – continued to promise peace.

From the window carved crudely into the mud brick wall, a thin sliver of the white moon shone luminously from the black night sky. It was a lovely contrast – the white light slicing a dramatic semi-circle through the dense, midnight sky. She was reminded of the God that she served, and of the wonders that His mighty hand had wrought from the beginning of time until now.

You still work wonders, Lord, she prayed. *And I know that Your work is not finished. You will continue to work in my life, just as You have promised to those who love You.*

Even as she prayed, she found that she could not deny the worry, the doubt, the concern welling up within her heart. The world was not a forgiving place – especially not to one as unfortunate as a widowed woman.

She couldn't help but wonder.

Lord, what now?

Chapter 9

PLANS

That very night in Bethlehem, Boaz knelt to pray at his bedside, the wind whispering softly though the open window, the shutters clattering lightly upon the outer wall of smooth stone.

Folding his hands upon the soft mattress before him, Boaz took a moment to appreciate the gentle breeze, the still beauty of the evening, the mesmerizing charm of the stars shimmering gallantly in the immeasurable depths of the melancholy sky.

What breath-taking phenomena the Lord's hands had wrought! And to think that He had fashioned such beauty not only for His own good pleasure, but also for the enjoyment of His children here on earth.

Closing his eyes and bowing his head, Boaz began his evening prayers in the deep, hearty tone so familiar to those fortunate enough to know him.

He made special mention of his foreman, Kemuel and of Kemuel's sweet wife, Adara, in his prayers. Both had weighed heavily upon his heart for the course of several weeks now, and he was faithful to lift them up in prayer and to ask the Lord to work mightily in both their lives. After all, he knew firsthand what it was for a heart's most cherished desire to remain unmet. He thanked the Lord for their faithfulness in serving Him despite the fact that their sincerest prayer remained yet unanswered. He prayed fervently that it would not remain unanswered much longer.

It was in the midst of this intimate conversation with the Lord that Boaz felt an unmistakable stirring within his heart. His prayers stopped short, he lifted his face in the direction of the open window and his eyes were instantly drawn to the pale sliver of moon rising high in the inky blackness of the night sky.

Drawing himself up to his full height, Boaz stepped purposefully toward that window and allowed his hands to rest upon the smooth, tiled sill.

There was something about that moon... how it spoke volumes about the One Who had spoken it into existence, suspending it from raw space with the skilled hands of a passionate artist intent upon his work.

In fact, hanging there suspended like a slender silver arc in the heavens, the moon looked very much like the half-sphered sickle used by the workers in his wheat and barley fields...

Still marveling at such a heavenly, other-worldly wonder casting silvery beams of light upon an otherwise dark world, Boaz found himself puzzled at this unexpected turn of events. Why had the Lord drawn him away from his bedside moment of prayer simply to gaze upon a sight that – though stunning in every respect – he had witnessed many a night?

Perhaps it was merely to allow him a moment to worship the Lord in the splendor of His awesome might and power, in awe of His holiness and matchless creativity. And if that were so, Boaz would take full advantage of it.

Lord, You are so good. With every new day, I find myself completely astounded by Your awesome might and Your powerful deeds. And somehow, even after all that You are and all that You do, You still have time to comfort the weary spirit of a simple man like me.

Though only weeks before, Boaz had been content to accept that this reality in which he now found himself may truly be all the Lord had intended for him, he now realized that perhaps the most challenging and rewarding moments of his life may very well be soon in beginning. He continued to cling to the promise that the Lord had spoken to his heart and also to the heart of his dear housekeeper, Ada.

Pray for the one I have chosen for you.

The admonition was so clear, so concise, and so undoubtedly meant for him that Boaz reeled away from the window, stunned. Was the Lord prompting him to pray for – could it be so– his future wife?

Pray for her.

There was no doubt in his heart or mind. The woman whom God had prepared especially for him – the woman whom God had equipped to bring completion to his life, to his God-given mission, to his household – was now in dire need of his prayers. He did not know how or why. He could not even begin to gauge the circumstances surrounding the command to lift her up in prayer. The one thing that he *did* know – he would obey.

Dropping to his knees, his hands clasped in fervent prayer upon the windowsill, Boaz presented his petitions to the God of the universe, asking the Lord to minister to the heart of the woman that would, one day, hold his own heart.

~

Ruth had risen from the uninviting straw pallet and now stood poised at the large rectangular window, drinking in the splendor of the glittering stars that seemed to beckon towards the wondrous sliver of moon rising higher and higher in the evening air.

She had prayed, she had wept, she had wondered, she had worried, and somehow... she now felt nothing but peace.

She could feel the Lord's loving presence enveloping her shivering form like a warm, wool blanket draped pleasantly about her aching shoulders.

Lord, You truly are with me. You do *hear my prayers,* she thought in awe.

Mere moments before, she had felt the relentless talons of fear and despair clutching at her very soul. And then, suddenly, it was gone. The worry. The anxiety. The gnawing distress of one who – according to the world's standards – had no future, no hope, no chance. And yet, all of those foreboding thoughts and grasping fears had been dispelled instantly.

How could it be? How could such a heavy burden be lifted so simply, so quickly? She did not know, nor did she care. The one thing she *did* know was that the Lord had come through for her... *again*. He was so faithful, so good.

She wondered if perhaps Naomi was lifting her up in prayer at this very moment. She could think of no other explanation. And suddenly, she felt an overwhelming need to know, for there was absolutely no doubt in her mind that *someone* – bless their wonderful, generous heart – was praying for her!

Creeping soundlessly from her dim chamber, Ruth ventured to the small room that Naomi had once shared with her own husband Elimelech.

It was a piteous sight. Ruth almost wished she had not left her own chambers.

Naomi lay in an awkward heap in the middle of the room, her tear-stained cheek resting numbly against the cold, dusty clay floor. Her eyes were shut tightly, her features ragged and drawn, her lips taut. Chalky dark ash was still smeared upon her forehead, her nose, her face. Her silver-streaked hair hung loosely about her face, and her shoulders rose and fell softly, steadily, indicating that she had finally managed to slip off into a deep, troubled sleep.

Ruth felt tears stinging her eyes, and she somehow suppressed the sob that had risen instantly and unwantedly in her throat.

Poor Naomi. Poor, sweet, wonderful Noami. Would she ever be the same again?

Swallowing her own pained cries of bitterness, Ruth turned and walked stealthily, purposefully, back to her own bedchamber.

Then it occurred to her. Naomi could not possibly be the one lifting her up in prayer to Almighty God.

If not Naomi, then who could it possibly be? Certainly not a soul from this depraved pigpen called Moab!

Returning to her serene perch at the window, Ruth rested her tired arms upon the sill and attempted to quiet her curious thoughts.

Lord, I know not who dares to lift this lonely widow up in prayer to You this night, but regardless, I thank You. I thank You for lifting this heavy burden from my shoulders and carrying me in Your gentle arms.

Right then and there, Ruth resolved to pray for her despairing mother-in-law with all the strength that she possessed. Her God was faithful. He *would* hear her prayers. And by His great grace, He would answer them.

And with that fact firmly settled in her busy mind, Ruth continued to gaze out the lone window upon the beauty and sweet tranquility of the Lord's creation, allowing the Creator to whisper and administer comfort to her weary heart.

The week which followed inched forward with the painstaking slowness and progress of a lone snail traveling the length of the River Jordan.

Ruth was thankful for the endless tasks that continued to present themselves at home, as they kept her hands quite busy and averted her anxious thoughts from the bleakness of her present situation and foreseeable future. She continued to praise the Lord for His goodness, for His protection, for His loving guidance. She often lost herself completely in prayer as she labored intently at home, feeding the gentle donkey in the pen outside and scattering seed for the few scrawny chickens that hobbled pitifully about the property, scrubbing the dusty floors, baking the daily bread, fetching the pail of water, and polishing the few dishes that she and Orpah managed to dirty over the rare, meager meals they happened to share.

Naomi was refusing to eat for the most part, remaining tucked away in her dark chamber, the rough sackcloth pooling about her sickly frame as she sat in a sorrowful state of blank stupor upon a filthy pile of ashes.

Ruth had tenderly and kindly carried meals to her each day, imploring her to eat, to keep up her strength, to press on. The first few days following the deaths, Naomi had outright refused to eat. Fortunately, at this point, Naomi reluctantly accepted small doses of bread and water, eating silently like a fearful little bird and pushing the leftovers aside. Ruth was thankful to see even this slight bit of progress, however small. She continued to pray heartily for the frail woman, constantly reminding herself not to lose heart.

Orpah, on the other hand, seemed to embrace her newfound freedom with both spirit and complete disregard to the feelings of her bereaved mother-in-law. Much to Ruth's dismay, she saw more and more of the uncouth character named Balak, and Ruth seriously doubted that Orpah would remain a widow much longer. Despite Balak's blatantly wandering eyes, Orpah seemed bent on securing the man's attention and affection. Ruth wondered how Orpah could disregard such obvious flaws in the man's character and integrity. And as she watched the budding romance taking shape between Orpah and Balak in the week following Chilion's death, a new fear began to well up in Ruth's cautious mind...

What if another man seeks to claim my hand in marriage, as Mahlon once did? The very thought sent unwelcome shivers dancing up and down her spine. She could not bear the thought of being freed from one oppressive, abusive relationship with a man who despised the very thought of her God, only to be chained down to another man of the same hardened mindset.

I must remain invisible, unseen, she had decided forcefully the moment the frightful thought had assaulted her. *If no one knows of me, then no one can come seeking after me.*

In her heart, she knew that she must place this burden also in the capable hands of Almighty God. Surely He would protect her, guarding her beneath the shadow of His mighty wing. Surely He would not allow her to stumble into the very horror from which she had so recently been released.

I must trust my God, she reminded herself unceasingly. *I must not lose myself in despair over a worry that may never come.*

Taking a deep breath as she uttered yet another feeble prayer to God, Ruth wiped her floury hands on her apron and adjusted the comfortable woolen head covering that threatened to fall over her eyes, which often burned bright with intensity and determination these days. She had taken to wearing her shawl each day even while performing the sweaty house chores that demanded attention, as Balak's unwelcome surprise visits were growing more frequent and his eyes were anything but unobserving.

"Where is the water, Ruth? I am dying of thirst!" Orpah barreled through the entryway with the grace and poise of a herd of angry cattle.

Ruth glanced up from the rounded, slender loaves of bread she had set upon the windowsill to cool. "Good morning to you as well," she murmured petulantly. She wearied of keeping up the chores day after day with absolutely no assistance from the person who demanded the most attention.

"Whatever happened to little Miss Sunshine this morning?" Orpah rasped caustically, groping for the heavy urn of water that Ruth had drawn from the well early that morning and drawing the ladle brimming with fresh water to her gaudily-colored lips.

Ruth directed her attention back to her cooling loaves, refusing to take the bait that Orpah dangled before her eyes day after day. Ruth knew that Orpah only wished to catch her in a bad temper and corner her there like a trapped animal, long enough to jab a critical finger in her face and pronounce that, despite Ruth's newfound faith, she was just as capable of being nasty and retaliatory like everyone else.

Ruth knew that, aside from Naomi, she may very well be the only example of a truly dedicated God-fearer that Orpah would ever encounter. She understood the immense responsibility resting upon her shoulders. She must not stain the Lord's holy name nor damage His reputation by the way she behaved underneath the scrutinizing gaze of her sister-in-law – even when provoked.

"Oh, you are refusing to talk to me now, is that it?" Orpah pressed in a sing-song tone, dropping the ladle with a loud splash and turning in Ruth's direction.

Ruth glanced over her shoulder, both surprised and irked by Orpah's sheer pettiness. "Of course not," she responded evenly. "I am simply absorbed in the daily tasks. I assure you that is all."

"Of course. Why, everyone knows that the *holiest* member of the household remains shut away at home, grinding away at the daily chores – while the irresponsible one actually has the nerve to go out and seek a better life for herself."

Here we go again, Ruth thought in dismay as Orpah's lower lip curled up into its usual pout, and her painted eyes rolled dramatically.

Snatching one of the flat loaves of bread, Orpah perched herself on a narrow, stone ledge across from the kitchen and cocked her head to one side, her eyes following Ruth's every move.

Ruth said nothing as she swept the crumbs and fine dust into a pile on the corner of the kitchen floor, keenly aware of Orpah's viperous green eyes seemingly boring holes into her back. Something was coming. She sensed that Orpah was holding back, storing up some type of despicable insult for just the right moment.

And then it came.

"Balak has a brother, you know."

Ruth stiffened, her hands gripping the broomstick so tightly that she feared it might snap. It was as if Orpah had peeled away all of Ruth's protective layers and peered into her very soul, reaching for her deepest, most daunting fear and hurling it straight at her face.

Ruth considered throwing aside the broom and facing Orpah's threat head-on, despite the fallout that might ensue. However, still turned away from her sneering sister-in-law, Ruth took a moment to clench her eyes shut and utter a silent prayer.

Her blurred thoughts of utter panic immediately cleared, and she realized that to respond defensively to Orpah's threat would merely place even more power in Orpah's greedy, groping hands. Allowing a quick sigh to escape her lips, Ruth resumed her sweeping as nonchalantly as if Orpah's insulting comment had slipped away unnoticed into the steamy afternoon air.

"Well?" Orpah demanded, obviously incensed that Ruth had not responded to her taunting jest. "Aren't you going to say anything?"

Turning to face Orpah, Ruth somehow managed to flash her a carefree smile. "Alright, I'll say something. Aren't *you* going to get to work? I could use an extra set of hands around here, if you are willing!"

Orpah's jaw nearly dropped at Ruth's sparkling eyes and playful invitation to assist her with the daily chores, even in the face of such a crude affront. She stammered dumbly as Ruth tossed her the broom and grabbed up a thick gray cloth in preparation to scrub the floors.

Neither woman was prepared for the version of Naomi that emerged from her own private quarters before Ruth could even bend to polish the newly-swept floors.

"Why, she lives after all! Thank the gods!"

Not at all surprised by Orpah's tactless cry, Ruth shot her sister-in-law a silent warning against any and all sarcasm and thoughtless remarks. Rushing to Naomi's side, Ruth took the frail woman's arm and declared softly, "I knew you would come back to us, Naomi."

"Quite the opposite." Naomi's voice sounded hollow, void of all expression or meaning. The very sound of it chilled Ruth to the bone, diminishing any glimmer of hope that might have arisen upon Naomi's grim presence.

"Quite the opposite?" Ruth repeated, nonplussed. "I'm not sure I understand."

The grieving woman looked as though she had aged an additional ten years in the course of a few short days. Her eyes – once alive with wonder and zeal for life– appeared dark and vacant. Her lips were drawn taught and drained of all natural color. Her cheeks were pale and ghostlike, and her long, slender hands were clenched arthritically by her sides. Ruth had noticed with a sigh of slight relief that the sackcloth was gone; however, Naomi still donned the drab mourning garments of the bereaved.

Naomi wrung her bony hands anxiously, appearing to study her own dusty, sandaled feet. "I have come to say goodbye."

Goodbye? Any and all hope that Ruth had been so desperately clinging to vanished in that awful instant. Ruth wanted to ask what her mother-in-law could possibly mean by such a statement, but her throat had constricted so tightly upon hearing Naomi's foreboding announcement that she found it impossible to speak.

Orpah had no trouble voicing her own inquiry. "Goodbye? And where exactly will you be going?" Sneering, she added, "To the marketplace?"

Orpah's brazen insolence loosed Ruth's frozen lips and she wheeled around to face her mouthy sister-in-law, almost violently. "Orpah, that is *enough*!" She had never known such a fierce desire to strike the mouth of another person. She reminded herself that such violence was certainly not her Lord's way.

Orpah's green eyes were as wide as marbles as she quickly backed away and checked her sarcastic tongue.

Turning to Naomi, Ruth asked in a broken whisper, "Are you leaving us, Naomi?"

Naomi's eyes never left the floor. She responded softly, "I am."

"Is it something we have done?" she managed weakly, her voice broken. If Orpah's shameful misconduct had instigated Naomi's departure, Ruth knew she would never forgive her. Or allow her to get away with such a thing.

For the first time, Naomi lifted her head and met Ruth's gaze.

Ruth had never felt a deeper sorrow in all her life. The eyes that met her own were filled with love and tender compassion, even while brimming with relentless pain and immeasurable loss. Ruth knew that this was the dearest friend she had ever known, the closest thing to family that she had ever had. *Oh, God,* she pled numbly, *please spare me this great loss, I beg of Thee.*

"Oh, my darlings," Naomi spread her arms wide, inviting both women to come to her, the black folds of her garment dropping far below her outspread hands. "This has nothing to do with you." She must have read the hesitation in Ruth's eyes, for she added quickly, "Nothing to do with *either* of you."

In her heart, Ruth was still unconvinced. "Then why are you leaving?"

Taking a hand of both Ruth and Orpah, Naomi said quietly, "This land is not for me. I have always known this... long before now."

Uncomfortable, Orpah quickly pulled her hand away, but Ruth grasped Naomi's tighter than ever.

"But, Naomi," Ruth was nearly weeping, "where will you go?"

"To Bethlehem." Naomi lifted her gaze and, for the first time in weeks, Ruth detected a sense of hope, of renewed purpose, behind those deep gray eyes.

Ruth's heart leapt within her chest. *Bethlehem?* She had heard such stories of the place – why, Bethlehem was a small town nestled snugly within the Land of Promise! The great men and women of the Scriptures had trod upon those very paths, walked among the rolling pastures, gazed upon the star-studded horizon washed pink and purple beyond the gently sloping hills! Her heart was instantly drawn to a land that she had never known, yet had seen in many a peaceful dream. Oh, if only she could travel with Naomi! If only she could dwell among her God's very own, special people as well! But would they accept her? Could a foreign woman ever find a place among the chosen people of God? Why, if the Lord Himself had accepted her in the land of Moab, surely His people would accept her in their own land as well!

Then it occurred to her. Gripping Naomi's arm, Ruth met her gaze with such a will and a purpose that she herself was surprised. "Both Orpah and I were married to your sons. By law, we are legally bound to you and your family, Naomi – "

Naomi shook her head dolefully, "Nonsense. I have no family."

"That matters not. We are legally bound to you. Your

family paid the bride prices and the dowries. We are no longer our own, but we belong to you – " Ruth paused long enough to catch her breath, noticing Orpah's unmistakable scowl as she glowered at Ruth from her perch on the stone bench. Ruth swallowed hard and plunged ahead anyway. "You must take us with you, Naomi. It is lawful, and it is completely acceptable. It is the only way."

Naomi looked visibly stunned at Ruth's shocking proposition, and Orpah look downright furious.

"It is the *only* way," Ruth insisted, her voice level.

"Well!" Naomi planted her hands firmly on her hips and looked from Ruth, to Orpah, then back again. She didn't seem to notice that Orpah was about to come out of her skin with suppressed fury. "It seemed so much to ask of you, my darlings. But, Ruth, what you say is indeed true. Lawfully, it is right. And I would certainly not object to the company of the two people that I love most in this world."

"When do we leave?" Ruth's jaw was set firmly, and she purposefully turned her eyes from the invisible daggers that Orpah's fierce expression conveyed.

Naomi placed a hand on the crumbling clay wall to steady herself. She had certainly not expected all this! "Why, I had planned to leave upon the morrow if I could locate a traveling caravan, but perhaps that is too sudden if the two of you are to accompany me."

"We'll be ready."

"Ruth!" It was the first time Orpah had spoken since the conversation's sudden and drastic change of course had occurred. "I've had quite enough of you speaking for me."

Ruth did not back down. She met Orpah's gaze evenly. "You are a grown woman, Orpah, and quite capable of speaking for yourself. I had expected you to chime in at any time – whether it be in agreement or not."

Orpah's rouged cheeks deepened in color, but she bit her lower lip resignedly, her eyes narrowed.

"Why, Orpah, do you have any objections to Ruth's proposition?"

Orpah's emerald eyes flashed from Ruth, to Naomi, and back again. It was rather obvious that she had *many* objections; however, even brash, impetuous Orpah understood the binding nature of the marriage contract between herself and Naomi's late son. She had no right to object.

Naomi's gaze was fixed on Orpah, and Orpah squirmed uncomfortably at the disconcerting change of events that had occurred quite unexpectedly. She stammered a few broken strings of syllables before she nearly spat, "Of course I'm not objecting, but I will need more than a few short hours to prepare for this journey. Anyone should be able to understand that!"

"Of course, my darling!" Naomi took Orpah's hand before the girl could protest. "How much time do you need?"

Orpah appeared to be carefully calculating the proper response. Ruth knew that Orpah's mind was busy plotting and scheming, and it made her feel uneasy.

A slow smile crossed Orpah's face, and she responded easily, "Three days."

Naomi looked slightly troubled. "Three days? I had hoped to leave at once."

"Give me three days, Naomi. You owe me that."

She owes you nothing! Ruth nearly screamed. Who did Orpah think she was? To mistreat and abuse and backstab a woman as kindly and trusting as Naomi, then to be so arrogant as to demand something in return for such abuses!

"What could you possibly want with three days to prepare, Orpah?" Ruth dared, feeling protective of this little bit of progress which Naomi had thus far demonstrated. "Our few belongings could be packed in a matter of minutes!"

Orpah tossed her head calmly – too calmly – and responded, "You might be willing to completely uproot yourself from the only life you have ever known, to venture unprepared to a strange, new place filled with peculiar customs, but I am not. I have a right to prepare myself for such a journey and to make the proper preparations."

Ruth knew that Orpah was up to no good. She could feel it just as plainly as the bile rising bitterly within her throat. *You must trust the Lord, even in this. He has good plans for you. He will not forsake you,* Ruth reminded herself, steeling herself against the torrent of unkind speech which she wished to release for the benefit of Orpah's haughty ears.

For the first time, Naomi seemed aware of the obvious tension existing between her two young daughters-in-law. Wringing her hands nervously, she offered quietly, "You are both sure you wish to go through with this?"

A slow smile spread across Orpah's deceptively fair face. "Why, Naomi, we wouldn't have it any other way."

The sweetness dripping from Orpah's every word was downright offensive to Ruth. She knew that every ounce of kindness Orpah could muster up was completely false – nothing but a show, a means to obtain whatever it was that she desired upon any given moment. Ruth prayed desperately that whatever crooked plans Orpah might have already fabricated would prove unsuccessful.

Shaking off the immense feeling of discomfort that was mounting in her own spirit, Ruth took Naomi's arm and added, her eyes glowing softly, "There is nothing in the world I desire more than to leave this place, and to take shelter among our God's very own people, Naomi. I cannot wait to make this journey."

Naomi almost smiled. "My daughters, I cannot fully express the gratitude that I feel. Thank you, my daughters. You have brought great comfort to my old heart." Naomi reached for Orpah's hand and, this time, Orpah did not wrench away. "Orpah dear, regarding your request to prolong our departure for three days..."

Ruth noticed Orpah's eyes flash indignantly, yet she somehow managed to keep her composure.

"At this very moment I am on my way to town to inquire about the nearest departing caravan. We three women are by no means able to make such a journey alone, without the help of an experienced guide and pack animals to assist with baggage, parcels, and such."

"Naturally," Orpah responded knowingly, although it was quite obvious that she had not thought of that. A look of mock disappointment crossed her face. "And suppose a caravan will not be departing for many months? Perhaps even longer? That would be a shame."

Again, Ruth bit her tongue and fought the urge to comment sharply.

Naomi smiled. "I have prayed long and hard about this. I have no doubt that the Lord is leading me back to my own land – *His* land. He will make a way for us. I am not concerned."

"And suppose the next caravan is to depart immediately?"

"I should like to be counted among those leaving then." Naomi's jaw was set, and Ruth realized that no amount of pleading or cajoling on Orpah's part would convince her to delay this journey. She allowed a short sigh of relief to escape her lips.

Orpah tossed her head defiantly and disappeared into her chambers without another word.

Ruth turned to Naomi, her eyes brimming with tears. "To see you looking more like yourself, Naomi – trusting in our God and acting on His behalf once again – is an answer to prayer."

Naomi managed a lop-sided smile, leaning gingerly upon the clay-hardened wall. Her eyes appeared to be roving across many distant memories as she spoke slowly, resignedly, "When I first lost my husband, Ruth, I felt rather as I feel today... aimless, empty, broken. For several days after his death, I could do nothing but weep. I loved him, Ruth. I loved him dearly."

Ruth wondered if this was a good idea – to reopen old wounds and discuss painful memories that had long-since been pushed aside, swept under the rug... especially given Naomi's present circumstances. "Naomi, you don't have to tell me..."

"We were so young when we married, Ruth. And we were both quite foolish, I am afraid."

Ruth wrinkled her nose in dismay. "You? You are the least foolish person I know, Naomi!"

"Ah, but I was! I was young. Naïve. I viewed the world through the dreamy eyes of a very young woman in love with a very impetuous young man."

Ruth couldn't help but smile. How she wished she could have known Naomi as a young woman! She must have been absolutely beautiful – stunning, in fact. She imagined her with a much younger-looking, slender frame, vibrant with restless energy and enthusiasm, her sleek black hair cascading down her shoulders and framing an exquisite face all aglow with the prospect of young love.

Naomi actually smiled – a faint, distant smile, full of

longing and pain and... could that possibly be *hope*? She shook her head emphatically and chuckled. "Oh, but you have far better things to do than listen to the regretful musings of this old woman!"

Ruth reached for her arm. "But, no! Oh, Naomi, I would love to hear all about it – your story, I mean. There is so much I do not know."

Was that a twinkle in Naomi's eye? Or had Ruth simply imagined it? Shaking her head once again, Naomi pushed away from the wall and brushed some dust from her long cloak. "Perhaps, then, you would like to help me hitch up the wagon and join me on my little visit to town? I can't deny that I would enjoy your company. Perhaps we can talk more on the way."

Ruth beamed. "I would like nothing more!"

Chapter 10

NAOMI

Ruth could not remember the last time she had left the safety of their obscure little home and the similar dwellings of nearby neighbors. It did not take her long to harness Dag – their pitiful gray donkey – and hitch him up to the creaky old wagon.

Soon, Naomi sat straight-backed on the bench of the wagon, which seemed to be groaning painfully with every hazardous turn of its rusty wheels, with Ruth gripping the reins beside her. Ruth wondered if any passers-by would laugh at the sight of a woman driving the wagon on her own, but perhaps the news had spread about the fate of Naomi's two sons. Perhaps they would be spared the tell-tale laughter and degrading comments out of sheer sympathy.

But, then again, this *was* Moab.

"Thank you, Ruth, for coming with me," Naomi said quietly, her eyes warily scanning the bleak, dusty path that would take them to town where they would find the marketplace and the gates to the city. "I am not sure I could have faced them alone."

Ruth smiled. "You are stronger than you think, Naomi, but I was glad to come."

Naomi nodded and set her jaw as with firm resolve. Ruth knew that she was contemplating the dreadful possibilities that might assault them along the way – not to mention the obscenities that went on in a place as busy and bustling as the center of the city.

"Now I believe you owe me a story," Ruth prodded playfully, glancing sideways at her mother-in-law, who had suddenly become quite stoic.

Naomi's posture relaxed slightly, and that distant, thoughtful look returned to her soft gray eyes. "Ah, yes. It is a fascinating story, to be sure. I only wish it had a happier ending."

Ruth smiled. "But the story hasn't ended yet."

Naomi couldn't help but smile at Ruth's gentle optimism. "Hmm. I believe you are right about that, my daughter."

Ruth kept her eyes steeled on the dusty landscape before them, fighting the urge to study Naomi as she proceeded with her long-forgotten tale. Dag's gray ears stood straight up as his hooves clip-clopped on the hard-packed trail before them.

"I was but a girl – thirteen years old, I was. So young and full of life – in fact, I was very much like *you* when my son chose you to be his bride."

Ruth managed a weak smile for Naomi's sake. Those were memories she preferred to leave buried with her dead husband. "How did you meet Elimelech?" she asked casually, subtly changing the subject.

Naomi smiled. "Where I come from, each son or daughter must marry within their clan. It is our way – rather, it is God's way."

Ruth had never heard that before. "Does that not feel strange? Marrying someone from your own family?"

"No, no, not from our own *family*, you see! From our own *clan*. There is a difference. There are many, many families within each clan, and therefore, many prospects to choose from!" She gave Ruth a playful wink.

Ruth was nearly taken aback. She wondered if her own eyes were fooling her – or if perhaps this was but a dream, and she would awaken the following morning to find dear Naomi still a muddled heap on the dusty floor, covered in ash.

No, she reminded herself firmly. *My God is good. He is working in Naomi's heart at this very moment, giving her the strength to laugh again – the strength to move on.*

To Ruth's immense delight, Naomi was just getting started! Ruth quickly directed her attention back to her talkative mother-in-law, uttering a silent prayer of thanksgiving even as she did so.

"Do you know why I believe God put it together that way?" Naomi was asking her. "To marry within one's own clan?"

Ruth shook her head dumbly.

"Well, as it is the father's responsibility to select a spouse for his son, I believe this is so that each parent has the ability to select a suitable partner for their child. Imagine – if the father should pick just anyone? No, but you see, since each clan lives grouped together, the parents are given a very special privilege to observe the marriageable prospects for their children and to make a wise decision based on what they see."

"And is that what happened with you and your Elimelech? His father chose you to be his bride?"

"Well, I suppose you could say that. Our fathers were

good friends – both upstanding leaders of the city, both men of excellent character. Elimelech and I grew up together. But as he became a young man and I became a young woman, naturally we were separated for a good deal of time as he was apprenticed to learn a trade and I was taken under my mother's wing and taught to keep house – you know, such things as cooking and cleaning and the taking care of children."

"Your mother must have been a wonderful teacher," Ruth commented kindly.

"Oh, she was! She certainly was. My mother was a wonderful lady – gentle and soft-spoken and so very caring. Now there I was – a young girl of thirteen – minding my own business, taking care of the household chores, when who do you suppose came knocking at our door?"

"Your Elimelech!"

Naomi smiled again, and this time, there was more pain in her smile than fond recollection. "My Elimelech. Oh, he'd grown, alright – grown right into a strong young man. And that boy – he was more than my poor heart could take! Of course, he didn't come to see me. *His* father had sent him with a message for *my* father... those sly devils! They knew good and well what they were up to!"

"They hoped you would fall for each other?"

"They did. And they got what they hoped for. Elimelech later told me that I was the most beautiful woman he had ever laid eyes on. And my desire for him was every bit as strong. He went home and immediately spoke with his father – who in turn spoke with *my* father – and within two weeks we were betrothed!"

Ruth shook her head, taking it all in. It was all so crazy, so impetuous! Why, the whole affair sounded nothing like the wise, cautious Naomi she knew and loved! "It all happened so fast," she mused.

"Too fast," Naomi agreed. "I did not truly know him. Yes, we had grown up together, but much had changed since we were children. I believe my father had hoped that Elimelech's character would be much like that of his father – nearly flawless. Sadly, that was not the case. Though Elimelech's father was a good, hard-working man, he had become quite successful, and Elimelech had been given too much. He was far too accustomed to luxury and the fleeting pleasures of this life to care deeply about the things that truly mattered."

Ruth nodded sadly. She had observed the same traits in Elimelech's son – the man who had been her husband.

"As is typical of any Hebrew betrothal, we were engaged for a solid year. During that year, my father began to feel some reservation. I despised him for it. After all, Elimelech was a dashing young man – and I wasn't the only Hebrew maiden pining after his love. I wasn't about to relinquish the prize I thought I had won."

"Your father had second thoughts about Elimelech?"

"My father was a very wise man. The more he observed Elimelech, the more he realized that Elimelech had little in common with his worthy father. My father expressed this to both my mother and me on several occasions. But being a senseless, impractical teenage girl, I begged and pleaded with my father to give Elimelech a chance. Besides, my father could not very easily revoke the marriage contract between Elimelech and me. After all, in my homeland, a betrothal is legally *marriage* – excepting any physical intimacy, of course. My father would have had to obtain a certificate of divorce – which would have brought terrible shame upon our household."

Ruth realized that she was paying little attention to the bumpy road on which they traveled, being so engrossed in the intriguing romantic saga that her mother-in-law was so animatedly depicting. She quickly tightened her grip on the donkey's reins and did a careful sweep of their desolate surroundings. The brutal sun was already rising high in the sky, and Ruth began to wonder if they should have simply waited to make the venture until early the following morning. She shoved those troubling thoughts aside, deciding that if Naomi was ready, there was no reason to hold back. After all, she was enjoying Naomi's tale far too much to complain about the sweat that was beginning to dot her fair brow.

"We were married and the festivities were glorious!" Naomi continued. "As we both came from well-to-do families, they held back not a single shekel which they believed might contribute to our happiness. The feasting and dancing, the music, the laughter, the look in my young husband's eyes as he took my hands in his own and whispered that I now belonged to him... Oh, Ruth, I truly believed that my greatest hopes and deepest longings had been realized! It was all so perfect – *too* perfect. Why, I still remember the look on my father's face when Elimelech and I were pronounced man and wife... his jaw was set grimly, firmly. His eyes conveyed every ounce of concern that he had expressed since my betrothal. I could see the doubt etched across his every feature. And I – such an ignorant little girl – nearly hated him for that one look. How dare he put even a chink in the immense happiness that I felt on that day! Looking back, I saw a million times over how right he was. And how gullible *I* was."

Ruth freed one hand of the reins long enough to touch Naomi's arm. Her gray eyes were beginning to dim with disappointment that was decades old. Ruth longed to cheer her heart, to offer up the slightest bit of encouragement, but her spirit told her to remain quiet and to simply listen.

"Those early days quickly faded from pure bliss to sheer disillusionment. I quickly learned that Elimelech was very, very committed to one thing... *his own happiness.* I do not fault him for it. Though his parents were wonderful people, they had granted him his every wish and desire from the day he was born. He knew nor understood any other way. Though I did all I could to please him, to be a stellar wife and housekeeper, certain things were beyond my control. And when circumstances rose up that were not in his favor, his temper would quickly get the best of him. I learned to stay out of his way and busied myself tirelessly with the household chores."

Ruth was taken aback. So Naomi had also found herself desperately entrenched in a piteous union with the wrong man! No wonder she had proven so understanding in Ruth's own situation with her young son. Naomi had already been there. She knew the pain. She knew the regret. And yet, in Naomi's case, the husband was of her *own* choosing! How heavily that must have weighed upon Naomi's heart and mind! To have been given the rare privilege of choosing one's own husband, only to stumble into the wrong relationship... And to think that Ruth had never known or even suspected!

"Why, Naomi," Ruth breathed softly, "I had no idea."

Naomi sighed. "Well, my child, I never saw any sense in burdening others with the consequences of my own carelessness..." she turned and looked ruefully in Ruth's direction, and her eyes twinkled ever-so-slightly, "But... you asked."

Ruth couldn't hold back a smile, and she bit her lower

lip to discourage any unwanted laughter from escaping her unruly lips. *Thank you, God,* she prayed silently, fervently. She could hardly fathom the unspeakable change that had overtaken Naomi this day. Just a few short hours ago, Ruth had despaired that her tender-hearted mother-in-law would never again be the same. And yet God was working a miracle before her very eyes – strengthening Naomi's aching heart and giving her the grace necessary to cope with her grief.

Ruth wondered if it was safe to change the subject, but she could scarcely contain her excitement as she thought about leaving this dreadful city and taking refuge in the Holy Land! "Naomi, it almost feels like a dream," she broached the new subject cautiously, half-frightened that over-discussing the issue might overwhelm Naomi and encourage her to abandon the idea entirely.

Naomi raised a brow ever-so-slightly. "A dream?" she obviously was not following Ruth's rapid switch of subjects.

"To live in a land belonging to the Lord God Himself – why, it is nearly too much to fathom!"

Naomi chuckled slightly. "Well, now, let's not forget that *all* land belongs to Him. Even the unhallowed ground beneath this very wagon."

Ruth wrinkled her nose in a display of conscious disgust. "I suppose the difference being that the people in the Holy Land have accepted the fact that it belongs to *Him*."

Naomi nodded, her dark, gloomy head covering slipping back from her forehead. She did not bother to adjust it.

"It must be wonderful," Ruth mused on, reminding herself to stay focused on the well-worn path before them even as pleasant daydreams danced about in the forefront of her mind. Dag's heavy hooves sent little puffs of red dust trailing behind him as he plodded steadily along beneath the sun's unforgiving rays.

"Living among God's chosen people?" Naomi picked up where Ruth had left off, and her eyes again looked weary and very distant. "It is certainly quite different from Moab. But always remember, Ruth, that in Bethlehem live many *people*. And people are never *perfect*. I don't want you to arrive only to find yourself disappointed to learn that God's own children make mistakes as well."

"We all make many mistakes," Ruth readily responded. "I would not expect perfection from any place apart from Heaven!"

Naomi dipped her head in a slow nod and Ruth found herself slightly perplexed at the nervousness she detected in Naomi's lowered eyes. What could she possibly be worried about in a place so remarkable as the Land of Promise? Feeling slightly uncomfortable with Naomi's sudden silence, Ruth went on, "Why did you leave?"

Naomi's thoughts had evidently already trailed elsewhere, for she shook her head as if to draw herself back to reality and repeated, "Why did I leave? Leave *where*?"

"Bethlehem," Ruth pressed on, determined to keep Naomi talking and thinking positively. Too much time to ponder the loss of her children could not possibly be a good thing. "Why, you have already mentioned that your family as well as Elimelech's lived there. And both were well-to-do. Why would you leave the security and promise of home as well as the comfort of family to travel to a place such as *this*?"

Naomi sighed, and Ruth thought she saw a slight flash of fire in those deep gray eyes, as if the question had rekindled a bitter frustration long-since forgotten. "Elimelech."

Ruth looked questioningly to Noami. Elimelech had

dragged poor Naomi to this blasphemous land, far from her home, her people, and her Lord? She tried to calm the anger rising within her against a man she had never even met. How could he do such a thing to a woman as kindhearted and deserving as Naomi?

Naomi seemed to notice Ruth's inward struggle, for she placed a gentle hand on Ruth's arm and smiled. "Don't trouble yourself so, my dear."

"How could he do it?" Ruth managed, careful to keep her voice even.

"In a way, Ruth, I thank him for it."

Ruth turned to Naomi with both brows lifted, her large eyes round and skeptical. "But why?"

"Had he not uprooted our family and brought us to Moab, I never would have had the honor of meeting *you*, my dear."

Ruth swallowed hard and fought to hold back the tears that stung her eyes and threatened to spill over both cheeks. To hear Naomi speak with such love and genuineness in the midst of such dreadful circumstances touched her heart and warmed her to the core of her being.

"So, see?" Naomi asked with a smile. "Our God truly does know how to take evil circumstances and turn it into something good – beautiful, even."

Ruth nodded emphatically as a stray tear slipped down her cheek. How she prayed that the Lord was working in such a way even in this moment! The deaths of Naomi's sons were tragic to be sure, but perhaps Almighty God was working even in these dark circumstances to take them to a place they could actually call *home* – a place where they belonged.

Adjusting her shawl to shield her face, Ruth warily scanned the horizon and observed the taut, coarse, animal-skinned projections of countless, thrown-together ramshackle tents that lined the outskirts of town. They had nearly reached their destination! She felt sharp anticipation course through her, as well as a hint of reserve. What would they encounter upon reaching the town? Would the men at the city gates laugh at them or taunt them? Would squealing, squawking animals and shabby merchandise be shoved invasively under their noses and in their faces? And what news concerning the traveling caravan would meet their eager ears upon their arrival? Could they set off sooner rather than later? Would they be maddeningly delayed? She certainly hoped not.

The brutal Middle Eastern sun had risen high in the sky by this point, and Ruth began to feel sweat trickling down her back and neck in the stickiest, most unpleasant way. With firm resolve, she shoved aside any and all disturbance at such discomfort and reminded herself that soon – the Lord willing – they would be free from this godless land and it would all become quite a distant memory. That promise in and of itself was worth all the temporary discomfort in the world!

Ruth looked to Naomi, and she saw her own determination and resolve reflected in the eyes of the older woman. "Are you ready?" she inquired calmly, hoping that her own peace of mind could somehow overtake Naomi as well.

The weathered skin around the corner of Naomi's eyes crinkled delightfully as she responded lightly, "I'm ready to get out of Moab."

Chapter 11

TROUBLE

Adara was busily working her loom and spinning another outer garment to replace her husband's weathered one when she heard an unexpected knock at the door.

Tal, the yellow, stiff-eared dog and honorary member of the household, who had been lying lazily in one of the warm sunbeams slanting across the floor at Adara's feet, lifted his head and uttered a low, guttural growl. Because most people considered dogs filthy, vile creatures, and viewed them as the dirty dredges of society, they were often left to roam the dark streets and alleyways at night, seeking out their next meal. Not so with Tal. Kemuel and Adara enjoyed his company as well as the protection he offered, and Tal enjoyed the scraps he received from his adopted masters' own table. The relationship was certainly beneficial for both sides.

Strange, Adara thought, rising from her loom. *I was not expecting company today.*

Before she had even tread the short length from her loom to the door, which she kept propped open during the day to allow the stifling heat an easy exit, a heavily-shawled head appeared around the sturdy wooden beam of the doorframe.

Adara instantly recognized the plump, full-faced woman.

"Reba, how are you? Good morning! Come in, come in!"

Reba was Adara's mother-in-law. She did not pay frequent visits, as she clearly loathed Adara's very existence. Still, Adara sweetly attempted to make amends with this difficult woman, hoping and praying that her kindhearted efforts would one day pay off.

Reba was wearing her highcap, which was customary for most women of Bethlehem to sport when out in public. It was a rather large, awkwardly-fitting headpiece, with a full length of silver coins stitched across the band that ran across her forehead. The pale blue fabric flowed some four feet in length, trailing behind her like the tail of some pompous, colorful bird. Adara did not care to wear hers often, for she found it burdensome and it often halted her progress when she was hard at work scrubbing clothes clean or elbow-deep in bread dough. But the crisp *jingle-jingle* of the loose coins was always a handy tip-off that other women were in the vicinity, giving Adara plenty of time to flee from the judgmental stares and critical looks.

At this moment, she wished that she could flee from the scrutinizing gaze of her huffy mother-in-law as well. The middle-aged woman's cheeks were as red as a pair of plump apples from her journey across the courtyard, and her sharp little eyes glinted with cruel resolve.

Adara wondered how a woman so unkindly could have produced a son so noble. She had often reminded herself that Reba had every reason to refuse to accept her – a childless woman was regarded as a curse and a disgrace. No doubt Reba abhorred her because she had besmirched her son's reputation among the locals – the people wondered whether *he* was the vile sinner and harborer of some secret sin, or if his wife was. After all, one of them must be responsible for her accursed infertility.

Wringing her hands with a hint of nervousness that amused Adara, Reba accepted the cheerful invitation to enter and allowed her eyes a quick, suspicious glance about the room.

Leading her toward the stone bench hewn beneath the window overlooking the courtyard, Adara began invitingly, "What brings you here this morning, Reba? It is good news, I should hope!"

But Reba pursed her fat lips and shied away from Adara's gentle hand as if it were a poisonous viper. "I will not stay. Nor will I take much time from your morning." Her breath was coming in short puffs, and Adara wondered if it were from the physical activity or sheer nervousness.

Tal must have sensed her discomfort and agreed with a low whine, his large brown eyes seeking out his master's with concern.

Reba took several hurried steps back, catching her first glimpse of the yellow beast still lying peacefully on the floor, his long tail *thump-thumping* with friendliness. Reba's carefully-preened brows shot up derisively. "Why, what on earth is that... that... that *creature* doing in the house?!" she protested in disgust as well as a bit of fear.

Adara noted that Reba's response to the animal was quite the same way she responded to *her*. But she kept her peace and smiled gracefully. "The poor thing had no home, and he took a liking to Kemuel immediately. We hadn't the heart to turn him away."

"He's a threat to the cleanliness of this house!"

Adara bit her lip to curb any sharp remarks, for she knew that her home was far cleaner than Reba's had ever been. She almost dared the woman to find even a speck of dirt in the carefully-kept home, but she thought better of it. Whether she liked the woman or not, Reba was Kemuel's mother, and she would respond respectfully.

"How might I best refresh you this morning, Reba? I still have some cool water from the well..."

"I wouldn't dream of taking water stored in the same quarters as that beast," Reba retorted haughtily, her chin lifted in a stubborn set. "Why, I'm sure there would be filthy little animal hairs floating all in it."

Suit yourself, Adara wanted to say, for she knew the heavy woman was most certainly parched even after a short walk in the scorching afternoon sun. "Well, then," she replied instead, "what brings you here this fine afternoon?"

"Oh, enough of the pleasantries, you little fool! I should like to know if you put up such a friendly front for my sake or for my son's!" Reba's cheeks had flushed an even deeper shade of crimson – if that was even possible – and she clenched her chubby fists angrily at her sides.

Adara was completely taken aback by her mother-in-law's unexpected outburst. Why, the woman had given her plenty of angry looks and disapproving scowls over the years, but this was the first time she had ever verbally attacked her. Adara felt enraged at the gall of this woman – to come into her *own* home and begin shouting out preposterous accusations – and in such a cowardly fashion as to wait until she knew that Kemuel would not be home! Why, the nerve –

Taking a breath to steady herself, Adara quieted the racing thoughts that were coursing through her mind at lightning speed. It was obvious that something was terribly wrong, and perhaps she would be able to work through this little misunderstanding if Reba would behave like a mature adult rather than a spoiled, little child. Carefully, Adara countered, "I can assure you that this is not a front. Kemuel and I have resolved to treat people kindly because it is the Lord's way. But there appears to be a serious misunderstanding between the two of us – "

"A misunderstanding?" Reba scoffed. "Is that what you think this is – a *misunderstanding*?"

"I can't imagine what else it might be," Adara answered measuredly, refusing to flinch even as Reba shook an angry fist in her direction. "But I am willing to work through it."

"Well, I've got some news for you, *honey*," Reba nearly spat, "and this is *not* a matter that we will be *working through* – as you so delicately put it."

Though Adara's head was spinning, she was determined not to let this spiteful woman get to her. She must appear calm, together. "Perhaps this is a matter that should be discussed once Kemuel has arrived home. He is, after all, the head of this household – "

"You leave my son out of this, you filthy, ungrateful little *sinner*!"

The way Reba emphasized *my son* sounded is if she had reclaimed him as her own, voiding any ownership that Adara might have possessed. It angered Adara. In fact, it infuriated her far more than Reba's groundless accusations did. Her spine tingling, Adara straightened and took a step closer to her mother-in-law, who was now trembling with rage. "This is no way to speak to your daughter-in-law – in her own house – whom, I might add, has done you no wrong. Now, I respectfully ask you to leave. This issue must undoubtedly be resolved, but I refuse to pursue the subject further without my husband."

"Your husband! Your husband! As if you have any right to claim him – you have no right to him at all! You have shamed him, disgraced him – our entire family! I know Kemuel, and I know that he is blameless, above reproach in every single way! You childless wretch, you have brought shame upon him! But no more!" Reba's eyes narrowed, and a fiendish smile spread across her face in the most disturbing way. "I have spoken with the elders at the city gates. We are in agreement. They will be speaking with Kemuel, and they will be urging him to obtain a certificate of divorce."

Divorce. The word stung like a hard slap in the face. In fact, Adara would have preferred it. She felt hot tears burning her eyes, but she refused to let them have their way. She would not give this woman the satisfaction. Instead, she said lowly, evenly, "He would never do it."

"Oh, but he will. Now that the elders – not to mention his entire family – are involved, he will have no choice. It is only a matter of time." Having said this, Reba cast a final, gloating smirk in her direction, then, looping her long blue train over one arm, she waddled out of the room like an overweight goose quite pleased with the golden egg she had just delivered.

Tal was on his feet at this point, yellow fur bristling, teeth slightly barred. He was no doubt waiting for a simple command from his mistress, and that would have been the final golden egg for the goose named Reba. Adara was quite tempted to give the command. With pulse racing and head throbbing, Reba threw herself into the wall and allowed her flood of tears to burst forth. Pounding a fist gently against the wall, she took a deep breath and slowly lowered herself to the ground.

Now quite concerned, Tal moseyed up to his distraught

mistress and settled down beside her, his large head resting on her lap, his expressive eyes soft with care. Adara received the comfort he provided and gently stroked his coarse fur, having emptied her angry tears.

Her fear was not that Kemuel would succumb to such pressure and seek to divorce her. No, Kemuel loved her. Even more than that, Kemuel loved God, and he would not dishonor the Lord's holy name for anything in the world.

Rather, Adara's fear was that Reba – and now the elders of the town as well – had the power to make her husband's life quite miserable. And all because of *her*...

How she hated it! How she longed to thrash and scream and unload every ounce of righteous fury upon that haughty, arrogant woman whom had caused both she and her husband so much unnecessary pain! How could she do it? How could a mother be so brazenly heartless, so hideously arrogant?

Adara realized that she must now brace herself unlike ever before. The looks would become even worse. The critical stares would increase. The backstabbing and the vicious gossip would circulate all the more. Reba had knowingly and willingly heaped fuel upon that fire.

She wondered if the flames would ever go out.

And what about Kemuel, her poor husband? What would the other men say to him? How would they treat him? Would they take his side, or ally against him?

And how on earth was she to tell him of the exchange that had taken place with his own mother? Would he be capable of remaining calm and objective regarding a dispute between two people that he greatly loved? She was sure that he would; nevertheless, she began to pray that the Lord would be with him, administering strength and clarity.

Chapter 12

PRAYER AND PREPARATION

The city gates were buzzing, alive and crawling with people. The filth and the stench that assailed Ruth's delicate nostrils was anything but pleasant. The rows and rows of makeshift tents harbored a vast array of interesting people and commodities. Children ran pell-mell in the narrow, crowded streets, seemingly begging to be run over by the numerous, rickety mule-led wagons. Long-faced beggars and all counts of unfortunate invalids howled and cried out for mercy and a few meager coins from their pathetic straw mats arranged in rows along the busy streets. Shabbily dressed women bargained at the fruit and vegetable stands, carefully inspecting potential purchases. Decently-clad servants and half-naked slaves rushed hastily to and fro to do their masters' bidding. Ruth nearly exhausted her weary eyes – already burning from dust and grit – attempting to count the rows of booths, each one attended by eager merchants badgering and cajoling and nearly assaulting each passer-by, bartering, trading, manipulating, and negotiating. As if the sea of wanting voices, the moaning of beggars, the mischievous laughter of children, and the shrill cries of the merchants was not enough, donkeys brayed, cattle lowed, pigs squealed, and chickens clucked in a state of utter panic.

Naomi had surprised Ruth with a distinctly cosmopolitan air upon their arrival at the city gates by calmly stepping down from the wagon, throwing back her shoulders, and walking headlong into the crowd of grimy humanity. She appeared to be a woman of the world, quite certain of what she was looking for and even more determined to obtain it.

Shocked and feeling rather befuddled, Ruth had blinked back her surprise and hurriedly followed after her mother-in-law, careful to keep her wits about her so she would not spoil Naomi's resolute presence. She imagined that, with the attitude Naomi now possessed, her request – whatever it might be – would not be denied.

Somehow amidst all the madness, Naomi had managed to locate her desired venue with the effectiveness of an arrow bursting forth from a bowstring. Again, Ruth was impressed.

Naomi's stance alone commanded attention and respect, and as she stood talking with a rough-looking, stocky man of medium height and strong build – Ruth assumed he must be the caravan master – several harried young mothers with screaming babies on their backs appeared to take note of her and attempt to compose themselves. Naomi's direct manner and ease must have shamed them.

As Ruth stood a respectful distance away from her bartering mother-in-law, she tried to avert her eyes from the madness of the streets and instead attempted to read the roughshod mass of men under the authority of the caravan master. It was rather disturbing to acknowledge that these ill-bred, potentially dangerous men were soon to be her traveling companions. She was particularly startled by the large, savage-looking brute of a man standing at the caravan master's side. Even more startling was the fact that Naomi paid no more attention to him than if he had been one of the pesky flies buzzing heavily in the air.

I have seen another side to Naomi that was yet to be discovered, Ruth thought with a small smile. *The fearless side.*

But as she continued to study the motley caravan crew – especially the beastly one near the master – she began to wonder if it was fearlessness Naomi possessed or sheer insanity. *Perhaps it* would *be safer to travel alone,* she thought, ill at ease.

Quickly, Ruth turned aside and shifted her gaze to the street, for the brute-man hovering near Naomi and the master had suddenly redirected his attention from the two in his circle to Ruth's small form, and he eyed her every bit as suspiciously as she had studied him.

Ruth stood motionless, feeling his beady animal eyes taking her in, and she fought to still the shiver that wracked her entire frame. She must be strong, fearless, like Naomi. She could not give these ruthless creatures the upper hand. Even still, with her attention fully averted, she could envision the steely gaze lurking within those black eyes, magnified by the dark, swarthy complexion of an Ethiopian.

Surely he is not from around here, she thought, bemused. *Perhaps he appears so beastly simply because he misses his family and his homeland...* she chanced one more look in the man's direction, only to find his lion-like gaze still fixed upon her. *Then again, perhaps not.*

Ruth sighed with a feeling of utter relief when she saw Naomi press a few silver coins firmly in the caravan master's large hand. It appeared that the transaction had been made and their spot secured among the traveling caravan!

Ruth was more than ready to flee to the safety and comfort of their small home, as lonely as it might have been. She had had plenty of excitement for one day. So she was greatly dismayed when Naomi turned and beckoned her with a commanding air. "Ruth."

Sighing and nervously adjusting her shawl, Ruth approached.

The caravan master eyed her with a little too much interest as Naomi introduced them. "Ruth," Naomi was saying, "this is Ahmad, the caravan master. He will be the man in charge as we venture forth."

Ahmad was certainly an intimidating man, with dark eyes that glinted with steely resolve, a long, slanted knife belted at his waist, and a strong, set jaw, but he seemed quite harmless standing beside the Ethiopian giant that continued to eye the small party with boundless suspicion.

"Your slave?" Ahmad asked Naomi carelessly, after rudely looking Ruth up and down.

"No," Naomi answered firmly. "Daughter-in-law."

Ahmad shrugged his powerful shoulders as if to say, *Same thing.*

Ruth knew better than to act offended in front of the man's personal bodyguard. She would bear the insult with grace and poise, and beg the Lord to somehow lead them safely to His blessed land despite any assistance they must receive from these tactless ruffians.

Ahmad obviously had better things to do than indulge in meaningless introductions and small talk with strangers *after* the business transaction had been made. "We will depart in three days at dawn. Meet at the city gates. We will not wait."

Ruth's heart leapt into her throat. Three days! How soon the moment would arrive! Momentarily, she wondered if Ahmad meant that the two women would depart from Moab or depart from this life, but she quickly pushed aside her doubts and instead committed the journey to the Lord.

As she and Naomi climbed the creaky old wagon and prepared to journey homeward, Ruth kept her eyes fixed ahead and focused on maneuvering poor Dag and their clunky wagon through the bustling throng of humanity. It was not until they had left the tumultuous unrest and busy chatter of city life behind that Ruth dared a glance in Naomi's direction.

Naomi remained seated rigidly straight on the uncomfortable wooden bench, her shoulders proudly squared and her head erect. Her hands remained folded in her lap, and a small smile was playing about the corners of her lips.

Ruth couldn't help but smile herself. Stately Naomi looked as though she ought to be lounging on a queen's royal litter carried upon the strong shoulders of doting servants, rather than bouncing and jostling noisily on a clumsy wooden bench beneath the scorching desert sun. Still, Ruth could hardly fathom that this was the same woman who had so recently lain in a dusty pile of filth in the corner of a dank, empty room, her hair snarled and her face smeared with ash. Once more, Ruth breathed a silent prayer of thankfulness to her mighty God.

"I am curious... have you conducted much business in the city before now?" Ruth had waited in silence long enough. She could not hold back the deluge of questions that threatened to spill out at any given moment.

Naomi turned to Ruth and chuckled good-naturedly. "Every time I ventured to town, of course. Why do you ask?"

Ruth wrinkled her brow. How often did Naomi frequent the town? She supposed more often than she had realized.

"You seemed to know exactly what you were doing back there."

"I quickly learned that you cannot make yourself the victim. If you cower before those men trembling with your head tucked low, and are fearful to look the vendors in the eye and tell them exactly what it is that you want, and exactly what you are willing to pay, you will find yourself completely at the mercy of those horrid badgers and swindlers, dear."

"You were certainly no victim!"

"I learned much from my Elimelech. Dear me, the poor man desperately lost his way, but I am grateful that I was able to learn a trick or two in the art of business before he passed. Otherwise, I fear that my boys would have suffered greatly and been much in want upon his death."

Ruth detected the slight tremor of Naomi's lower lip as she managed this last painful statement, and Ruth thought it best to change the subject quickly rather than to allow Naomi to dwell on the deplorable past. "Well, I was quite impressed, Naomi. I must admit, I was nearly scared out of my mind!"

Naomi shook her head as if the idea were preposterous. "Whatever for? You did look a mite pale."

"I felt more than a mite pale!" Ruth admitted with a humorous laugh. "But he looked so fierce! Are you sure you want to travel with him?"

Naomi clicked her tongue chidingly. "It is the only way. We will be much safer traveling among a large group. Three women venturing alone would not stand a chance. Besides, there will be respectable merchants and businessman – possibly even their wives and children – traveling along with us." She grinned teasingly. "No fears, Ruth – we will not be alone with the beastly man and his ruffian crew."

The two women locked eyes and shared a hearty laugh.

After traveling along in silence for a good while, Ruth ventured quietly, "Three days. We shall leave for our journey in three days?"

"Precisely."

"Was that his idea or yours?"

"His, of course. I cannot give the orders. I do not run the caravan!"

"I would have thought otherwise when we were back in town."

Naomi laughed. "You ask because Orpah requested three days before departure?"

Ruth nodded solemnly. "I am grateful that she is willing to accompany us, Naomi, but I am afraid that she may try to interfere with your good plans. I wish not to speak ill of Orpah, but I also desire to protect you and your plans for a good future, Naomi." Ruth would have dropped her gaze and stared sheepishly at her own feet if Dag's continual jerking of the wagon did not require her constant and steady attention.

Naomi smiled lovingly and touched Ruth's arm reassuringly. "I know this, my daughter. Do not worry. My love for Orpah has not blinded me as to the condition of her heart. I pray for her every single day, that she might find the truth for herself and accept it."

"As do I," Ruth responded heartily.

Naomi gave Ruth's arm a gentle squeeze. "I know you do. I, too, thought it was rather interesting that the caravan departs three days from now. Who knows? Perhaps the Lord has given us these three days to prepare Orpah's heart for the journey to come?"

Ruth tried to smile, but she found that rather difficult to

believe. She knew Orpah well, and she knew that the young woman was definitely up to something.

Straightening her shoulders, Ruth shoved such disturbing thoughts aside and committed the entire venture to the Lord.

He would guide them.

He would sustain them.

Just as He had led the Israelites to the magnificent land of promise, He would lead her as well to that precious land of old, and He would be right there beside her every step of the way.

Again, those sacred, ancient words scrawled so beautifully across the aging parchment dawned fresh and clear in Ruth's troubled mind, and she felt her entire being calmed at the gentle reminder...

Do not be afraid. Stand still, and see the salvation of the Lord...

Do not be afraid. Stand still. Let the Lord show Himself in all His glory and might and splendor.

For the Lord shall fight for you, and you shall hold your peace...

The Lord would indeed fight for her. Until then, she would wait. No matter what conniving schemes Orpah might throw her way, no matter how fearful the prospect of the traveling caravan might seem, no matter what difficulties they might encounter upon their journey home, Ruth determined that she *would* wait for the Lord.

She would hold her peace.

Boaz was proud of all his workers. He was careful to hire reputable men to work in his fields, and even when the occasional questionable straggler came along needing work, he was quick to see the ministry opportunity and lend a helping hand – along with the much-needed work – smiling to himself as his good men continued to set an example by their conduct and actions.

Kemuel – his foreman who oversaw all that went on in his most prized field – was by far the most dependable and trustworthy of them all. Along with all the administrative responsibilities that accompanied the duties of a foreman, Kemuel was often seen setting his hand to hard, manual labor in the fields, leading the others in jubilant songs of praise to the worthy God they served, or dropping extra heads of wheat or barley – with his master's approval, of course – for the poor and destitute of the community who were allowed to gather the leftovers of the collected harvest. He kept a strong stance, his head held high, his knowing eyes vigilantly observing the fields, a hint of a smile softening his set jaw.

But not today.

Boaz knew something wasn't right. His keen eyes and perceptive spirit immediately sensed the change in this man that was not only his best worker but also his trusted friend. He wondered if he should offer some word of encouragement or even pray with the man, but he also knew that he did not want to invade the man's private life.

So he had held back. At least for the first few hours of the day's work. But the more he had prayed about it, the more inclined he felt to minister to his friend whose confident shoulders now appeared to droop, whose friendly eyes seemed thoughtfully distant.

Kemuel remained standing with sandaled feet planted firmly apart as he observed the workers with sweaty backs bent in the sandy-colored fields. He looked up in surprise when Boaz clapped a strong hand down upon his shoulder.

Boaz's eyes were kind, but serious. "What troubles you, my brother?"

At first Kemuel appeared startled, but he managed a lopsided grin and his stance relaxed ever so slightly as Boaz gave his shoulder a quick squeeze before folding his hands casually behind his back as if he had all the time in the world to share his worker's pain and frustration – whatever it might be.

Kemuel continued scanning the fields, the yellow heads of grain bending and bowing to and fro at the wind's gentle bidding, appearing much like curling, foaming golden ocean waves at high tide. He smiled. "You noticed?"

"How could I not?"

"Am I really that transparent?"

Boaz grinned, amused, his eyes dancing. "To others, no. To those who know you very well, perhaps."

"Shame on me, then."

"The only shame owed would be due to those who love you but didn't notice."

This time, Kemuel's smile appeared less forced. "It's a small matter, really. Family business."

"I consider you family."

"And I consider you as close to kin as well."

"Then?"

Kemuel sighed, and there was a sudden fierceness about him that Boaz had not previously observed – as if it were with great struggle and difficulty that he were holding his anger in check.

Boaz admired him for it. Many men claimed to possess full mastery of their emotions, but very few knew how to control the most threatening emotion of all – cold, raw anger. Boaz cleared his throat and waited patiently for Kemuel to continue on at his own pace.

"It's my mother," he finally ventured, his brows knit threateningly together. "And my wife," he added in a much softer tone.

Boaz nodded with understanding. Though he had never been married, he had heard plenty of colorful tales and unlikely stories. "That can be an interesting combination," he commented somewhat good-naturedly.

"More like a ruthless combination in this case, I'm sorry to say."

Boaz's brows lifted in surprise. "Ruthless?"

Kemuel kicked a pebble with the toe of his sandal and watched it bound a few feet before entangling itself in the tall prairie-like grasses beyond. "My mother never liked Adara. Never. Said she was too pretty. She thought I was only marrying her for her good looks."

Boaz realized that his own brows were still lifted skeptically, and he quickly lowered them. "Your mother should know you better than that."

"She should," Kemuel responded calmly. "But practicality is not one of her strongest points."

Boaz gave Kemuel a sideways glance. No, the man wasn't speaking disrespectfully of his mother. He was simply stating a fact. This was the way his logical mind worked.

As testy as the situation between a mother-in-law and daughter-in-law could be, Boaz sensed that Kemuel's unrest was due to a far deeper issue than his mother's stubborn dislike. He knew Kemuel well enough to know that he would not allow something as trivial as a woman's petty jealousy or doubt to cloud his even temper and better judgment. Still, he did not pry.

"When we were unable to have children," Kemuel

continued after what seemed like an eternity of waiting, "my wife's fate was sealed. My mother despised her with a ferocity that stunned me. My father – though kind and steady – appeared more and more disapproving. I hated the way the women of the town gossiped and slandered Adara's name, but I also understood that the Lord is our Judge and ultimately He will bring everything to light in His own due time. I know my wife's character and her heart. That is enough for me."

Boaz smiled softly and for an instant longed to trust a woman in that same unflinching way.

"However, my mother was not content to leave us be. She has gone to the elders of the city. She seeks to obtain a certificate of divorce... for me to present to my wife."

For a moment Boaz's head reeled with anger and a nauseating disgust. What a noxious, viperous woman Kemuel's mother had proved to be! But he quickly steadied himself and reevaluated his initial response. It would not do to make Kemuel's situation worse by fueling his intense anger, which already threatened to spill over at any minute. Softly, but firmly, Boaz replied, "That is not your mother's decision to make."

"That is exactly what I have told her."

"And how did she respond?"

"She insists that it is only a matter of time. With the family and the wise elders of the city on her side, she believes that she has placed me in a real bind."

"Only if you allow her that much."

Kemuel's jaw was firmly set, and he nodded his solemn agreement. "I have already given this to the Lord. I trust that He will somehow bring good out of a very unpleasant situation. He has done this many times before."

Boaz couldn't help but to smile broadly at this young man's steadfast faith. "Indeed, brother, he has."

"I hurt for my wife. Already we are considered castaways – shunned by society and our very own people. Now our situation has only worsened. But I will continue to pray. God hears."

Boaz nodded decidedly, giving Kemuel a firm pat on the back. "That He does, my friend. Don't lose heart. I will be lifting you and your family up in prayer as well. Every day."

"Thanks for lending an ear. A man doesn't always like to admit that he needs it."

Boaz simply nodded. "Anytime." And he meant it.

Chapter 13

HEARTBREAK

The crumbling, hovel-like dwelling looming on the distant hill had never appeared more inviting to Ruth.

After a long and tiresome journey to town, Ruth felt hot, damp, smelly, and nauseated. Her long, heavy hair hung in wet strands about her face and clung to her fair forehead, and her thick garments felt damp and heavy with sweat.

I suppose we make a lovely picture right about now, Ruth thought ruefully as the wagon finally pulled to a stop at the decrepit corral near the dilapidated old house. Forcing herself to climb quickly down from the wagon bench, Ruth's aching back screamed for a soft bed to lie in sweet, forgetful repose after so many hours of sitting stiff and tall with nothing to support herself beneath the bumpy, jolting, jerking wheels of Dag's wagon. She hurriedly made her way to the other side of the wagon, firmly grasping Naomi by the arms as she helped her make her way to solid ground again.

Poor Dag was breathing in labored, smelly puffs, his sides heaving and lathered in foam from the exertion of pulling such weight in the intensity of the afternoon sun's heat.

You poor beast, Ruth thought sympathetically, gently stroking his neck and ladling out a nice long draught of water from his trough. She was careful to supply him with the refreshment he needed, even as her own sore throat cried out for water. Even as she revived the poor gray creature, Ruth reminded Naomi, "There is still cool water from the well inside. Help yourself, Naomi, and I will be in shortly."

Naomi was about to acknowledge Ruth's thoughtfulness but was interrupted when rushed, angry voices wafted out from the windows, carried by the wind straight to their ears.

"You can't do this to me. You love me. I know you love me!" The voice sounded desperate, distraught, and tight with emotion. Ruth and Naomi instantly recognized it as belonging to Orpah.

A male voice – slimy enough that it could only belong to *one* person, Orpah's revolting companion Balak – responded easily, "You are making this harder than it has to be. Of course I love you. I even enjoy loving you. But there are others I love as well – other women. Am I supposed to forsake all of them for the love of *one* woman?"

"That's how it works!" Orpah retorted.

"Look, I see that you want me to marry you, but I am not interested in chaining myself down like that. I'm not your man."

"Then tell me why – WHY – you lied to me for so long? While my husband was still living! I risked everything for you!" Orpah was nearly beside herself.

Ruth winced and didn't dare look in Naomi's direction. Unwittingly, Orpah had admitted downright infidelity to Naomi's son. Besides that, the fact that a woman so recently widowed should be found alone in a house with another man was positively dreadful. Preposterous. Blatantly disrespectful. Ruth could only shake her head in horror and disbelief.

The angry voices rose and fell for several minutes, and Ruth wasn't sure if she and Naomi should walk away and feign complete ignorance or barge in and put a stop to such godless nonsense.

"Listen, we had our fun when you were a married woman, and I kept you smiling and plenty entertained. But that is all it was – something to keep us occupied, and certainly nothing more. I'm telling you that I will *not* marry you... so, have a nice trip to Bethelville, or wherever it is you're about to end up."

With that, Balak barged out of the house and found himself face to face with a very dismayed Naomi and a very indignant Ruth.

"It's Bethle*hem*!" Orpah screamed after him, emerging behind him in the doorway. She halted instantly as if hitting an invisible wall the moment she saw her mother-in-law standing wide-eyed and bewildered before her faithless lover.

Balak looked suddenly grim, and his eyes traveled back and forth between the three women for a very confused moment before he began to stammer out a string of unintelligible excuses.

Ruth couldn't help but feel a slight satisfaction at the thought that she probably looked and smelled every bit as unpleasant as the donkey whose nose she now cradled in her soft hands. *I don't see you feasting your eyes now, you wicked man,* she thought coolly.

Straightening her back stoically, with one long sweep of

her arm, Naomi said firmly, "I prefer no explanation. I must ask you to leave my home and my property. Now."

That was all that Balak needed to hear. Without even a backwards glance at the woman he had deceived for so long, he hastened down the hill with the speed and agility of a frightened animal.

Feeling repulsed, Ruth realized that *that* was exactly how men behaved when they chose to shut God out of their lives – like confused, carnally driven, raging animals. It was truly horrendous.

Naomi brushed past Orpah and entered her house without a word. It was quite unsettling.

Ruth longed to escape the brutality of the sun's rays and follow after Naomi into the coolness of the home's stone walls, but she sensed that the poor woman needed a few minutes alone after such a rude affront, even if it had not been intended for her ears. Ruth could have wept knowing that Naomi must suffer yet another unexpected blow... from a daughter-in-law that she had thought she could trust.

That's when she remembered Orpah. The young woman who was so pretty outwardly, yet so broken within, stood still as a stone just beyond the door. She hadn't budged since Balak's untimely exit. Her eyes remained locked on the figure that was now a vague, blurry shadow at the foot of the hill, continuing its forward march into a future that did not include her.

Turning away from Orpah's still form, Ruth continued to stroke's Dag's soft gray neck and whisper comforting phrases near his long, twitching ears.

"Go ahead."

Startled, Ruth turned in the direction of Orpah's defiant voice "Excuse me?"

"I said, *go ahead*. Laugh. Judge. Mock. Do whatever it is

that you obviously want to do right now!" Orpah's emerald eyes were fierce, and her voice was menacing.

Ruth sighed and turned her attention back to Dag. Hot, weary, and frustrated, she hadn't the patience to deal with Orpah's accusatory, manipulative temper flares today. She feared she might say something she would deeply regret if she remained where she was much longer. "I am not your enemy, Orpah," she stated evenly, slowly removing Dag's harness and letting him loose in the corral. "Do not take your anger out on me." With that, she closed the gate behind her and prepared to follow after Naomi.

But Orpah stood tall and unyielding in her path, her eyes continuing to flash fire and her lip curling tauntingly. "Is it really *so* dreadfully sinful of me? That I wanted to find *love*? *Love*, Ruth! I thought that's what we had – Balak and I. If he would only marry me, I could stay here with my father and mother and live my life!"

Ruth breathed a silent prayer and managed quietly, "I don't fault you, Orpah. I have no desire to laugh at you or mock you for your misfortune. Now please let me pass."

"No!" Orpah cried out belligerently. "No, I *won't* let you pass – just to go find Naomi and gossip about what a wicked heathen *I* am and how perfectly angelic *you* are!" And then Orpah did something completely unexpected – she collapsed upon a nearby stone, buried her face in her hands, and began to sob as if her heart would break.

Ruth felt her reserve and frustration slowly begin to melt away as she observed the pathetic figure before her. Though she felt much too warm and even a bit faint from her journey to town, Ruth swallowed her own desires for shade and refreshment and stepped carefully alongside Orpah, daring to place a gentle hand on the heaving shoulder.

Orpah jerked her shoulder away fiercely and continued to bawl like an injured child, dark paint streaking ugly black lines down both cheeks.

"Orpah," Ruth said quietly.

Orpah continued to sob.

"Orpah?"

"*What do you want*?"

Ruth exhaled softly and silently implored the Lord for strength yet again. "I don't judge you. And I don't think less of you after all this." *I already knew. I have always known,* she thought sadly. *How could I think any less?*

Orpah's crying was stilled and she glanced suspiciously at the young woman standing beside her. "You don't mean that. You only say it to make me feel better about myself."

"The only thing that comes to mind is this: You say you seek after love, but, Orpah, you already have it. If only you could see that the love you crave is freely offered to you – by the Lord God Who created you, and by your mother-in-law, and by *me*."

Orpah's exquisite eyes filled with tears, and she shook her head harshly. "You just don't understand."

"But I do! Orpah, whatever it was that you thought you had with Balak – it was not love. Love does not run from trials, and love does not lie. Love is a *decision* we must make – to be committed to seeking after each other's interests ahead of our own. What a perfect state our world would find itself in, if we each resolved to love each other as we love our own selves!"

"Oh, Ruth, you sound like someone's grandmother! What of *love*, what of passion, what of fire and flame and desire? Surely you don't expect to find any of that subjecting yourself to becoming the world's doormat and chasing after the wants and needs of a crotchety old woman!"

Ruth actually smiled; Orpah's expression was so desperately comical. She shook her head kindly. "You speak of the love between a man and a woman?"

"Must I explain it to you?" Orpah grumped, exasperated.

Ruth laughed. "Of course not. Don't you see, Orpah? *That* kind of love is impossible without the love of God first. I believe that a man and a woman can love each other passionately. But without the determination to do right by God and each other, no relationship can last. It doesn't matter how much passion or desire you may feel for each other. Eventually, someone else will come along that will give your man those same passionate, desirous *feelings* – and then what? Where does that leave you?"

"Exactly where I am right now," Orpah huffed emphatically.

"That's right. If you desire to find happiness with a man *first*, it will never happen, Orpah. You must choose to put *God* first in your life. Then share your needs with Him. Ask Him to bring the right man into your life – "

"And what if He doesn't?" Orpah snapped.

"Then you trust that He loves you enough to do what is best for you."

Orpah gave her head a defiant toss and crossed her arms. "No, thanks."

By this point, Ruth was so parched that she considered helping herself to Dag's drinking trough, but she felt that she couldn't leave this conversation dangling. Orpah had shown more transparency in these last few moments than she had in all the years Ruth had known her. Quietly, she ventured, "Let me ask you something, Orpah. Even if the Lord did not grant you your every wish, do you think you could possibly be any more miserable than you are right now? Do you truly desire to wager away your very *soul*, even as you believe that you will be miserable either way?"

Orpah bit her lower lip and turned her head obstinately. As clearly as if it were happening all over again, Ruth saw Chilion set his jaw as he turned his face away, rejecting the only One Who could save him for the final time. A terrible tremor wracked her frame. She attempted to shake it off, but her entire body felt strangely chilled.

Oh, Orpah, you are so close, she silently pled. *Don't make the same dreadful mistake your husband made! Turn from your wickedness and your pride. Be saved!*

It seemed like an eternity had passed before Orpah finally spoke again. "I understand that you are only trying to help," she said, her voice distant, eyes vacant. "But I'm not sure you can."

Ruth did not hesitate. "*I* cannot," she stated firmly. "But my God can."

"I want Balak," Orpah whispered, her lip trembling. "I love him."

Lowering herself to the ground at Orpah's feet, Ruth replied, "You cannot force love, Orpah. Believe me when I say you have been spared great pain and loss. After all, if he was willing to pursue you knowing that you were a married woman, why in the world would that keep him from pursuing another woman even after entering into a relationship with you?"

"Well, apparently he already has. Several, in fact." She snorted her disgust.

"That is no life for you, Orpah."

"But it's better than being dragged halfway around the world with a grieving, miserable old woman to some remote, miniscule little town called Bethlehem."

"Don't you mean *Bethelville*?" Ruth asked, her eyes gleaming with mischief.

For a moment Orpah gaped at her, open-mouthed and repulsed. But then she caught the playful glint in the eyes of the young woman kneeling humbly at her feet, and Orpah couldn't help but utter a genuine laugh.

"If you abhor the idea so very much, why did you agree to go along?" Ruth wondered.

"You know I can't tell that woman that I'm forsaking her for my own selfish interests!"

"She would not be forsaken. She will have me along with her."

"Well, thank the gods for Saint Ruth."

Ruth shrugged her shoulders lightly and changed the subject. "Honestly, I can't imagine a more glorious opportunity! Imagine living in the Land of Promise – "

"Only if you believe in all those old wives' tales."

Ruth grew serious. "Naomi has already spoken with the caravan master. We leave in three days. Just as you requested."

"A lot of good that does me now!" Orpah scoffed. "I had planned to be happily betrothed to Balak – planning my wedding – by then."

Ruth smiled. "Perhaps God has better plans for you."

"A little bit of a heads-up would have been nice."

"I don't believe you ever asked Him."

Orpah exhaled loudly, then stretched her arms and legs. "I believe I've had enough of your lectures for one day." Somehow, her words didn't sound quite so antagonizing this time. There was a hint of a smile behind them.

Ruth couldn't be happier to end the discussion. She felt as though she might drop into a faint at any moment if she did not help herself to a cup of cold water. She gave Orpah's shoulder a final squeeze as she rose to enter the house.

Orpah is in the Lord's hands, she reminded herself. She would leave it be for now. She also realized that there was much to be done in preparation for this journey. It would be a long, treacherous venture, to be sure. The journey would last a stretch of several days, at least. And, of course, they must bring several days' worth of travel-safe food and provisions, along with any other items necessary for daily life in their new home. Ruth wondered how she and Orpah – for Naomi would certainly not be in any condition to carry heavy baggage – would possibly shoulder such burdens alone.

But we will have Dag and the wagon, and that should provide ample space to store our few belongings, she reminded herself calmly.

For now, she would help herself to their supply of cool water, and from there proceed to check on poor Naomi. After all, their return from the city had not been a pleasant homecoming. Naomi was bound to be a little shaken up.

Before long, we will be dwelling in the Promised Land among God's very own people, Ruth mused pleasantly as she tilted her head back and felt the cool, clear water trickle down her parched throat. *And then... all will be well!*

Chapter 14

A PAINFUL GOODBYE

The third day dawned bright and unusually warm, and Ruth agonized over the few leather sacks that had been packed, along with the meager belongings she had painstakingly loaded onto Dag's rickety old wagon. Every single goatskin canteen Ruth could get her hands on had been filled to the brim with fresh water, along with several tall, earthenware pottery jugs balanced hazardously in the back of the battered wagon.

Naomi had assured Ruth that there would be several stops along the way to refresh the animals as well as the travelers with fresh food and drinking water, but Ruth was certain that one could never be too prepared. She would definitely prefer to error on the side of caution.

Along with their ample water supply and several pieces of tumble-down furniture, Ruth had also carefully tucked away several weeks' worth of travel-safe, nonperishable foods to keep them sustained for the long journey ahead. Naomi insisted that the trip should take no more than five or six days, but again, Ruth knew that certain circumstances were beyond their control, and she resolved to hope for the best even while preparing for the worst. Discreetly, she had stowed away a bounteous supply of parched grain, recognizing that it would feed not only herself, Naomi, and Orpah, but their faithful mule as well. She had also scrupulously pored over their supply of essential dried edibles – dried olives, figs, and dates – carefully wrapping them in rough, waxy cloth and storing them in a safe location among the other necessary supplies.

She had found herself thanking the Lord that Naomi had already traveled this stretch of land that was so foreign to her. The wise, motherly Naomi had been able to offer plenty of practical advice as Ruth had struggled over which items would be the most feasible to take. She had even instructed Ruth to load up the small clay oven in which she could stack hot coals or stones, light a fire, and bake bread. Along with the clay oven, Ruth had set aside several measures of freshly ground flour and oil for the important process of bread-making. Fresh bread would be such a treat when the caravan was brought to a halt for the night! As fresh loaves would not keep for more than two days, Ruth had checked and re-checked her inventory to make sure she had tucked away plenty of precious flour and oil. She eventually convinced herself that she had set aside more than enough.

Per Naomi's instruction, Ruth had painstakingly wrapped and labeled several small packets of promising young seeds – hoping to plant a small garden where they might grow some of their own food when they reached their new home. Already, Ruth could envision the tempting little green sprouts of carrots, onions, cabbages, and cucumbers peeking out at them from beneath fertile soil in their very own vegetable garden. She could hardly wait!

Of course, the three women had also remembered to

bring rough straw mats that would serve as their sleeping quarters along the way, along with the few extra shawls, wraps, and garments that belonged to them, several wool blankets, and various cooking pots and utensils that would prove helpful on the journey as well as in their new home.

Now as Ruth strolled casually alongside Dag's bumpy wagon, her fingers lightly gripping his leather bridle, she could barely suppress the thrilling excitement welling up within her very soul. Though her eyes carefully scanned the horizon ahead and the hundreds of animal-skin tents that marked the beginning of the town, Ruth didn't even attempt to hide the broad smile that stretched across her face, lighting up her every feature.

Naomi and Orpah sat side by side on the bench in Dag's wagon, Naomi gripping the reins with hands that trembled with nervous excitement. Orpah, on the other hand, sat stiff and rigid beside her mother-in-law, her jaw gruesomely set, her slanted, emerald eyes even more intense than usual. The obstinate young woman had insisted that she be the one to ride along in the wagon with Naomi, even as she refused to take the reins and lead. Ruth had felt her frustration beginning to rise, but she had reminded herself that the journey would be brief and it might be best to simply humor Orpah, understanding that she would make the journey quite miserable if she did not have everything done in her own way. Though Orpah had promised that she and Ruth would take turns resting in the wagon, Ruth was doubtful that her turn would ever arrive.

The exercise will do me good, she thought ruefully, an amused smile tipping up the corners of her full lips. *Today, I do not mind. Nothing can steal my joy today. We are venturing to the Promised Land! Just as Moses and the Israelites did so many years before us!*

Oh, the miracles Almighty God had wrought for those stubborn, hardheaded people! Ruth could only imagine what it must have been like to be guided by a massive pillar of cloud by day, and a blazing pillar of fire by night!

We may not be guided by a pillar of flame and fire, Ruth thought cheerfully, *but perhaps with the Lord's help those unruly caravan men will prove every bit as helpful...* It was doubtful, but she smilingly opted for optimism.

By now those dilapidated old tents were looming closer and closer on the horizon. The sun had not quite peeped out from behind the rolling green hills of the land of Moab – the land of Ruth's birth, the land of her fathers, the land of her people. Yes, whether she liked it or not, she was a Moabitess. The Lord had seen fit for her to be born here, raised here, and – praise God – delivered from her many sins and set free here. And yet, she was about to walk away from all of it. Forever.

In the three days she had been preparing for this journey – as she had flown about the house like a whirlwind, checking and rechecking the list she had mentally thrown together in her mind – she had found herself pondering over memories that she had long-since dismissed, permanently shelved in the back of her many thoughts, wistfully hoping to forget. But, no, she could not shove them aside. She could not get rid of them. They were here, they were staring her in the face, screaming for her attention... and they needed to be addressed.

She had thought about her mother. For years, she had intentionally set aside any and all thoughts and memories of the woman who had borne her. Though her mother had given her life, Ruth felt that her mother had snatched away any hope of ever finding that life to be fulfilling. Her mother had willfully – intentionally – ignored her young daughter's pleas those dreadful nights that had occurred before the wedding. She had shut her ears and her heart to every single one of her daughter's desperate entreaties. She had seen the raw pain and despair and agony etched all over her little daughter's face, and yet... she had done nothing. "This marriage will greatly ease your father's heavy load. It will be one less mouth to feed," she had said quietly, her eyes lowered as she had turned her attention to the garment she had been mending. "You must be a brave girl and accept it."

So Ruth had done as she had been bidden. She had been a "brave girl." If her mother had ever been proud, Ruth never would have known. The woman had died shortly after her daughter's wedding.

And her father? He had wasted no time finding himself a perky, young wife – a girl about Ruth's own age. Ruth had been appalled when she had been informed of the shocking events– not by her father, but rather from several chatty women at the well one drizzly, gloomy spring morning. Ruth wondered if this young bride of her father's had also sobbed as if her heart would break the night before her wedding.

Ruth also had three brothers – along with several new additions to the family that had been borne to her father by his second wife. She had never met her new half-brothers and half-sisters, and she hadn't been close to her brothers, either. As the only daughter of the family, she had remained at home with her mother learning the art of keeping house, while her brothers had gone their separate ways pursuing their various trades.

Even as her heart fluttered with excitement and her cheeks flushed with anticipation and unbridled zeal, she found herself silently wishing that her own family could have accepted the truth with willing hearts as she had. Upon her conversion to the one true faith in the one true God, she had paid a visit to her father's house. She had introduced herself to the pretty little woman he had married, and held the newest member of their family – a tiny, crooning baby girl – in her arms. And she had explained to both her father and the young woman that she had discovered an undeniable truth and longed for them to experience the glory of it for themselves.

Her father had shut the door behind her with a dogged warning never to return. "No daughter of mine who blasphemes the gods of our fathers is welcome in this house," he had stormed violently.

Bravely, Ruth had squared her shoulders and strode calmly – and with great dignity – down the winding path that would lead her back to her own home.

Despite the cold reception she had received the first time, Ruth had paid her father one last visit the day before she was to leave for Bethlehem. To her great dismay, it had ended on the same note as her first visit. Her father had become even more obstinate this time, taking her by the shoulder and throwing her out of his home – the home that had once been *hers* as well – bellowing that the country would be better off without her.

Sadly, she had realized that her father had made his choice. He would have to live with it. Still, she would continue to pray for him each day. Though the situation pained her greatly, she had already given it to the Lord. By God's grace she had found closure, and she could proceed onward, traveling this new journey with a willing, cheerful heart.

Ruth wondered if Orpah had said goodbye to her own family before setting off with Naomi. After a time of walking alongside the wagon in silence, Ruth decided to voice the question.

"Of course I said goodbye to my family!" Orpah exclaimed incredulously. "What kind of daughter would I be to forsake them without a single word?"

"I don't believe you have forsaken them, Orpah," Ruth countered quickly. "You are honoring your mother-in-law and fulfilling your duties and obligations as her daughter-in-law."

"They would never see it in such a way," Orpah snorted defiantly. "In their opinion, their contract with Naomi became null and void the moment her son decided to up and die on us. *He's* not exactly fulfilling *his* obligation to love and protect now, is he?"

Ruth blanched at the sheer audacity with which Orpah spoke. *And this after we allowed you to ride comfortably in the wagon,* she fumed inwardly.

However, outwardly she kept her peace. She looked to Naomi, and though the woman's eyes had clouded over with saddened tears, she returned Ruth's glance with a look of her own that was so knowing, tender, and patient that Ruth had to turn her face away to hide tears of her own that threatened to spill over her soft cheeks.

Dag plodded along, his strong hoofs clip-clopping rhythmically against the hard-packed earth and stone beneath. Something about the creaking, gently-turning wheels of the wagon, the rhythmic beat of Dag's rough hooves, and the soft whisper of the early morning wind as the soon-to-be rising sun cast long, melancholy shadows across the graceful hills was calming, soothing, to Ruth's eager yet troubled spirit. She closed her eyes for a brief moment and whispered a prayer of thanks to the God Who had given them such a glorious morning on which to begin their journey.

Sooner than Ruth had expected, she found herself carefully guiding Dag by the bridle through the hustle and bustle of a very busy city in the chaotic and hazardous process of waking up for the day.

For the first time in weeks, Orpah's eyes widened with interest as merchants hollered from behind their richly-draped booths, thrusting all manners of finery and miscellaneous merchandise beneath quick eyes and eager noses.

"Oh!" Orpah cried out as they passed a booth glittering with every imaginable type of expensive jewelry – silver, gold, and bronze, rubies, onyx, lapis lazuli, and emeralds, rich strings of colorful beads and odd little charms, tokens, and trinkets. "Perhaps we should visit a few of the merchandisers' booths!" Orpah attempted to suggest casually, though she was nearly begging, her eyes bulging with desire. "Perhaps we might find some wares that would prove helpful for our journey!"

Ruth followed Orpah's gaze straight to the stand of expensive jewelry and laughed aloud. "The only help such 'wares' might provide would be for the bandits and thieves along the way who would rob us blind for traveling with such foolishness!"

Orpah folded her arms across her chest with a loud huff and resumed her pouting as they carefully threaded their way through the bustling sea of humanity toward the city gates, where they were to meet the caravan master along with his crew.

Ruth caught her breath in amazement at her first sight of the city gates. Besides the usual throng of activity surrounding the imposing brass gates, a winding line of pack camels loaded down with packages and parcels, their long necks arched gracefully, their busy black eyes bulging and ever-observing, dominated the impressive scene. The strong smell of the beasts caught Ruth surprisingly off-guard, and she realized that poor Dag would look much like the small black sheep of the caravan among so many tall, stately camels. Large wagons – much sturdier than the one housing the women's meager provisions – were still in the process of being loaded with heavy burdens, barrels, buckets, leathern bags, straw, caged birds, and a number of wrapped items of unusual shapes and sizes. Men of many varying shades and statures bustled about, bellowing orders and rushing to obey gruff commands. The camels moaned and whined, a few lonely donkeys brayed impatiently, the birds clucked and squawked anxiously, the men roared with laughter and a hundred different commands. All of it created quite the commotion, and Ruth felt her grip tighten around Dag's weathered bridle. She quickly dismissed the temptation to feel overwhelmed.

This is an adventure, to be sure! Ruth reminded herself, a smile playing about the corners of her lips. At first, the prospect of traveling with such rough-and-ready, wild guides was simply unbearable, but she had somehow managed to reconcile herself to the idea and even felt a bit of enthusiasm at the unknown adventures that might await them on the road to Bethlehem.

The caravan guards stood tall and at the ready, swords belted at the waist and spears in hand. Ruth would have felt enormously safe had she been convinced that they were on *her* side.

"So you have arrived."

Ruth tore her attention away from her silent reverie, jolted by the cool, level voice. Ahmad – the caravan master – stood calmly before them, arms crossed over his barrel chest, his sword a grim omen strapped to his belt. Ruth saw that he was addressing Naomi, which was proper. It would not be respectful for a strange man to address two unmarried women – particularly women so recently widowed. *So he does have a few manners tucked beneath that frightful exterior*, Ruth thought with some relief.

Naomi was already stepping down from the wagon, and Ruth hurried to the opposite side to assist her. Naomi gratefully took the arm that Ruth offered her and steadied herself by gripping the side of the wagon. "Nothing could keep us away," Naomi replied decidedly.

Ahmad remained firmly rooted in the dusty path and appeared to be surveying the bed of their wagon, cluttered with sacks and various household items. "Our journey is short."

"And our items are many?" Naomi's eyes glinted mischievously.

Ahmad shook his head ever so slightly, apparently resigned to the fact that he must endure the illogical whims of the three women... at least for the next few days. "Your place will be at the rear of the caravan. The caravan will be fully guarded, so fear is unprofitable and unnecessary. We embark within the hour. Be ready." With that short speech, Ahmad gave the women another brief nod before disappearing into the sea of carts, wagons, men, and beasts.

Ruth noticed Naomi's brows knit together thoughtfully at Ahmad's departing speech. "Something he has said troubles you?" Ruth ventured quietly.

Though Naomi's tone was laced with concern, she maintained a confident stance. "The back of the caravan may not be the most desirable position," she stated calmly.

"Why not?" Orpah demanded loudly, leaning towards the other two women from her wagon perch.

Naomi drew a knowing finger to her lips. "We will not complain. We will graciously accept our position and make the most of it."

"Is there danger?" Ruth asked soberly, careful to emanate the surety of Naomi's expression and posture.

"Danger? No. We will be very close to the rear guard, which is quite an advantage. However, I'm afraid it will be a dusty ordeal – traveling behind the majority of the wagons and animals all along the way."

At this unwanted disclosure, Orpah scrambled down from her perch like some exotic, haughty bird perturbed at having its feathers ruffled. "You don't mean to say that we will be eating everybody's dust the entire way?" she protested cynically.

Naomi patted Orpah's cheek in a comforting manner and said rather merrily, "Only for a few days, my dear."

With that unpromising bit of news, Orpah dropped her face into her hands dramatically and set up a despondent wail. "Ohhhh!"

For once Ruth was thankful for the tumult and deafening chaos that engulfed them, for it distracted the rest of the travelers from Orpah's pathetic behavior. Ruth felt her cheeks flush with embarrassment. Why couldn't Orpah behave like a mature adult for once in her life?

Naomi appeared to be more sympathetic. Her eyes soft with motherly affection, she reached out and touched Orpah's shoulder with patient understanding. "My child, is this truly what you want?"

Orpah had already broken down, and she sobbed into her trembling hands like a mother bereft of her only child. "No! This is not what I want! Not at all!" Sobs continued to wrack her small frame, and she shuddered, horror-stricken.

Ruth cast several nervous glances about them, but no

one seemed to be paying any attention to Orpah's childish tantrum.

"Oh, my dear girl," Naomi's own eyes were welling with tears. "This is too much for an old woman to ask of you – to ask of *anyone*." She turned to Ruth, her eyes pleading. "Listen, I want both of you to return to your fathers' homes. Let them arrange decent marriages for you."

Ruth was so taken aback by this sudden, shocking turn of events that her head fairly spun. "Naomi – "

Naomi raised a firm hand. "No, I mean this. You have both sacrificed so much for me – more than anyone else would ever even consider. I cannot keep asking for more, my daughters, when you have already given so much. Go. Please."

Now it was Ruth's turn for the tears to flow unchecked. "Naomi, I won't. I will not go. I will not turn back!"

But Orpah brushed aside Ruth's firm assertions. She looked to Naomi, her dark lashes framing red-rimmed eyes. "Oh, Naomi, do you mean that?"

"I do. With all of my heart."

"But, Naomi, how could you possibly think we would be wiser to remain in this idolatrous country? How could you even say it?" Frightened, Ruth wondered if Naomi had begun to crack beneath the emotional strain and pressure.

"Oh, my darling, do you not see it?" Naomi looked severely tormented even as she spoke. "With me, there is no future for either of you. I am getting old – long past the child-bearing years. And even if I were to marry some unfortunate man tonight and bear sons, would you wait for them to grow up rather than find happiness with another? Of course not!"

Orpah's tears had somehow miraculously subsided. Her paint-smeared eyes had grown instantly brighter. "Oh, my dear mother-in-law!" she gushed. "You're an angel – an absolute *angel*! If you truly mean it, then I accept your kind offer with a grateful heart!"

Naomi appeared to have aged an additional five years in the few brief moments since the discussion had begun. "Will you find safe passage to your father's home, my child?"

"Of course I will! Don't worry about me, Naomi, I will be just fine! Wonderful, in fact!" Orpah was already slinging her bags over her shoulder from the wagon's bed, tremulous with enthusiasm and sheer relief. Scrambling down from the bed of the wagon, Orpah took a quick inventory of her belongings and flashed a brief smile of satisfaction.

Naomi took that opportunity to place both hands firmly on Orpah's shoulders, looking her squarely in the eyes with much sadness and grief. "My daughter, I will not question you nor the path you have chosen. I want you to know that I will never forget you, Orpah, and I will keep you in my prayers with each passing day."

Orpah was looking increasingly uncomfortable. She fidgeted uneasily, her eyes roving about the engulfing clamor and confusion as if to escape the intensity of Naomi's gaze.

"My daughter, will you promise me this one thing?" Naomi's tears traced two slender lines down her dust-caked cheeks.

Orpah nodded nervously. "Of course," she conceded half-heartedly.

"Promise me that you will seek the Lord with all your heart. He truly does love you, Orpah, and you will never be happy without Him. Though your girlish heart finds it quite difficult to believe, all the merchandise and money and men in the world cannot bring you long-term happiness, my dear."

Orpah did indeed look as though she found it very difficult to believe, but she nodded her consent.

Naomi kissed Orpah's cheek, still salty with tears, and smiled. "God be with you, my child."

"Goodbye, Naomi." Orpah then turned to Ruth, giving her a cool nod.

Ruth returned the gesture, and yet somehow she longed to throw her arms around Orpah's neck and beg her to reconsider. How could she not see that she was making the biggest mistake of her life? How could she be so foolish? But as was the case with Ruth's father, Orpah was in the Lord's hands now. Ruth could not force her to make the right decision any more than she could force her father's hand.

With that, Orpah turned with great self-possession and strode calmly back through the crowd with the air of a woman who had just been crowned queen of her very own empire.

Ruth kept her eyes steeled upon Orpah's scarlet-clothed form, her matching head-covering brazenly shoved aside, the warm desert breeze tugging at her long black tresses, until she was swallowed up by the tumultuous crowd and could be seen no more. A sob caught in the back of Ruth's throat, but she refused to let it have its way this time. Ruth turned back to Naomi with squared shoulders and determined resolve.

"Well, that is that." Naomi's lip trembled, even though her tone sounded evenly matter-of-fact. She turned to Ruth. "Well," she asked softly, averting her eyes before they could contradict her brave composure. "Will you go, too?"

"No." The resounding strength, the iron will with which she spoke, stunned even Ruth herself. She hardly recognized the sound of her own voice. "I will *not* go. *Don't* ask me to leave you or turn back."

"Your sister-in-law has returned to her people and to her gods. She recognizes that life in Bethlehem will not be easy for two foreign women from Moab."

"I am *not* Orpah. I have already given my heart to Almighty God. He has directed my steps every single day of my life – even before I knew it or felt His hand upon me. He brought me straight to you, Naomi. I will *not* be deceived. I will *not* forsake Him – nor *you*, for that matter. So I say again... Don't ask me to leave you, to turn back. Wherever *you* go, Naomi, *I* will go. Wherever you live, I will live. Your people will be my people, and your God shall be my God. Wherever you die – there I shall die also, and there I will be buried. May the Lord punish me – be it ever so severely – if I *ever* allow anything but death to separate us!"

Naomi said nothing, for she had begun to weep. Her shoulders heaved and she drew her hands up to her face as tears streamed past her feeble fingers.

Ruth gathered the distraught woman in her arms and held her close. "The Lord has given us each other, Naomi. I will not leave you. Don't cry, Naomi, I am here. I am here."

Chapter 15

THE JOURNEY

It didn't take long for Ruth to discover *exactly* why it was so unpleasant to be last in line in a traveling caravan. The journey had scarcely begun, and already her eyes stung with unexpected ferocity, her nostrils itched and burned, and her dry throat cried out for relief. She had already swallowed enough coarse dust to fill her belly for a week, and she imagined that there was plenty more where that came from. *Well, perhaps with our bellies full of dirt, our rations will last even longer than expected,* she thought ruefully. She could feel the dry grit crunching between her teeth, and it was quite irksome.

Though Naomi had declared the back of the caravan to be particularly safe – thanks to the rear guard, of course – Ruth now had her doubts. A heap of doubts, in fact. Much to her dismay, the beastly-looking Ethiopian had taken his position at the back of the caravan – in an unsettlingly close proximity to their wagon. Apparently, *he* was the rear guard.

There were several other men scattered about here and there near the rear, and two others flanking either side of the Ethiopian. However, they appeared dwarfish and pallid in the dark shadow of the fierce-looking foreigner. Ruth's wide eyes observed that his spear was several sizes larger than those belonging to the other men, and his sword was curved viciously rather like a scythe, the hilt a huge brick of dull, molded bronze. She made up her mind right then and there that she would do all in her power to remain on the good side of that man and his savage-looking weapon.

Ruth ambled alongside Dag's wagon at a somewhat comfortable pace. They had not been traveling long enough for fatigue to set it, and fortunately the camels were too burdened down with heavy packs and merchandise to hurry. At that moment, however, Ruth felt that she wouldn't mind picking up the pace just a little bit. She felt nearly overwhelmed with nervous energy and zeal and restlessness. There was a delighted bounce in her step that sent up a tiny explosion of reddish dust with every slap of her sandals upon the dry, cracking desert floor. Awed, she wondered how the men leading the caravan could so easily navigate these barren desert wastelands. The road seemed nothing but a mere imprint – a slight indention in the endless miles of rolling sand, dotted here and there with dull stones or occasional hardy desert shrubs.

The minutes rolled quickly by and somehow morphed into hours. Though Naomi remained seated as comfortably as possible in the wagon, Ruth alternated between the jostling wagon bench and trailing alongside the wagon for a bit of a stretch and some exercise. She couldn't stomach remaining still in the wagon much longer than half an hour, for then she began to feel the sun beating ruthlessly upon her covered head, back, and shoulders. Sweat dripped from her brow, trickled down her back, dampened her thick, scratchy garments, and accumulated with great stickiness in the most unpleasant places. Ruth found herself constantly swiping the flowing sleeve of her tunic across her forehead to mop up the sweat and to discourage the gritty, stinging grains of sand from sticking to her face. She worried constantly about Naomi, and regularly encouraged her to drink water from the rations for fear of dehydration. Most of the time, Naomi declined with a forced smile, and Ruth knew it was because she worried about their supply.

Hopefully we will be able to refill at the various rest stops, Ruth thought time and time again. The water was going much faster than she had anticipated.

As the caravan trekked along, carefully winding its way through the gently rolling desert plains, the wind whistled and blew, so dry and warm that it hardly provided any relief from the glaring afternoon sun. The caravan was forced to halt several times throughout the day's journey, as the taxed animals required another bout of dried oats and water for nourishment.

When the sun began to ride low on the hills, giving off a faint orange glow, Ruth felt her heart leap with relief. From the ground alongside the wagon, she turned and looked up to Naomi, who was beginning to nod off even as she gripped Dag's reins with her white-knuckled hands. "We will break for camp before nightfall, I suppose?" Ruth wanted to be sure before she allowed herself the pleasure of imagining how delicious it would feel to curl up beneath a woolen blanket – protection against the notorious desert chill that crept up on travelers at nightfall – and drift off into a carefree slumber beneath a dazzling array of shining stars.

Naomi was past the point of forcing smiles by now. She nodded wearily. "Of course. When the sun finally sets beyond those hills, you will not be able to see your own hand held before your face – much less able to see well enough to traverse this rugged landscape."

For the first time in several hours, a genuine smile graced Ruth's pretty lips. Oh, to rest! To halt from this weary journey, to kindle a small fire that would glow and crackle delightfully, to refresh her hungry stomach with dried dates and olives and figs!

She dared a quick glance over her shoulder. Yes, he was still there. The Ethiopian continued to march menacingly along, the jagged scar slashed across his cheek glowing red and angry in the faint light, his beady eyes glinting and steeled like polished onyx. He did not appear even slightly winded after an entire day of such brutal travel.

A slight shiver traced its way up Ruth's slender spine. As beautiful as sleep would feel for her tired body, she wondered if she would have the courage to allow herself that luxury alongside such fierce traveling companions.

When the time finally came to set up camp for the night, Ruth no longer fretted about their companions. In fact, she didn't even give them a second thought. She was convinced that she had never felt more exhausted in her entire life! They had not made good enough time to reach the small outpost that functioned as a rest stop, but at this point, few of the travelers even cared. Everyone was ready to settle down for some much-needed rest.

Just imagine, she thought as she spread out two sleeping pallets – one for herself and another for Naomi. *I feel this way after a single day of travel. Think of how the Israelites must have felt after traveling through the desert for forty years!* It was quite a daunting thought, and she realized that the stories she cherished were coming to life, leaping off the pages of Naomi's weathered scrolls in a way that was both thrilling and awe-inspiring. She felt as if she were being given the unique opportunity to trod in the Israelite's own shoes – to feel the fatigue, the exhaustion, the anticipation, the wonder, the doubt. She hummed a happy little tune as she arranged the coals to start a fire, glorying in the coolness that had swept across the desert floor upon the brilliant setting of the sun, basking in the wonder of all she had experienced in such a short time, and thrilling over the blessings that were sure to follow them straight into the Promised Land.

"Ah, my Ruth. How I love to hear that gentle voice of yours," Naomi said fondly as she offered a handful of dried oats to Dag, stroking his soft neck with a stiff hand.

Ruth glanced up from the fire she was kindling, unaware that she had been humming. She smiled. "I can't help but sing. My heart is so happy!"

"To say such a thing after the exhausting day of travel we have just endured is quite a feat."

"In but a few a days, it will all be worth it!"

Naomi smiled faintly. "I'm sure it shall, my dear. I'm sure it shall." After carefully securing Dag by rope and harness, Naomi joined Ruth by the pathetic little fire she had managed to coax from the stubborn coals.

For a moment neither woman said a word. Both were too fatigued, and the small flames that rose and fell were mesmerizing to their tired eyes. All across the desert valley, small fires much like theirs were being brought forth, and the smell of flatbread baking and even some meat roasting wafted through the camp in the most delightful manner. Overhead, the stars dazzled and sparkled with the majesty and brightness of a thousand gleaming gems.

Ruth and Naomi had carefully selected this spot to set up their own little camp – sheltered by a large outcropping of sharp, desert stone at their backs, yet open enough to observe the breath-taking canopy of glistening stars overhead.

A short distance away, a group of men burst forth with deep, heartfelt laughter, shaking Ruth from her trancelike stupor. She realized that she had sat idle long enough, and quickly snapped into action. Reaching into the sack that she had carefully selected from the back of the wagon, she asked Naomi, "What will you have to refresh yourself?"

Naomi shook her head decisively. "Nothing for me, thank you, dear. I am much too weary for that. Sleep sounds the most welcome to me."

Ruth frowned her disapproval. "Now, you have traveled long and hard this day, and I will not have you dropping like a fly by the wayside because you refuse to refresh yourself!" Eyes twinkling, Ruth reached into the sack, retrieving a handful of dried dates. "Eat!"

"Oh, my darling, I couldn't."

"But you must, and you *will*," Ruth responded readily, taking Naomi's hand and firmly pressing the dates into her palm. "At least a small handful. You really must have something."

"Now, Ruth, I already said – "

"Never mind what you already said," Ruth retorted playfully. "Heavens, it's a good thing I'm here to look after you, Naomi!"

Both women laughed at that remark, and Naomi settled comfortably against the cool stone at their backs and slowly began to munch the sweet dates that Ruth had provided.

Ruth reached into another sack and retrieved a small rounded loaf of bread. Breaking it into several pieces, she handed the largest piece to Naomi.

The dates seemed to have awakened Naomi's appetite, the refreshment emphasizing the hunger that had previously been dulled by her fatigue. Naomi eagerly accepted the fresh bread, which Ruth had baked with loving care the day before their journey had begun. "Thank you, my daughter," she managed eagerly before helping herself to a large bite.

It was not until Ruth was sure that Naomi was comfortable and cooperatively devouring her supper that Ruth drew forth the goatskin flask and offered it to her mother-in-law, who took it gratefully and allowed herself a nice long draw of the fresh water. Wiping her moistened lips with the back of her leathery hand, Naomi held out the welcome flask with a satisfied grin.

Ruth willingly accepted the flask, her hands nearly shaking with eagerness. She had never known or experienced such thirst. Her graceful head covering fell back and gathered like a pool about her shoulders as she tilted her head back for a drink, and she didn't bother to adjust the unruly shawl. The chilly night air felt absolutely delicious upon her flushed cheeks. Eagerly, she took her first sip. The water tasted cool and refreshing as it cascaded down her severely parched throat, washing away the dust and muck and grime that seemed to have accumulated and settled there during their long trek.

Naomi thought about how stunning Ruth looked, carefully poised before the fire's gently leaping flame, the orange glow accenting her bright eyes and delicate features. She looked quite lovely, even after the day's exhaustive travel.

Oh, Lord God, Naomi prayed silently, her eyes moist. *Ruth has sacrificed so much for You... and for me. I ask that you flood her heart and mind and life with the same happiness and peace that she has brought to me. Do not rob her of the joys these early years ought to bring a faithful young woman. Bless her, Lord. Bring a godly, worthy man to love her, to protect and provide for her. Bless them with children, Lord. Bless that girl, Lord! I pray with all my might that You bless her.*

Ada, always the careful one, was meticulously arranging her master's supper on a large platter when she heard heavy footfalls behind her.

Samuel's, no doubt, she thought to herself as she arranged a healthy bunch of plump, deep purple grapes about a large loaf of freshly baked bread. She added a generous slab of strong goat cheese, along with a handful of ripe olives and glistening dates. She stepped back a pace to proudly examine the work of her calloused hands.

There, she thought, rather pleased with her own effort. *Perfect.*

"What a pretty picture you have made, my dear Ada!"

"Master Boaz!" Ada wheeled around in surprise upon hearing the master's voice. "What brings you to the kitchen this evening?"

She appeared rather shocked, as it was unusual for the man of the house to join the servants at work in the kitchen. Customarily, she would deliver Boaz's meal as he lounged in the spacious chamber overlooking his Eden-like courtyard, then make herself scarce so he could enjoy his evening meal in peace. However, Boaz was unusual in every single way – not just in this instance. She smiled to herself, thinking of how fortunate she was to gain employment at the hand of such a godly man. Though she depended upon him for her daily wages, she viewed him more as a son than a master.

As a young girl, she had waited upon his own mother – a woman of unusual common sense and beauty. Boaz's mother had been older than Ada, yet Ada had thrilled at the woman's many questions and delighted exclamations as she learned more and more about the Lord God and grew in her faith. While serving Boaz's mother, Ada had felt more like a teacher than a lady in waiting, but she had gloried in every minute of it, answering questions, poring over the Scriptures, and marveling at the might of God as He delighted them through answered prayer. What could possibly be more beautiful than to witness the daily growth and maturity of a woman in love with her Lord?

Ada was an older woman now, her hair far more gray than chestnut, wrinkles slowly beginning to set in. Yet the inexplicable joy and youthful vigor of one who found their value in the sight of God rather than men was still evident upon her worn features.

Boaz pulled up a stool before the sprawling island countertop behind which Ada spent many an hour throwing together every type of culinary masterpiece and delectable delicacy imaginable. Folding his large, work-hardened hands upon the countertop, he began somewhat teasingly, "I may have had a few ulterior motives in visiting you..."

Ada threw her flour-dusted hands up in the air. "For shame! And here I thought you simply enjoyed my company."

"That I do," Boaz responded wholeheartedly.

Feigning a look of mock offense, Ada asked carelessly, "Shall you take your meal right here then, seeing as you enjoy my company so much?"

Boaz laughed heartily, delighted by the inviting display of edibles that Ada lifted and now carried towards him. "Absolutely."

"As you have arrived several minutes ahead of schedule, Samuel has not quite finished roasting and seasoning the lamb," Ada reminded him shortly, nose in the air. However, she couldn't hide the playful sparkle that often hid behind her dark eyes.

"Actually, Ada, the lamb is prepared according to the

master's liking. And it is prepared early at that, as I am well aware of the master's habits." With that, Samuel emerged from the hall and an inviting aroma followed after him. Samuel was a soft-spoken young man no older than fourteen. He had lost both his parents to a terrible sickness that had claimed both their lives, and nearly taken his as well. Boaz had lovingly taken the boy in, provided him with employment, and instructed him in necessary schooling such as reading and writing, hoping to enable him to have a better future even without the security of living relatives. Initially, Boaz had hoped to apprentice him under Kemuel's steady hand at the fields, but the intense heat and back-breaking labor had not suited Samuel's gentle spirit. Though he had worked hard and with no complaint, Boaz quickly realized that this was not the path of the boy's choosing. Despite his difficult childhood, Samuel had learned to smile readily and enjoyed ribbing his master and Ada, as well as Amal– the third and final member of Boaz's staff.

Boaz's mouth watered at the sight of the roasted lamb, stacked high upon the silver platter that Samuel balanced proudly above his head. With a daring little spin, he brought the tray down before Boaz's nose, and the tempting aroma of seasoned meat filled the air.

"Well, Samuel, I believe you have outdone yourself," Boaz remarked, eager to help himself.

Samuel beamed boyishly as he set the tray before Ada and Boaz, then turned to leave.

"Wait." Boaz held up a hand. "I imagine you are both famished after working so hard to prepare such a glorious feast?"

Ada and Samuel eyed each other questioningly at the odd inquiry.

"Well?" Boaz prompted, popping a ripe olive into his mouth.

"To tell you the truth, we are rather hungry..." Samuel began first.

Boaz looked to the matronly woman standing behind the counter, arms covered in flour up to the elbows, apron still in place. "Ada?"

"Well, I am a mite hungry myself," she replied hesitantly.

"Well, then, what are we waiting for? Let's help ourselves to some of this delectable fare!"

Samuel looked as though he might bury his entire face in it, but Ada was a bit uncertain. "Oh, sir, we couldn't – "

"You *could*, and you *will*! Do you expect one lonely man to attempt to devour this feast all on his own? Now shall we thank God for this blessed meal fit for a king?"

Both servants nodded eagerly, and Boaz lifted up his voice to God, deeply thanking Him for His provision, loving kindness, and generosity.

After the prayer, Ada chuckled in wonder as she helped herself to a few juicy grapes.

Samuel tore into the roast lamb as if he hadn't eaten in a week. "I am an even better cook than I thought!" he winked at Ada, who threw up her hands and clicked her tongue in a chiding manner.

"Your humility is inspiring," she quipped.

"Now," Boaz began after taking a long drought of cool water scented with fresh fruit. "About my ulterior motives..."

Ada arched a brow, delicately helping herself to another grape. "What about them?"

"I've had something on my mind for some time now, and I'm afraid that it is an issue that only a woman can help me resolve."

Now her other brow shot up as well. “Master Boaz, might I mention that I’m nearly twice your age, and a servant at that! Couldn’t you find a lovely young lady your own age to meet such demands?”

Clearing his throat uncomfortably, Boaz nearly choked, “Ada!”

Though Ada appeared riled and much appalled, Boaz knew that the lively little housekeeper was only poking fun at him. He felt his face flush and his ears burning red as crimson despite that fact.

Samuel was fairly howling. “Good one, Ada! You had *me* fooled for a minute there, too!”

Ada wiped her hands upon her apron loudly, a gesture that indicated she was quite pleased with herself.

“Shall we proceed forward as mature adults or not?” Boaz managed a chuckle in spite of himself.

Ada waved a dismissive hand. “By all means, proceed.”

Boaz chewed the tender lamb thoughtfully, turning a proposition over in his mind. “It’s about a young woman – the wife of my foreman, Kemuel.”

Ada’s brows shot up again, and Boaz hurriedly explained himself before she could make another embarrassing wise-crack. “The sad truth is, she is barren, and both she and her husband desire children very much.”

Ada looked instantly solemn, and she nodded in deep understanding. “I see.”

“As you know, most women unable to bear children are shunned, slandered, rejected. I strongly disagree with those haughty enough to claim that barren women are cursed – often considered sinners far more reproachful than the rest of us. Why, has the Almighty not made Himself perfectly clear? Sin is *sin* in the sight of God. We are *all* sinners. We are all in desperate need of His mercy.”

Ada nodded more emphatically. "Amen."

"As if being ridiculed and shunned is not enough, Kemuel's own family has taken action against his wife. They have involved the elders of the city. Their desire is to convince Kemuel to divorce his young wife."

Now Ada was ruffled. "The nerve of some people – "

"It is what it is. We cannot change it. But perhaps we can ease their burden just a bit."

Ada looked very interested.

"Kemuel is a dear friend of mine. I would do anything to offer my support during this difficult season of their lives."

"Any friend of yours is a friend of mine," Ada put in firmly.

"I can offer my support and encouragement to Kemuel daily at work in the fields. We discuss the progress of the situation and pray together often. However, I cannot rightly offer such encouragement to his wife."

Ada gave one long, slow nod. "Ahhhh. I see."

"Obviously, the women of town will offer her no such support. But you, Ada... God has gifted you. He has given you the ability to turn the stormiest days into pure sunshine."

"Well, I don't know about all that," Ada blushed modestly.

Boaz sat a little straighter on the bench, looking directly into Ada's eyes. "Will you pay her a visit, Ada? Offer her some encouragement, some support? Heaven knows she needs it."

Ada smacked both hands resolutely against the countertop. "Why, I'll do far more than that! I'll make it a habit to visit that poor girl regularly! That's what we're called to do, after all."

Boaz was nearly brimming with pride and admiration. "You're an angel!"

"That's doubtful, but I'm much obliged," she quipped mischievously. "Now what is the name of this unfortunate young lady?"

"Her name is Adara. According to her husband, she is a perfect saint. I believe the two of you will get along wonderfully."

"I'm sure we will! And the Lord knows this will do my old heart some good as well – after all, a woman does get a bit lonely for female company, being the only lady on staff around here."

She winked teasingly, but Boaz realized for the first time that this arrangement would probably be quite beneficial for his tenderhearted housekeeper as well. *God is so good,* he thought.

Samuel, who had remained thoughtfully quiet throughout this conversation, clapped a hand upon Ada's shoulder and smiled broadly. "That's really good of you, Ada."

Boaz felt deeply relieved. "A hundred thanks, Ada. And you needn't ask my permission during the workday to take your leave. As soon as you see fit to go for a visit, head right on out."

Ada gave one last, final nod. "It's all settled then. I shall pay the girl a visit first thing tomorrow morning."

Chapter 16

THE CARAVAN

Naomi stretched herself out upon her sleeping pallet, perfectly content to allow sleep to claim her beneath the dazzling display of glittering, diamond-like stars. It did feel rather odd to slumber fully aware of the presence of so many men, their cooking fires and sleeping pallets dotting the nearby landscape.

Ruth had tactfully parked the wagon directly in front of their own camp site. Naomi was thankful that their sleeping forms would be mostly sheltered by the large outcropping of stone, as well as Dag's wagon.

Already their small fire had reduced itself to a few burning embers. Ruth knelt before it, hoping to coax it back to life in order to provide some warmth from the nippy desert chill.

Naomi had nearly drifted off into sweet nothingness when she heard the gentle droning of a woman's voice. She pushed herself up on her elbows for a better look.

Ruth sat comfortably near the fire, their beloved scroll open before her face. She was reading softly.

Naomi grinned. "I see I have the honor of a bedtime story!"

"Only if I may have the honor of reading it," Ruth replied, returning Naomi's smile.

Noami settled back down on her pallet, her mantle draped about her small form to protect her from the chilly breeze. Ruth had also placed an extra woolen blanket at Naomi's feet, but she didn't feel the need for the added warmth and protection quite yet.

"As we ventured forth today across the vast, endless miles of desert landscape, I could not help but think about God's chosen people – the Israelites – and how they wandered about in such agonizing conditions for decades! I could not wait to read the tale again for myself once we were settled down for the night. If you agree, I thought it would be perfect to resume our reading from the beginning of the Israelites' long journey – as we are at the beginning of our own – after the Lord God brought the mighty waters of the Red Sea crashing down upon the Israelites' Egyptian foes!"

"I couldn't think of a better place to start myself!"

"Oh, good!" Ruth redirected her attention to the aging scroll, her eyes tenderly scanning the faded lines of carefully-penned script. Softly, she began to read.

"*Then Moses and the children of Israel sang this song to the Lord, and spoke, saying: 'I will sing to the Lord, for He has triumphed gloriously! The horse and its rider He has thrown into the sea! The Lord is my strength and my song, and He has become my salvation...*'" Ruth had to pause, for her eyes had filled at the beauty and the genuine gratitude that leapt from the writings of the scroll. How she could relate to such Scriptures now! The Lord truly *was* her strength and her song, and He had become her salvation as well. Clearing her throat as silently as possible, she continued. "*'He is my God, and I will praise Him; My father's God, and I will exalt Him. The Lord is a man of war; The Lord is His name.'"*

Again, Ruth paused. She *felt* rather than *heard* or *saw*... something. A presence. Disconcerted, she sensed that someone was watching her... someone who wished to remain hidden in the shadows. It was not a pleasant thought. Though the breeze was cool, she knew the breeze itself was not what caused the hairs on the back of her neck to stand upright. She looked to Naomi, who was nearly dozing on her sleeping pallet. Shaking off the uncomfortable feeling, she decided not to disturb the weary woman.

Surely my mind is playing tricks on me, she thought with some surety, though she was not entirely convinced. Again, she resumed her reading.

"'...*Your right hand, O Lord, has become glorious in power; Your right hand, O Lord, has dashed the enemy in pieces. And in the greatness of Your excellence You have overthrown those who rose against You*..." Seeing that Naomi was already resting in sweet, blissful repose, Ruth scanned over the next few verses before she closed their night's daily devotions. "... *Who is like You, O Lord, among the gods? Who is like You, glorious in holiness, fearful in praises, doing wonders? You stretched out Your right hand; The earth swallowed them. You in Your mercy have led forth the people whom You have redeemed; You have guided them in Your strength to Your holy habitation... You will bring them in and plant them in the mountain of Your inheritance, in the place, O Lord, which You have made for Your own dwelling, the sanctuary, O Lord, which Your hands have established. The Lord shall reign forever and ever.'"*

The people You have redeemed... What joy and inexplicable beauty in that one, simple word: *redeemed*. Redeemed by the God of the universe, the Creator of all things. What a privilege God's people had received – to be redeemed by the One who created them and loved them.

Rolling up her beloved scroll, Ruth tucked it carefully away. She then stretched out on her own sleeping pallet across the fire from Naomi.

You will bring them in and plant them in the mountain of Your inheritance... The stirring words echoed quietly in Ruth's tired mind. They brought such comfort, such peace...

Lord God, her heart prayed, *I ask that you do the same for Naomi and me. Bring us safely to Your chosen people, to Your chosen land, and plant us firmly and safely in the mountain of Your inheritance.* She paused, hesitant. Dare she even ask? Mustering up her courage, she plunged ahead with her silent prayer. *Redeem us, O Lord, for only You can. Please, Lord, redeem me.*

Then, having shaken her prior paranoia of being watched, she curled up beneath the warmth of a woolen blanket, closed her eyes, and slept.

Ada paused just outside the door of a very modest home – one of many identical dwellings, all of which surrounded a bustling central courtyard. She imagined that everyone living within the tight-knit square must be related – one big, not-so-happy family.

Must be difficult to live lumped right in the middle of such a large family that despises you up one side and down the other, Ada thought sympathetically.

Though Ada felt convinced that she was doing the right thing by paying this young lady a visit, she also felt a bit nervous and ill at ease. Would Adara be comfortable visiting with an aging woman she had never even met? Would she accept and appreciate the company, or would she feel like Ada was simply sticking her nose where it didn't belong?

Well, Ada thought in her usual no-nonsense manner, *there's only one way to find out.*

Taking a deep breath, she balled her hand into a fist and gave the door – which was already propped open – a quick tap.

Ada hadn't given Adara's appearance much thought up to this point. She had pitied the girl, and perhaps imagined a fleeting glimpse of a sad, bitter wraith of a woman with taut features and eyes dark with anxiety. But she was certainly not prepared when a vibrant young woman with dancing eyes appeared in the doorway.

The girl was striking – beautiful, really. A small cloud of dark ringlets framed an exquisite face with bright eyes, a lovely sun-kissed complexion, and a charming smile. She appeared slightly surprised at the sight of a strange woman at her door, but she quickly regained her composure, smiling invitingly. "Good morning, and the Lord bless you! Is there anything I can do for you?"

The girl's s voice was sweet, melodic. Ada was fairly taken aback. Here she had been expecting to meet a distraught, needy young woman, and instead she was greeted by a bright, charming young lady brimming with life, vigor, and enthusiasm.

Ada sputtered a few unintelligible words before she finally found her tongue. "Oh, good heavens, forgive me, child!" she chuckled heartily. "I ought to have already introduced myself. You see, my name is Ada. I am the housekeeper of a kindly man named Boaz – I believe your husband works for him?"

Adara's eyes lighted with recognition. "Yes, he does! Boaz is indeed very kind." Though Adara continued to smile hospitably, it was clear that she was pondering several unasked questions.

"I simply came to introduce myself and pay a visit to a fellow daughter of the Most High God," Ada rushed to explain, feeling awkward and unsure as how to proceed. She certainly didn't want to tell the girl that she had decided to pay a visit because she felt sorry for her.

Upon hearing Ada's last comment, Adara's entire countenance seemed to brighten even more. With one wide sweep of her arm, Adara said, "I fear I have been quite rude! Please, do come in!"

Ada looked about, wringing her hands nervously. "I wouldn't want to intrude, my dear –"

"Why, you wouldn't be intruding!" Adara assured her. "If you are familiar with my husband Kemuel, then I am sure you have heard of *me* as well. My name is Adara. I'm sure you understand that I receive few visitors, and the exceptional visitor that *does* appear at my doorstep rarely has anything nice to say!" Though her words were quite serious, Adara's eyes twinkled with merriment.

Smiling with deep understanding, Ada followed behind Adara as she led her into the simple house. The living quarters were spotless and meticulously well-kept. Ada was quite impressed, and she was quick to say so. "You keep a lovely home!"

"Thank you!" Adara beamed happily. "Please, have a seat! Make yourself at home." Already, Adara had poured a fresh cup of cool water for her guest and carried it across the room as Ada seated herself on the stone ledge beneath the window.

Ada accepted the cup with thanks.

Adara quickly put together a tray of fresh fruit, cheeses, and freshly baked flatbread. How long had it been since she had been given the privilege of entertaining a guest? Her spine tingled with excitement. She realized that her hands were trembling as she sliced a cucumber of the deepest shade of green.

Adara placed the tray on a wooden stand before her guest, wiping her hands nervously on the apron she had fastened about her slender waist. "Now tell me," Adara asked with great interest as she seated herself beside her visitor. "What brings you all the way out to see me this day? I must admit, this is quite an unexpected blessing."

Ada felt the relief washing over her at Adara's eager reception. "Well, quite honestly, my dear, I thought that some female company might greatly benefit the both of us."

Adara was already aware of the fact that this kindly woman was reaching out to her – despite the fact that they had never met before. Ada was very much like her kind-hearted master, Boaz. Adara was touched. She reached out and grasped Ada's hand. "Your kindness is greatly appreciated, and I hope you know that."

Ada felt her eyes moisten – something that had not happened to her in quite some time. She managed another smile. "I appreciate yours as well, my dear. I am greatly blessed by your company also. You know, there's not a whole lot of womenfolk back at the master's place. I'm the only one, in fact." She grinned. "I find myself starved for a bit of female company and a bit of intelligent conversation as well!"

Heartily, both women laughed together.

The second day of travel had progressed very much like the first. The air was hot, sweltering, and rather suffocating.

Overhead, the torrid sun shimmered from its perch in the cloudless sky, sending undulating, steamy waves of heat bounding across the imposing dunes of sand. Oh, and that *sand*! It stung Ruth's eyes and throat, swirling about their bodies in the dry wind, all-encompassing, penetrating. She found herself constantly daydreaming of how glorious it would be to finally arrive at their destination, to shake the grimy, gritty, obstinate sand from their worn clothing, and to say goodbye to nature's nuisance once and for all. Only two days into their daring venture, and already she had come to loathe the gritty, grainy dust of the desert-like terrain.

Poor Dag had courageously pressed forth upon the first few hours of the journey, but already the older animal was beginning to protest. His knees shook and often buckled beneath him, and his sides heaved, lathered in foam.

Ruth's sensitive heart went out to the poor beast, and she intentionally denied herself many draughts of water in order to preserve extra for the tired animal. She knew that Dag was old and in no condition for the yoke that had been placed upon his bony shoulders. She found herself praying for the animal every bit as often as she prayed for Naomi. She could not bear to lose their beloved donkey on the wayside.

Dag's ears had risen with pleasure as they crossed a shallow streambed, the muddy water winding its way to and fro through miniature cataracts and stony ground. Ruth had opted for the wagon with Naomi upon one glance at the murky waters. She feared that the creaky wheels of the wagon would be no match for the persistent lapping of the small waves.

"There is nothing to fear here, my daughter," Naomi said calmly, reading into Ruth's thoughts. "Part of the year, these waters do not even exist. The thirsty ground devours it in the summer months."

Seated straight-backed and stoic beside Naomi, Ruth simply nodded and begged the Lord to keep them safe.

"Dag certainly seems to be enjoying himself," Naomi chuckled, watching as he pranced almost playfully through the shallow waters. "I almost wish I could dance through it myself!"

"I shall not hold you back," Ruth teased, though she still felt a bit nervous as the wagon lurched and bumped over the uneven, stony streambed.

Far ahead of them, the never-ending line of pack mules and camels had already safely crossed the desert stream. Ruth felt that she would breathe much easier once they had made it safely across as well. She dared a quick glance behind. The Ethiopian waded through the choppy waters easily. The current barely reached the shins of the tall man. For once, Ruth envied his size. The fierce-looking man noticed her gaze and met it with an intimidating, expressionless stare, and Ruth quickly looked away. *Someone really ought to teach that man how to smile,* she shuddered.

With a gentle lurch, the wagon's wheels – first the two front, then the back – crunched upon the smooth pebbles that lined the shoreline of the shallow stream. Ruth breathed an audible sigh of relief, realizing that they had safely traversed the width of the narrow streambed.

Laughing, Naomi covered Ruth's hand with one of her own. "Do you fear the water, child?"

Ruth felt her cheeks flush with embarrassment. *How silly of me to fret like a frightened child,* she chided herself.

"I understand," Naomi went on, scarcely giving Ruth a moment to respond to her inquiry. "When we first traveled this way so many years ago, I was rather terrified myself."

"One doesn't come across a great deal of water living in the desert, after all," Ruth pointed out with a smile. "Perhaps it is the fear of the unknown."

"Most certainly! Be thankful that your first experience in river-crossing was with that tiny stream. I nearly lost my wits when, traveling from Judah to Moab, we came across the tumultuous River Jordan first!"

Ruth wondered if her heart had stopped. "The River Jordan?"

"One and the same. I suppose we will be fording it within the next day or so, once we reach the Jericho Pass."

Ruth no longer wondered if her heart had stopped, for now it pounded so heavily against her chest that she feared Naomi might hear it! "The River Jordan..." Ruth managed, attempting to keep her voice steady. "You speak of the same River Jordan which the Israelites crossed with the mighty leader Joshua? The river that God Himself parted so that His chosen people could walk across on dry ground?" Just repeating the facts of the stories she loved so dearly calmed and strengthened her timid heart.

Naomi laughed at Ruth's anxiety and enthusiasm. "That's the one!"

"And we will be *crossing* it?"

"Very soon, indeed."

Ruth crossed her arms and shook her head in wonder. "I can hardly believe it! The very river your forefathers walked across, turned to dry ground beneath their feet by the mighty hand of God Himself! What it must have been like to see those roaring waters stop mid-flow and pile up upon each other like a massive wall of water! Naomi, we truly are following in their footsteps! We long to reach the Promised Land, just as the Israelites did. It nearly takes my breath away."

Naomi laughed and gave Ruth's arms a gentle squeeze. "I thank the Lord that your enthusiasm is so contagious, my dear. Such zeal and merriment does these old bones of mine much good!"

Ruth laughed nervously, hoping that her squeamishness wouldn't be too apparent to Naomi and the others who traveled among them. She considered the fact that it was late spring, and the rivers were still very much inclined to be full, rapid, and turbulent. She wondered what the Jordan must look like this time of the year.

Very, very full, most likely, she thought hesitantly. Taking a deep breath, she sighed and shook her head resolutely. *It matters not.* The Israelites had come across far greater obstacles – the great Red Sea included – and still they had safely reached their destination under the divine protection of their God. The very same God who had guided them would watch after her and Naomi, as well. She was sure of it.

Perhaps God will part the waters for us as well... This time, Ruth's smile was genuine. Despite the intense heat, the sweat, the grit, the grime, and the discomfort, this truly was a unique and thrilling experience. Ruth had no idea how the Lord might work in both hers and Naomi's lives throughout this journey, but she did not doubt that He would. It was exciting, invigorating. She thanked God for the strength she felt pumping through her veins, prodding her to press forward, to keep going. She knew that any and all strength she might muster up was strictly a result of her trust in the Lord.

The large caravanserai loomed upon the distant horizon just before dusk – a welcome beacon of hope for the weary travelers. This is where the men and their animals would rest for the night – a tall, two-story shelter standing alone in the dismal wilderness. As the caravan approached the caravanserai at a frustratingly sluggish pace, Naomi explained, "The animals will be cared for, watered, and fed in the central courtyard. Once the animals have been taken care of, we travelers will bed down for the night in the upper room. It is cool and sheltered from the harsh winds and muck and other unwanted outdoor elements, and it will make a fine place to rest for the night."

"The upper room..." Ruth mused, a few scattered thoughts harassing her tired mind. "Is it a single room? Or many separate chambers?"

"Most often a single room," was Naomi's unsatisfactory response.

Ruth blanched. "And we will be sharing that single room with all the men of this caravan?"

That statement halted Naomi in her tracks. She appeared to be considering Ruth's question for some time before she allowed a weary sigh to escape her lips. "I had not thought of that. You are right, Ruth, it would not be proper. Especially for an unwed woman like yourself without the protection a husband could offer."

"What shall we do then?" Ruth feared she would not like the answer.

"Well," Naomi said slowly, "I suppose we will spend another night beneath the stars."

Ruth accepted the disappointment graciously and resolved not to utter any complaints.

The lonely, ramshackle desert dwelling instantly hummed with activity as the men of the caravan converged upon all four sides, lining up at the well and filling the troughs with water for their mules and camels. There were shouts and roars of laughter as the men filled leather canteens with fresh drinking water and unloaded the few supplies that would be necessary for a brief night in the upper room.

Though most of the men of the caravan had not bothered to introduce themselves, Ruth had begun to familiarize herself with the rugged characters, and already she could match several of the rough faces with names, simply by hearing them call out to each other at various instances throughout their desert trek.

Of course, she had known of Ahmad, the master of the caravan, since Naomi had secured their spot three days prior to the journey. *Has it truly been only five days since?* Ruth could scarcely believe it. It seemed as if an eternity had passed since they had agreed to journey forth with the caravan, setting out three days later.

She had reasoned that the tall man with the easy stride was called Azad. His eyes, a rare green and honey-speckled swirl of color, often glinted with a fierceness and a ferocity that bespoke a deep-rooted love of freedom as well as an iron will to defend it if threatened.

Rashid was the quiet one. His narrow eyes were nearly as dark as his hair and beard. Most of the time he appeared to be thinking, musing, brooding – even as the merciless sun beat down upon their aching backs. He rarely spoke, and Ruth wondered how a man of such quiet thought and intellect could have stumbled upon such difficult work. Surely he would be far more content in the city – beneath the shade of a merchant's tent or contentedly scrawling line after line as a scribe in some beautiful palace.

Ruth especially enjoyed her observations of the small, energetic fellow named Yusef. Whatever the man lacked in height, he certainly did not lack in enthusiasm or valor. Though his beard was nearly white, and the hair beneath his tightly turbaned head had long-since gone gray, Yusef was every bit as quick and nimble as the strong, young men who were his juniors by twenty years or more.

Then there was the Ethiopian. Though they were two full days into their journey, Ruth had yet to hear the man speak. She wondered if he *could* speak, or if he were severely impaired in some way. Rarely did the other men address him, and if they did it was not by name. Ruth wondered if he even had a name. She was slightly temped to ask Yusef, who often traveled alongside the man, but she thought better of it. She was not sure how the large, silent man would respond if he knew she had been inquiring about him. She certainly did not want to give him the wrong idea.

There were many other men accompanying them on the worn, ancient pathways as well, but Ruth was too tired at this point to think about them or even care. As the men disappeared into the upper room one by one, Ruth and Naomi prepared to settle down for the night just outside the large building. Ruth hoped that the sturdy walls would shield them from most of the wind and dust.

The previous day, Ruth had thought she couldn't possibly be happier to settle down on her sleeping pallet, simply to be claimed by blissful sleep. However, as the sun nestled itself into its sheltered bed behind the rolling hills, Ruth once again praised her God for the privilege and comfort of a full night's rest. She found herself to be even more exhausted than the night before, which was no surprise considering the immense amount of ground they had covered.

Ruth sat transfixed, gazing into the gently leaping flames of the fire she had carefully built, a woolen blanket draped about her shoulders. She forced herself to slowly munch at a handful of dried dates, reminding herself that it was vitally important to keep up her strength. Opposite the flickering flames, Naomi did the same.

Raising another date to her lips, Ruth struggled to think clearly. The fatigue was beginning to set in, and she attempted to shake it off. Her body longed to curl up on the pallet and sleep, to ignore the sustenance she held in her hands and simply drift off into sweet nothingness. But her common sense encouraged her to be wise, to fill her empty stomach, and to make sure Naomi was safely and comfortably settled in for the night before she allowed herself to rest.

Dag appeared quite content, munching at the grain from the feed sack he wore strapped around his neck. Ruth smiled, thankful that he was finally comfortable and satisfied. "Bless you, Dag," she whispered fondly. "You have proven to be more valuable than a hundred young steeds could ever be. Take heart, we are almost home."

Home. Ruth nearly wept at the beauty of such a word.

"I believe I shall call it a night, my dear one." Naomi was finishing the last few dates she held nestled in her palm, quite unaware of the quiet exchange going on between Ruth and their beloved mule. Spreading herself out as comfortably as possible upon the sleeping pallet, Naomi buried her face in the crook of her arm and sighed tranquilly. "I believe I could sleep for years," she breathed, looking as relaxed as possible for one finding repose on the rocky desert floor.

"Shall I read from our scroll tonight?" Ruth almost didn't ask. She wasn't entirely sure she could keep her eyes open long enough for reading, but she would surely try.

Naomi remained as she was, her shoulders rising and falling along with her relaxed breathing. "Oh, would you, Ruth? I would love to hear a few lines if you feel you are up to the task!"

"Certainly," Ruth managed cheerfully, though she doubted her own optimism. Retrieving the scroll, she lovingly unrolled the delicate parchment and, clearing her throat softly, began to read. "*...All the congregation of the children of Israel came to the Wilderness of Sin, which is between Elim and Sinai, on the fifteenth day of the second month after they departed from the land of Egypt. Then the whole congregation of the children of Israel complained against Moses and Aaron in the wilderness. And the children of Israel said to them, 'Oh, that we had died by the hand of the Lord in the land of Egypt, when we sat by the pots of meat and when we ate bread to the full! For you have brought us out into this wilderness to kill this whole assembly with hunger...*'"

At this, Ruth paused and shook her head sadly. "Just imagine," she remarked to no one in particular, "they had just witnessed some of the most miraculous signs from Heaven, the Lord God had rescued them and delivered them from the hands of their enemies, and *already* they were complaining. Oh, Lord, we are so stubborn, so dense. Forgive us, Lord." With a sigh, she continued to read.

"*Then the Lord said to Moses, 'Behold, I will rain bread from Heaven for you.*'" Again, Ruth shook her head in wonder. "I cannot even fathom the mercy God has for His children. How could He possibly love us so much? He is so full of mercy and kindness and forgiveness and love..." Here, Ruth halted mid-sentence, suddenly becoming aware of Naomi's gentle snoring. She was not even awake to listen to Ruth's ponderous reverie! Ruth smiled and began to put the scroll away, but her heart was still thirsty. She was not ready to lay it aside yet. Smiling softly, she angled the scroll in the direction of the fire, hoping the flickering light would aid her tired eyes in their late-night reading.

"*And the Lord spoke to Moses, saying, 'I have heard the*

complaints of the children of Israel. Speak to them, saying, "At twilight you shall eat meat, and in the morning you shall be filled with bread. And you shall know that I am the Lord your God.' So it was that quails came up at evening and covered the camp, and in the morning the dew lay all around the camp. And when the layer of dew lifted, there, on the surface of the wilderness, was a small round substance, as fine as frost on the ground."

Setting aside the scroll, Ruth leaned back on her palms and surveyed the open sky. The stars glinted from beneath a thin, wispy layer of hazy clouds. She imagined that same sky during the day, as countless measures of God-given manna rained down upon the Israelite camp like gentle snow carpeting the desert floor. It must have been marvelous, truly breath-taking. She wondered how the Israelites could have doubted the Lord's loving care and provision.

Sniff.

Ruth stiffened, her aching muscles protesting from the sudden strain. Someone was nearby. Again, she felt the hairs prickling like tiny spines on the back of her neck. Instinctively, she turned to look in the direction of the arched entryway – a gaping black hole chiseled into the relentless stone. *There*! – her searching eyes glimpsed the slight flit of a shadow somewhere within the dark recesses of the entrance.

"Hello?" Ruth dared to call ever so quietly, a slight tremor in her voice. "Who is there?"

The shadow froze.

"Hello?"

Ruth was not prepared for the dark form that slowly rose, emerging from the dense shadows and looming frighteningly before her. Ruth cast a frightened look in Naomi's direction. The older woman's tranquil features and steady breathing convinced Ruth that she was still asleep. Ruth wondered if she would be able to protect Naomi should the need arise.

That's when the form took several daring steps closer, the gently leaping flames of Ruth's fire eerily illuminating the fierce face, an angry red scar glaring even more frightfully in the unsteady flickering of the flames' weak light.

It was the Ethiopian.

Chapter 17

MOSES

Ruth caught her breath in a short little gasp, and her heart began to hammer uncontrollably within her chest. The gravity of her situation dawned on her with ugly recognition, and she realized that if something were to happen to her and Naomi way out in the middle of the desert, they would not even be missed. She was completely at the mercy of this cruel-looking monster of a man. And she was very afraid.

That's when she noticed something strange – something glittering upon the man's rough, scar-torn cheek. Could that possibly be... a tear?

Fear gave way to concern, as well as to sheer curiosity. What could have possibly caused this big man to weep so freely?

The man knelt before her fire, and indeed tears streaked both sides of his face. Burying his face in his large hands, he wept for a moment, then lifted both arms heavenward, a smile transforming his stony features.

Ruth wasn't sure how she should respond. Had the man

lost his mind? Was he insane? Should she cry for help, or offer some type of consolation? She hadn't the slightest idea.

"Sir, are you alright?" she asked, afraid that all this commotion would wake the sleeping Naomi.

The man was muttering unintelligibly but excitedly. His voice was unusually deep and rather daunting, and Ruth struggled to make out the words proceeding forth from his lips. His arms waved hysterically and his eyes shone. He was obviously trying to tell her something.

"Do you need help?" Ruth emphasized each word slowly, carefully, hoping that the man would understand.

"No – no help," he exclaimed, his words running together in a jumble of confusion. By this point, the man was nearly hopping from one foot to the next in his excitement, arms still waving about like bulrushes in the wind.

Ruth realized that he must be attempting to communicate in a language that was not familiar to him. *Our own language must not be his native tongue,* she thought desperately. No wonder he had remained so silent! She wondered how they were ever to reach a conclusion or an agreement at this rate.

Seeing that he was being sorely misunderstood, the man attempted another method of communication. Kneeling before Ruth, his big form nearly quaking with intensity, the Ethiopian snatched the precious scroll from Ruth's trembling hands and stretched it open in one swift movement.

Ruth uttered a little gasp, followed by a cry of dismay. "Wait! Please, give it back!" She couldn't bear to see the words of her Lord so carelessly handled, or – even worse – destroyed.

"Good heavens! What is the meaning of this?"

As if the situation could have gotten any worse, Ruth

turned to see Naomi slowly pulling herself up on her sleeping pallet, her eyes wide with fright.

"Well, I'm... I'm not sure..." Ruth stammered, her eyes darting back and forth between Naomi and the crazed man still kneeling at her feet, her precious scroll in hand. "Naomi, perhaps you can help! I think he's trying to tell us something!"

Naomi raised her eyes toward the Ethiopian, struggling to maintain her cool composure. In such close proximity to them, the man appeared mammoth and even more brutish. Naomi was clearly fighting to remain calm.

The man was speaking again in rough, labored tones. "Ma-nna!" he cried, waving the scroll in the air as if he were gesturing towards the sky. "Ma-nna! MA-NNA!"

Ruth's brown eyes widened as she realized what the man was saying. "Manna?" she repeated questioningly. Had this man been listening to her as she read about the Israelites in the wilderness? Furrowing her brows, she recalled that she had not yet read aloud the Lord's term for the sweet, wafery bread supplied from Heaven. Surely this man did not know the story...

Thrilled beyond belief, the man nodded so vigorously that Ruth feared his head might spin off. "Yes! Yes! *Manna*!"

Ruth looked to Naomi in stunned belief. Of all the people she had met on this venture, here was the *last* one she would have expected to know a single thing about the ways of their God! Daring to reach out a hand for her scroll, Ruth ventured softly, "You have heard the story, then?"

The man studied her fair palm for a brief moment, obviously unsure about what to do with it. He seemed to remember the scroll he had impulsively snatched from her, and, sheepishly, gave it back. But the shyness was only momentary, and the corners of his eyes crinkled as his broad face widened with yet another grin. "Yes, know story! Great God... send bread... from Hea-ven!"

Ruth was enthralled by the man's zeal, made even more apparent as he struggled to express himself in a language that was wholly unfamiliar to him. He dragged out words that Ruth had always heard briefly-spoken, and the *s* pronounced at the end of each *Yes* seemed to last forever, emphasized by a strong *uh* at the end. She wondered about his native tongue, and how he had come to learn of the holy Scriptures belonging to a people not his own. Though she was dying to ask such questions, she certainly did not want to offend him and she also knew that he probably did not possess a wide enough word base to express himself in a way that could be understood.

It matters not, she reminded herself, her eyes filling with tears. *God has sent us an angel to guide us along the way – someone familiar with our customs and our ways!*

Ruth shook herself from her present state of stupor and realized that Naomi was already at the man's side, her own small body dwarfed by the imposing frame. "Bless you!" she was saying, her own eyes glistening. "May the Lord bless you! How good the Lord is to lead us straight to your traveling caravan!"

The man did not seem to comprehend the whole of Naomi's speech, but he understood enough. His own joyful tears had not quite subsided, and he took the small hand in his own and gave it a tight squeeze. Smilingly, Ruth hoped that all of Naomi's delicate fingers remained intact.

Naomi turned to Ruth and shook her head in wonder before smiling kindly at the man standing next to her, who – a few brief moments before – had been no more than a stranger to them. "Our brother."

"God...be...praise!" The man managed roughly, his eyes shining even more brightly than the gleaming desert stars. "Yes! God be praise."

Ruth wondered if this third day journeying forth seemed a bit brighter because the sun glimmered in golden brilliance as majestic pastel fingers of light streaked across the pink desert sky, or because she was ecstatically aware of the fact that she and Naomi had a brother traveling right there among them.

The caravanserai had sprung to life long before the sun had even begun to rise, with the men shouting out orders, commanding stubborn beasts, and laying up the sacks of grain they had removed from their wagons the previous night in order to feed the animals.

As the caravan began its long, winding trek across the fading desert pathways, Ruth hummed softly to herself and strolled alongside the wagon, thankful that they had been able to replenish their water supply from the well at the caravanserai. She watched Dag's alert, twitching ears and smiled. She knew that he was appreciative for the water as well. Even as she smiled, she remembered the haunting words that Ahmad had spoken before the caravan had set off that morning...

"Today we cross the River Jordan."

The Lord will be with us, Ruth reminded herself firmly. *There is no need to fear.* Though she felt extremely apprehensive about such a feat, she also felt enthused about crossing the very river the Israelites had been led across by the mighty hand of God.

Behind Dag's wagon, the Ethiopian made his usual

bounding strides, but today he wore a smile that greatly contradicted his typical bearing. Each time Ruth glanced over her shoulder, she was acknowledged with a wide, pearly-toothed grin. It did her heart much good, and she could see that Naomi was touched as well.

As their journey progressed, Ruth was surprised to discover that Yusef strode alongside her, his step carefree and springy. She wondered how a man his age could be so packed full of energy, despite his small stature. Typically the Ethiopian's traveling companion, she wondered why he had deserted his post at the very back in order to walk alongside her.

"Greetings, friends," Yusef enthused, his white mustache twitching even as it blended with the thin beard that fell in stages upon his chest.

Ruth acknowledged him with a polite nod, and Naomi smiled kindly. "Good morning, sir."

"Please," the little man argued with a smile on his face. "I am not a *sir* – I am just Yusef."

Again, Naomi smiled. "Yusef, then. How are you this unusually warm day?"

"Used to the heat, so it no longer disturbs me," he responded readily. "You must wonder why I am here."

Ruth grinned. This man did not beat around the bush.

"As a matter of fact, I do," Naomi admitted with a chuckle.

"I speak to you on behalf of Moses."

Naomi's thin brows shot up in confusion. "Moses?"

"The Ethiopian."

Ruth was instantly intrigued. "His name is Moses?"

Yusef shrugged. "Doesn't have a name. Not that we know of anyway. I'm one of the few men who bothered to get to know the man when he joined up with this caravan."

"Bless you, then," Naomi asserted approvingly.

"We take to calling him Moses, because that's just about the only name we've heard him say that we can understand. Doesn't speak much, hardly at all. Doesn't understand much of what we say. The others thought he was mute at first, with all his strange grunting and frantic gestures. But I quickly learned otherwise."

"And you call him Moses," Ruth repeated, curious.

"Took me forever to understand him," Yusef continued, keeping a steady pace. "Apparently the name means something to him, so when he began speaking of it, we took to calling him that. He doesn't mind."

Ruth looked to Naomi, her eyes bright. "Of course the name Moses means something to him! He knows the stories of old, and he loves them."

Naomi nodded her agreement.

"I think it is a fitting name for him," Ruth stated, satisfied with the small bit of information Yusef had provided.

"And what prompted you to tell us all this?" Naomi asked, somewhat suspiciously. Had the man been eavesdropping on their little meeting with *Moses* the night before?

"He asked me to," Yusef explained, nodding in the dark man's direction.

Ruth and Naomi instinctively followed Yusef's gaze, and the Ethiopian grinned and nodded enthusiastically.

"Not in so many words of course," Yusef went on, "but I understood what he was asking of me. I know the man well enough by now." He paused long enough to wipe a trickle of sweat that slipped out from beneath his turban and added, "Of course, I wondered why he would make such a request, but obviously it is not any of my business." Yusef's tone clearly indicated that he would be glad to listen if an explanation was offered.

Naomi smiled. "We recently discovered that we share the same faith," she stated simply.

"You? The same faith as Moses?" Yusef looked surprised.

"Most definitely. He worships the God of Abraham, Isaac, and Jacob – the God of our fathers."

"The one true God," Ruth added, her heart beating with passion. "The Maker of Heaven and earth."

Yusef stroked his beard thoughtfully. "You speak of the Hebrew God, then?"

Naomi's eyes burned with intensity. "You have heard of Him?"

"Who hasn't? I make frequent trips to the land of the Hebrews with this very caravan. You are headed there now, in fact?"

"We are," Naomi replied.

"Now I see why you journey such a long way from home," Yusef responded thoughtfully.

"Moab is not home," Naomi gently reminded him. "I was raised in Bethlehem, the land of my fathers."

"A proud race, your people," Yusef commented, and it did not sound like a compliment. "Your God – His laws – they are quite rigid, unbending."

"He is the same yesterday, today, and forever," Ruth spoke up, feeling slightly peeved at the man's skepticism. "Nothing like the gods of other lands, who change as often as the shifting shadows."

"That is true," Yusef agreed carefully.

Naomi wisely understood that now was not the time to pressure the small man. Skillfully, she turned the course of their conversation back to the original discussion. "You say the caravan stops at the Holy Land often? Perhaps that is how the Ethio – er, *Moses* – was introduced to our God."

Yusef shrugged. "Perhaps, though doubtful. From what I have understood, the man was a slave. Ran away from his master, unwilling to bear the yoke of any man. Maybe he ended up there – maybe even joined the caravan from the outpost there. Who knows? Either way, after finding this God, he returned to his master only to find that the man had died. He felt terrible, but there was nothing left for him to do. He joined our caravan, and has carried more than his share of the load ever since. And I'll tell you one thing – you would have to be one crazy bandit to attack this group with Moses standing guard."

The journey progressed much as the previous two days had, the sun's rays beating mercilessly upon the backs of the weary travelers. Frequently Ruth found herself reaching for water to soothe her parched throat, and she insisted that Naomi and their beloved donkey drink twice as much as she allowed herself to consume. Each time she felt her spirits start to sag, she immediately resorted to prayer and reminded herself that the journey was already more than halfway over.

Ruth had long since lost track of time, but she guessed by the sun's high position in the sky that the caravan still faced much travel before bedding down for the night.

That's when all her thoughts stood still.

Ruth *heard* the mighty River Jordan long before she *saw* it. A low rumble – deep, guttural, strong – had met her ears. For a moment, Ruth nearly succumbed to an overwhelming desire to turn and flee. But then she reminded herself that they had nearly reached their destination – as they had come upon the River Jordan, they were already within the boundaries of the Promised Land! The thought nearly stole her breath away.

"Ah, the River Jordan," Ruth overheard one of the unidentified men breathe several paces ahead.

"And Jericho is very close by," another agreed.

Ruth busied her racing thoughts by conducting a thorough observation of the landscape. She wasn't greatly impressed, and secretly she hoped that the rest of the Promised Land would not prove to be so drab, lifeless, and arid as this stretch of land seemed to be. A few hardy desert shrubs dotted the rust-colored ground, and here and there a frightened lizard would skitter across the land, disappearing into an ancient crevice. Other than that, there was not much to see.

The land grew greener and healthier as the Jordan River loomed into view. The sight of it nearly took Ruth's breath away. She reached for Naomi's hand, having to stretch quite a bit since Naomi was still seated in her usual spot at the wagon's front.

"Are you ready for this, my child?" Naomi asked in a very motherly tone.

Ruth simply bit her lower lip and nodded.

Many of the animals balked as they reached the turbulent waters' edge. Ruth was thankful to see that this section of the river wasn't nearly as broad as she had expected, and it did not appear to be exceedingly deep in this location either.

"We were fortunate this time," Yusef brooded, coming alongside the women's wagon. "This venture is always a bit risky this time of year."

Ruth lifted a brow. "How so?"

"Well, it's not exactly flood season – it being the end of spring and all. But we are at the tail-end of high-water season. The best time for travel is at the end of the summer months, or even the beginning of the autumn season. But it looks good today. Must be due to this cursed heat we've been having."

Ruth smiled. She had to admit that the summer heat's unwelcome, early arrival had been quite miserable, yet now it had proved to be a blessing in disguise. She uttered a silent prayer of thanks.

Ruth watched with a queasy stomach as the men waded eagerly out into the rushing waters, pulling their balking and protesting animals along behind them. At this shallow point of the river's crossing, she observed that the water barely reached chest-level.

Well, a quick swim will certainly cool us off, she thought wryly.

Naomi surprised her by scrambling down from the wagon and taking a firm hold on Dag's bridle.

"Why, Naomi, would it not be best for you to remain in the wagon?"

"Not if the entire wagon tips over!" Naomi laughed mischievously, but she quickly checked herself when she saw the concern creeping into Ruth's eyes.

"Perhaps we should tie down the provisions more carefully," Ruth faltered, preparing to climb into the bed of the wagon.

Naomi gripped her arm. "Dear girl, I have already seen the job you did with those ropes. We'll be fortunate if we are able to get them untied once we finally have need of them in Bethlehem!"

Ruth relaxed slightly.

The man and beast directly before them began to wade out into the muddy brown flow of river water, and Ruth realized that it was now their turn. Her legs felt weak and shaky, and her knees nearly buckled.

Why are you so afraid? She chided herself. *A little water never hurt anyone. Besides, the Lord will be with you!*

That's when the unexpected happened. Before Ruth could carry her troubled thoughts any further, both Moses and Yusef had drawn themselves up beside the two women. Yusef immediately took charge of Dag, whose gray ears lay fearfully back against his smooth head. Moses, their new friend and brother in the Lord, drew Ruth and Naomi close to himself, looping his left arm about Ruth and his right arm about Naomi. Apparently, he was ready and willing to guide them through the hazardous river crossing.

Ruth's eyes welled with tears. How kind these new friends were to take charge and guide them with such tender strength and compassion! She was not ashamed of the tear that trickled down her cheek. Looking up into the once-fierce, ebony eyes, she offered up a heartfelt whisper. "*Thank you.*"

"God be with us," Moses struggled to properly enunciate each meaningful word. "God go behind and before us."

Ruth's fear and anxiety melted away as she realized that Moses was referring to the pillar of fire and cloud that guided God's chosen people as they traveled through the perilous wilderness. The Lord went before His people and protected them from behind. He would do the same even now.

Skillfully, little Yusef guided Dag into the water that lapped about the river's edge. The donkey hesitated and brayed, but Yusef urged him forward with an iron hand and a strength that greatly contradicted his smallish stature.

Moses led the trembling women into the rushing current of the Jordan River. The water was thick with mud and silt, despite Ruth's picturesque imaginings of a crystal-clear stream. The moment the water flowed smoothly across her sandaled feet, she felt the suffocating heat that seemed trapped within the heavy folds of her robe seep away. The water felt cool, refreshing. And instantly, she thought of the priests who had carried the sacred Ark of the Covenant directly into the raging tumult of water that momentous day when the Lord God caused the waters to pile up upon each other, allowing the children of Israel to cross the riverbed on dry ground.

"It was not until the priests had set foot into to the turbulent tide bearing the holy ark of the covenant that the Lord God performed a mighty work for them," Naomi had once explained. "You see, the Lord God is always ready to work in mighty ways on behalf of His children. Sometimes, however, He calls us to take the first step. Truly, a step of faith."

Ruth glanced around the large figure that guided them deeper and deeper into the rushing river and caught Naomi's gaze. She wondered if Naomi was remembering the same story.

In answer to Ruth's silent inquiry, Naomi smiled broadly and nodded. "A step of faith!" she cried. She could barely be heard above the river's angry roar.

Slowly, the water climbed to the knees, then the hips, then the chest. Ruth feared that the waters might bury the slight Yusef, but he had crossed this river many times before. Holding his head high, he sealed his lips tightly and proceeded forth, expertly tugging Dag along by his bridle.

When Ruth, Naomi, and their gentle leader emerged from the opposite side of the Jordan River, Ruth's hair was matted and gnarled and her garments were heavy and dripping wet, but she had never felt more exhilarated in her entire life.

Moses released his iron grip, and Ruth staggered at the unexpected realization that she stood on dry ground on her own two feet again. She felt uncommonly heavy with her drenched woolen garments hanging about her and clinging to her damp form. Then, with an unexpected burst of jubilee, Ruth threw her arms around Naomi and cried out, "We did it, Naomi! We crossed the Jordan!"

Naomi was laughing and crying all at once. "We have but a short distance left to travel, my dear. God has been gracious. He has been with us every step of the way."

Moses pumped a fist in the air, unable to understand the women's words of thanks but clearly jubilant that they had been given a safe passage. "God be praise!" he proclaimed joyously.

Yusef, a few steps ahead of them, was removing his heavy outer garments and shaking his head skeptically. "You three are something else," he muttered, slinging the dripping cloak across the side of the wagon.

Naomi ignored the sarcasm and addressed him warmly. "Thank you so much for your help, Yusef. Your service was invaluable."

Yusef wasn't accustomed to receiving compliments. He shrugged it off. "Shall we proceed forth with our journey? The caravan will leave us behind for sure."

Smiling, the two women nodded and, after thanking Moses again, they followed willingly after the spritely Yusef.

"There's another outpost quite near this area," Yusef was explaining as he trudged along, his fingers still curled around Dag's leather bridle. "There you can discard your soiled clothing and change into something more comfortable."

Ruth breathed a quick sigh of relief. It would feel good to wear fresh clothes again, and she was convinced that her soaked garments added an additional twenty pounds to her slight frame!

Even as they walked, Ruth silently expressed her thanks and praise to God. *You are so good,* she exonerated, her heart fairly soaring. *You are faithful. Thank You for taking me by the hand even as I took that very first step of faith.*

Chapter 18

CONFRONTED

Kemuel was shocked when his spritely young wife suggested that they pay a visit to the marketplace upon his return from the fields. He had arrived home much earlier than usual, as much work had been completed early in the day and the kindly master Boaz dismissed many of his working men early to spend a pleasant evening at home with their families.

Adara was clearing away the leftovers from the evening meal, careful to preserve even the paltry amount of food remaining. She had been taught from childhood not to be wasteful, and Kemuel respected her all the more for it. He had seen many frivolous women roaming the streets and marketplaces, their arms burdened with packages and parcels that they could not possibly make use of before they were spoiled. He knew that Adara was meticulously careful to be sure that his hard-earned income was put to good use, rather than squandered away thriftlessly.

Kemuel stood by the window overlooking the courtyard. Several women were hurriedly gathering in the day's laundry or preparing meals over glowering stoves. He and his wife had certainly received an early start to their evening, and he was grateful. They had shared a pleasant supper, and Adara continued to bubble over delightedly with details about the visit she had shared with his boss's housekeeper, Ada, the previous day.

"She was just delightful, Kemuel! I wish you could have met her!" Adara was saying over her shoulder as she removed her apron and hung it on a peg on the wall.

Kemuel smiled thoughtfully. "If she's anything like her master, I'm sure she was."

"Oh, she was! So kind and thoughtful, too. She asked questions but she didn't pry, and she truly took an interest in all that I had to say. I felt comfortable with her immediately."

Again, Kemuel could not hold back a smile. He couldn't thank the Lord enough for Boaz's thoughtfulness in sending Ada to visit with his lonely wife. He was surprised when two slender arms circled about him from behind, clinging to his chest playfully. He remained firmly planted where he was, a smile still playing about his lips, as Adara whispered into his ear from behind, "About the marketplace...?"

"And why such a hurry to get down to the busy market?" he asked playfully, his tone matching hers. He turned to take his wife in his arms, and the hope that he saw reflected in her eyes touched him to the very core. Her spirits had been so lifted by Ada's visit. He wasn't sure a trip to the marketplace was such a good idea. The women would gossip and stare, and the men would turn their backs. He didn't wish to see Adara hurting tonight – especially not when the evening had gotten off to such an enjoyable start.

"Well," Adara began, her tone quite persuasive, "Ada plans to visit again within the next day or so, and I feel it would be kind and hospitable to have something special prepared for her when she arrives..."

Kemuel lifted his brows. He hadn't thought of that, but his wife was right. If the kindly older woman could take the time to walk away from her chores and cross town just to brighten his wife's day, then they could certainly be hospitable and have some refreshments waiting for her.

Adara seemed to interpret his brief hesitation as a definite *no*. "That's alright. I can certainly make do with what we have here, my love."

Her cheerful acceptance of a verdict he had not even given only fueled his desire to please her. "I might be talked into a quick venture to the marketplace," Kemuel said slowly, his eyes dancing.

Adara's eyes widened with glee. "Truly?"

"Hurry now! We have but a few hours of sunlight left and the market will be closing!"

"I'm ready now!" Adara threw herself into her husband's arms and rewarded him with a confiding kiss. "Thank you, Kemuel!"

The breeze was somewhat cool and the evening was pleasant, so Kemuel and Adara walked the short distance from their home to the marketplace near the town gates.

"What did you have in mind to prepare for your kindly guest?" Kemuel asked with interest as they strode in the pleasant evening air.

Adara looked to him and smiled. "You seem rather interested in the menu. Perhaps you would be willing to try my silly experiments and tell me if they are any good!"

"I would willingly make the sacrifice, my lady."

Adara laughed pleasantly and took her husband's arm. "I had thought perhaps cucumber and onion and dill tucked inside some freshly baked flatbread. Perhaps some garlic as well. Oh, and goat cheese, too."

Kemuel nodded his approval. "I have no objections there."

When they reached the marketplace, the hustle and bustle of the day had almost subsided. Kemuel was grateful for Adara's sake. Fewer people meant fewer sneers paired with scathing remarks.

Adara carefully selected each item, always looking to her husband for his approval. He nodded his consent with each item she held up for his inspection, and was pleased to see that, though she had made careful selections, she had thoughtfully abstained from purchasing any more than necessary. He knew that she had chosen enough to make several savory sandwiches for him as well, and he looked forward to enjoying them.

Kemuel doled out the proper amount of coins to the pot-bellied shopkeeper, who appeared to enjoy his fair share of the groceries he provided. The man gave a curt nod as the two turned to leave.

Adara did not seem fazed. She continued to chatter enthusiastically as they prepared to journey home.

"Kemuel."

Kemuel stopped in his tracks and turned in the direction of the firm voice that had addressed him from behind. Immediately, he recognized the bearded man standing there as Ezra, one of the elders of the city. "Good evening, sir," Kemuel began, in no mood for small talk and rather eager to get home to spend the rest of the evening with his pretty wife.

Ezra's leathery old features appeared quite stony, and his jaw was set intensely. His eyes – a very rare blue – appeared icy and cold set within the grim face darkened from hours in the sun. His white hair and beard created an even starker contrast, and he appeared somewhat fierce, wizened, contemptuous. "Good evening."

Knowingly, Kemuel draped a protective arm about his wife and began to steer her around the stoic elder. "If you will excuse us, sir, we had better be on our way."

Adara turned questioning eyes toward him, but she did not say anything. It was unlike Kemuel to make it clear he wished to avoid polite conversation, regardless of what kind of a hurry he might be in.

Ezra was not to be put off. "Might I have a word with you?" It sounded more like an order than a request. His cold eyes briefly acknowledged Adara's presence, and he added coolly, "Alone."

Kemuel's chest tightened. Already he knew what this was about. He could almost visualize his mother's puppet strings dangling above the man's snowy head. And he had no intentions of listening to ignorant and slanderous accusations. But to refuse a meeting with an elder of the city? It would greatly disrespect the man, as well as heap even more shame upon his own family name. He sighed and uttered a silent prayer. *Lord, when will it all end?*

Refusing to relinquish his protective hold on his wife, he squarely met Ezra's gaze and smiled amicably. "I have a rather pressing matter to take care of tonight, sir," Kemuel said politely but firmly. "I also need to escort my wife home."

"I ask for only a moment of your time." Again, it was not a request.

An idea occurred to Kemuel, and he nearly smiled in spite of himself. As calmly as ever, he said cordially, "I have an even better idea, my good man. My wife and I would certainly enjoy the honor of entertaining you and your gracious wife sometime in the near future. Perhaps one evening this week?" He turned to Adara. "Why have we not thought of such a thing before?"

Adara looked cornered and considerably confused, but she managed a lopsided smile and responded heartily, "Why, I haven't the slightest idea, my love! But it is certainly an excellent suggestion." She offered her sweetest smile to the flinty elder. "I haven't yet had the honor of meeting your lovely wife, sir."

Upon Adara's acknowledgment of his presence, the older man visibly flinched. Fleetingly, Adara wondered if the man feared he had been defiled simply because he had been addressed by a barren woman. Her smile deepened gleefully at his obvious discomfort, though she silently rebuked herself for it.

Kemuel turned his attention back to Ezra, fully knowing that the man would never accept such an invitation. He and his haughty wife would not be caught dead in the home of such *sinners*. "What say you, sir?"

Ezra began to look exceedingly uncomfortable, and he shifted positions restlessly. His eyes darting about like a cornered animal, he was about to protest when sheer frustration must have overtaken him, because he barked rather sharply, "Now why on earth is it a complete impossibility to allow a respected elder just a few moments of –"

"Ezra! My good man! Why, you're just the man I was hoping to see!"

Ezra's neck wheeled around like that of a stunned camel at the unexpected, hearty address. A heavy hand clamped down upon his shoulder, and he wrenched away rather suddenly, disconcerted.

Kemuel could scarcely believe his eyes. Somehow, Boaz stood right there in the midst of them, his tall, imposing form towering over the fragile elder. Kemuel could not hold back a smile. *Ah, Boaz, you are Heaven-sent!*

Ezra managed a string of unintelligible stutters before he was finally able to breathe in deeply in a very righteous manner and recompose himself. "Boaz. You startled me."

Boaz squared his broad shoulders, grinning good-naturedly. "So I gathered."

"Unfortunately, I am otherwise engaged. I must speak with Kemuel here – "

"Is that so?" Boaz asked innocently. "I had no intention of intruding..." As they often did when working together in the fields, Boaz and Kemuel communicated without a word. An arch of Boaz's brow and a clearing of Kemuel's throat, and both were instantly tuned in to the other's plans.

"Ah, it's not a problem, brother," Kemuel assured Ezra with a hearty slap on the shoulder. "I'm sure Boaz's business with you is far more pressing. I shall see you again soon, I am sure. As I mentioned before, there is a rather pressing matter that I must attend to at home. Good evening, sir."

"Good evening, my brother!" Boaz called after Kemuel, a triumphant smile broadening his features.

Kemuel telegraphed a grateful, silent *thank you* as he led his baffled wife around the corner before Ezra could protest any further.

It wasn't until Kemuel determined that they were a safe distance away before he released his hold on Adara's shoulders and took her soft hand in his. He slowed his pace, enjoying the cool evening breezes as they whispered about his face and neck.

Adara looked to him with wide, luminous eyes. "I hadn't the faintest idea about what was going on back there," she confessed.

Kemuel gave her hand a squeeze. "Do not let it trouble

you, my dear. All I can say is... I owe Boaz a thousand *thank yous*."

"How did he know to step in?" Adara asked, curious.

"That man Ezra – he may be a respected elder of the city, but he is not good."

Again, Adara turned questioning brown eyes toward her husband. It was rare for Kemuel to make such a strong statement against any man.

"He sees only with his eyes, Adara, not his heart. The Lord God gives us faith and the ability to see past the surface. Ezra is easily influenced by outward appearances, and by what others think."

"It is an easy trap to find yourself in," Adara admitted humbly.

"It is," Kemuel agreed. "But he was up to no good tonight. My role is to protect you, Adara. I take that role very seriously."

Adara appeared slightly frightened. "What did he wish to do?"

Kemuel sighed. "Merely talk tonight, I suppose. But I wasn't willing to grant him an audience. Not tonight. I had my wife to look after," he added with a playful wink.

Adara's smile appeared to be a forced one. "He wanted to talk about *me*, yes?"

Kemuel would not lie to her. "Most likely."

"About his conversation with your mother, no doubt."

"Most likely." Again, that seemed to be the safest answer.

Adara nodded, her jaw set. She appeared to be deep in thought, though still very much composed.

Kemuel ran his free hand through his copper colored hair, suddenly fatigued. He was grateful to see the cluster of white-walled houses and garden courtyards just a few short paces ahead.

Tal greeted them with several friendly barks, his yellow tail whipping happily back and forth like a streak of lightning. He pranced about his masters' ankles as they unlatched the door and made their way inside.

It was getting dark. A single oil lamp flickered upon a stand near their home's entrance, and Adara hurried about to light the rest.

Kemuel remained firmly rooted where he stood near the door. He had closed it and bolted it shut behind him, and now his eyes followed his attractive young wife as she coaxed the olive oil lamps back to life and prepared for a quiet evening at home. *She is beautiful,* he thought, feeling strangely choked with emotion. *Beautiful on the inside and out.* He knew that it mattered not what the elders of the city or anyone else said. Adara was a strong, caring woman who loved the Lord deeply. He had no doubt that the Lord was not holding out on them. If it was in His will to bless them with children, He would do so when the time was right.

Adara turned, having lit the last candle, and flushed slightly. She apparently sensed her husband's watchful eyes upon her. Brushing aside a stray curl, she asked quickly, "Is everything all right?" Instinctively, her eyes fell upon the neatly wrapped parcels she had set near the door upon their arrival. She reached for them, but Kemuel caught her hand instead and pulled her close to him.

"They can wait," he said softly, his eyes never leaving hers.

She searched his face questioningly, and seeing nothing but deep love and longing there, she drew her arms around his neck and smiled shyly. "Kemuel," she asked, "you mentioned that there was a pressing matter you must attend to at home?" She was slightly afraid to remind him of his own hasty words. She didn't want to lose him to a monotonous task he felt he must tend to.

Kemuel nodded, his eyes still locked upon her. "There is," he assured her, drawing back her head covering and smoothing her hair.

Adara looked curious, perplexed. Again, she preferred to keep her husband right where he was, but she dared ask him anyway, "And what is the pressing matter, my love?"

Taking her face in a strong hand, he replied calmly, "You."

Chapter 19

THE PROMISED LAND

Ruth could hardly believe her eyes when the final outpost loomed into view. She looked to Naomi, fierce expectation defining her every feature. She felt rather like a small, impatient child as she asked in a voice that trembled with excitement, "Is this the one, Naomi? The final outpost?"

Naomi glanced down from her lofty wagon seat and smiled, her body rocking in rhythm to the jilted movements of the wagon. "Indeed, it is. Here the caravan will remain. You and I shall press on to Bethlehem alone. It is quite a short distance from here."

Ruth felt her entire body quiver with excitement. After the hours and the days she had hoped and dreamed and longed for this moment... it had finally arrived! She could scarcely take it all in. How she longed to dance, to shout, to break out in a glorious song of praise to the God whom had brought them safely to the Land of Promise! Swallowing hard, she instead forced herself to remain calm, cool, and collected. She certainly didn't want her future friends' and neighbors' first impression of her to be that of a leaping, bounding madwoman.

The final outpost proved to be a noisy one. As was the case with many others Ruth had encountered over the last few days, makeshift tents, booths, and even a few flimsy stone structures had been thrown together in a ramshackle assembly line that wound about rather like a crowded maze of boisterous, narrow tunnels. The tents were comprised of a variety of materials ranging from rough animal-skin to light linen sheets. An uncommonly pleasant breeze whispered its way through the hum and the activity, and excess tent material flapped sharply in response to the welcome breeze.

This was only the second outpost Ruth had visited in this wonderful Land of Promise called Israel. All the others had dotted the dusty plains of Moab and the uncharted land in between. As was the case with the first Israelite outpost near Jericho, Ruth was delightfully surprised at the absence of filth and grime. Though far from the wealthier residences of the area, this outpost was nearly spotless. As was the case in Moab, Ruth had expected her nostrils to be assaulted by the usual smell of unkempt, sweaty humans and animals that so often dominated any overcrowded area. Though both Israelite outposts had been humming with human activity, the unpleasant odor had not yet assailed her senses here.

"This land is so fresh, so clean," Ruth commented, her voice nearly drowned beneath the boisterous activity.

Naomi nodded in agreement. "The Lord God gave our people strict laws to govern every aspect of our lives in order to make our living better, safer. Cleanliness has always been a priority to both the Lord and our people."

Ruth smiled. She already liked this new world in which she found herself.

The caravan slowly, painstakingly, worked its way through the narrow, unpaved streets of the outpost. Ruth thought she would burst with excitement as she waited for her turn to enter. When that moment finally arrived, Ruth carefully guided Dag by the bridle, dodging pack animals and harried pedestrians as they bustled past with hardly a second glance. Ruth supposed that the arrival of a foreign caravan must be an everyday occurrence in a place like this.

Naomi reached beneath her tunic and retrieved a small pouch of coins which had been securely tied in the fabric about her waist. "We may make some purchases here at market to take with us to Bethlehem. After all, most of our dry goods were ruined after crossing the Jordan."

Ruth nodded her agreement. Plenty of water had worked its way into the wagon bed and claimed the small amount of dried edibles remaining. Moses had been most thoughtful the previous evening, willingly sharing provisions with them from his own meager store.

Ruth turned to smile at their newly acquired friend. He stalked cautiously along, his eyes and ears evidently open. He had become quite protective of the two small women traveling the road before him since the discovery of their shared faith. Yusef bounded along beside him, unimpressed with the wares spread out upon crude wooden tables beneath the overhanging tents.

Naomi halted the wagon's progress occasionally to make a few careful purchases. Soon she had acquired a sack of parched grain along with some fresh produce, among which rested a large, juicy bundle of grapes that appeared most tantalizing.

Ruth found herself far more interested in observing the

people of the area rather than the merchandise they sold. *Mostly men,* she noted, however she did spot a few women among the hustle and bustle of the trade. And she was quite impressed with the few women she saw. They were humbly dressed in casual, homespun garments. Every single one of them wore a head covering, and many wore veils or drew their head coverings about their shoulders, hiding the lower halves of their faces. Many of them were seated behind booths owned by their husbands, and they busily counted coins, sorted through merchandise, or busied their hands with sewing of some sort. She was grateful to note the absence of brazen young women hiding beneath a mask of provocative paint.

The men, too, carried themselves in a very different manner than the lazy dreamers she had observed in her own country. They seemed to move with purpose in every stride. They wore less clothing than the women, with leather-thonged sandals that were tied up near the backs of their shins. They appeared dark and strong from long hours of manual labor beneath a brutal sun. Their eyes were ever watching, their features staunchly alert, their hands ever busy with the tasks set before them.

Ruth watched from a safe distance as Naomi spoke with them and bartered for goods, asking the proper questions and conducting thorough examinations of each product. *She fits right in, even after all those years away,* Ruth thought with a deep sense of pleasure. She wondered if Naomi already felt the comfort of home – the healing that must come from being among one's own nation and people after a long, painful absence.

When Naomi returned to the wagon once more carrying several carefully wrapped parcels, Ruth read in her expression that they had lingered long enough. "It is time, my darling," Naomi stated firmly. "Are you ready to see my hometown?"

Ruth's heart leapt into her throat. She felt her temples pounding with both nervous energy and anticipation. "I am," she managed hoarsely.

"Wait." The booming voice of Moses interrupted their homeward thoughts.

Both Ruth and Naomi turned to see their tall, intimidating companion standing behind them, his stance firm and his arms crossed.

"Moses," Naomi whispered, her eyes filling with tears. "I thank the Lord God for placing us directly in each other's paths. You were a blessing, and we will never forget you."

Much to the surprise of both women, the man's dark eyes brimmed with tears. One tear slipped down his cheek unbidden, tracing a wobbly line through his dust-caked features. "Never meet God-fearer," he stammered out, each word sounding labored and well thought-through. "Never know sister in God."

Naomi gently touched his arm. "We will always be your sisters in the Lord, Moses, no matter how far apart we might find ourselves. That is a promise."

"You travel..." he struggled to find the right words, "...by your own?"

Naomi nodded, understanding. "Yes, we travel alone." Seeing the concern that clouded his dark features, she added briskly, "But it is a very short distance, and I have made the trip before. We will arrive long before dark."

Moses did not look appeased. "Must not. No make trip... by your own."

Naomi patted his arm in a motherly fashion. "God has brought us this far. He will protect us."

"Your trust, dear woman, is inspiring." Yusef had joined

the teary threesome at some point during the conversation. Ruth wasn't sure exactly when. She felt slightly peeved at his comment, yet when she looked into his eyes she saw no sarcasm there. Only admiration.

Naomi must have observed the same, for she gave him her warmest smile and said softly, "Our Lord is worthy of our trust. Of mine, as well as *yours*, my dear friend."

Yusef pushed at a pebble with the tip of his sandaled foot, uncomfortable. "I haven't a pressing need for such trust, I'm thinking," he mumbled quietly. "Perhaps someday, but not today."

Naomi's gray eyes were intense. "Please do not wait long, my friend. We never know how much time we have left on God's earth."

The sincerity of Naomi's gaze must have greatly impacted Yusef, for he answered with conviction, "Perhaps I shall look into it. Very soon. There are few people in the world whom I admire more than Moses, and quite honestly, *you* as well, Miss. Your courage and your devotion to this God of the Hebrews is inspiring."

Naomi smiled deeply and exchanged a knowing look with Moses. The Lord in His wisdom had given the former slave a very unique opportunity to impact the life of a very secular man. Naomi hoped and prayed with all her heart that Yusef would take a stand for the Lord before it was too late. Turning her full attention back to Moses, she asked, "How long will the caravan remain at this outpost before turning back?"

Moses looked expectantly to Yusef, his unofficial interpreter. Yusef replied, "We will not remain. We continue to journey forth, and once we have safely delivered our wares, we shall return to Moab. We have several outposts yet to reach."

Awed, Ruth stared at the unlikely pair standing before her. These nearly five days of travel had drained her of strength as well as vigor. She could not imagine walking in the footsteps of these hardy men whose lives were one continuous trek through barren desert wastelands.

Taking Moses's large hands in her own, Naomi said softly, "God be with you." She turned to Yusef, and added with the deepest sincerity, "God be with the both of you."

Yusef appeared slightly emotional and at a loss for words. Swallowing hard, he managed, "And with you as well. It was a pleasure. Until we meet again." And with a slight bow of his turbaned head, he turned on his heels and disappeared into the raging sea of humanity beyond.

Almost simultaneously, Ahmad emerged from the chaos, his countenance bearing his usual grimness. He held himself a respectful distance from the two women, appearing somewhat uncomfortable. "I must admit," he said gruffly, his alert eyes roving about the crowded area, "when two women approached me seeking safe passage, I was not excited about the prospect. The rugged land we must traverse is not for the weak-willed or simple-minded. However, it was a pleasure traveling with you. You held your own and I was impressed."

Ruth was visibly stunned. Ahmad had just spoken more words in four seconds than he had in the past four days! She found that she wasn't quite sure how to respond, so she remained safely silent as she had done for most of the journey.

Naomi beamed warmly. "I am humbled. Thank you for guiding us so skillfully."

Shrugging off the compliment, Ahmad continued, "Moses is right in what he says. He expressed his concerns about the two of you traveling alone... at least, he *tried* to express his concerns. You may thank Yusef for his clever interpretation. I have arranged for a guide to lead you to your final destination."

Ruth saw the concern crossing Naomi's face. Surely she was mentally calculating the cost of a personal travel guide, and worrying that they would not have enough coins left over for bare necessities should she invest in one. But Ahmad hurriedly waved aside her concern. "No payment will be necessary. I have already taken care of that."

Naomi's eyes widened in surprise. "Oh, but we couldn't accept – "

"It has already been arranged."

A lanky young man stepped forward, his bright eyes still dancing with boyish enthusiasm. Ruth knew he couldn't be a day older than fourteen years of age. But Ahmad had proven himself trustworthy and quite capable handling the dangerous tasks that befell a caravan master. If he believed that this young man was capable of escorting them safely to Bethlehem, then she would trust his judgment.

"This is Jacob," Ahmad explained, his jaw firmly set. "He has assisted me upon many an occasion. He's a trustworthy fellow. He shall escort you to Bethlehem, and return to his father once you have comfortably settled in."

Naomi's expression spoke more than her words ever could. "Thank you so much. You have truly blessed us, Ahmad."

"I extend my best wishes to you both." And just as suddenly as he had appeared, Ahmad turned on his heels and was gone.

Ruth was surprised at the unexpected stab of pain in her gut. She had known these men for only a few brief days. Yet, in those few days of trying travel, thirst, and discomfort, she had learned to admire her faithful traveling companions – even if they were a bit rough around the edges.

She was drawn out of her silent reverie when she realized that Moses was still attempting to communicate with Naomi. "Where you travel?" he was asking, furrowing his thick brows and wearing the expression of an anxious father.

"To Bethlehem, the land of my fathers," Naomi readily responded. "There we shall live. There we shall stay."

Moses nodded knowingly, apparently familiar with the city. Then, he surprised both women by gathering them in his big arms for a brotherly embrace. "Go with God," he whispered, his voice cracking with emotion. "Go with God."

As they parted and walked their separate ways with young Jacob in the lead, Ruth couldn't help but smile through bittersweet tears. *Go with God.* She could not have said it better herself, for that is exactly what she intended to do.

~

Naomi had assured Ruth that the remainder of the journey would be quiet, uneventful. For that, Ruth was grateful. However, Naomi's promise had been made *before* meeting their exuberant guide.

Jacob had the appearance of a young colt – with long, lanky arms and legs that he had not quite grown into. His limbs swung freely back and forth as he expertly led the two quiet women across gently rolling pastureland and towards their ultimate destination.

"Bethlehem – it's not much, but I've seen worse," he was saying, his endless chatter rather grating on Ruth's worn nerves after four full days of seemingly endless travel. "It can be stifling hot at times, and you will certainly get to experience some of that with the summer months soon approaching. The land is, well, sandwiched between two drastic features – with a sea on one side and a desert on the other. Still, the cool breezes from the Great Sea often reach the little town, which certainly makes the climate a bit more bearable."

Ruth couldn't help but grin through her exasperation as a thought crossed her mind. This energetic young man would certainly make an excellent tour guide.

Naomi surprised Ruth by making an unexpected inquiry of the young man. "Jacob, is it? I liked you the moment I heard your name. You must be one of us?"

"If by 'one of us' you mean a child of the God of Abraham, Isaac, and Jacob, then yes, I am."

Ruth felt a thrill course through her. An Israelite! Here she was, annoyed with the boy's rambling conversation, and yet he was the first true Israelite that she had been given the pleasure of meeting in the Land of Promise. Inwardly, she chided herself for her impatience and resolved to curb it from this point forward.

"It is indeed a pleasure to meet you, Jacob," Naomi said genuinely. "What a joy it will be to dwell among my own people again."

"I see you have brought a foreigner with you."

Ruth felt her face flush. Jacob's brusque statement was not aimed to demean. He was simply speaking with the brashness of a blunt youth. However, she realized that if her foreign ethnicity was so blatantly obvious to one as young and inexperienced as this Jacob, she would indeed stand out like a sore thumb among Naomi's people.

Naomi chuckled casually. "And what makes you say that?"

Jacob shrugged. "She's more colorful – dresses differently. Not that I'm complaining – I think she looks very nice."

Again, Ruth blushed and wished she could bury herself beneath the blankets stacked haphazardly in Dag's creaky wagon.

"And she carries herself differently – with confidence," Jacob continued. "Many of our own carry themselves with something a little more like arrogance, or pride." He halted abruptly and turned to look at the two women. "Don't tell my mother I said that."

Naomi laughed outright. "You needn't worry about that, son."

Sighing, Ruth tightened her shawl about her shoulders despite the warm beams of sunlight that beat down upon them. She felt self-conscious, and wished that Jacob would spend more time elaborating about Bethlehem rather than her wardrobe. *Well, at least he spoke well of me... I think.* She could not wait until they had safely arrived and could fully recover from this draining excursion.

From that point forward, the threesome mostly traveled in silence. Jacob seemed aware of the fact that he had conversationally overstepped his bounds, and Ruth felt sorry about that. She wished she knew of an appropriate way to tell him that she preferred his rambunctious chatter to this awkward silence.

The wheels of their cart creaked and groaned in protest as it climbed the uneven, bumpy terrain. Ruth thanked the Lord for the green grass and the healthier-looking shrubs and trees that dotted the path along the way. According to Jacob, Bethlehem was a fertile pastureland near the southern end of the Judean Mountains – nothing like the barren wasteland they had left behind them. And Ruth was quite grateful.

Jacob now strode several paces ahead of the wagon pulled by Dag, with Naomi riding in the driver's seat and Ruth strolling alongside. In the silence, Ruth had noticed that Naomi's expression grew more and more troubled as they neared her beloved hometown. Ruth could not understand it. Wasn't Naomi's heart burning within her chest at the prospect of arriving home so soon?

Ruth spoke softly so as not to alert their young guide as to the nature of their conversation. "Naomi, is everything all right? Are you well?"

Naomi managed a lop-sided smile. "Perhaps just eager to arrive."

"You look troubled."

Naomi gave her hand a careless wave and attempted to laugh it off. But Ruth continued to eye her with concern. With a long sigh, Naomi conceded. "Is it really so obvious?"

"Nearly as obvious as the fact that I am a foreigner," Ruth responded with a playful smile.

Naomi remained silent for a long time, her weary eyes scanning the green hills. "We are so very close, Ruth, I can feel it."

Again, Ruth felt the familiar thrill. "Is it not wonderful?" she nearly gushed.

Naomi smiled faintly. "I suppose, though the closer I find myself nearing Bethlehem, the more anxious I feel."

Ruth was perplexed. "And why is that? Are you not anxious to reunite with family and long-lost friends? Will it not be a most joyous reunion?"

Naomi pursed her lips, her forehead creased with concern. "I hope so, my daughter. I left them many years ago. They may not even remember me. Or worse, they might despise my very existence, the way I abandoned them so."

Ruth reached for Naomi's arm, however she merely grasped at the air due to the inconvenient jilting of the wagon. "Naomi, you had no desire to leave them. You longed to stay. You were merely devoted to your husband, and they could not judge you for such a thing."

Naomi's expression indicated that she believed otherwise, but she did not say so. Instead, she called ahead to their guide, who appeared restless and uncomfortable with the growing silence. "Jacob, you have been a worthy guide. You are so knowledgeable about the land, the terrain, the surrounding areas."

The boy's head perked up at the prospect of another conversation. "I make it my business to be knowledgeable about my surroundings. My father is a very successful merchant, and one day I hope to oversee the caravans and the distribution of his goods." Pride in his father was evident in his voice. It was pleasant to behold.

Naomi smiled. "I believe you will make him very proud."

"I plan to," Jacob responded with the easy confidence of a trusting child. As if afraid that silence might once again penetrate the remainder of their brief journey together, Jacob plunged forward with another one of his lengthy narrations, a springy bounce to each step and his hands flying about animatedly with each new announcement. "Being a native Israelite, I'm sure you recall that at one time the Tabernacle of the Most High God was actually located in Gilgal, quite near the place from whence we just came. A few years later the tabernacle was relocated to Shiloh, of course, where it has remained. Many devoted Israelites attended the ceremony."

Ruth and Naomi exchanged knowing smiles as Jacob

continued to debrief them about every possible aspect of the long-awaited town of Bethlehem.

As the humble, white-walled dwellings of the city of Bethlehem loomed into sight, Ruth caught her breath. They were close. Exceedingly close. Before nightfall, they would have set foot in the new land that was to be called *home*. A thrill coursed through Ruth's entire body. Her joy bordered upon sheer hysteria. She wondered if she must be experiencing a very small taste of what the Israelites must have felt upon their arrival at the blessed Promised Land.

A good distance ahead, the white-stoned city gates towered majestically, their clean-cut, symmetrical lines appearing to slice through the hazy blue sky. The massive walls seemed to encircle the city like a gargantuan pair of arms. As the three drew even closer to the impressive stone structure, Ruth was enamored by the many graceful arches that had been constructed within the walls of the city. She guessed that the shade beneath such large arches chiseled into the cool stone must feel simply delicious on a day as sweltering as the many she had recently endured.

Already, the typical sounds of the hustle and bustle of a busy town met Ruth's eager ears. She could hear the melodic laughter of the women as well as the deeper, heartier laughter of the men, the low rumble of hundreds of voices engaged in casual conversation, the enthusiastic shouts of children, the wailing of tiny babies, the braying of donkeys and the bleating of sheep.

What a place this must be! Ruth thought, catching her breath in wonder as Jacob led them beneath one of the tall arches in which had been constructed a solid gate of impenetrable bronze.

"These gates are open for us now," Jacob was explaining, although his once-captive audience paid little attention to his words. “They will be closed each evening, of course. As well as on the Sabbath Day.”

As the small, weary party of travelers crossed beneath the intimidating archway and emerged on the other side within the city gates, Ruth felt many probing eyes upon her. Carefully, she pulled the edge of her shawl over her shoulder, shielding the lower half of her face. She certainly did not want to appear too bold. Still, the elders who often stood discussing civic matters at the city gates eyes her with suspicion and even contempt.

Expertly, Jacob weaved his way through the tight throng of people that had gathered to chat or conduct business in the public square, and led his two quiet charges to a safe corner near one of the city’s towering stone walls. “Well, we have arrived,” Jacob stated with a grand flourish of his hand and a slight bow. “Would you like me to escort you to your family’s house?”

Naomi smiled gratefully. “You have been most helpful, Jacob. Thank you so much for your kindness. I believe we can make it from here.”

Jacob appeared relieved. Still, he asked cautiously, “You’re sure?”

“Completely sure,” Naomi was quick to answer. “And what of you? Surely you will not travel back to the outpost alone?” Her matronly eyes were quick to observe the rapidly setting sun. The daylight would not last much longer.

“Of course not,” Jacob replied quickly. “Not that I fear the dark. Or traveling alone,” he quickly amended. “But many friends of my father reside here in Bethlehem. I plan to spend the night with one such family, and I shall venture home early tomorrow morning.”

Naomi gave his shoulder a motherly squeeze. “Enjoy your evening, then. And many thanks for all your help.”

"The Lord be with you!" Jacob called out heartily as he disappeared into the crowd.

"And with you also, my son!" Naomi smiled after him, shaking her head in a motherly fashion. "So much like my own sons when they were but small children – " Naomi choked on her own words before she could finish the statement, her eyes welling with tears.

Instinctively, Ruth reached for her, but Naomi waved her away and forced a smile. "Enough of that. Enough of the past. We have our future to attend to, do we not?"

Ruth smiled. "That we do, Naomi. I thrill at the prospect of meeting your family, perhaps even before this week has drawn to an end – "

Naomi set her jaw firmly. "I am afraid that is impossible, my dear. They are gone."

"Gone?" Ruth nearly gasped in her shock and displeasure. "What do you mean *gone*, Naomi?"

Naomi looked very solemn. "We learned by way of a messenger of my own parents' passing, which is to be expected. They lived a full life and they were very old."

"What of your brothers and sisters?"

"My sister has passed. Of my brothers... I haven't the slightest idea if they are still living. Or where to find them, for that matter. They were all many years older than myself."

"And Elimelech's family?"

"His parents also rest with their fathers. They passed even before my own parents."

"And his siblings?"

"He had none."

Ruth raised her brows in awe. "That is very unusual."

"Yes, very. His parents believed he was their miracle from the Lord. He saved them from the disgrace of childlessness. And his father would have been distraught had he died without an heir to inherit his life's work." She sighed sadly. "Unfortunately, that is exactly what happened, regardless. After we left for Moab, we received word that his father was very ill. And he decided to leave his estate to another – his highest servant – after Elimelech betrayed him so."

Ruth cringed. What a tragic story.

"We will seek lodging for the night. In the morning, we shall visit the land of my father. Perhaps one of my brothers is still living and would be willing to grant us shelter."

Ruth felt her mouth go completely dry. She barely squeaked, "Are you saying… that we have no plan? No place to stay?" *Why had Naomi not mentioned this before?*

Naomi managed a small chortle. "Look around you, child. We will find a place. When Elimelech and I left many years ago, we disgraced our families. I doubt we will find any refuge among those that remain, but God is good. He will provide a safe haven for us."

Ruth nodded dumbly as she followed after Naomi, who had helped herself down from the wagon and led Dag by his harness through the busy throng of last-minute shoppers and merchants preparing to shut down their market stalls for the night.

A tall man in dark robes stepped directly in their path, his blue eyes – cold as ice – set deeply within his fierce, sun-darkened features. His white beard was neatly trimmed and appeared almost luminescent, starkly contrasting with his dark robes and complexion.

Ruth stifled a small gasp but Naomi appeared calm. She squinted up at the man, recognition slowly crossing her face. "You are an elder of the city, yes? As was your father before you. I know you, sir, though I apologize that I do not remember your name."

The man looked surprised, somewhat less tense after her acknowledgement. "I am Ezra, son of Reuben. Yes, I am an elder here at the city gates. Pray tell, how you have come to know me."

The haughtiness of his tone was undeniable. Ruth thought he might as well have demanded to know how such worthless rabble could have ever been privileged by his awesome presence.

Naomi did not look the least bit fazed. Apparently, she had come across arrogant men before. "I am Naomi, the wife of Elimelech who was laid to rest over ten years ago."

"Elimelech?" His exquisite blue eyes appeared distant as he grappled for recognition. A slow scowl crossed his leathery face. "Ah, Elimelech. Yes, I remember. And as I recall, he packed up his wife and children and herded them away from the blessed country... to find refuge in a heathen land."

Ruth winced. This was not the warm reception she had hoped for. Surely he would not send them back after traveling all this way! Could he? Did he possess the right? The authority? She began to pray.

"He did," Naomi answered unwaveringly. "And now I have returned to the rightful land of my fathers – "

"I see that your husband has been punished for his rash acts and wrongdoing. We all knew that such judgment was inevitable. And your sons?"

Again, Naomi did not cringe. She stood straight as a rod, her flashing eyes never leaving the elder's. "They, too, are gone – "

"I see."

Ruth fought to remain composed as fierce indignation welled up within her. Her entire being chafed at the smug satisfaction that appeared to cross the man's face upon hearing of Naomi's misfortune. How could one of the Lord's very own, chosen people find such glee in the misfortune of another? It was despicable, unthinkable! She wondered how this pompous man had ever obtained such a prestigious position at the gates. Surely the others were unaware of his true character!

"We have traveled long and we are very weary. I have brought my daughter-in-law with me. Her name is Ruth, and she is a jewel. We seek lodging for the night."

The elder named Ezra arched one grizzly white brow in Ruth's direction. "You have brought a heathen woman with you? Into our gates?" He looked absolutely incredulous, and Ruth's cheeks burned with suppressed indignation and mortification.

The only heathen I see is ***you****,* she longed to cry out. But she knew such disgraceful behavior would only serve to confirm this critical man's doubts. Even now, he eyed her as though she bore the marks of leprosy or a deadly plague.

By now, a crowd had pressed in and gathered about the two women. Ruth could hear whispers of wonderment, as well as gasps of surprise.

"Could it possibly be Naomi?"

"She has come back from the dead!"

"And where is her family?"

"Struck dead, by the mighty hand of God Himself."

Ruth longed to bury her warm face within the folds of her shawl and flee to the safety of... well, perhaps there was no safety available. Here she was – in the Land of Promise, among God's own people – and already she was being shunned. She could sense the animosity rising among the crowd, and she silently cried out to God to give her strength, to steady her. She felt engulfed by a sense of panic even more overwhelming than the pressing crowd.

"As I previously stated," Naomi continued, her firm voice rising above the crowd, "we simply seek lodging for the night."

Again, Ezra lifted his grizzled brows and appeared to communicate non-verbally with the pressing crowd. He stroked his long white beard. "Have you any coins – any method of payment?"

"A sparse few."

"I suppose the innkeeper would be willing to humor you for the night." With arms folded importantly across his chest, he gave a curt nod towards a tall, imposing stone structure near the entrance of the city.

"Ah, I remember now," Naomi said calmly. "Still run by the same family, I suppose?"

"Naturally. And probably will be for generations and generations to come."

"I vaguely remember the family who ran the Bethlehem Inn. Thank you, sir. Good evening and may God bless you." With that, Naomi took hold of Dag's worn bridle and surged past the elder with an authority that defied her small stature, the creaky wagon bumping noisily behind her.

Ruth chuckled inwardly as Ezra pushed himself back up against the rim of the crowd, as if he feared he might be rendered unclean should the shadow of a heathen woman slant across his tall frame.

Chapter 20

ARRANGEMENTS

The innkeeper was a slight man with showy garments and bulky gold rings upon his fingers. Ruth imagined that he was the only supplier of shelter for weary travelers, therefore he could charge a hefty fee. She prayed that Naomi would have enough to spare.

And whatever will we do when those few coins have been spent? she thought wearily, discouraged by the response of the Bethlehem villagers. Oh, well. The Lord would provide. Hadn't He faithfully done so in the past?

The innkeeper appeared quite interested in the two women who had caused such an uproar within the city gates. However, his shrewd merchant's eyes plainly told him that these lowly female travelers had little coin to offer and were merely wasting his time. Slightly peeved, he accepted the two small coins which Naomi pressed into his sweaty palm, and led them to a central stone courtyard where their animal could rest and be refreshed with oats and water.

Ruth immediately set to work tying Dag's reigns to a slender post and filling his feed sack with tender oats, of which he began to chomp with a fury. She hadn't even noticed the innkeeper slip soundlessly from the open-air resting place.

There was very little that escaped Naomi's shrewd eye, however. "Excuse me," Naomi called after the man. "Our animal is well-taken care of, and for that I thank you. And where shall my daughter and I stay?"

Ruth's heart was warmed. This was the first time Naomi had simply referred to her as *my daughter*. It touched her heart and she nearly wept. Especially knowing that – as a foreigner – *she* was the one who had caused Naomi the most grief upon their arrival.

The innkeeper wrung his hands nervously for a moment, then gave a careless shrug of his shoulders. "For the price we agreed upon, you will stay here."

"Here?" Naomi looked incredulous. "With all the animals?"

"Unless you can find it within your heart to make me a better offer."

Ruth felt as if the breath had been knocked out of her. They hadn't much to offer, but they had clearly given this man all they could afford. What more could he possibly want?

Naomi shook her head helplessly. "Is there no room available in the inn?"

"Not for the price you have offered."

"It is all that I have."

"Unless you would prefer to sleep out in the dilapidated old cave where we house animals when we are too full, this will have to do. The cave is not much, but there is a manger for your animal and plenty of soft straw to sleep on."

Naomi appeared to be weighing her options. The cool, tiled courtyard seemed to be more appealing than a dusty old cave that served as an overflow stable. "I suppose we shall remain here for the night, then."

The innkeeper merely offered another shrug of indifference. "Enjoy your stay." And then he was gone.

Ruth looked to Naomi, her eyes wide.

And – much to Ruth's surprise – Naomi doubled over, laughing hysterically.

Ruth felt irritated. "Naomi, what on earth could possibly be so mirthful?"

Naomi dropped to a stone bench and clutched her stomach, still laughing heartily. "I do apologize, child!" she giggled. "But I wish you could have seen your expression!"

Ruth sighed, finally beginning to accept the humor of the situation. "I must admit, I am beginning to wonder if we will ever sleep with a roof over our heads again."

Naomi caught Ruth's hand and gave it a confident squeeze. "Things will be difficult for a while, my daughter. But the Lord will be with us. He will continue to provide."

"I suppose He already has. At least we have a place to rest."

"That is true. And we will feel much better after a good night's rest, I'm sure. First thing tomorrow morning, we will set out to find a home."

As the two women spread out their pallets and bedded down for the night, Ruth couldn't help but voice a few quiet concerns.

"Naomi, what shall we do if we cannot find any of your relatives? Or if they refuse to offer shelter?"

Naomi slowly lowered herself to her pallet and nestled beneath a soft woolen blanket. "We will pray."

"Do you truly believe they will turn us away?"

"They might."

"But they are your *family*!"

"Ah, my darling. They were once. But, you see, I was a headstrong and rebellious young girl. I married against my father's wishes. I know that he forgave me – why, he even felt responsible for introducing me to Elimelech. But when my husband and I turned our backs on our fathers and the land of our God... it was a direct affront to them, Ruth. It was not wise. I begged my husband to reconsider, but he did not trust the Lord with our lives. When that famine struck, and so many of us were losing everything and watching our children starve... he just gave up, Ruth. Nothing that I said could sway him."

"Surely your family knows that his decision was not of your choosing."

"It matters not. The hurt is there. The bitterness is there. But I have prayed long and hard that the Lord would work a miracle in their hearts. Perhaps they will provide a safe haven for us."

Ruth drifted off to sleep that night deep in prayer. She prayed that the Lord would restore Naomi's broken relationships. She prayed that the villagers would accept them, and not turn away from Naomi on account of a foreign woman. She prayed that the Lord would provide a safe place in which they could abide.

But above all else, she prayed for His will to be done.

Ruth awoke with a start, aware of the cool tiles beneath her sleeping pallet and the insistent braying of several unruly donkeys. Throwing herself to her feet, she looked about frantically. Where was she? What had happened to her?

Then, as full wakefulness dawned upon her, she remembered the strange happenings of the previous evening – the critical elder, the curious crowd of onlookers, the stingy innkeeper, and a night spent in an open-air courtyard filled with protesting animals.

Sighing, Ruth dropped to her knees and rubbed her throbbing temples. *Oh, Lord, this is not at all how I imagined it would be...*

But enough of that! Today was a new day, and she was determined to hope for the best. After all, today was the day that Naomi might be reunited with her family – it was a day full of questions and promise.

Already the sun's warm rays slanted down lengthwise across the courtyard. She judged by the sun's high position in the sky that she had carelessly overslept, and her cheeks flushed warmly in her shame.

So much to do, and here I am sleeping the day away like a careless child! she thought, chagrined. *And where on earth is Naomi?* Ruth realized that she must have been physically exhausted from their journey. She could not even remember the last time the sun had beaten her out of bed.

Hurriedly, she ran her fingers through her tangled hair and quickly managed to tame her long tresses enough to form a loose braid. She then reached for her shawl and placed it modestly over her head and shoulders, slipped into her sandals, and led Dag to the large, water-filled trough in the center of the courtyard.

Wherever Naomi was, Ruth determined to be ready to go the moment she arrived.

She did not have to wait long. Naomi entered the courtyard looking exhausted and dejected. Her shawl had slipped off her head and hung heavily behind her back. She was covered in dust from the road and her forehead was slick with sweat.

Ruth hated herself for sleeping through whatever ordeal Naomi had just faced.

"My child, I thank the Lord you were finally able to get some satisfying rest."

Ruth left Dag alone at the watering trough and hurried to Naomi's side. "And why did you not awaken me? I feel so ashamed – "

"I slipped out as quietly as possible in hopes that you could rest and regain your strength," Naomi confessed, falling to the stone bench and looking much like a rag doll.

Ruth quickly seated herself beside her weary mother-in-law and waited. She could sense that Naomi bore news that she would eventually share, and she felt that she shouldn't pry. She would wait.

Ruth had no idea how long they waited there in silence, the unforgiving bench pinching their sore backs as the merciless sun heated the tiles beneath their sandaled feet. However long, it seemed like an eternity.

Finally, Naomi spoke. "I have been out inquiring about my family."

"Have you met any of your old friends or neighbors, Naomi? Were they happy to see you?" Immediately, Ruth regretted asking such impulsive questions. The shadow that crossed Naomi's face was enough to answer any and all future inquiries.

"My worst fears were merely confirmed, Ruth. My family is gone."

Ruth realized that her mouth had dropped open. She quickly closed it. "All of them?"

"All of them. I knew it would be so, Ruth. I just had this feeling, this dreadful sense that they would not be waiting for me."

"Oh, Naomi, I am so sorry..." Ruth's mind was flooded

with a thousand different questions, but right now she knew that her sole intent should be to comfort Naomi. She draped her arms about the old woman's shoulders and realized that Naomi was trembling.

"It's going to be alright, Naomi," Ruth assured her, her own voice quavering. "We know that the Lord will take care of us..." *But where will we live? Where shall we stay?* Even as she whispered reassurance to her bereaved mother-in-law, she wondered if she could muster up the strength to believe in her own hollow reassurances.

Naomi eventually straightened and Ruth dropped her hands into her lap, her eyes lowered respectfully.

"Oh, just look at me," Naomi chided herself, swiping impatiently at her tears and readjusting her cap. "A fine example for you, I have been!"

Ruth shook her head stubbornly. "Naomi, you have been the most beautiful example a young woman could ever hope for!"

"Shah, forgive me, Ruth. We may not have any relatives or a home that we can call our own, but I have no doubt that the Lord is going to provide. He would not bring us this far to no avail."

"Of course He wouldn't."

"I already knew the fate of my father, mother, and sister. But my brothers..." again, the tears threatened to spill over Naomi's cheeks and she took a moment to compose herself. "Rueben has passed. I am not surprised to hear it. He is – was – much older than I am. His two younger brothers – still my elders by many years – fell greatly into debt. Apparently their sad family situation was more than they could bear. They sold my father's beloved land and made off like bandits in the night. No one knows where they are."

The silence reigned for several moments before Ruth

finally spoke up. “What shall we do, Naomi? I am prepared to follow wherever you lead.”

“Wherever *God* leads,” Naomi corrected, rising to her feet and gathering the few belongings they had brought with them from the wagon. Ruth noticed her handle the scroll with added fervor and care.

“Where will we go?”

Naomi met her gaze and smiled. “Where did Abraham go? And his lovely wife Sarah?”

Ruth managed another smile. “To the land that God would show them.”

“I suppose we will do the same.”

“Excuse me.” Both women stiffened at the unexpected greeting from a clearly male voice.

Ruth turned to see a tall, solidly built man standing in the entryway. He wore simple garments and his skin was darkened from numerous hours in the sun’s brutal heat. His eyes were bright and the color of dark honey. Something about him felt familiar and unthreatening despite his tall stature.

Respectfully, he fastened his gaze on the older woman present, rather than allowing it to rest on the beautiful young woman by her side. “Forgive me for the intrusion, but I assume you must be Naomi?”

Naomi looked startled, but she nodded dumbly. “I am.”

“My name is Kemuel. I work out in the fields, and it was only by chance that I was sent to town early this morning. It was there that I was informed of your predicament.”

Ruth looked questioningly to Naomi. She wondered why their *predicament* held any weight at all to this young man standing before them.

“I was disturbed to discover that none of our fine villagers offered up any hospitality to two widows in need. I have spoken with my father. We abide in a small, modest cluster of homes near the fields where I work. He has granted me permission to provide lodging until you have had the chance to work things out."

Naomi stared at the man, her eyes wide with astonishment. Ruth knew she must be wearing a very similar expression.

"Is your father aware that I have brought my daughter-in-law with me?" Naomi asked meaningfully.

"He is. And my wife would not have it any other way."

Naomi visibly relaxed, and she smiled at the young man with admiring eyes. "Young man, I do not possess the words to thank you for your kindness and your generosity. You are heaven-sent, a true gift from God."

The young man named Kemuel seemed to dismiss the praise with a small smile. "If you are prepared to leave, I would be glad to escort you to your new home before returning to the fields."

Kemuel led the two women down a winding path that led to his simple homestead. He remained respectfully silent. They appeared more comfortable with quietness, and he could not blame them – especially after hearing about the noisy reception they had received the night before.

Silently, he thanked the Lord for the opportunity to reach out to the brokenhearted. He knew that it was by the Lord's own hand that he had stumbled upon the two widows – very rarely did Boaz ever send him to town during a shift. Upon hearing of the widows' plight, he had hastily informed Boaz and asked for permission to seek his father's approval on the matter of allowing them to stay in one of his own vacant dwellings. Kindhearted Boaz had graciously agreed to let him go, and Adara had been thrilled at the prospect of meeting the new women and making them feel welcome. He hoped with all his heart that these women would not shun or reject her.

However, he also wondered if this was not yet again the Lord's hand subtly at work in their lives. This new young woman – he believed her name was Ruth – was a Moabitess and would most certainly be rejected by the majority of the villagers. Especially after a certain touchy incident had taken place between the Israelites and the Moabites in the somewhat distant past...

But all that aside, perhaps his gracious wife and this new young woman could find refuge in the company of each other.

He had been so lost in thought that he hadn't even noticed the large cluster of whitewashed houses loom into view. He turned to the women apologetically. "I apologize for the silence, I have been rather lost in thought."

Naomi returned his smile. "I believe we have as well! And you have nothing to apologize for, young man. You are an answer to prayer."

The small dwellings seemed quiet enough from this deceptive angle – but Kemuel knew full well that the inner courtyard boxed in by a large rectangle of nearly-identical dwellings would be bustling with morning activity as young wives and mothers hurried about to accomplish the day's chores.

Kemuel led the two widows past his own home, and Tal bounded to his feet – his tail wagging an enthusiastic greeting. Kemuel laughed and caressed the yellow dog's head fondly as he passed. He was grateful that neither woman seemed startled or unsettled by the large animal. In fact, the younger woman appeared enthralled. Her eyes shone with interest as the pointy-eared beast resettled himself on the dusty ground, his head resting thoughtfully between his paws.

A mere two dwellings down from his own, Kemuel released Dag's bridle and guided him to a nearby trough for a well-deserved drought of water. "It isn't much," he admitted humbly, "but there is a roof over your head, shelter from the elements, and plenty of room for two small women."

Naomi's eyes were brimming with tears. "Bless you," she managed, her voice catching in her throat. "Bless you, Kemuel."

Chapter 21

HARVEST

Kemuel pushed open the weathered wooden door, flooding the small space within with dazzling light.

Ruth drew in a deep breath, surprised. A young woman knelt in the middle of the room, the sleeves of her tunic rolled up to the elbows and a large vat of water at her side. She appeared to be elbow-deep in the process of scrubbing the neglected clay floor clean of dirt and grime.

"Adara? What on earth are you doing, love?" Apparently, Kemuel, too, was surprised.

The young woman looked up from her work, curly brown tendrils framing a lovely face. She reached for her hair, obviously aware of the fact that she had neglected to wear a shawl. Then, laughing, she wiped her hands on her soiled tunic and allowed Kemuel to help her to her feet. "I must be quite a sight!" she laughed, her voice every bit as arresting as her melodic laughter. "Kemuel, I had no idea you would have them here so quickly!"

Kemuel grinned, holding the young woman by the

elbow. "I knew they would be eager to have a place called home."

"And that they will!" the young woman put in decisively, a smile lighting her every feature. She turned to both widows apologetically. "I am so sorry to present myself in such a manner! I'm afraid I am not fit to be seen!"

Naomi smiled warmly. "Actually, my dear, I have yet to see a prettier picture than the one you have just presented – a lovely, young woman with a servant's heart, working tirelessly to help those in need."

Adara flushed pleasantly. "I am so thankful for the privilege of meeting you – both of you! I had hoped to have this place spotless before your arrival, but I am afraid the task has proven to be a bit more demanding than I expected!"

Ruth could scarcely believe her own eyes. The dwelling was indeed small – consisting of only one box-shaped room – but this young woman had worked wonders with it. The cobwebs had been scraped and cleaned from the corners, the clay floor fairly shone after a fresh scrub, and there was no trace of dust or grime on any surface anywhere. She wondered how long this poor woman had been scrubbing away the filth in order to make it pleasantly livable for two complete strangers.

It must have been quite a sight before she got hold of it, Ruth thought, awed. *It appears to have been abandoned for years!*

"Adara, you have done a fine job, my dear," the young man declared, his eyes filled with pride. Pulling the young woman close, he announced tenderly, "This lovely young woman is Adara, my wife."

Naomi found her voice first. "I am Naomi. And this is my daughter-in-law, Ruth. She has been my strength for many years."

Ruth felt slightly embarrassed by Naomi's unexpected

praise, but she managed a smile anyway, feeling suddenly very shy. "This is... this has been such a gift," she stammered, touched to the core of her being. "Thank you for your kindness."

"You may stay here as long as necessary," Kemuel assured them.

"And I will always be around," Adara added brightly. "I would be glad to help with anything you may need – the cooking, the cleaning, the sewing... Please let me know if there is anything I can do to help you get settled in."

Naomi fairly beamed upon the young couple standing before her. "You have done more than you will ever know. I thank you from the bottom of my heart, I do."

"Well, then, I suppose we will leave the two of you to get settled in. Is there anything else I can help you with before we depart?" Kemuel's voice held an immense amount of strength, but also humility.

Ruth gazed in wonder at the young couple and felt that they must be perfectly matched. These were the kind of people she had dreamed of meeting in the Land of Promise. The Lord had indeed answered her prayer. "I would like to offer my services as well," Ruth heard herself saying even before she was aware of her own thoughts. "You have both done so much for us. Adara, if I can be of any help to you and your family, please let me know. I don't mind hard work, and I would be honored to be of help to you in any way."

Adara's luminous eyes held a serenity that Ruth longed to claim as her own. Here was a woman who had accepted her lot and allowed peace to reign in her life. "That means a lot to me, Ruth, and I will certainly let you know if anything comes up. Thank you so much."

As Kemuel helped Adara gather up her urn of clean water and guide her towards the door, she turned to face

Ruth and Naomi once more. She gestured toward another slender urn resting in the corner. "I drew some fresh water for you, but I'm sure you will need more by morning. I would be glad to show you to the well. Also, there is a central courtyard just outside the back door. You can use our oven whenever you'd like, and your donkey will be perfectly safe in the pen. Make yourselves completely at home, and don't hesitate to visit me or send for me if you have any questions!"

Naomi offered up her warmest smile. "Thank you, my dear. I do have one question."

Both Kemuel and Adara waited expectantly.

"It is mid-April, is it not? And if I am not mistaken, the beginning of the grain harvest?"

Kemuel ran a hand through his hair and smiled easily. "You are right about that. And the harvest is bountiful this year. My men have been scrambling to harvest the abundance of grain the Lord has blessed us with."

Naomi appeared to color slightly with her next question. "And the poor are still permitted to follow behind the threshers and gather the grain that has fallen?"

Ruth noticed the sympathy in Adara's eyes, and she had to force herself to swallow the lump forming in her throat. She knew it must take a considerable amount of humility for Naomi to comfortably ask such a question.

Kemuel nodded, his jaw firm. "That is correct. The poor may gather whatever grain may fall. And it is indeed a good year to be gathering grain – the Lord has provided more than we ever thought possible."

Naomi nodded agreeably. "That is good news indeed. Thank you."

The couple started to leave, then Kemuel seemed to think better of it and turned back to face them. "If you should choose to follow behind the harvesters in search of grain, I insist that you do so in my master's field. He is a good, God-fearing man, and daily he seeks to meet the needs of the poor and the destitute. I know that he would not have it any other way."

Ruth looked to Naomi, and in an instant she realized what Naomi planned to do. Emphatically, she stepped in. "Naomi, you are in no condition to be gleaning out in the fields each day. That is my responsibility and I will take care of it." She turned to Kemuel, shocked by the authority in her own voice. "I will do as you say. Tomorrow I shall glean in your master's field."

Adara's eyes widened in protest, but she remained respectfully quiet. Ruth had no doubt that this kindly woman would gladly go without food herself if it meant she could keep others from the backbreaking labor of the fields.

"Ruth, it was *I* who desired to come here. I will support us now, whatever it takes," Naomi put in staunchly.

Ruth shook her head with a glint in her dark eyes that indicated the matter was completely settled. "That is not even an option, Naomi." She smiled playfully. "After all, who would keep house if you were out in the fields all day? I will take care of it. The Lord has already provided a place in which I can gather grain for us. What more could we ask for?"

Naomi bit her lip and looked away, defeated.

Adara looked to her husband, and they seemed to communicate momentarily without a spoken word. Turning back to Ruth, Adara said quickly, "The gleaning begins just before daybreak. I can take you to my husband's fields if you would like. The fields lie just below the town, not far at all from here."

Ruth gave her a heartfelt smile. "I would like nothing better. Thank you, Adara."

Adara's eyes lit up with anticipation. "Then I suppose we have a plan. Until tomorrow, then!"

Ruth couldn't believe the sense of peace that was gradually engulfing her entire being, chasing away her fears and doubts. Resolutely, she replied, "Until tomorrow!"

Ruth caught her breath at the sight that met her eyes – a vast, undulating sea of gold glistening beneath the dazzling light of the rising Bethlehem sun. Thousands upon thousands of golden heads of grain swayed to and fro in the whispering morning breezes, the sky above them washed a pale pink and lavender and orange and gold.

Gazing upon the spectacular sight, Ruth turned to her companion and, awe-struck, whispered, "Is it like this every morning here?"

Adara's own delicate features were lively and animated, as Ruth's wonder was almost contagious. "Well, this *is* Bethlehem – the House of Bread. God has surely blessed us with plenty."

"It is beautiful," Ruth breathed, inwardly thanking God for graciously meeting each and every one of her needs. Not only had He provided a home for her and Naomi – He had provided a dear friend in this sweet young woman named Adara, as well as a means with which to support herself. Whereas her circumstances had seemed hopelessly bleak a few short hours before, it was now abundantly clear that the Lord had been watching out for them the entire time. He had not abandoned them.

True to her word, Adara had knocked on the coarse

wooden door of Ruth's new home just before daybreak to escort her new friend to her husband's fields. They had made excellent time in reaching the swaying fields of wheaten gold, despite lively conversation along the way.

"Are you going to be alright, Ruth?" Adara asked as they reached the simple row of structures where the workers often ate their meals or slept overnight.

Ruth felt extremely nervous about the prospect of attempting a backbreaking form of labor – a task that she was completely unfamiliar with – before an entire regiment of perfect strangers. But she refused to allow her resolve to weaken. She was convinced that the Lord had provided this means of nourishment for her small family – herself and Naomi. She would be grateful and she would go about the task with both determination and zeal.

Smiling, Ruth placed a hand on Adara's shoulder. "I will be fine. God has surely blessed me – I know that He will remain with me along the way."

Adara smiled comfortingly. "My husband says that he works with good men. I pray they will treat you fairly, but I have also asked my husband to keep an eye out for you. He can be trusted, that I assure you. And I could say the same about the man who owns this field. My husband and I have yet to meet a man who loves the Lord more passionately than Boaz."

Ruth nodded her understanding. *I am so blessed,* her heart cried out. *So blessed!*

Ruth was surprised when a door creaked open behind them and Kemuel emerged from a ramshackle storage hut. Smiling, he took his wife in his arms and planted a firm kiss on her forehead. "Good morning, my love."

Adara's entire countenance lit up in her husband's presence. She smiled up at him, almost teasingly. "Good morning to you."

"I see you have brought another worker this morning?"

"And a more diligent worker I doubt you will find!"

"There is none more diligent than you, my dear..."

Ruth shied away slightly, afraid that she was intruding on an intimate moment between husband and wife. But Adara merely chuckled and, reaching for her arm, pulled Ruth back into their circle.

"Oh, Kemuel, we are embarrassing Ruth with our silly talk!"

Kemuel grinned and released his hold on his wife. "The workers are already beginning the day's work. Do you know what to do?"

Ruth shook her head slightly. "Not exactly. But I'm sure I will catch on quickly."

"The concept is actually quite simple, though the work isn't easy. See those men setting to work in the fields with the curved sickles? They will be cutting the barley, and other men will tie it into bundles. Anything left on the ground behind them is available for keeps. Simply tuck it within your tunic and gather as much as you possibly can. I have already informed Boaz that you would be here today, and he is thankful that the Lord has led you here. He says that you are most welcome in his fields."

Ruth nodded her thanks.

"And don't you worry about Naomi either, Ruth," Adara spoke up, her eyes shining. "I will make sure that she learns her way around today. We will visit the well as soon as I return. And I will acquaint her with her new best friend – our bread oven – as well! I would even love to give her a few lessons on my loom if she would be willing. I will look out for her in your absence – I promise."

Throwing her arms about Adara's shoulders, Ruth gave her new friend a genuine hug. "Thank you, Adara. That means more to me than you'll ever know."

Adara returned the embrace warmly, then stood on her tiptoes to give her husband one quick, parting kiss. She then turned back in the direction of their homes. "God be with you, Ruth! I will see you when you return!"

"God be with you as well, Adara."

Ruth watched Adara as she skipped her way back along the winding path they had taken to the fields. With little success, she tried to suppress the panic that was rapidly rising in her chest. Way out here in the fields, without the watchful eye of Naomi or Adara's caring smile, she felt terribly alone.

But I'm not alone, she reminded herself staunchly, her eyes following the dozens of workers who were converging upon the fields like hungry locusts. *The Lord is with me. He is always with me.*

Behind her, Kemuel cleared his throat, and she realized that he probably felt uncomfortable standing alone with her in the field. She had no desire to make him feel uneasy, so she quickly adjusted her mantle, preparing to fill it with grain. "May I begin gleaning behind the workers, sir?"

Kemuel nodded his assent. "Of course. For as long as you wish."

"Thank you," she responded heartily, hurrying out to the open fields.

Ruth was glad to see that she was not the only woman huddling behind the men, gleaning from the stalks that were left behind after their busy threshing. A handful of poorly-clad women had scattered about behind various groups of harvesters, eagerly gathering up the leftover grain. On several occasions Ruth attempted to meet their gaze and exchange a friendly smile, but the women remained distant and aloof. She noticed that many of the women had gathered together in throngs, chatting and laughing lightly as they worked. She longed to join them, but their threatening scowls and venomous stares warned her to keep her distance. She sighed and continued her solitary work without further glances in their direction.

Soon she found herself completely lost in her work. The reapers seemed to work and move as one giant wave of humanity, reaping the benefits of a bountiful harvest with incredible speed and agility.

That's when she noticed the workers straighten as one, seeming to come to attention like the soldiers of some vast army. Confused, Ruth straightened to her full height as well and glanced around curiously. What had they seen that had brought them to full attention so quickly?

That's when she saw him. He was tall, broad-shouldered, and strongly built. Clearly, he did not belong out in the fields. His beard was neatly trimmed, cropped close to his firm chin unlike many of the workers'. He wore flowing robes of rich hues with intricate embroidering, which appeared quite imposing draped about his massive frame. Ruth guessed him to be in his late thirties, if not his early forties, but he had aged very well. He strolled near the fields as one with authority, and his gaze was firm, decisive.

Here is a man who knows what he is about, Ruth thought as she observed the impressive, stately figure and wondered who he could possibly be. A political figure? A prophet? Perhaps even one of the mighty judges of Israel?

That's when she saw Kemuel standing close beside him, his arms crossed before his chest and his eyes calmly following the man's every movement.

Perhaps he is the owner of this field, Ruth thought, remaining standing as the other workers did.

Curious, Ruth watched intently as the man began to speak. His voice rang out, deep and strong, easily carrying over the distance of the vast field. "Good morning, my good men! And the Lord be with you!"

As one, every single worker in the field responded heartily, "The Lord bless you!"

The man's face stretched into a smile expressing genuine pleasure, and Ruth was surprised at the way that smile closed the distance between herself and the tall stranger, warming her to the very core. Surely this man must be Boaz – the bold man of God that Kemuel and Adara had previously mentioned with such deep respect.

The harvesters then returned to their work, and Ruth was left standing alone, confused... but in the most pleasant way.

Perhaps it is customary for him to greet his workers in like manner each day, she mused as she resumed her work retrieving the unruly stalks of barley.

At first the work did not seem too burdensome. As the wayward stalks fell from the men's quick hands and tightly-bound bundles, Ruth would wait a respectful distance behind them before scooping up her golden prizes and tucking them away into her mantle.

However, as the sun rose higher and higher in the hazy blue sky, drenching the workers in a layer of glistening sweat, Ruth began to feel dizzy and even slightly nauseated. The sun beat mercilessly upon her aching back and shoulders, penetrating her heavy garments and drenching her entire body in a slick layer of sticky sweat. Her legs and her back ached from the constant crouching and scooping movements, and her throat cried out for even a drop of water. Her hair – dripping with sweat – clung to her damp forehead, as well as the back of her neck – in the most uncomfortable manner. She shuddered to think how frightful she must look to the other workers, but her own eyes confirmed that they looked terribly unpresentable as well.

After what seemed like an eternity of walking then bending, scooping then rising, and repeating the painful process all over again, Ruth straightened and struggled to remain standing on her own two feet as her entire world tilted and spun. She felt ridiculously light-headed, and she prayed that God would grant her the strength to press on without passing out.

Shaking her head and regaining her senses, Ruth knelt once more to retrieve several stalks of leftover barley. However, just as her slender fingers curled about the tender stalks, two sandaled feet appeared directly in front of her. A small gasp caught in her throat, and she peered up to find herself gazing directly into the kindly face of the man she had seen earlier that morning as he had greeted the workers in the fields.

Chapter 22

BOAZ

In her haste to scramble up onto her own two feet, Ruth's mantle slid from her hand and much of the grain she had gathered plummeted gracelessly to the ground.

"Oh, no," Ruth breathed, frantically kneeling to gather up the mess.

The man standing before her immediately knelt and began to gather up her losses. "Do not be afraid, my daughter. Here, let me help you."

Ruth looked to the man with large, questioning eyes. The tenderness and warmth with which the man spoke rendered her speechless. Nodding dumbly, she continued to gather her spilled grain.

The man seemed to sense her unease. With a reassuring smile, he spoke to her softly. "My name is Boaz. The Lord has blessed me with this field. I have spoken with my foreman, Kemuel, and he says that both you and your mother-in-law are honorable women."

Ruth could not bring herself to meet his gaze. She realized that she must be making quite an unimpressive picture, squatting in a pile of upset grain even as the sweat trickled down her brow. Mortified, she fought for composure and prayed that this embarrassing moment might come to a swift end.

Gently, Boaz took her by the arm and helped her rise to her feet. Again, her head swam with dizziness and she felt herself begin to tilt.

"Steady, now." Boaz held her arm firmly, and she was astonished by the combined strength and gentleness with which he upheld her. That's when she realized that he was gazing directly into her eyes.

Her cheeks aflame, Ruth managed a wobbly smile and carefully tucked away the remaining grain in her mantle. "Thank you, sir," she nearly choked. "You have been very kind."

Just when she thought this awkward encounter had drawn to a close, he surprised her by saying, "I have heard such reports about you – reports of your kindness."

Ruth felt her brows rise in surprise. *This* man had heard reports about a nobody such as *her*? News traveled fast in Bethlehem.

"As I mentioned, I spoke with my foreman. He says that you left everything – your relatives, the land of your birth, seemingly everything promising of a bright future – to care for your aging mother-in-law."

Desperately, Ruth busied herself by arranging the stalks of barley within her mantle. She felt terribly cornered and longed to throw aside her precious bundle of grain and flee to the safety of her small abode. She knew not how to answer this kind stranger, but she was certain that he could hear her heart beating violently within her chest.

"This indeed is hard work, and you have been at it for

many hours now. Do you see our well, just beyond that gentle rise?"

Thankful for an excuse to look at something – *anything* – other than the impressive figure standing before her, Ruth quickly followed his gaze and strained to see the well from which the workers drew water. She nodded.

"There you will find many large vessels of cool water, drawn fresh from our well. Help yourself to the refreshment as often as you wish."

Ruth lowered her head, tears stinging her eyelids. How could a perfect stranger speak to her – a foreigner, a *heathen* – with such warmth, such kindness?

"I have also spoken with my men. I have commanded them not to touch you. They will leave you be, so you may gather your grain each day without fear. These are good men – my workers – and they have shown me that they respect my word. Please, gather only here in my field. You will be safe here."

Slowly, reverently, Ruth lowered herself to a kneeling position before the man. A puzzling assortment of emotions had washed over her like a relentless deluge, and she knew no other way to fully express her gratitude. "Sir," she whispered, "what have I done to find such favor in your sight, that you should take notice of me – a foreigner? I do not understand..."

"Frankly, I admire your servant's heart. Ruth, is it? May I call you Ruth?"

Again, she nodded.

"And you may call me Boaz."

Ruth remained kneeling where she was, studying the brittle blades of yellow grass that scratched at her knees and palms. She couldn't imagine addressing him as such – after all, he was the owner of this field, and she was an impoverished woman from a pagan land! Why, she had not a coin to her name! How could he expect her to elevate herself to such a level?

"You have done much for your mother-in-law – more than you may ever know. She is blessed to call you her daughter. After the loss of her husband as well as her sons, I know that she must have found such solace in your tender compassion and selfless care. And I pray that the Lord will repay you for all you have done, and a full reward be given to you by the Lord God of Israel, under whose wings you have taken refuge."

It was altogether too much. She could sense the depth and the sincerity behind those words – every bit as solid and strong as the strength that upheld him. She gazed up at him in awe even as the tears traced two slender lines through the dust upon her cheeks. She fought for composure as she formed her next words. "Thank you, sir. Your words have both strengthened and comforted me."

"And your unshakable trust in the God of my fathers has indeed strengthened my own faith as well." There was a pause as Boaz lifted his gaze to the surrounding fields. The many eyes that had been gapingly taking in every detail of Boaz's introduction immediately shifted back to the work at hand. Boaz chuckled under his breath. The sound was low, rumbling, pleasing. "I suppose my workers must wonder why I am keeping you from your urgent task. Forgive me."

"There is nothing to forgive," Ruth startled even herself with the straightforwardness with which she spoke. Just being in the presence of Boaz seemed to banish her own petty anxieties and insecurities, feeding her new strength. She found herself marveling at the wonder of it all, and then realized that she was blushing beneath his gentle gaze. She hoped he couldn't read her silly thoughts. But those eyes – not brown, nor green, but a shade of hazel somewhere in between, rather like that of polished bronze – appeared so knowing, so intuitive. She feared that he could read her every thought like the lines of an opened scroll.

"It is customary for the workers to rest with the intensity of the afternoon heat, and break bread together, and enjoy a meal. Please join us. I imagine that you've worked up quite an appetite."

Ruth hadn't realized how famished she was until now. Just the thought of a fresh meal and a cool draught of water nearly sent her trembling. She managed a lopsided smile of gratitude. "Thank you, sir. That sounds most welcome at this moment."

Boaz returned her smile kindly. "Come along, then. I will show you the way."

~

Naomi spent the morning in prayer – her prayers brimming with thanksgiving and gratitude and wonder.

You are so good, Lord, she found herself repeating over and over. *So good. You have truly worked wonders for us. I could never truly thank you enough. You are SO good, Lord!*

So much had come together in such a brief amount of time! Her greatest fears had been realized, and then scattered – rather like the morning mist that encompassed the gentle hills, only to be immediately dispersed upon the day's first breath of wind.

She had feared her family would not be there to meet them. And they were not. Yet the Lord had provided her with a daughter more devoted than a dozen blood-relatives could have ever been.

She had feared they would have no home. And upon

their arrival, they had found themselves truly homeless. Yet the Lord had provided a sturdy little home for them, completely free of charge. They would be sheltered from the rain and the elements. Safe.

She had feared they would be despised and rejected. And they had indeed been shunned upon entering the city gates. Yet the Lord had sent a lovely young couple to accept them and draw them into warm, like-minded fellowship – a healing balm for the wounds inflicted by those gawking spectators in the town square.

She had feared they would have no food, no sustenance. And it had certainly seemed as if they would remain empty-handed. And yet again... the Lord had provided a law in ages past that foresaw the needs of the poor and the destitute. Now they could gather as much grain as would be needed to satisfy their hunger.

Naomi marveled at all that the Lord had set into motion on her behalf – once she had been stubborn, unyielding, bitter, unfaithful. And yet... her God had been faithful. Steadfast. Merciful. He had gathered His aching child in His arms and led her to a better pasture, to a place of comfort and safety. It was truly unfathomable.

Now as she bustled about her new abode – righting this, tweaking that – she wondered about her gracious daughter-in-law out in the fields, smilingly accepting a task that would prove harsh and unyielding, perhaps even unfruitful.

I do hope she has been treated with kindness, Naomi fretted as she fumbled with the panels on the small window overlooking the central courtyard beyond. She admired the intricate lattice-work, but at the moment she felt that she would appreciate the sunshine streaming through an open window even more. *Perhaps it won't be so evident that she is a foreigner beneath all those heavy garments. And surely Kemuel will keep an eye out for any signs of trouble...*

She caught herself mid-thought, and instantly chided herself. *You silly old woman! You ought to be ashamed of yourself! Look how God has already provided, and yet you still trouble yourself with anxious thoughts!*

She started at an unexpected rap at the door. She had not expected company. Why, Adara had already helped her draw the day's fresh water from the well and given her a thorough tutorial on the workings of the large bread oven out back. Who could possibly be seeking her out now?

Cautiously, Naomi moved toward the door and placed a hand on the latch. "Who is there?" she called raspily, her brow furrowed with concern.

"Oh, Naomi, it is only me – Adara! I did not mean to startle you!"

Naomi's heart fairly sang when the joyous young voice met her ears. *So much like my Ruth,* she thought as she unlatched the front door.

The door creaked open on unwilling hinges, and Naomi was surprised to see another woman standing smilingly beside Adara.

"I brought a surprise!" Adara announced, her eyes sparkling with delight. "I hope you don't mind!"

The girl's enthusiasm was infectious. Naomi felt the corners of her eyes crinkle with pleasure. "Not a bit!"

"This is Ada – a dear friend of mine," Adara explained, guiding the aging woman through the doorway and leading her to a stool.

But Ada had no interest in sitting down. Without hesitation, she took Naomi's hand in both her own and said with a straightforwardness that delighted Naomi, "I am so pleased to meet you, Naomi. Adara has told me much about you and your daughter-in-law."

Naomi liked the woman immediately. She was short and pleasantly plump, with rosy cheeks and a no-nonsense manner. "What a joy to meet you as well!" Naomi readily replied.

"Ada has been such a comfort to me," Adara was explaining, pleased that the two older women appeared to be quite comfortable together. "She is the only kind soul who ever came to call on me, and she has made my long days at home such a delight. I eagerly await her visits."

Naomi wondered why Ada would be Adara's only caller – after all, the girl was lovely, kind, and very gracious. Didn't the other neighbor women find the time to drop by every now and then? But she knew better than to overstep her bounds by asking such a personal question. Instead, she simply nodded her understanding.

"And now the Lord has blessed me with yet another sister in the faith," Ada put in emphatically, her hands on her hips. "Well, two sisters, actually – including your daughter-in-law. Whom I am quite eager to meet as well!"

"She will be sorry that she missed you. She is gleaning in the fields today, but she promised to return before nightfall."

"Ah, a hard worker, is she? I like her already!"

Naomi returned Ada's smile. "She is truly a gem."

Always the hospitable one, Adara quickly arranged two small stools near the window– the only real pieces of furniture in the room – so the women could be seated comfortably. She led Ada to one stool and helped Naomi settle into the other one. "I have a few chores to attend to at home," she explained apologetically, although Naomi suspected that she was simply giving the two older women an opportunity to get to know each other. "I must return home, but I will be back shortly to see you out, Ada. Is that alright with you both?"

Ada waved a hand good-naturedly. "By all means, don't keep your chores waiting, missie! When you return, I suspect you will find that neither Naomi nor I will be ready to call it a day."

Adara grinned, pleased to pieces at the outcome of her little introduction, and ducked out the door. "I will see you both very soon!"

~

The sun was just beginning to settle in for the evening, tucked comfortably between the sheltering western hills, washing the lovely sea of golden grain in soft, russet-colored hues.

With great effort, Ruth straightened from her stooped position, her aching back crying out for relief. *If my sore body is able to budge tomorrow, it will surely be a miracle,* she thought ruefully, carefully tucking away her last load of grain and preparing to make her way back to the small cluster of buildings near the homeward path.

After helping herself to a long draught of water at the well, she carefully folded heaping piles of collected grain into her mantle and settled herself upon one of the ancient rock walls, her blistered feet dangling just above the ground. Adara had promised to meet her at the well at the day's end, and both she and her husband would escort a very tired Ruth home.

"I daresay if all workers shared your diligence, my daughter, this entire field would be harvested in but a day's time."

Blushing slightly at the subtle praise, Ruth turned to meet Boaz's serious gaze and aptly helped herself down from her perch. "Your workers appear very diligent indeed," she quickly amended, lowering her eyes to study her own two feet. Severe blisters were already forming where the harsh leather sandal straps had rubbed against her tender flesh. *This man has quite a habit of appearing out of nowhere... when least expected,* she thought deplorably. And she wasn't entirely sure what to do with herself. After all, how was a lowly widow woman such as herself – and a foreigner, at that! – supposed to relate to an important landowner such as Boaz?

Boaz did not even seem aware of the glaring difference in their social statuses. He regarded her with the same respect that she suspected he offered up to the esteemed elders at the city gates. It was refreshing, but also unnerving. She could never imagine being addressed with such kindness and sincerity by anyone of his status in her homeland, yet she suspected that Boaz might very well be an exception to the rule here in Israel as well – especially after the unfriendly reception she and Naomi had received upon their arrival that first night.

I had dreamt that living among God's chosen people would be much like heaven upon earth, Ruth thought quietly, even as she struggled to think of something useful to say to the impressive man standing before her. *But I suppose Israel is no different than anywhere else. There are those who love the Lord and desire to do what is right, as well as those who have closed their minds and hearts to His gentle instruction.*

Her tumbling thoughts were interrupted by yet another thoughtful remark from Boaz. "The Lord was surely with you and your mother-in-law as you journeyed here. My father spoke none too fondly of such travel through the barren wastelands – both unforgiving and treacherous are the paths."

Ruth's brows lifted in surprise. Irrepressible questions rose up in her throat, but she forced herself to remain silent. What had this man's father known of harsh wilderness travel? Had he not been born in the Promised Land? Perhaps he had been a merchant or a caravan guide like the ones she had grown to admire and respect on her own journey. But no – most likely Boaz's father had also been a man of the fields. According to Naomi, the Israelites were extremely rigid about keeping land within the family. In fact, the Lord had even given directives to Moses about such things. Biting her lip, she resolved not to allow such questions to come tumbling out. She had no desire to offend the man whom had so readily come to her aid.

"Ruth! It is so good to see you!" Ruth was relieved to see Adara hurrying along the path, her eyes aglow and her cheeks ruddy from her walk in the fresh evening breeze.

Adara's arrival meant the closing of this disconcerting, nearly one-sided conversation. Not that Ruth didn't enjoy conversing with Boaz – surprisingly, she had found herself scanning the fields in hopes of sighting him several times throughout the day – but now she struggled to find just the right words to say, and it left her feeling sorely inadequate.

"It is good to see you as well, Adara," Ruth responded warmly.

"Naomi has worked wonders with your new home," Adara informed her with a twinkle in her shining eyes. "She has scrubbed every surface and gathered water from the well. She has a lovely row of fresh loaves cooling on the windowsill, and she has found a becoming place for each item brought from your homeland!"

An entire row of fresh loaves? Ruth had no doubt that

Adara had donated the ingredients, and she prayed that the generous woman would not suffer for the loss. She resolved right then and there to offer a portion of the grain she had already gathered to replace the ingredients Adara had so willingly sacrificed.

"I see you have met Master Boaz," Adara rushed on enthusiastically. "Have you decided to remain here in his field?"

Ruth avoided Boaz's steady gaze, fully aware of the fact that his eyes were upon her. She nodded decidedly. "I have. He has been very kind to me."

"Kemuel knew he would be," Adara replied surely, offering her husband's employer a grateful smile. "God has been so good to us, Ruth. Forgive me for speaking so bluntly, but I feel that God has brought us all together for a purpose. Perhaps to strengthen and encourage one another."

Boaz nodded grimly. "I couldn't agree with you more."

"Nor could I," Kemuel added as he joined the group and placed a strong arm about his pretty wife. He turned to Boaz. "Tomorrow then, brother?"

"Tomorrow, God willing."

"I look forward to it."

Secretly, Ruth wondered how *anyone* could possibly look forward to another day of such backbreaking labor.

Adara turned questioning eyes toward her new friend. "Do you plan to gather grain behind the reapers tomorrow as well, Ruth?"

Ruth glanced about the group and stuttered slightly. She hadn't expected the direct question, nor thought much about it. Regardless of how hard and unyielding her makeshift straw pallet might be, all she could think about at the moment was settling down and drifting off to sleep. She desired nothing more than to be lost in a delicious state of nothingness. She realized that those gathered around her were waiting for her to answer the question. She flushed slightly and quickly attempted to steady her voice when she realized that Boaz's eyes were riveted on her. "Um, I had not yet considered the possibility, but..." *Oh dear.* As much as her entire body ached and yearned for a day's rest, she knew that she must gather enough grain during harvest in order to store enough food to get through the hot, dry summer. She forced a smile. "But, yes. Yes, I shall work tomorrow as well." Somehow, she found the courage to meet Boaz's intense gaze. "And I am exceedingly grateful for the opportunity to work in these fields, sir."

"You will always be welcome here, Ruth."

Something in his gaze caused Ruth's cheeks to grow warm. She lowered her eyes, but not quickly enough to miss the look of surprise and recognition that flashed across Adara's soft features. Clearly, Adara had noticed something that Ruth had not.

"The sun is nearly set," Kemuel observed, his eyes slowly scanning the distant horizon. "Let us be on our way."

Boaz gazed at the young Moabitess standing patiently at Adara's side, her features soft in the waning light. He then looked to Kemuel, and some unspoken message passed between them. "You will see her safely home?"

Kemuel nodded, looking quite capable. "I will."

"Blessings to all of you, then," Boaz said. "The Lord be with you."

Kemuel gave one last, firm nod. "And with you as well."

Chapter 23

A SURPRISING DISCOVERY

The evening breezes were fresh, and Ruth enjoyed the walk home despite her sore muscles. It felt good to stroll along the pathway without the constant stooping motion that had been required of her during the many hours of gleaning. She straightened her back and shoulders, wincing slightly at the searing pain that gripped her lower back, and enjoyed this opportunity to stretch her cramped legs.

Adara chattered animatedly as they strolled, aware of Ruth's fatigue and hoping to distract her from her intense weariness if at all possible. Kemuel remained stoic and silent, but the protection he provided proved reassuring.

Naomi was waiting at the door upon their arrival. Her cheeks were aglow with delight. "Oh, my darling! How I've missed you! Kemuel, Adara, thank you for bringing her home to me."

"Is this not what neighbors are for?" Adara asked, giving Naomi's shoulders a squeeze. She turned to Ruth. "I shall see you in the morning, my friend."

"I look forward to it," Ruth replied, fighting her fatigue and forcing a grateful smile.

After friendly goodbyes had been said, Ruth and Naomi retired within their humble abode.

"You have truly turned this little house into a home!" Ruth breathed, taking in the freshly-scrubbed walls and floor. Oil lamps had been lit and distributed about the room, and a vase of spring flowers created an unexpected burst of color from its perch on the windowsill. The smell of freshly baked bread was homey and inviting.

Naomi's eyes were twinkling as she arranged a generous slice of bread with goat cheese and olives on a small tray for Ruth. "I had plenty of help."

Though she felt famished, Ruth's aching body cried out for sleep. She began to spread out the sleeping pallets on the floor, hoping that she could stay awake long enough to swallow the fresh meal that Naomi had prepared for her.

Dropping to her sleeping pallet, Ruth removed her head covering as well as her shawl, setting them aside for the following morning. Her stiff fingers fumbled clumsily with her sandal straps as Naomi brought her the tray of food and seated herself upon the stool a few feet away.

"You poor child!" Naomi shook her head in dismay. "You look exhausted, Ruth! It must have been quite a day!"

"Oh, it was," Ruth responded, enjoying the thick slice of bread smeared generously with goat cheese.

"Once you have finished your meal, I would like to hear all about it!" Naomi declared, her gray eyes as insistent as a child's. "That is, if you feel up to it, my dear."

Ruth had nearly finished her meal before she remembered something. Reaching for her mantle, she carefully unfolded it to reveal the leftover parched grain she had tucked away from her afternoon meal. She had carefully set some aside for Naomi, little knowing that Adara had already helped the woman with the baking and even offered up some fresh vegetables from her own garden.

Naomi was too involved in conversation to notice the parched grain. "What a day, Ruth! So many blessings packed into such a short amount of time! With the grain you shall be gathering, I will be able to bake bread, and Adara has already given me a wonderful variety of seeds so that we may plant a garden! We will need a bit more furniture, of course, but that is not an urgent need and I have no doubt that the Lord will provide a way for such things when the time is right..."

"I have no doubt about that," Ruth replied, setting aside the empty tray and smiling at Naomi's enthusiasm.

Naomi noticed the empty tray and carried it to the small row of shelves where their utensils were now kept. Ruth noticed that Naomi had unloaded most of their possessions from the wagon, making the place feel even more like home.

"I also drew water from the well – which is thankfully a very short distance from here! And I found a suitable place for most of our belongings. Dag enjoys the fresh water as well as the company of the other beasts in the corral. I believe we have found a fine place to call home, Ruth."

"I believe you are right, Naomi."

Naomi's eyes lit with anticipation. "Oh – and I couldn't wait to tell you, Ruth – I made yet another friend today. I met the most wonderful woman!"

"And I met the most wonderful man!"

There was an awkward pause as Naomi froze, obviously considering the gravity behind the first real words Ruth had spoken since arriving home. She arched a brow, both playful and questioning. "*Did* you, now?"

Recognizing how such a statement must have sounded

to her astute mother-in-law, Ruth blushed, her cheeks a flaming scarlet. "Oh, Naomi, it's not like that!"

"Oh?" Naomi seated herself once more upon the stool, her eyes round with curiosity. She did not sound convinced.

"Truly, Naomi, it's nothing – nothing! Why, he must be at least fifteen years my senior – maybe more."

"Hmm. A mysterious older man, is it?"

"Oh, Naomi!"

"What is he like?"

Ruth wanted to bury her face in her shawl to hide her mortification. She had no interest or desire to seek after male company. She had made herself look foolish to Naomi. Oh, why had she not guarded her tongue more carefully?

"Well, are you going to keep an old woman waiting?" Ruth saw the twinkle in Naomi's eye and relaxed slightly. At least the good woman realized that her comment had been a careless blunder and did not feel disrespected by Ruth's mention of another man so soon after Mahlon's departure.

"He is the owner of the field. He was very kind. I was so fearful, Naomi. I did not know how I would be received, but he is a godly man and he accepted me right away. He even asked me to join the workers for the midday meal, and I set aside a portion for you." At this, Ruth offered up the mantle filled with leftovers, and Naomi looked surprised.

"That's quite a bit of food, my dear! He didn't mind?"

"Not at all. In fact, he encouraged me to take more."

"Goodness! He *does* sound kind."

Ruth felt warmed by the memory. "He is. And just look at all the grain we have acquired after only one day's work!" She swept her arm in the direction of a large sack she had propped up by the doorway. It bulged from all sides with excess grain.

"Heavens, child! All that in one day? How hard you must have worked!"

"It was indeed hard work," Ruth admitted, wincing as she attempted to settle herself down on the sleeping pallet. How sore she felt! "But I believe it was the Lord looking out for us, rather than anything I might have done. The owner of the field seems to care very much for the poor and the unfortunate. I was stunned by the amount of grain his workers were required to leave behind."

"Required? Surely he does not require the workers to leave a surplus amount for the many poor – "

"Oh, but he does! Kemuel explained to Adara and me that he feels burdened to provide for those in need, and that his workers are instructed to leave behind a fair amount for those gleaning behind the reapers."

"Bless him!" Naomi cried compulsively, shaking her head in disbelief. "You were not misguided in your claim – he is a wonderful man! The Lord bless him!"

Ruth smiled, her face serene. "I pray that He does."

"And does this wonderful man have a name?"

"Boaz. His name is Boaz."

Naomi's face went white as her hand flew to her mouth.

Startled, Ruth shot up from her sleeping pallet and knelt before her aging mother-in-law. "Naomi? Are you all right? What has happened?"

The older woman trembled, and, lowering her eyes, she shook her head back and forth in utter disbelief. "Surely my ears deceive me," she managed, her voice nothing but a whisper. "But I was certain you said that his name was Boaz."

Ruth bit her lip, fearful of confessing to Naomi that she had indeed heard correctly. She had no desire to invoke another response like the one she had just received. Still kneeling before the startled woman, Ruth took Naomi's hands in her own and said very carefully, "But his name *is* Boaz, Naomi. Your ears have not deceived you. He owns the field in which I gleaned."

When Naomi lifted her face, tears rolled down both cheeks. "It couldn't be so! It just couldn't be so..." she gasped, appearing to be in some state of shock or stupor.

Ruth wondered if she should call for Adara. Was Naomi having an anxiety attack or a nervous breakdown? She could not be sure, but she felt extremely concerned at this unexpected turn of events. "Naomi..." she ventured, fighting for control. "I do not understand. Is something wrong? Do you know the man?"

"Do I? *Do I*?" Naomi repeated, her voice rising in pitch. Unexpectedly, she thrust herself to her feet, drawing Ruth up with her. "Blessed be the Lord, the God of my ancestors! He has not forsaken his kindness to us, my daughter! His mercies never fail! How good He has been!" Overcome, she buried her face in Ruth's shoulder and relieved herself of her tears.

Ruth had no idea what was happening, but she remained still, stroking Naomi's quivering back and waiting for the woman to regain her composure.

When Naomi finally pulled away, her eyes were puffy and red, but her face was radiant with joy. "Ruth," she managed, her voice hoarse. "Just when I thought the Lord's tender blessings could not be any greater..." she had to pause for a moment, but she quickly recovered and continued. "That man... he is a close relative of ours – of mine. Rather, he is a close relative of my husband's."

Ruth searched Naomi's eyes, stunned. Boaz – a close relative of Naomi's? She could scarcely believe her ears! She wondered if Boaz knew who she really was. But he couldn't possibly – she had simply given him her own name, and a foreign name at that. Naturally, he would suspect that she had traveled with a companion from the same land.

"Ruth."

Ruth was instantly drawn from her reverie by the urgency in Naomi's tone. The gray eyes held the same message of urgency and importance as she reached for Ruth's shoulders and held her at arms' length.

"Ruth, I want you to listen to me. Stay in Boaz's field. Do not go seeking after another place to glean, do you understand?"

Ruth nodded slowly, confused. Why should she seek the field of any other man, when Boaz had already been so kind to her? "He has already asked as much," she explained, her dark eyes betraying her curiosity.

Naomi drew in a sharp breath, apparently pleased. "He has? Good! Remain with him, my daughter. He is a good man – a godly man. Even before Elimelech and I left for Moab, Boaz's love for the Lord was evident, even as a very young man."

Ruth wondered why so many questions lobbied for her attention. Naomi had known Boaz? What had he been like as a young man? How old was he *really*? Reluctantly, she pushed such questions aside. After all, such things were none of her business, and she really had no idea why she cared. *Perhaps simply because he has demonstrated such kindness...*

"It has been many years since last I thought of Boaz," Naomi mused, her eyes distant with far-off memories of another time, another life. "Ah, but he was so good. So many ladies vying for his attention, his affection. A good-looking man he was, and I warrant he still is. "

If Naomi intended this last statement as a question, Ruth

didn't dare answer. Yet mentally she recalled the intense eyes the color of bronze, the strong, firm jawline, the becalming aura that seemed to emanate from his sturdy frame. Flushed, Ruth hoped Naomi's searching eyes would somehow overlook the fact that she had indeed caught the question.

Naomi smiled. "Oh, but Boaz always had an astounding sense of discernment. He knew those Bethlehem women saw but a tall, handsome stranger – not to mention the great wealth he was quickly accumulating. He had barely reached the marrying age when Elimelech and I set out for your country, Ruth, but when we left Judah he was still unwed. I wonder if that remains the case..."

Again, Naomi's musings were beginning to sound strangely pointed, a little bit too curious... Ruth felt uneasy and sidestepped the question in what she hoped to be a skillful manner. "I am very thankful that the Lord has brought us directly to his field, Naomi. It must be so good to learn of a relative so close by. I'm sure he would be delighted to see you again, after all these years – "

Naomi laughed. "Heavens, child! I doubt he would even remember me. He knew well my husband, Elimelech, but I had little to do with him – other than to admire his obvious love for the Lord from a distance."

Ruth nodded, relieved that the conversation seemed to be taking a different turn.

"Yes, my dear, the Lord has indeed been good to us. Better than this old woman could ever deserve! Continue your work with Boaz, my daughter, and trust me when I say this – the Lord is surely at work in this, Ruth. He has a very special plan for you, my daughter. This I know." She chuckled, her eyes aglow yet vague, as though gazing directly into the future and rejoicing over the obvious blessings in store.

Ruth was puzzled. Something about Naomi's look – her tone – unsettled Ruth. She was fully aware of the fact that Naomi understood something that she clearly did not – and the older woman was glorying in whatever it was.

Ruth was reminded of a very similar expression worn by Adara earlier that evening – before they had begun their lengthy trek home from the fields.

What was it about this strange yet wonderful new land that so thoroughly perplexed and intrigued her? These customs she had read about for years in the sacred texts with Naomi... yet reading about them and living them were two different things entirely.

And now, as Naomi's aging face had transformed before her very eyes at the prospect of something marvelous – something that Ruth did not know or understand, something that even young Adara had clearly understood even before Naomi had – Ruth found herself both invigorated and overwhelmed. She longed to ask Naomi directly what she meant, and yet she held back. A soft voice within her stirred, reminding her that everything was in the Lord's hands. The timing was not right.

But when the time was right, she would surely know. As well as understand.

Despite the mysterious questions that lingered heavily in the air, fatigue washed heavily over Ruth's entire being like a lead blanket, and she realized that her body was in desperate need of reprieve. Especially if she was going to start the same wearying process all over again before sunup... The thought was overwhelming.

Naomi appeared to notice Ruth's exhaustion and her motherly instincts kicked in. "My goodness, look at me! Keeping you up at this late hour after the long day you've had – giggling and carrying on like a little girl! And at my age! To bed with you now! I fear you have another long day ahead of you, child."

Ruth did not argue. And she didn't mind that Naomi fussed over her as she collapsed upon the straw pallet. The work-worn hands gently tucked a woolen blanket about Ruth's shoulders before she hurried to extinguish the majority of the oil lamps burning brightly about the cozy room.

As she stretched out her legs and attempted to ignore the screaming pain cramping her back, Ruth wondered if she would have the strength to continue on this way for... well, she had no idea how long. Perhaps forever.

Yet somehow, the future didn't seem quite as daunting as she remembered Boaz's quiet strength, the genuine concern for her that she had sensed in his eyes, the way his smile had reached across those endless, rolling waves of grain and gripped her very heart.

Silently, she lifted the man up in prayer to the Lord, asking God to grant him a special blessing for his kindness and generosity.

He is a good man, Ruth sighed contentedly.

And that was her very last thought before desperate sleep claimed her entire being.

Chapter 24

PROMISING DAYS

"Master Boaz! I feared the servants and I would have to consume your evening meal before it molded from age!"

Boaz realized that he was standing in the kitchen, and Ada remained planted behind the massive stone counter, watching him with great amusement. He had been so lost in thought that he had hardly noticed where his heavy steps had carried him. "I do apologize, Ada," Boaz offered, mustering up a pacifying tone. "I was unaware of the late hour."

"And the setting sun and ensuing darkness was not reminder enough?"

Boaz gave Ada a startled second glance. A mischievous smile split her rosy face in the most pleasant way, and he realized that she was once again teasing him.

"We had a new gleaner working the fields today. I simply felt responsible to see that she was escorted safely home."

Ada raised a brow with one smooth, fluid motion, her eyes wide with interest. "*She*?"

Boaz caught the hidden connotation right away, but he

refused to take the bait. "Kemuel and Adara took her home. I'm sure Adara will tell you all about it during your next visit."

"On the contrary, I already know all about it." Ada tossed her head with an air of superiority that greatly amused Boaz. A thousand questions chased through his logical mind, but he had no intention of satisfying the smug housekeeper by demanding answers.

"Well, then, I suppose that spares me from having to recount the entire story all over again," he stated matter-of-factly, a slight gleam of mischief in his own eyes. He pulled himself up to the large table meant for the servants and helped himself to the roast lamb seasoned with fresh mint, onion, and thyme. Several large slabs of bread were piled near the savory meat, and fresh vegetables had been roasted along with the lamb, releasing a tantalizing aroma.

"I met the young woman's mother-in-law today," Ada stated abruptly, attempting to appear casual as she filled Boaz's mug with fresh goat's milk and set it before him. "Her name is Naomi."

Naomi... the name sounded vaguely familiar, as if triggering some distant memory that he had long since forgotten. But, no. It was a common enough name among Hebrew women. Surely his mind was playing tricks on him.

"She was a very pleasant person," Ada continued. "But, my! She has been through so much. That poor woman lost her husband and both her sons – one of them being the young woman's former husband. And yet she still finds reason to smile, to rejoice. She is truly an inspiration."

"She must be deeply rooted in her faith. I pray that the Lord will bless her," Boaz responded around a large bite of lamb. He hadn't realized how famished he was until he had begun eating.

"And the woman's daughter-in-law – Ruth, is it? – I imagine she is quite something as well?"

Boaz glanced up around yet another bite of lamb, suspicious. What exactly was Ada hinting at with those conniving eyes of hers? "I imagine so," he responded, supplying her with what he hoped to be a safe answer. "She seems determined, strong. She appears to have great strength of character as well as a quiet spirit. A rare combination among today's women, to be sure."

Ada did not miss the admiration that had unknowingly colored his response. She grinned, satisfied. "It is said that she left everything to support her mother-in-law. Such loyalty is a novelty these days."

"That it is."

"Adara says that she is very kind. And very beautiful."

Boaz kept his eyes glued to his meal, attempting to appear indifferent. Especially towards the latter statement. "Oh?"

"Are her assessments true?"

Boaz felt his jaw tighten, and he realized that he was adjusting himself uncomfortably in his chair. He did not appreciate being interrogated over dinner.

Ada smiled triumphantly. "*That* beautiful, is she? I daresay the lovely young maiden has rendered you speechless!"

Boaz felt indignation rising within his throat. He knew that his relationship with Ada was quite different from the relationship between most servants and masters – theirs was much more like that between a mother and son – and yet for the first time in his life, he was tempted to brusquely inform her that she was overstepping her bounds.

Ada must have sensed his mounting irritation – a sensation quite foreign to her disciplined employer – for she relaxed her grip on her serving utensil and laid a gentle hand upon Boaz's strong forearm. "Enough nonsense. Forgive me, Master Boaz. I am thrilled that you may count this diligent young woman among your workers now. And the Lord has surely blessed her by guiding her to your fields. You honor our Lord through your kindness and generosity to the many poor."

Running a hand through his hair – which was still quite abundant, unlike that of other men in their early forties – Boaz rose to his feet, drained the remaining goat's milk, and pushed the mug away from him. He forced a smile. "Thank you for the meal, Ada. As always, it was delicious and very satisfying."

Ada acknowledged his praise with a warm nod. "I am glad to hear it."

"I am feeling especially weary tonight. I believe I shall retire."

Ada watched as her stoic master disappeared beyond the massive, arched entryway. She had no doubt that he sought refuge in his lush garden courtyard before choosing to retire for the night.

And even as he disappeared among the many shadows, her heart leaped with joy. She had never seen staunch Boaz so flustered, so easily provoked. His short, uncertain replies as well as his not-so-subtle avoidance tactics were proof enough to grant her heart an eagle's wings, because her motherly prayers for her dear, former mistress's son were being answered... before her very eyes.

Boaz did indeed seek refuge among his luxuriant courtyard haven, his mind feeling uncharacteristically muddled and his body aching with unusual fatigue. Kneeling before the tall fountain, its gentle spray gleaming and golden in the light of many lamps, he spoke to his Creator in scattered, broken sentences. He found that he could not keep his mind on his prayers. And he felt that he was not sharing the events of the day in their entirety as he so often did at the end of each day.

Even as he knelt in prayer, Boaz felt a stab of guilt. He feared that he was not being entirely honest – not in his prayers, not with Ada... not even with himself.

Sighing, he reverted to silence, leaning his head on the cool marble surface of the bench before him. He listened... to the gentle patter of the fountain's spray, to the palm branches swaying softly in the whispering evening breeze, to the serene, contented call of a night bird.

And, in that moment, he was reminded of the promise he had been given many, many days before.

Soon.

He pondered the meaning of that one, simple word, wondering at the depth and the magnitude of what it might possibly imply.

Oh, Lord, why is my soul troubled? Why do I feel so disturbed? Even as he asked the question of the One who created him, he knew. Yes, he was unwilling to admit the truth even to himself, but he knew.

He just couldn't get that beautiful young woman off his mind.

Ruth rose before the sun, awakened by the shrill cry of a neighbor's confident rooster. Though the grating screeches had awakened her with a start, she was grateful that the bird had not allowed her to oversleep.

Ruth winced in pain as she pulled herself wearily up from her pallet, every muscle screaming in protest. She feared that her morning prayers were a bit redundant, as her mind was not fully awake and she found her thoughts to be constantly wandering.

Lord God, I pray that You grant me strength to work another day... she repeated over and over as she slipped into her sandals and adjusted her shawl. She chose to believe that her body would eventually adapt to the strenuous labor required of the field workers and gleaners.

Naomi rose moments after Ruth and fluttered about their small home like a zealous little sparrow, fussing over Ruth and humming as she prepared to begin her daily chores.

Ruth thanked the Lord for His goodness. The wounds in Naomi's soul were healing far more quickly than Ruth had ever dared to hope or expect.

"How did you sleep, my dear?"

"Better than I ever have," Ruth responded ruefully. "Heaven knows I needed it!"

"I can imagine!"

"Naomi, I realized that I did not get to hear about the wonderful woman you met yesterday."

"Oh, yes, yes. I suppose I became distracted with your own tale, my child."

"What happened?"

"Adara introduced us. Her name is Ada, and she is about the same age as I am, I suspect. A spritely, pleasant, rosy-cheeked woman she is! I was delighted to meet her. And she is quite eager to meet you as well, Ruth."

"You may tell her that I share the same sentiment."

"Hopefully you will have the opportunity to meet her soon. I know you will love her, Ruth."

"Is she a relative of Adara or Kemuel?"

"No, no. She is a housekeeper, and a good friend of Adara's. I believe she works for Kemuel's – my word!"

Ruth glanced up in surprise. "Is everything all right?"

"My word!" Naomi repeated, shaking her head in disbelief. "She must work for Boaz!"

"Oh? Why do you think so?"

"Because Adara explained that the woman worked for her husband's employer – as a housekeeper."

"A housekeeper?"

"Yes. So the man must have never married," Naomi mused as she offered Ruth a handful of dried dates from their meager store of food.

Ruth felt strangely relieved. "But what makes you say that?"

"I know Boaz. He would never marry a woman who refused to keep house. He was – is – very traditional. You know, he stands for the old values, old ways, old traditions... He would want to find himself a woman who delighted in her role as a mother and a wife – a keeper of the home."

Ruth nodded and turned her attention back to her breakfast, unsure about what to say next. She had barely drained the mug of fresh well water Naomi had provided when there was a gentle rap at the door.

Naomi was quick to answer. Adara stood smiling at the door, her tall husband standing alongside her.

"Adara! Good morning, dear! And Kemuel – so good to see you, as well!"

"Good morning, Naomi!" Adara's voice was musical – even in the wee morning hours. "And Ruth! How good to see you!"

Ruth greeted the cheerful young woman with a warm embrace. "It is wonderful to see you as well, friend!"

The two women started off, with Kemuel trailing a short distance behind, his eyes always watchful.

"I hope this morning finds you well?" Adara's luminous brown eyes were thoughtful, inquisitive.

Ruth managed a smile. "I am a little sore, perhaps, but overwhelmed with gratitude."

"The Lord be praised! I admire your attitude and your strength, Ruth."

Ruth was surprised. "Why, I have thought the very same about *you*, Adara!"

"It must be a great relief to you – knowing that tomorrow is the Sabbath."

Ruth could have shed tears of joy at that welcome realization. Today was Friday – tomorrow would indeed be the Sabbath Day, the seventh day of the week, the blessed day of rest sanctified by the Lord God Himself. There would be no gleaning out in the fields on the Sabbath Day – only sweet, life-giving rest, as well as time spent poring over the Scriptures and basking in the glory of the Lord.

Ruth's smile was genuine this time. "That is a blessing, indeed."

"What does the Sabbath Day look like for you and Naomi?"

Ruth felt warmed by the many sweet Sabbath memories she had shared with her dear mother-in-law. "Well, there is always rest. We do no work on that day."

"Today is Friday – preparation day," Adara mused, her eyes distant. "With such a small family, however – just Kemuel and myself – there is not nearly the amount of work to do compared to that which was required in my mother's household."

Ruth nodded her understanding. "Naomi will surely be busy making such preparations today."

"And I will see to it that she receives all the help she needs!"

"Thank you, Adara. Truly. I only wish I could be there to help her."

"But you *are* helping her – more than you ever could by remaining at home! What would she ever do without you to supply the daily bread?"

"I suppose you are right," Ruth agreed reluctantly.

"Of course I am!"

The walk down the well-trodden path was especially pleasant as the early morning breezes gently caressed their faces and whispered its way through the low, shrubby trees alongside the path. Ruth gazed in awe at the richly-colored sky as the sun made its grand appearance and bathed the gently rolling hills in breath-taking, glorious light.

"In your country – Moab, is it? – were the sunrises so brilliant as this?"

Ruth considered the question carefully before responding. "They were lovely, but nothing like this."

"Do you miss your home?"

This time, Ruth did not have to consider a thing. "Not a bit," she replied with a ready smile.

"No?"

"It was a godless place – brimming with every kind of wickedness imaginable. The pagan customs and rituals, the wicked neighbors... evil abounded at every turn. I never belonged. Traveling to Judah with Naomi has been the greatest blessing the Lord has bestowed upon me."

Adara smiled softly. "I believe it has turned out to be a great blessing to me as well. I value your companionship greatly, as well as Naomi's."

"And I value yours as well."

Adara paused, and Kemuel nearly bumped into her. "Is something the matter?" Concern creased his brow.

"Oh no, not at all!" Adara reassured him. "It's just that... I was just wondering... Ruth, would you and Naomi like to join Kemuel and me for the Sabbath meal tomorrow evening?"

Ruth had to swallow the lump forming in her throat. She managed a weak smile. "Thank you, Adara. We would be honored."

As they crested the hill, Ruth was again overwhelmed by the beauty and the bounty of the plentiful harvest below, the gently rippling sea of grain swaying majestically in the cool morning breezes.

Today is a day full of promise, Ruth decided as they drew nearer to the fields.

"Kemuel, the Lord be with you! Adara and Ruth, good morning to you both, and God bless!"

The hearty voice could belong to only one man.

"Master Boaz, the Lord bless you, sir!" Kemuel responded first, and Adara modestly echoed her husband's greeting.

Ruth turned eager eyes toward Boaz, but just as quickly lowered them when she realized that his gaze rested squarely upon her. "Good morning, sir," she repeated softly. "The Lord bless you."

Boaz's voice was surprisingly gentle. "And may the Lord bless you as well, my daughter."

Ruth noticed Adara exchange a knowing look with her husband, who appeared rather surprised. This time, Ruth didn't mind.

Yes, she decided firmly. *This day does indeed hold much promise.*

Chapter 25

A DISTURBING VISIT

The following weeks were joyous and filled with every imaginable delight. Ruth and Naomi settled into their new home with an exuberance and a zeal that was pleasant to behold. There was an abundance of grain to be gathered in Boaz's field, and a healthy friendship was blossoming between Naomi and Ada, as well as with Ruth and Adara.

Ruth spent most days gleaning in the fields, and she found that she had never slept so well in all her life. As she had hoped, her body had gradually adapted to the back-breaking labor required of all the field workers, though it was still very hard work. She wasn't sure if she would ever get used to the sweat that caused her heavy garments to cling to her body like a second soggy skin. Regardless of the undesirable aspects of field work, a day never passed that she did not thank her God for His goodness and His provision.

Though the relationships between Naomi, Ruth, Adara, Kemuel, Ada, and Boaz had flourished like the abundant harvest, it was obvious to Ruth that she had not been accepted by the rest of the village. The few times she had accompanied Naomi and Adara to the well, the townswomen had cast venomous glares in their direction and resorted to all manners of vicious behavior. They had snickered and whispered among themselves, appearing much like a small band of vultures waiting to pounce upon their hapless prey.

Ruth experienced a similar reception among the female gleaners of Boaz's field. Though they were clearly afraid to incite a riot against the pretty, young foreigner in the presence of their wealthy benefactor, they avoided her at all costs.

Ruth had found herself marveling at the malice of a people who claimed to be the chosen few. She wondered if they had ever stopped to consider how their spiteful behavior reflected upon the God that they served. At first, she had nearly succumbed to discouragement. She had expected something wholly different – a land brimming with righteous inhabitants, jubilant and full of praise for the propitious God they served. Yet, upon reaching the Promised Land, she had found something entirely different.

"You cannot allow them to beat you down so, my daughter," Naomi had gently admonished as Ruth had wearily returned home one evening.

"But these Israelites – they are so critical, so unaccepting. Will they ever see beyond my heritage and accept a willing and contrite heart?"

Naomi had simply smiled, her eyes distant. "Ah, if only God's children possessed an ounce of the wisdom of the Father. I fear, child, that even His own here in Judah forget that their own hearts were once wayward and distant – yet the Father called them home, accepted them as they were, and led them by the hand to become children more like Him."

"Will they ever accept me as one of their own?"

Naomi had spoken bluntly. "Perhaps, perhaps not. It does not matter."

Ruth had not looked convinced.

"You have the acceptance of the only One that truly matters, child – the Lord God Almighty. He will never leave you nor forsake you. You may rest assured in that promise."

Ruth had nodded her understanding. "You speak truth, Naomi."

"And you must remember that you are called to live a life set apart – of holiness and righteousness, regardless of what others may do. Each of us will have to answer for our own actions."

Ruth had taken to heart the gentle yet direct advice of her mother-in-law, and she found that the unwelcome stares and haughty chuckles did not disturb her nearly as much. She had learned to concentrate her efforts on doing the best that she could. She had also learned to thank the Lord daily for the precious individuals that He had seen fit to place in her life – people like Adara, her husband Kemuel, the plucky Ada and her master, Boaz – a man of uncommon quietness and strength. She appreciated all of them so much.

Arranging her shawl carefully about her head and shoulders in her typical modest fashion, Ruth drew up a carefully woven basket and prepared to make the short walk to Adara's house a few doors down. The two women had developed the pleasant habit of venturing to market together each week. It made the necessary duty so much more enjoyable, and Adara's husband approved as long as the women returned home before the daylight threatened to wane.

Ruth had been quick to catch on to the disdainful glances cast their way as they journeyed to the marketplace each week, and she feared that her presence might mar Adara's reputation. She had shared this concern with her cheerful companion on more than one occasion, but Adara had brushed it off nonchalantly each time. "Nonsense," she had declared with conviction. "I haven't any reputation to lose!"

Each time, Ruth had wondered what Adara could have possibly meant by that statement. After all, the woman was beautiful, vivacious, full of life, and brimming with kindness and gentle hospitality. Yet, with each trip that they took to market, it became more and more evident that the malice was aimed not only at Ruth, but at Adara as well. *Perhaps the other women are simply envious*, Ruth had thought, attempting to set aside her concerns. After all, these Israelite women did not seem to need a good excuse to dislike another.

Adara was emerging from her own doorway as Ruth drew near. The young woman was all smiles, her own basket resting easily upon her arm. "Ruth! Good morning, friend. How does this pleasant day find you?"

"I am doing well, and every bit as blessed as always," Ruth readily responded. "Shall we?"

"Of course!" The two women set off at a brisk pace, chattering happily as they went. Though warm, the day was still pleasant, and billowing clouds moseyed their way across a surprisingly blue sky.

Tal, the friendly yellow dog, continued to bark his welcome even as his lovely mistress disappeared over the crest toward market.

"I believe Tal is asking to go with us," Ruth laughed as the faithful mutt's barks slowly began to subside.

Adara laughed good-naturedly. "He would follow us all over town if we allowed him!"

Ruth smiled. "I would enjoy his company. Do you suppose he has any brothers or sisters nearby that would like to come live with Naomi and me?"

"When we found him, he was but a little, lost puppy," Adara mused, her eyes lighting with the tender memory. "Kemuel scooped him up and we have claimed him ever since. He has been a good companion, as well as an excellent guard when Kemuel is away from home."

Ruth nodded her understanding. "I imagine so."

Abruptly and completely unexpectedly, a small stone whistled through the air, striking Ruth squarely on the cheekbone. She let out a helpless cry, and instinctively her hand drew up to touch the tender bruise already forming from the careless missile.

"What on earth?" Adara spun on her heels to see two small boys scurrying to the shelter of the home along the pathway, raucous laughter erupting as they disappeared into their shoddy abode. Her brows drew together fiercely, and for a moment Ruth feared that the spunky young woman would follow right after the boys and drag them out of the safety of their home. She had never seen Adara indignant before.

Ruth quickly grabbed Adara by the arm. "It's alright. They are but children."

"Children deserving of severe punishment!" Adara bit her lip in an attempt to calm herself before another indignant outburst could escape. "Oh, Ruth, I am so sorry. So terribly sorry. Let me see your face."

Embarrassed, Ruth drew her shawl further about her

face and managed a shaky chuckle. "It's fine, really. I will be fine."

"Such rebellion, and so young, too!"

"I'm sure they were simply responding based on things they have heard their parents say about me," Ruth said quietly, determined not to lose her resolve.

"Well, then, their parents ought to be ashamed," Adara declared decisively, her eyes still flashing. "No matter," she managed after she had regained her composure. "The Lord will be their judge."

The women continued on with their walk and attempted to carry on with cheerful conversation as before, but the situation never fully righted itself.

As the bustling stalls at the city gates loomed into view, Adara said quietly, "Don't think too much of it, Ruth." Obviously, her mind was still on the disturbing episode as well. "As you said, they are only children. However, if any child of mine were to behave in such a way – " Her voice trailed off sharply, and in that moment the fire went out of Adara's eyes. Sadness filled her expression, but only for a moment. She swallowed hard, and a moment later she was her normal self again.

Ruth wondered what it was about. Still, she did not ask.

Despite Ruth's crowded thoughts, Adara seemed to read her mind. "You have never asked me."

Ruth's heart skipped a beat. "Pardon?"

"You have never asked why they shun me, too."

Ruth swallowed hard. She did not wish to intrude upon her friend's privacy. "I suppose because it is none of my business."

"Ruth, we are truly sisters – in the Lord. You can ask me anything you wish."

Ruth nodded, but still she did not ask.

Adara sighed, but there was no longer any sorrow within her countenance. "The women believe that I am a great sinner."

Ruth's brows shot up in surprise. "*You*?" she gasped, incredulous.

Adara laughed, tickled by her response. "I no longer say I *cannot* have children – because nothing is impossible with the God that we serve. *If* – and *when* – the time is right, then He can enable me to have a child, perhaps *many* children– if it pleases Him. But the women say that I am barren, and they see it as a great curse. They believe that some secret sin prevents me from experiencing the joy of children."

Ruth bit her lip in dismay, chagrined. What a stubborn, stiff-necked people these Israelites had proven to be! How did the Lord ever put up with them for so long?

"It used to tear me apart," Adara plunged ahead, as if attempting to get the conversation over with as quickly as possible. "But the Lord has brought me peace. Instead of dwelling on the one thing that I do *not* have – children – I have learned to glory in the countless blessings that I *do* have... and Ruth, I count our friendship as one of my greatest blessings."

Ruth was stunned to silence. She had never dreamed that Adara battled against such discouraging odds. She was both amazed and strengthened. And she felt a kinship, a comradeship, with this young woman even stronger than before. Though born in different lands, of a different heritage, of different backgrounds and different circumstances, the Lord had brought them together as dear friends. And despite those many differences, they had more in common than Ruth could have possibly imagined.

"I hate the way they snub you, Ruth," Adara continued. "But I still know that God brought you here for a reason.

And I thank Him for bringing you into my life. You are the only one on earth who can truly know what it's like – what I have endured from my own people."

Ruth held her tears in check, though they threatened to come anyway. She managed to clear her throat and give Adara's arm a loving squeeze. "As you said – we are sisters."

Adara beamed, her huge brown eyes glowing with warmth. "Sisters."

The loud, incoherent babbling of the merchants and market stall holders met their ears as they reached the inner gates of the city, cutting their conversation short.

Weaving their way through the crowded market stalls, the women made careful inspection of each item before tucking it away in their baskets for purchase. As usual, the other shoppers eyed them indifferently, while some eyed them suspiciously. Even the doggedly persistent stall holders left them alone, as if fearful that bartering with such outcasts might render them unclean – even if they were eager for their business.

"What do you think of this one?" Adara held up an unusually large cucumber for Ruth's inspection. "I have never seen one quite like it!"

Ruth smiled, thankful that the afternoon's mood seemed to be lightening up a bit. "It's marvelous!"

Carefully, Adara tucked it away in her basket. "Then we shall share it upon our Sabbath meal at the end of the week! Just imagine how many sandwiches it will make!"

Ruth froze instinctively, disturbingly aware of the fact that she was being watched. She had grown to trust her instincts, and she raised her eyes to see a tall, lanky man standing directly across from the market stall, his glittering black eyes fastened upon her. Even as passers-by weaved in and out around him like a raging human tide, the man remained rooted firmly in place, watching, leering...

In a manner that she hoped to be inconspicuous, Ruth breathed softly, "That man appears to be watching us."

"Who?" Not-so-subtly, Adara jerked her head up to meet the gaze of the intrusive man standing a few measures away from them.

Ruth felt her gut clench. It was now quite plain to the man that they were aware of his obtrusive eyes.

The man did not appear to care. He was a snake of a man, his features taut and viperous. He fastened his eyes upon them and offered a toothy yellow smile. He swayed ever so slightly, leering, his every move slow and reptilian.

Inwardly, Ruth recoiled. "Perhaps we should make our purchases and return home."

Adara met the man's stare head-on, plainly letting him know what she thought of his manners. "Perhaps you are right."

Even as the women pressed silver coins into the eager hands of the shopkeeper and turned toward the beaten path that would carry them home, Ruth sensed those black eyes fastened tightly upon them, boring into them, like a predator ready to pounce.

Chapter 26

THE RIOT

It had been a delightful Sabbath day, full of joyous psalms of praise, savory feasting with friends, delightful conversation, and plenty of much-deserved rest.

As had become their custom, Ruth and Naomi had joined Adara and Kemuel for the Sabbath meal. This time, Boaz and Ada had delightedly agreed to join them.

On Friday, the day of preparation before the Sabbath Day, Boaz always released his workers early from their labor in the fields. This way they could prepare themselves for sweet communion with the Lord and with their families. Ruth and Adara would then meet early in the afternoon to prepare the following day's meal. It was an immensely enjoyable time, as their busy hands worked to peel and pare the vegetables and carefully season and prepare the meat. Even as they worked, they compared stories and laughed together. Both women were eager to contribute towards the meal that would warm and fill their loved ones the following day.

Now, as the seventh day drew to a close and the setting

sun cast a rosy glow through the windows' latticework, the small family of believers remained lounging about the left-over Sabbath spread, the large candles beginning to sputter but never burning out.

Sensing the late hour, Adara rose to light the oil lamps, and Ruth promptly rose to help her with the task, strangely self-conscious. She felt annoyed with herself. *Why do I feel this way – fearful that I blunder with every move that I make?* she thought in frustration. After all, this Sabbath meal was no different than any of the rest. *Excepting the fact that Boaz and Ada have joined us,* she reminded herself, suddenly blushing. *Why, that doesn't make the slightest difference!* They were all friends, fellow believers. *There is no reason on earth to feel self-conscious,* she chided herself.

As she helped Adara light the small lamps, she wondered for the umpteenth time if Boaz had figured out the relation between himself and Naomi's family. Naomi had remained strangely silent about the matter, and counseled Ruth to remain silent as well. *Until the proper time,* the older woman had instructed her. Ruth had come away puzzled. What exactly *was* the proper time? And why did it matter?

"I believe you have both outdone yourselves," Kemuel remarked, leaning back on two elbows and watching his wife with admiring eyes. "That was a remarkable meal."

"I couldn't agree more," Boaz admitted, his eyes seeking out Ruth's.

She caught the esteem reflected in his copper-colored eyes, and, flushing prettily, lowered her gaze.

By now the sun had disappeared behind the western hills, and the stars were beginning to peek out one by one, winking playfully at all the inhabitants below.

Ruth always felt exhilarated as well as disappointed as

the Sabbath Day drew to a close. It was so joyous, so wondrous, so rejuvenating – God's gift to man. Naomi had told her about many devout Israelites who found the Sabbath to be dreary with its requirements, but Ruth could not imagine feeling that way. On the contrary, she wondered how she would ever manage to flounder through the incredibly difficult weeks of heavy manual labor without it.

The tranquil atmosphere as well as her mulling thoughts were interrupted by heavy pounding on the front door.

Instantly, the peace that had enveloped them began to drain away as if sucked into a swirling black whirlpool.

The musky odor of burning torches assaulted their nostrils, and brewing, angry voices could be heard distinctly just beyond the safety of the heavy wooden door.

Ruth felt suddenly paralyzed with fright. What was happening? A fierce stirring within her spirit warned her that something terrible was about to happen.

Boaz and Kemuel, their muscles tense, locked eyes, and another unspoken message passed between the two of them.

Ruth knew that they were communicating in a manner that would not frighten the women. They had each other's backs.

Being the man of the house, Kemuel rose first and, with a steady gait, reached for the door.

Boaz stood as well, remaining firmly planted behind Kemuel – a barrier between the women and whatever threat loomed just beyond that door.

His shoulders thrown back and his every muscle tense, Kemuel flung open the door to face a menacing mob outside. The men were armed with torches and a few even had knives strapped to their belts. Several women had also joined them, shrieking angry threats.

Kemuel's voice was nearly a roar. "What is the meaning of this?"

Ezra, the elder from the city gates, stared icily back at Kemuel, his cold blue eyes like two deep, cruel wells of turbulent water. He appeared to be the leader of the raging mob. "We come bearing witnesses against this mockery which you have called your *marriage*, Kemuel. The time of reckoning has come. You must make your choice."

A gasp of horror escaped from Adara's lips, and Ruth gripped her friend by the shoulders to steady her. An intense surge of righteous anger welled up within her, forcing the fear that had previously claimed her right out the door. She resolved to be here for Adara and for Kemuel, regardless of the outcome. Exchanging a swift look with Ada, she saw that the spunky old housekeeper shared the same resolve. Already she was on her feet, her hands balled into fists and her face flushed crimson with anger. Naomi remained seated where she was, her eyes wide in shock and disbelief.

Kemuel's eyes snapped angrily as he surveyed the riotous mob at his doorstep. "Begone, all of you! I will bear with none of this nonsense in my own home."

"Then step outside, if you will," Ezra's voice was too smooth, too calm. "And we will handle this *nonsense* – as you so call it – outside your little home."

His condescension was maddening. Ruth wondered how either of the men possessed the will to remain in calm possession of themselves.

Kemuel remained firm, unbending. "I will do no such thing."

"Stand aside, Ezra!" The shrill order came from a

woman – that was certain. Ruth watched with apprehension as a short, squatty woman pushed her way to the front of the crowd to stand beside Ezra. The coins of her headdress jingled like a thousand angry bells.

Kemuel appeared to shrink at the sight of the woman. She was middle-aged and heavyset, and the venom in her eyes was enough to paralyze most victims.

Adara stifled a cry with her hand, her eyes filling with tears.

Ruth wondered who this woman could possibly be to have such an effect on both Adara and Kemuel. She looked to Adara questioningly.

A little sob escaped Adara's tight lips. "That's Reba," she whispered shakily. "Kemuel's mother. This is going to hurt him so much."

Repulsed, Ruth caught her own breath in a short gasp. How could it be so? Kemuel was such a remarkable man – surely his mother would not stoop to such hateful measures! She couldn't believe her own eyes or ears. She forced herself to turn her attention back to the matter at hand.

"Now, son, you listen to me!" Reba was saying, her voice strangely high-pitched and burning with intensity. "That woman is no good for you! You know it. *I* know it. The entire village knows it!" Behind her, the mob erupted with angry shouts of agreement.

Kemuel drew himself to his full, intimidating height, his brows knit closely together. "*Enough*," he breathed, his voice low and threatening.

"You have been cursed with childlessness because of her!" Reba screamed, daring to step over Kemuel's threshold. "You are a good man, Kemuel. A good son! You deserve much more than this!"

Kemuel did not flinch. Behind him, Boaz remained

staunchly in place, his eyes afire. "I said *enough*," Kemuel warned.

"Do you even know what the Law says?" Reba pressed on, her voice rising feverishly. "Your testimony against this woman requires but two or three witnesses, Kemuel! Look behind me! You have far exceeded that number! You have an entire mob!"

"Enough!"

Unflinching, Ezra flicked open a weathered scroll and began to read aloud. "*When a man takes a wife and marries her, and it happens that she finds no favor in his eyes because he has found some uncleanness in her, and he writes her a certificate of divorce, puts it in her hand, and sends her out of his house –* "

"I SAID ENOUGH!"

This time, Ezra blinked. Reba took several steps back, stunned by the sheer force of her son's voice. Even the crowd was silenced.

His voice low, measured, and steady, Kemuel met the gaze of the elder head on. "My wife is a noble woman. I make no charge against her. She has done nothing save serve her God as well as love her husband. And should this crowd of *respectable* citizens be too blind to see that, it is to their own folly and their own shame."

At this, Boaz stepped forward, his eyes boring into the icy blue of the elder's. "And as for your two or three witnesses, we have them. Right here. Who will vouch for the character of this woman in question? Who will vouch for Adara?"

"Character?" Reba snorted, clearly enraged. "Just look at the company she keeps!Just look at that woman whom she calls a *friend* – a filthy Moabite seductress – that's what she is! Why, the presence of that pagan woman has rendered the entire house unclean!"

Again, the crowd erupted in feverish agreement. The torches whirred as the men waved them in the air, casting eerie shadows that danced upon the walls.

"Do you not remember what happens when foreigners creep into our midst?" An unidentifiable voice shouted.

"Thousands of innocent men – slain in a single day!"

"She'll do nothing but entice our own to follow after her pagan gods and her wicked ways!"

Ada could take it no longer. Like an angry bull, she pushed herself even with Reba and poked an angry finger in the fleshy woman's face. "Now you listen here, missy. That girl from Moab is a jewel – do you hear me? A *jewel*! And were you to stick your neck out for just a moment other than to make false accusations against the innocent, you would have already observed her pure and chaste conduct! That young woman has given her life to the Lord, and I daresay she is a far more observant God-fearer than *you* might ever hope to be!"

Ezra was clearly taken aback. Reba's face continued to redden like an overly ripe tomato. Clearly, the crowd was beginning to grow uneasy. Restless murmurs of doubt rippled through the sea of humanity like an unsettling wave.

Boaz placed a steadying hand on Reba's shoulder and gently drew her back. When he spoke, all the strength Ruth had grown to admire in him was there. He was in complete control of himself as well as his emotions. "Have you forgotten my own mother?"

Silence swept over the tumultuous crowd. Every man and woman of Bethlehem knew of Boaz – of his character as well as his status among the community. He was a respected man, and any word to proceed forth from his mouth held great weight. "Rahab – once known as the harlot."

Ruth heard herself gasp at the frankness with which

Boaz had spoken. His own mother – a *harlot*? Could it possibly be so?

"She was also foreigner – not from among us – once. But then she encountered the God of our fathers. When the mighty warrior Joshua sent spies among the city of Jericho, my mother Rahab was there to meet them. She hid them from evil men and, in turn, God rescued her when the walls of Jericho came crashing down about her. To hear her speak of such things, the conviction in her voice and in her heart, was truly remarkable. My mother may not have been a descendant of our father Abraham, but she loved the Lord more than any woman I had ever met, and the Lord God blessed her mightily. Have you already forgotten such a powerful testimony? Have you already forgotten the might and power and mercy of our God?"

Still, the silence reigned. Ruth could scarcely believe her ears. Thoughts whirled wildly through her mind as she remembered another story… a story Naomi had shared with her so long ago… a story about a woman exactly like this Rahab. Could Boaz possibly be the son of that woman in Naomi's story – the woman she had never met, yet had given her such hope? The very woman whose story had encouraged her to accept the Lord God for herself? She forced herself to pull her attention back to the matter at hand as Boaz continued to speak in his steady tone.

"I tremble to think of the impression you have left upon this young woman," he stated firmly, his gaze even. "She has left everything to dwell among God's people and to observe His laws, and *this* is the welcome she receives? Is this how you intend to represent the God we serve? Is this truly the desire of your hearts? I admonish each of you to consider your actions – as well as the consequences of such actions – and beg the Lord God to grant you forgiveness as well as wisdom. And as for the character of either of these young women – as I previously stated, you have the testimony of four staunch observers of the Law right here in this room, and we will gladly defend these young women with our dying breaths. If you have nothing more to say, then I must insist that you leave this residence in peace – at once."

The authority in Boaz's tone was unmistakable. One by one, the enraged onlookers began to drop away. The light from their torches wove an eerie trail of fire down the retreating path like a winding snake. Moments later, only two pathetic accusers remained – the stoic Ezra and the huffing Reba.

Ruth continued to steady her friend, and the poor woman began to feel more and more limp within her tight grasp. Silently, Ruth cried out to God for strength and wisdom – for herself as well as for all of her dear friends. A moment later, she was grateful that she could not see the expression on Kemuel's face, but only the rigid set of his shoulders. She knew it would pain her as well as Adara to see the hurt that must be etched within his strong features as he spoke in a low tone to his mother, Reba.

"Does my father know about this?" he asked, the fire gone out of his voice. "Does he know what you have done this night?"

For the first time, fear began to flood out the defiance in the woman's shrewd little eyes. She began to stutter.

"I cannot imagine that he would stand by and allow such a senseless display. Of course, I noticed that he did not stand among you."

Reba's pudgy lip began to tremble. Ezra stood motionless beside her.

Without another word, Kemuel shut the door.

There was a moment of awful silence. Dread hung

heavily over their heads, threatening to choke out any hope of restoring the warmth, the laughter, the comradery that had reigned undisturbed a few short moments before.

Then, flinging herself into her husband's arms, Adara began to sob. "Oh, Kemuel, I am so sorry. So terribly sorry."

Ada cleared her throat and Boaz shifted uncomfortably as Adara continued to sob, held tightly in the strong arms of her husband. Ruth looked helplessly to Naomi, and Noami appeared frozen like a stone statue, her face blanched with dread.

No one seemed to know exactly what to do or say.

That's when Boaz turned and met Ruth's gaze. The tenderness that she saw there, as well as the sorrow and the genuine sympathy, nearly sent her reeling. This man – this strong, capable, worthy man – had risked his own reputation and position to defend her. And staunchly he had done so, without wavering. Suddenly, she was overwhelmed with the desire to be held. As Kemuel held and comforted his hurting wife, she longed to be held and comforted in soothing tones as well. She was startled by her desire to run to Boaz, yet she held back. Such actions would certainly not be considered appropriate.

How was it possible to feel so very alone in a room full of people?

Though Boaz held her gaze in a manner that would typically unnerve her, she did not look away. And everything in the world that she found herself desiring to say to him was silently spoken in that one look. In the dim light of the oil lamps, his heart was revealed. And hers as well. It was almost too powerful.

A moment later, Ada was the first to speak, and Ruth found herself trembling from the intensity of that one look.

"I suppose we should call it a night." Ada turned to

Kemuel, his arms still wrapped tightly about his trembling wife. "The two of you certainly need some time to yourselves."

Kemuel nodded gratefully, still lost for words.

Boaz patted his foreman firmly on the back as he passed him. "I am here for you, friend. As is our God. He will never leave you."

Again, Kemuel nodded his thanks.

Boaz opened the door cautiously, but all traces of the ferocious mob had vanished. He turned to Kemuel one last time. "Ada and I will see that Ruth and Naomi make it safely home."

Taking Boaz's cue, Ruth took Naomi by the hand and led her towards the door. Normalcy seemed to be somewhat restored. Ruth looked to Boaz questioningly, wondering if she had merely imagined that secret moment that had passed between them, but he stood utterly at attention, his eyes wary, as he reached for Naomi and led her out the door.

Ada draped an arm about Ruth's shoulders and closed the door behind them as they made their exit.

Once outside, the crisp night air and twinkling stars captivated Ruth, and her heart began to cease its furious pounding. A cool breeze whispered softly through the night, as if promising to restore the peace and solitude that had been cruelly robbed from them.

Boaz fell behind them, clearly focused on keeping the three women within sight at all times. He looked to Ruth, and she felt as if his strength were flowing directly into her heart. Without a word, he encouraged her to press forward, to press on.

It was a short trek to the small dwelling shared by Ruth and Naomi.

Naomi surprised Ruth by taking both of Boaz's large,

work-roughened hands in her own and giving them a tight squeeze. "The Lord bless you, Boaz," she whispered, her eyes shining with trust. "You are a gift from God, a true blessing. Thank you for all you have done for us – not only tonight, but from the moment we first arrived."

Boaz returned her kindly squeeze and mustered up a confident smile. "The Lord be with you, Naomi. And with you as well, Ruth."

Was it just her imagination, or did Boaz's gaze linger a bit longer than usual as he breathed those familiar words tonight?

Before her thoughts could progress any further, Ada swooped in and enveloped both women in a tender embrace. "Try to get some rest, both of you!" Pulling away, she patted Ruth's cheek in a motherly fashion and offered her most cheery smile. "The Lord was surely with us this night. And it will continue to be so!"

With one last, warm smile, Boaz turned to guide the spritely housekeeper home. "Until tomorrow, Ruth."

Ruth's heart leapt. In all the excitement, she had not even considered what the following day might hold. Already, it was time for the workers to thresh and winnow the grain. God had truly blessed them with an abundant harvest. Though there was little grain left to gather, Ruth knew that she would return to Boaz's fields. Again, she smiled. "Until tomorrow."

Softly, Ruth closed the door. Leaning with her back against the cool wood, she allowed herself a moment to take in the overwhelming circumstances of the evening. How could such a tranquil, serene evening shared with friends turn into such a nightmare? Her heart ached for Adara and Kemuel. She wondered if their relationship with Kemuel's mother would ever be restored. What a tragic turn of events the night had taken. And yet how startling the results had turned out be!

She was reminded of the longing in Boaz's eyes, the overwhelming fear that had engulfed her entire being, and the desire to be held.

Chapter 27

A DARING PLAN

"Ruth?"

Ruth was drawn back to reality by the gentle urging in Naomi's voice. "Yes, Naomi?" she whispered.

"Are you all right, dear?"

Sighing, Ruth realized that she still remained with her back pressed against the door, her arms crossed. She pulled herself away and sank onto the bench opposite her mother-in-law. Several oil lamps flickered in the dim light. She had not even noticed Naomi hurrying about to light them. "I'm overwhelmed."

Naomi's gray eyes were strangely clear, glaringly perceptive.

Ruth found herself looking away, her strength slowly draining. She felt as though Naomi could read her very thoughts. "I suppose we should retire, Naomi. We both must rise early, before the sun."

To her surprise, Naomi reached for Ruth's hand. "I fear for you, child."

Ruth looked up, her eyes round with curiosity. "You fear for me? How so?"

Naomi did not release her grip on Ruth's hand. "You are so young, so full of life. You have many years ahead of you to enjoy, the Lord willing."

Ruth felt her body stiffen. She wasn't sure she would like the outcome of this conversation. Naomi was too calm, too cool, to be discussing such things. Especially after the trauma they had just endured.

"You deserve every happiness, Ruth. You have sacrificed so much for me. But you should not have to sacrifice everything."

No, Ruth certainly did not like the turn this conversation was taking. "Naomi, I have *you*, and I have our Lord. I have everything I need. I am greatly blessed."

"And *I* am blessed by your gratitude, your thankful heart. But Ruth, it is not just your happiness I consider. I fear for your safety as well."

Ruth was incredulous. "My safety?"

"You saw what happened tonight. That angry mob... their horrid accusations... their thirst for violence, for mayhem..."

"Naomi – "

"What if you had been alone, on your way to the fields? Or traveling to the market with Adara?"

Ruth fought to resist the urge to shudder, remembering her last foreboding visit to market. The stone that had struck her cheek, that leering monster of a man at the marketplace...

"Ruth, I want you to listen to me. I want you to be safe – "

"But I *am* safe!" Ruth's outburst sounded violent in her own ears. Why did she feel this way? Why was her mind reeling, her body quavering with a thousand confusing emotions? What was Naomi hinting at? She was afraid to ask. "The Lord will take care of me, Naomi. He will take care of *us*! He always has. He always will."

Naomi smiled, and the peace that engulfed her entire being was unnerving, especially considering the circumstances. "Indeed you speak the truth, my daughter. The Lord has been so good to us, and already He has provided a way for us."

Ruth fought to understand, but she could not.

"I have been earnestly seeking our God concerning this matter, Ruth, for many months now. I have asked Him to make it abundantly clear to me – as to when the proper time would be."

"The proper time for *what*, Naomi?"

"It's called Levirate marriage, Ruth."

Ruth visibly recoiled. "*Marriage*?"

Naomi chuckled and patted Ruth's hand in a motherly fashion. "Now don't look so alarmed, child. I have every confidence that the Lord Himself is moving – working in this. I have prayed too long and too hard to think otherwise."

"But – but it's so soon. We have only just arrived here, Naomi. And my first husband so recently gone – "

Again, Naomi shook her head. "Oh, my daughter. You are so faithful – even unto death. But you need not express such sentiments for my sake. I know that your marriage to my son was never easy for you, Ruth. He never made it easy. He made it a living nightmare."

Ruth swallowed the lump forming in her throat, loathing the memories that came flooding back. Yes, Mahlon's death had been a tragedy indeed, but she felt that the Lord had freed her from a cruel yoke of bondage that had never been of her choosing. Even so, she desperately hoped that the man had accepted the Lord before passing.

"Ruth," Naomi's tone had taken on new meaning, a new seriousness. "The days of grieving have passed. It is time to look forward to what lies ahead."

Ruth fought to maintain her composure, even as her entire body trembled. "The Lord has already given me everything, Naomi. How can I ask for anything more?"

Naomi smiled broadly. "Indeed, the Lord has blessed you, Ruth. He has blessed both of us – richly. And yet again He has met another need of yours – before it even occurred to you to ask Him, I suspect," Naomi continued, her eyes merry.

"Still, I do not understand."

"Have you ever stopped to consider what we will do once the season for gathering grain has passed? Already the men have begun their threshing – and soon there will be nothing left to gather."

"Perhaps if we store enough – "

"For entire seasons at a time? For months on end?"

"Surely it is not impossible."

Naomi smiled patiently. "It seems to me you have it all figured out."

"I could say the same to you," Ruth muttered under her breath. She felt irritated, testy.

"This is how remarkable our God is, Ruth. Just as He instituted laws to provide for the poor through the harvest – by allowing us to gather grain behind the reapers – He has also instituted another law to provide sustenance and protection for a woman bereft of her husband."

"Levirate marriage?" The term sounded harsh, unfamiliar.

"That's right. The Lord knows the world in which we live. A young woman deserves to be loved – to be protected, cared for, sheltered. And when a woman loses her husband, Levirate marriage comes into play."

"But – but what is it?"

"When a woman's husband dies, her husband's brother steps in. He marries the widow, and provides her with an heir to the family estate."

Ruth crinkled her nose. "It seems utterly unnecessary, as well as impossible. We haven't a penny to our names. Yes, the Lord has provided for us, but we have nothing to lose, Naomi." She hesitated before stating her last assessment, concerned as to the effect it might have on Naomi, yet determined to get to the bottom of this unpleasant business. "And Mahlon has no living brother to – to marry me."

Such relief! She began to feel more at ease, simply by stating the obvious absurdity of Naomi's suggestion. Why did the prospect of marriage disturb her so? Was it because she feared the possibility of being trapped in yet another loveless marriage? Her thoughts wandered to the look she had shared with Boaz earlier that evening. Perhaps the secret longing of her heart was to wait for a man who truly loved her... perhaps a man she already knew quite well... She shook her head violently, as if attempting to shake herself free from such disturbing thoughts. What sort of nonsense was this?

Naomi waited patiently for Ruth's passionate outburst to end, then smiled calmly. "Ah, but my dear, the law makes amends for that as well."

Well, of course it does! "How so?"

"If no living brother remains, then the woman is given in marriage to the husband's nearest living relative."

"But, Naomi, that too is impossible. We have no living relatives in Bethlehem – "

Something in Naomi's expression made her reconsider

her hasty assessment. Slowly, a new realization began to dawn upon her with the force of a massive tidal wave. "That is, no living relative except..." her voice trailed off, and for the first time since the conversation began, Ruth found herself utterly speechless.

"No living relative *except...?*" Naomi prompted, her eyes gleaming.

Her mind a dizzying whir of scattered and frantic thoughts, Ruth clung to the sides of the bench, her fingernails digging into the rough wood. Her heart pounded so thunderously within her chest that she was certain Naomi could hear it.

Gently, Naomi took Ruth by the arm. "My daughter, is the Lord's magnificent provision not abundantly clear to you as well?"

Ruth could not speak. She could barely even think. Her mind raced with a countless number of contradictory thoughts – wonder, doubt, excitement, fear, apprehension...

"My darling, I have seen the way you look at him," Naomi whispered softly. "You are ready."

"But is *he*?" The words had escaped her quavering lips before logic could suppress them. Mortified, Ruth flushed, her face crimson.

"Oh, my daughter, how could he *not* be? The man has waited long enough for a godly woman to come into his life. Do you not find it interesting that the man has remained unwed all these years?"

"But – but he is a prosperous landowner. I am nowhere near his station."

"A minor detail for a man like Boaz. His desire is for a woman who will serve the Lord with him. And I believe he has found her."

A thousand questions vied for Ruth's attention. She

wasn't even sure where to begin. "Naomi, he does not know who I am. How is he to ask me to... to marry him... if he is unaware of the fact that he is my dead husband's closest relative?"

Naomi smiled wanly. "Leave that up to me, child. The man is your *kinsman redeemer*. It is his duty by law to accept you as his bride. Boaz is a good man. He will not shirk such responsibilities."

Ruth gasped, appalled. "Oh, Naomi, please, no! I had no idea it was like that! Please, do not push me off on him like that! He is such a good man! He deserves to marry the woman of his choosing – not to be forced into marriage by some law! Oh, please, Naomi, let us not speak of this again!" Ruth was near tears. She couldn't imagine being so bold, so brazen, as to push herself on any man. Why, it was unthinkable!

"Oh, my daughter, do not fret! It is not like that. Why do you think I have held my tongue until now? The Lord is surely in this."

"Boaz deserves better!"

For the first time that evening, Naomi's voice took on a sharp edge. "Have you no eyes, my daughter? Do you not see the way the man looks at you – admires you – with love in his eyes?"

That was enough to stop Ruth dead in her tracks. Dare she even hope? "Did you say... *love*?"

"*Yes*, love! Is that so hard to believe?"

Again, Ruth was drawn back to that one tell-tale moment... and the memory was still so clear, so raw, so mind-numbingly powerful that she found herself gripping the sides of the bench once more.

"The Lord has brought Boaz into your life, Ruth. He is a good man, a godly man. Yes, young love is new and exciting and even thrilling. And I do not doubt that you will experience such marvels with this man that I see you have grown to love. But those are just *feelings*, Ruth, and they will waver and wane. Boaz is strength to his very core. Why, his very name indicates such – *in him is strength*. The love he has to offer comes directly from God. His love will remain strong, steadfast, regardless of trivial feelings or circumstances, because that is the kind of man that he is. You can count on him, Ruth. He would, in fact, be a *redeemer* in every sense of the word."

Ruth could not find her voice to speak. She kept her eyes glued to the floor, even as they brimmed over with tears. She had no idea if they were tears of joy or consternation – perhaps both.

"Now," Naomi prodded, reaching to brush aside several stray tresses of Ruth's glossy hair, "I need you to answer me truthfully."

"Have I ever answered you any other way?" Ruth's voice was barely audible, even in her own ears.

"Do you desire to wed this man, Ruth? Will you marry Boaz?"

Oh, Lord, help me! Ruth uttered one last, silent plea. A plea for strength, a plea for discernment, a plea for guidance. And instantly, her heart was at peace. Astonishingly, she had her answer. Lifting her gaze to levelly meet Naomi's intense gray eyes, Ruth responded without a trace of the former reluctance, "Yes. Yes, I will."

Naomi's shoulders visibly relaxed, and the soft glow that illuminated her every feature seemed almost ethereal. "Good. Now listen closely, child. You must do *exactly* as I say..."

~

"My love? Are you alright?"

Adara's long lashes fluttered as she slowly drifted from sleep to wakefulness. Something wasn't right – not right at all. Even as she lay comfortably upon the pallet she shared with Kemuel, her head reeled dizzily and her thoughts swam in an indecipherable blur. "Kemuel?" She managed, her voice sounding weak in her own ears.

Instantly, his arm slid beneath her shoulders. He lifted her close to him as if she were a small child. She could sense his concern by the tenseness of his muscles. "Adara?"

"Oh, dear." No other sentiment could fully describe her affliction. She clenched her eyes tightly shut, further dizzied by the small room which appeared to be reeling all about her.

Kemuel actually chuckled, despite his obvious anxiety. "Are you well?"

Adara considered this. No. Quite obviously, she was not well. Her head throbbed in pain, she had no sense of balance, and she felt as if she were about to heave up all the contents of last night's meal at any given moment. However, she had no desire to further concern her husband. "I'm fine," she managed as stoutly as possible, even as she relaxed within his clasped arms like a limp rag doll. "You must go to work. I'll be fine."

"You're pale, and you were moaning in your sleep."

"A nightmare, perhaps."

"Or you are coming down with something."

Oh, no! Heavens, no. She hadn't any time to waste getting sick. There was too much work to do! She shook her head vigorously, then grit her teeth in pain as her temples pounded in furious protest.

"Listen, I want you to rest. Do not move from this bed. I will speak with Boaz. Perhaps he will give me early leave."

"No, don't!" Adara found the strength to extricate herself from his grasp. She cupped his face in her hand. "I will be fine, truly. You have work to do! As do I."

Kemuel stared at her for a long moment, apparently unconvinced.

"Please, my husband. You have suffered enough on account of me. I will be fine."

Kemuel's eyes hardened unexpectedly, and he took her hand firmly in his own. "I have suffered nothing on account of you, and I do not want to hear you say it again."

"But last night – "

"You had no control over how those people behaved last night. None whatsoever."

Adara sighed shakily. Perhaps this unbearable nausea was simply a result of severe anxiety – after all, the previous evening had been shocking as well as traumatic. She shuddered, remembering the pounding of the fists upon the door, the flickering of the torches' flame, the harassing shouts of the furious mob. *Yes, that must be it*, she consoled herself, straightening her shoulders and attempting to rise from the bed. *I must get control of myself. This is ridiculous!*

Kemuel reached for her and pulled her back to his side. "Rest." From the look in his eyes, it was not a suggestion.

"But, Kemuel – "

"You must rest if you are to get well. And if I am to work the fields today, I must have peace of mind that my wife is safe and sound. Understand?"

Sighing, Adara nodded glumly.

Rising from the pallet, Kemuel slipped into his heavy mantel and sandals. "I will see Naomi before I leave for the fields," he assured her, stooping to kiss her forehead. "I will ask her to pay you a visit in a few hours to see how you are doing."

"And if I am doing well, may I get to my chores?" Adara asked hopefully.

"Based on Naomi's assessment, we'll see."

Adara bit her lip in consternation. This was simply maddening!

Kemuel turned to cast her a smile before he stooped out the door. "I love you, Adara."

Adara couldn't help but smile through her discomfort. "I love you, too."

Adara feared that she would die of boredom before a faint knock at the door startled her from her agitated state.

"Adara, my child, it is Naomi."

Adara's heart leapt in sheer happiness. "Yes! Come in, Naomi, come in!"

Naomi let herself in, a steaming bowl of broth carefully balanced in one hand. "Kemuel said you were not well. I threw together something warm and filling as quickly as possible and came straight over!"

"Naomi, you are an angel!"

"How are you feeling?"

"Fine! Absolutely fine!" The nausea and lightheadedness had passed shortly after her husband's departure. "Lounging in bed when there are so many chores to be done has been positively dreadful!"

Naomi chuckled. "Well, you look spritely enough." Drawing up a stool, Naomi seated herself beside the bedridden girl and offered her the bowl of broth.

One whiff of the strong-smelling soup and Adara's stomach turned violently. Clasping a hand over her mouth, she turned her face away and attempted to regain her composure.

Naomi looked puzzled. "My dear?"

Jumping to her feet, Adara flung aside the woolen blanket and made a mad dash for the door.

Setting aside the broth, Naomi waited patiently, her hands clasped in her lap. A sneaking suspicion crept into the corners of her mind, and she could not suppress a secret smile.

When Adara returned, she appeared slightly pale but strong enough.

"Everything all right?" Naomi asked innocently.

Adara sighed and smoothed out the wrinkles of her robe, anxious. "I suppose I am better now," she muttered a bit shakily.

"Perhaps the broth can wait."

Adara smiled gratefully. "I fear my husband is going to be very concerned. I hate to cause him trouble."

"How long have you been feeling this way?" Naomi questioned casually.

Adara wrinkled her brow, considering the question. "Come to think of it, I haven't felt quite like myself lately. Kemuel often kids me – he says I have an endless supply of energy, which is typically true. But as of late I have felt rather weary – tiring easily." Wringing her hands nervously, Adara glanced about the room at the unfinished chores that were vying for her attention. "I hope it is nothing serious."

A soft smile continued to play about the corners of Naomi's lips. Rising from her stool, she reached out to pat the girl's shoulder. "I doubt it. I'll be keeping an eye on you, just to be sure. But I wouldn't worry, dear. I'm sure it's perfectly natural. Most women experience it at some point."

"Dizzy spells and nausea, and weariness for no particular reason at all?" Adara looked skeptical.

Naomi brushed aside her concerns. "Shall I stay here with you this morning? Would that contribute to your peace of mind, my dear girl?"

Adara shook her head adamantly. "Oh, no. You have plenty of your own work to do! I will be fine."

"You're sure?"

"Absolutely."

"All right, then. I'll leave the broth with you – just in case you change your mind," Naomi informed her with a wink.

Adara followed her to the door. "Naomi!"

"Yes, child?"

"One last thing." Adara's eyes looked so large, so pleading. "My husband said I could stay out of bed if you gave me a positive assessment... please, please, *please* tell me that I may work now!"

Grinning, Naomi gave Adara's hand a motherly squeeze. "A few chores wouldn't hurt."

"Thank you, Naomi!"

"Don't overdo it now," Naomi advised as she slipped out the door.

No promises, Adara thought, grinning mischievously. Reaching for the broom, she set to work with a vengeance.

Chapter 28

LOVE REVEALED

Already the sun was beginning to set just beyond the western plains, casting soft golden hues upon the harvested fields and washing the earth in a beautiful, ethereal light.

Ruth surveyed the vast fields, so lovely and serene in the waning light, surprised by the fond attachment that had developed between herself and these endless fields of swaying grain. There was something about this field... so open, so faithful, so fruitful. She wondered what it would be like to cease her gathering once the ground lay fallow. Were the fields every bit as alluring when the ground was carefully tilled, and the sun beat down upon the rich earth, willing those tiny seeds to grow?

Hoisting her grain-filled mantel over one shoulder, she turned, sighing shakily to steady herself as she anticipated the daunting task which lay before her.

As the women prepared to return to their homes for the evening, the men belted their tunics and watered the oxen as they readied themselves to continue on with the threshing process late into the night.

The threshing was no easy task, but the men went about it with vigor and great enthusiasm, roaring with laughter and good humor as they celebrated the bountiful harvest. First, the golden sheaves were scattered upon the threshing floor, where the stalks were beaten with rods or flails. In order to save time as well as manpower, the oxen were often hitched to a heavy sledge – the underside of which was lined with sharp stones – and driven over the tender stalks. Even after this lengthy process was completed, the wheat still had to be separated from the chaff.

The threshing was to carry on long into the night, so many of the men planned to simply bed down there for the evening. After all, they must set to work again with a fury even before the rising of the sun.

I am not ready, Ruth thought as she walked the lonely trail home, her shoulders aching and her legs wobbly beneath her. *I can't do this...*

Ruth had not waited to bid Boaz a good evening, as had become her regular custom. In fact, she had avoided him the entire day. Surely if she had spoken with him, she would have given herself away. He would have known... through some word or gesture or look. He would have seen right through her, and all of her plans would become transparent. She couldn't risk it. Her fate as well as her future – not to mention Naomi's – rested upon everything going according to plan tonight. She must be patient. She must be strong.

Even as she forced herself to place one foot ahead of the other as she ventured home, Naomi's words from the previous evening swirled about her mind in a dizzying blur of confusion...

"Then it shall be, my daughter," Naomi had said, "when he lies down, that you shall notice the place where he lies."

"But what if I am seen before then?" Ruth had whispered, her eyes full. "Only the men are permitted to sleep there. Already I have been accused of being a pagan seductress – "

"Shah, child! That is nothing but malicious gossip, and anyone with half a head upon their shoulders knows it. Years ago – even before my time – many of our warriors were seduced and led astray by Moabite women. I fear that some of our own women continue to hold a grudge, even after all these years! It is to their folly and their shame."

Arriving home, Ruth found their small dwelling empty. *That's strange,* Ruth thought as she lowered her sack of grain to the floor and began to unbraid her long, unruly tresses.

Where could Naomi be? Kemuel mentioned that Adara was not feeling well today, she remembered. *Perhaps Naomi is paying her a visit.* Ruth certainly did not mind. In fact, she welcomed the quiet, the solitude. It would allow for ample time to pray and prepare for this night.

"After you return from your labors in the fields," Naomi had prompted her, "bathe and anoint yourself with our finest perfume..."

"But, Naomi," Ruth had protested, "we haven't any perfume."

Naomi had then reached into her garment and retrieved a delicate bottle from the pocket sewn into the seams. "I purchased this at market several weeks ago. I have been saving it for this very occasion."

Ruth had gasped. "Naomi! It must have cost you a fortune!"

"Wear this tomorrow night," she had instructed, "when you go to Boaz. And put on your finest garments."

"But why?"

Naomi had simply smiled. "You will see."

Just thinking about what she was about to do filled Ruth

with dread. She bathed as quickly as possible, and noticed that Naomi had draped an elegant robe over her stool near the window. Gingerly, Ruth lifted the garment for inspection. The fabric was dyed a deep scarlet, with bold golden embroidery chasing its way across the hemline and both sleeves. Ruth could not resist the surge of delight that coursed through her entire body at the thought of wearing such a garment. She wondered where Naomi could have possibly discovered such a breath-taking marvel – much less afforded to purchase it. Allowing her own thin garment to drop to the floor, she slipped the stunning new robe over her head.

The material felt warm and soft upon her smooth skin, and she began to feel the slightest bit of confidence creep into her heart. Running a comb through her abundant brown hair, she arranged it carefully about her shoulders. Though she would be modest and don the matching, gold-embroidered head covering, she would not tie her hair in a braid tonight. She would let it fall freely about her, framing her face in a manner that she hoped to be pleasing.

Retrieving the pleasing little vial of perfume, Ruth removed the cap and was astonished by the sweet scent that filled her nostrils. *What a lovely fragrance!* She wondered what it could be.

At last, she was ready. She could only hope that she was pleasing enough to the eye. She did not like the idea of leaving without saying goodbye to Naomi, but already the sun had nearly vanished, allowing a lustrous full moon to crest the opposing hills. Ruth knew that if she did not leave immediately, she would never find her way back to the fields in the inky blackness of night. She must leave now.

She had just emerged from the entrance of their small home when Naomi nearly ploughed into her.

"Ruth!" Naomi's gray eyes were wide as marbles. "Heavens, child! I hardly recognized you! You look stunning!"

Ruth dropped her gaze and blushed, embarrassed. "Thank you, Naomi. I am so afraid."

Naomi drew Ruth in close for a tight embrace. "There is nothing to fear, my daughter," she whispered, her tone brimming with confidence. "Our God goes with you. He will be with you every step of the way."

"Naomi, I don't think I can do – "

"Oh, but you *can*! And you *will*! And you must go *now*, before the sun disappears for good!" Naomi gave Ruth a gentle push in the right direction. "Go my daughter! Go in peace!"

"But, Naomi – "

"The Lord will be with you, Ruth! Now hurry!"

Harvest was a season of celebration, a time of jubilant thanksgiving and praise to God for a bountiful crop. All around him, Boaz's workers laughed and sang and ribbed each other good-naturedly. His ears rang with the familiar, joyous songs of the late spring harvest, the futile lowing and heavy tread of the oxen, and the animated conversation of strong young men hard at work. Above him, a canopy of shining stars glistened, and below a bonfire roared, casting twisting, writhing shadows that danced about the camp.

Even so, his heart was not in it.

Perhaps his spirit was still disturbed after the shocking events of the previous evening. Still, he suspected that his lack of peace was due largely to the fact that Ruth had clearly been avoiding him throughout the day.

Mentally, he evaluated the happenings of the previous

two days, wondering if he had said or done something that could have possibly troubled her. And each time he allowed his mind to amble down memory lane, he was assaulted with a memory so clear and so precise that it was nearly unbearable… A strikingly beautiful young woman with clear dark eyes, gazing upon him with admiration, with such a perfect innocence, with the most refreshing purity. In the soft glow of the scattered oil lamps, in that one moment of absolute trust and sure confidence, Ruth had allowed him a fleeting glimpse of her heart. He was awed that her inner beauty matched her physical beauty – possibly even surpassed it. He had never known a woman of such loyalty, such devotion, such willingness to serve the Lord. It moved him – utterly moved him.

He had never prayed so hard in his life. And though every fiber of his being burned with hope and the consuming desire to make this woman his, his constant prayer was that of complete submission. *Your will be done, Lord.*

He could conjure up no reason whatsoever to explain the unusual change he had witnessed in Ruth that day. It disturbed him. Greatly.

One of his workers clamped a heavy hand upon his shoulder, drawing him out of his private thoughts and back into the evening's festivities.

"A greater harvest we have yet to see!" The man announced, his eyes shining with anticipation.

Boaz clapped the man on the back. "God is good, friend," he agreed, breathing deeply as he took it all in. "God is good."

~

Ruth reached the fields just as the last dying rays of the sun slipped behind the distant hills, filling the earth with a darkness that was both fearsome and mysterious. Far above her head, the stars winked and twinkled from their respective homes, enshrined within a sea of black nothingness.

Crouching behind a monumental bale of hay, Ruth observed the threshing festivities from a safe distance away, praying desperately that she would not be discovered. She remained crouched there for what seemed to be hours. Finally giving in to the demands of her cramped legs and aching back, she lowered herself to a sitting position behind her haven of hay. Closing her eyes, she listened to the musical voices of Boaz's men, carried away by the rhythmic cadence by which they worked and sang.

This is a spectacular night, she thought, caught up in the wonder of it all. She longed to emerge from her secret hideaway and join in the triumphant festivities. Silently, her heart joined their songs of thanksgiving and praise to a God who always gave generously.

After what felt like an eternity, the men began to set aside their tools and unyoke the oxen. The laughter and singing dwindled down along with the bonfire. Despite the heavy smoke that streaked the air, the sky remained calm and clear. The festivities were rapidly coming to an end. After many, many hours of hard manual labor, the men were finally ready to settle down for the night.

Ruth remained in position behind the towering bale of hay, her heart rate accelerating with every passing minute. Her breath began to come in short puffs. Panic welled up within her throat, threatening to choke her.

Trust in God, she reminded herself, even as she trembled in fear. *Trust in God.*

Just as Naomi had instructed, Ruth's eyes traced Boaz's

every move. She could not lose sight of him. If he were to choose to venture home – which would be unlikely at this late hour – she had already decided that she would follow after him. But she prayed it would not be so.

Lord, grant me peace. Grant me favor – favor in Your sight, and favor in the eyes of Boaz as well.

One by one, the men straggled into the small huts that served as temporary shelters for long nights such as this one. Ruth kept her eyes trained on Boaz, though she had to dodge behind the bale of hay on numerous occasions, fearful that she might be seen. Even after the last few stragglers had given up for the evening and retreated to the shelter of the wooden huts, Boaz remained pacing before the smoldering embers of the bonfire.

Oh, Lord, Ruth moaned inwardly, *how much longer must I wait?* Already, her nerves felt completely frazzled. Somewhat playfully, she feared that if she had to remain waiting in such breathless anticipation much longer, she might be claimed by cardiac arrest. But Boaz appeared to be in no hurry to retreat for the night, even after a lengthy day of hot, tiresome labor. With strong arms clasped firmly behind his back, he paced back and forth, back and forth, before the faint light the glowing embers scarcely provided.

In the inky blackness, Ruth could see little more than a chiseled profile, the outline of powerful shoulders, and flowing robe as he continued to pace. Then, he did something completely unexpected. Dropping to his knees, Boaz clasped his hands and lowered his head, clearly caught up in fervent prayer.

For a moment Ruth watched, overwhelmed by the power of a man on his knees before His Creator. Then her cheeks grew warm and, respectfully, she lowered her eyes. Who was *she* to share this intimate moment between Boaz and his Maker? She felt as though she had been caught eavesdropping.

A moment later, she heard the soft rustling of fabric and the scraping of sandals upon the gravelly dirt. Lifting her head, she saw that Boaz had risen to his feet and finally appeared to be retiring for the night. She swallowed hard as he disappeared into the closest hut.

For a moment, the panic began to rise yet again. *What if I cannot locate him in the dark? What if I kneel at the bedside of the wrong man?* Her mind raced with a thousand dreadful possibilities and foreseeable mishaps. But then she took a deep breath, calmed her racing heart, and reminded herself that she was not in this alone. The Lord was with her. She could trust Him to guide her steps. After all, hadn't He done just that – guided her every step – from the moment she had set out for Bethlehem?

Taking a long, shaky breath, Ruth rose to her feet, pressing her back firmly against the scratchy bale of straw. She knew what must come next, yet she wondered if she had the strength to go through with it.

First, I must wait until the man has had time to fall asleep... Oh, dear. She had no idea how long she should tarry before boldly stepping across the threshold of that stoic little hut. Would Boaz fall asleep quickly? Or would he lie awake for some time before sleep claimed him? He had certainly undergone an exhausting day of great physical exertion, so perhaps he would doze the moment his body hit the sleeping pallet. Then again, he had seemed to be immensely restless while pacing before the fire. Perhaps she should allow him more time than she had formerly anticipated...

Oh, Lord, help me! I don't know what to do, but I must do this right.

Clamping her eyes shut tight, she mentally reviewed

Naomi's careful instructions. "Then it shall be, when he lies down," Naomi had instructed, "that you shall notice the place where he lies. Go in to him, and set aside the edge of the blanket to uncover his feet. There you must lie down. And he shall tell you what to do."

Oh, Naomi, you make it sound all too easy.

Ruth had no idea how much time had passed, but she knew that she could no longer tarry. It was time to carry out her task. Sighing, Ruth lifted her head bravely and willed her feet to carry her forward.

As Ruth approached the simple dwelling, she was appalled by the rude chorus of deep snoring that met her ears.

Men! she thought with a hint of annoyance, then repented just as quickly. Straightening her shoulders and offering up one last desperate plea to her God, she took a deep breath and crossed over the threshold.

All about her, the still forms of sleeping workers littered the floor. They were but mere shadows in the gathering darkness, and she wondered how she would possibly be able to discern one from the other. Imagine the humiliation if she were to uncover the feet of the wrong man! She shuddered at the thought.

Taking careful, silent steps, Ruth glanced about the small room. She closed her eyes tightly for several seconds then reopened them, hoping to adjust to the all-encompassing darkness of her surroundings.

Yes, now she could just barely make out the still forms upon the sleeping pallet. There was Zacharias, and that form over by the window was Jedidiah, and a little further beyond was Eli. These men were little more than names to her – familiar names that she had heard repeated time and time again during her long hours in the fields. She prayed that all would remain at rest – at least long enough for her to carry out Naomi's instructions.

Cautiously, like a frightened, wary animal, Ruth's eyes continued to scan the room's sleeping inhabitants.

There! Beneath the window cut into the eastern wall! Ruth smiled wryly to herself. She should have known that Boaz would bed down in a place where he could rise with full view of the sun's dazzling glory. She offered a silent prayer of thanks when she realized that the other men had chosen to spread their pallets a respectable distance from the master's. Perhaps she would actually get through this trying ordeal without awakening any of them.

Drawing in one last, shaky breath, Ruth gathered the remaining fragments of her strength and moved stealthily towards Boaz, wincing at every *swish* made by her elegant, trailing robe. Kneeling at the foot of his pallet, Ruth was relieved to see his large shoulders rising and falling in time with his rhythmic breathing. The man was definitely sleeping soundly.

Silver moonlight washed through the open window, partially illuminating the man's face as he slept. Ruth took this moment to inspect the face of the man that might one day become her husband. Emotions that she had never experienced flooded her entire being, and with great difficulty she fought the urge to lean forward and gently kiss the fine forehead creased with care.

Enough of that, Ruth warned herself. There was little time to act, and she knew that she was wasting it. Glancing nervously about her, Ruth reached for the light mantle that Boaz had draped over his still form. With trembling fingers she drew it back, revealing bare, work-hardened feet rough, worn, and scarred. She had never seen the man without his sandals.

She had barely settled herself uncomfortably at Boaz's feet when the man lurched forward, instantly awake, swiftly pulling himself up into a sitting position. "Who – "

Acting much faster than she would have previously given herself credit for, Ruth drew herself up and placed a steady finger upon his lips.

Boaz visibly recoiled.

He does not recognize me, Ruth's mind screamed in panic. *It is much too dark!*

"Shhh. It is only me," she whispered tremulously.

Though she could barely make out his prominent features in the darkness, Ruth could sense the recognition that must have relaxed his expression. She could almost feel his muscles relax right along with it.

"Who are you?" he whispered softly, a very real longing hidden in his deep voice.

Ruth knew that he had his answer even before she could form her gentle response. "It is I – Ruth." She fought to remember the words Naomi had bidden her to speak. "Please, take your humble maidservant beneath your wing, for you are a close relative, Boaz."

"A relative?" Boaz's whisper was filled with awe. "Ruth, could it be so?"

Ruth fought to speak around the huge lump forming in her throat. Boaz's voice communicated everything she needed to know. All of her unanswered questions were indeed answered this night, simply by the tone in which he spoke. "Yes, Boaz. You are a relative of my dead husband's father – Elimelech."

"Elimelech!" Now there was a name that he had not heard in a long, long time. "But why did you wait? You know that I would have taken you to be my wife, Ruth."

His wife! Ruth could no longer speak. She fought against the tears that threatened to come.

Boaz seemed to sense her deep emotion. Taking her arm with a steady hand, he leaned forward and whispered directly into her ear, "Come. Walk with me."

Ruth allowed Boaz to help her to her feet. Silently, he led her away from the snoring men and into the open night air.

The bonfire's embers emitted a faint glimmer, even at this late hour. Ruth guessed it to be somewhere around midnight. Taking a long stick, Boaz poked at the charred embers and slowly coaxed a small flame back to life – small enough to provide a bit of light, yet also small enough not to awaken the others.

Ruth was unprepared when Boaz turned to face her, his face shining with love. He caught both her hands in his own. Her heart raced.

"Ruth, tell me, how did you know this?"

Ruth looked to him questioningly.

"How did you know that I am a relative?"

Ruth lowered her eyes, her cheeks growing warm. "Naomi."

Boaz had to stoop to catch her faint whisper. He smiled down at her. "You should have found me sooner."

Ruth could not meet his intense gaze. "I have only recently learned the truth," she whispered softly.

"Ruth, you amaze me! Blessed are you of the Lord, my daughter. Your kindness overwhelms me. Even in this, Ruth – you are a beautiful woman in both character and appearance. You could have had any man you wished. And yet you have not gone after the younger men – whether rich or poor. But you have been obedient to your mother-in-law – coming here to see me this night?"

Something in his tone caused Ruth to look up, and she

realized that he sought the answer to a very important question. *Why, he thinks I am simply following Naomi's orders!* she realized in horror. *He still does not know that I... love him.* Why, yes, she was indeed obeying Naomi's instructions regarding Boaz, but she had loved him even before she knew he was eligible to redeem her! With a boldness that she did not know she possessed, Ruth tightened her grip upon Boaz's hands and peered up into his face. Smiling, she said calmly, "And why would I chase after the younger men – rich or poor? None of those men are *you*, Boaz. None of them."

Boaz was clearly taken aback, but he laughed – a deep, heartfelt laugh – and drew her a bit closer. "I have no doubt that you would have been obedient to Naomi, regardless. That is your character, Ruth. That is what I admire so deeply about you."

Ruth flushed. "Only by God's grace," she whispered. "He supplies me with the strength that I need to make hard decisions."

Boaz gazed tenderly upon her. "Do you need more time, Ruth? Are you still grieving the loss of your husband?"

For a moment, Ruth said nothing. She felt her jaw twitch, and a tear slipped unbidden down her cheek. Looking up into Boaz's understanding eyes, she whispered, "He did not love me, Boaz. I was forced into marriage at a very young age. It was – somehow God gave me the strength to get through it."

Boaz nodded in recognition. Apparently, he had been wondering for a very long time. Now he had his answers. "Ruth, it would be an honor to take you to be my wife. You are indeed a virtuous young woman. Willingly, gladly, and with a full heart, I will redeem you."

Now the tears broke forth, and Ruth did not even care.

She smiled through her tears, overjoyed. "Thank you," she breathed, her voice shaky. "Thank you, Boaz."

"Tomorrow I shall visit Naomi and formally ask – " But there he halted abruptly, and even in the dim light Ruth could see the color drain from his face.

Ruth's heart skipped a beat. She grew instantly fearful. "Boaz? What is it?"

"Naomi – wife of Elimelech..." Again, his voice trailed off. "Elimelech. Oh, no."

"Boaz?"

The look in his eyes unnerved her. What terrible truth could have possibly disturbed him so?

Boaz appeared to be thinking very carefully about the words he was about to speak. "Ruth, it is true that I am a close relative. Yet, I fear that there may be one even closer than I..."

Ruth could not move. She could not speak. She felt completely paralyzed as merciless fingers of fear clutched tightly about her heart.

Boaz shook his head, and clearly he was attempting to appear calm. "But do not be afraid, my daughter. Surely the Lord will work in this as well. He would not have brought us this far..."

Ruth attempted to steady her breathing. She gazed up into his eyes in sheer desperation. "What will happen?"

Boaz released his grip on her hands, and she could have wept to see such a perfect moment come to a crashing end. "I will speak with this man tomorrow. His name is Yigal."

Yigal? The name itself sounded repulsive to her ears.

"If he should desire to redeem you, then by law you must..." Boaz's voice trailed off. Obviously, it pained him to go any further than this.

Ruth had never heard her own voice sound so small. "By law, what must I do?"

Boaz's mouth was nothing but a grim line, and he ran his hand through his hair in an agitated gesture. "You must marry him."

Chapter 29

STAND STILL

Marry him! Why, it was absurd! And *wrong* – so terribly wrong! How could she be forced to marry yet another man that she did not know, did not love, did not *want*?

Ruth felt as if her entire world was crashing down upon her. For a moment, her legs threatened to give way beneath her and she swayed precariously.

Boaz sensed her distress and gripped her by both shoulders. "Steady. Ruth? Can you hear me?"

But Ruth appeared dazed. Her eyes had taken on a desperation that frightened him. "Ruth?"

Before she could stop herself, Ruth flung herself into Boaz's strong arms. Burying her face in his chest, she wept like a distraught child. She no longer cared if anyone emerged from the hut to stare upon the shocking spectacle. She no longer cared if the entire town jabbered about the scene the following day. All that she knew was that she needed this man – she needed to be comforted, to feel his steady strength.

Boaz held her for several moments and let her cry.

When Ruth drew back, her face was streaked with tears. She buried her face in her hands and attempted to dry her own tears. "I shouldn't have – I should have never flown at you like that – " she managed shakily.

Again, Boaz steadied her by the shoulders. "Ruth, I would be entirely dishonest with you if I were to say anything other than this..." he took a deep breath, appearing to gather the courage to plunge forward. "I love you, Ruth. I always have."

At this, Ruth's tears broke forth anew, but she didn't care.

"It pains me greatly to think of anyone else... taking you as a wife."

"Please, I cannot do this. I cannot marry anyone else, Boaz."

"If I do not confront this man before the village elders, then we could never marry, Ruth. But at least this way... at least this way we have a chance. Yigal could refuse. In that case, we would be free to... to wed."

Despite his pain, hope glimmered anew in his eyes, so soft in the firelight. Ruth willed herself to draw strength from him. "Oh, Boaz."

With gentle fingers, Boaz tipped her chin upward, forcing her to meet the intensity of his gaze. "Do you trust our God, Ruth?"

It was as if her mind had unleashed a whirlwind of memories – some recent, others distant. Some painful, yet others joyous... She saw herself on her wedding day – her eyes swollen from weeping and her entire frame trembling with fear... Naomi seated before the fire the night that Ruth accepted the Lord God of Israel as her Savior... Mahlon cold and dead upon a straw mat... Orpah turning her back and walking away with stubborn determination, never to be seen again... an endless journey through the whirling sands of the barren wilderness of Israel... that imposing man called Moses as he wept and bid them a safe journey home... their first night in Bethlehem sleeping among the straw and bawling animals... Adara kneeling in the hard-packed earth, scrubbing clean a home for strangers she had never even met... and this man – this good, strong man – Boaz, as he strolled confidently through his fields, warmly greeting his workers in the name of the Lord.

The Lord. *Their* Lord. The Lord God Almighty – the very One who had led His children through a wilderness of trials and hardships and directed them to the land He had promised – the very ground beneath her feet!

It was as if Ruth had opened her eyes for the very first time that evening. Drawing in another shaky breath, she managed a very wobbly smile. "Yes, Boaz," she whispered softly. "Yes, I trust Him."

Boaz's eyes welled with tenderness and pride. "As do I," he managed. His voice sounded slightly choked, and Ruth loved him all the more for it. "First thing tomorrow morning, the moment the elders arrive at the city gates, I will lay this out before them. I will find this Yigal and we will work this out. I will do all that I can, and I trust our God to take care of the rest."

Ruth could only nod weakly.

Taking her gently by the arm, Boaz began to guide her toward the shelter. "Come. Stay this night. You must rest. Tomorrow will arrive very early. It always does."

Not early enough, Ruth thought wistfully as she allowed herself to be guided through the narrow doorway and directly to Boaz's mat.

She couldn't help but wonder if it would be proper to remain there for the night. She knelt near his feet and shivered despite the dense humidity of the crowded room. "Boaz?" she whispered faintly.

Boaz drew himself up to a sitting position, leaning in close. They could not risk waking anyone – not now.

"Is it, well, is it proper for me to stay?"

Even in the darkness, Ruth could sense his soft smile. "You have asked me to become your kinsman redeemer. This is the custom. You must remain here at my feet until morning. Fortunately we are in a room filled with men to keep us accountable – not that they are aware of it," he added wryly. "But before God we will conduct ourselves respectfully according to the custom set into place by the Law."

Ruth's conscience instantly eased. And she became fully aware of how exhausted she truly was. It did not matter that she lay on the hard-packed earth without even a mat to soften her slumber. The Lord was with her, and by His mercy perhaps this would be the last night she would have to fear losing the man she had learned to love so deeply.

"Goodnight, Boaz," she whispered softly.

"Goodnight, Ruth."

Moments later, sleep utterly claimed her.

Ruth was awakened by the sound of a man's voice whispering her name. She liked the sound of it. Warm and soft and strong. The sensation of it surged through her veins like warm honey, and for a moment she felt completely safe. And then she pushed herself up to a sitting position, startled and disoriented. Where was she? Why was she not at home?

Before panic could fully claim her, her eyes adjusted to

the encompassing dimness. The room felt warm and clammy just before dawn. Beyond the window fixed above her, she could see the sun threatening to break through the heavy mist.

Boaz knelt before her, offering his hand. "We must go."

The events of the previous night whirred through her mind at an unsettling pace. She suddenly remembered why she was here. She felt sickly, unsettled, and yet... hopeful. This day could result in two vastly different outcomes... one, beautiful; the other, heartrending.

Understanding the need for discretion, Ruth accepted his hand without a word and allowed him to guide her out the door and away from the suffocating confines of the sleeping hut. She noticed that Boaz had hoisted a large sack of grain over his shoulder. Undoubtedly, it was for her and Naomi. She swallowed a lump that had risen unexpectedly in her throat.

Boaz must have caught her staring, for he smiled and simply said, "Shall I return you to our dear Naomi empty-handed?"

Ruth offered him a smile that she hoped fully expressed her heartfelt gratitude.

From that point forward, neither spoke until they were a discreet distance from the fields. The winding path felt cool and damp beneath the morning dew. Ruth gathered the courage to look at Boaz, and saw that his gaze was fixed straight ahead, his jaw set in determination.

"What shall you do?" Ruth dared, keeping her voice low.

"First, we shall pray."

Ruth waited, sensing that he had more to say.

"Our closest friends shall join us in prayer – Naomi, Kemuel, Adara, and Ada. Then Kemuel and I will approach the elders at the gate."

"Alone?"

"It is better that way."

Ruth paused in the center of the path and touched his arm. "May we go with you?" she requested.

Boaz turned to study her. "A few of the elders I greatly respect. The others – not to mention may of the townspeople – are a brood of vipers. It is your safety that I take into consideration, my dear."

"What could they possibly do to me in the presence of all the elders, as well as those gathered at the city gates?"

Boaz's mouth was a grim line. He did not desire to share that he feared the kinsman redeemer – the man named Yigal – might instantly agree to redeem the lovely, young woman after a mere glimpse of her exotic beauty. And yet... something within him urged him to consider her request.

When they reached the small cluster of white-washed stone dwellings near the outskirts of the village, the sun was just beginning to rise above the eastern hills, washing the world in a golden spray of sheer warmth and light.

Naomi stood framed in the narrow doorway, wide awake and alert despite the early hour. Ruth's heart leapt into her throat at the sheer happiness that permeated the older woman's soft features. Obviously, the sight of Boaz and her pretty, young daughter-in-law traveling side-by-side was enough to convince her that her orders had resulted in a shining success.

But just as quickly, Naomi's rapturous expression faded and was replaced by one of deep concern. Her silver brows knit closely together as she observed the solemn expressions of the handsome couple before her. "Greetings, and the Lord be with you both," she announced, wringing her hands nervously and ushering them into the house. "Whatever is the matter?"

Calmly, Boaz set the sack of grain upon a low stand, then carefully explained their dilemma. Though Naomi appeared deeply disturbed, she did not panic or lose her sense of calm. Ruth was exceedingly grateful. Her nerves were worn and raw as it was.

"Well, that does present a problem," Naomi observed once Boaz had relayed the entire story. "And you have chosen to take it before the elders at the gate?"

Boaz looked to Ruth and she managed a weak smile of affirmation. "We have," he said, his jaw set.

Naomi merely nodded. "We must take this before the Lord."

Boaz went to find Ada while Ruth and Naomi sought out Kemuel and Adara. Before long, the six fellow believers were gathered together in a tight circle, their heads bowed, their eyes closed, their hands joined. Together, they fervently poured out their hearts to God, making known their request, and seeking His will first. Ruth felt strengthened and encouraged by the sound of her dear friends' voices as they whispered heartfelt petitions to their loving Father on her behalf.

Ruth had no idea how much time had passed when Boaz finally rose to his feet and addressed everyone huddled in the room. "I believe it is time. I had thought to go alone – Kemuel and I. But after much prayer and consideration, I sense that your prayers and support throughout this situation are vital – as well as a great encouragement to me. Naomi, Ada, I would ask that you and the younger women follow at a discreet distance behind Kemuel and I. Once you reach the square, simply blend in with the crowd. No good can come from drawing attention to yourselves," he paused, exchanging meaningful looks with the two older women. Clearly, they understood his quiet caution. Both women nodded purposefully.

Kemuel clamped a decisive hand upon Boaz's shoulder. "Let us be off, then."

For the briefest moment, Boaz allowed his eyes to rest upon the young woman he loved, his eyes silently communicating all that she needed to know. Then he turned smartly on his heel, purpose in his every step. "God be with you all. May He give us strength."

Ada and Adara waited respectfully outside the door as Ruth changed into simpler, less conspicuous garments. All four women had been careful to wear simple clothing and to heavily veil themselves.

Naomi stood, quiet and resolute, as Ruth adjusted her veil. Her hands trembled so that she struggled to drape the long end over her shoulder. Chuckling softly, Naomi padded over to her helpless daughter-in-law and assisted her with the unruly strip of fabric. "Everything is going to be all right, you know," she said softly, her deep-set gray eyes merry despite the stressful circumstances they now faced.

Ruth's face had grown especially pale. "I pray so," she whispered, her voice catching in her throat.

"Oh, but it will!"

Ruth lowered her eyes, one slow tear tracing its way down her cheek.

"Oh, my child." Naomi drew Ruth close to her, enclosing her arms about the trembling girl in a motherly fashion. "Here, sit down, my daughter. Let us have a quick chat, you and me, before we set off."

"But, Ada and Adara – they are waiting – "

"Neither of those wonderful women would want to set foot on that path before you were ready to do so," Naomi chided in a matronly tone. "Now what troubles you so?"

Ruth lifted a brow. Such a question! How could Naomi even ask such a thing?

"Tell me," Naomi insisted, her eyes deep and sincere.

Ruth sighed. She felt cornered. "I am afraid."

"Of?"

Ruth couldn't bring herself to say it. In truth, she was terrified. She had found herself in the very situation she had feared the most. What if she were to find herself trapped in yet another prison of a loveless marriage? Or – worse – a dysfunctional, abusive marriage? A shudder wracked her entire frame, and she found that she could not speak. Closing her eyes, she said nothing and simply allowed the tears to fall.

Naomi draped a protective arm about Ruth's shoulders and remained silent for a long time. Finally, she ventured, "You are afraid that this other man might redeem you."

Ruth wrenched away, surprised by the magnitude of her own emotions. "*Redeem* me? *Redeem* me, no! *Trap* me, yes! And what if I do not wish to be redeemed?"

Naomi simply smiled. "God will work it out for us, Ruth. He always has. We must trust Him."

"*We*? It seems to me that only one of us is struggling in that respect."

Again, Naomi chuckled. "It is only natural to fear. But we must not."

"I am so afraid." It was nothing more than a whisper.

Another pause. Another long moment of silence. Then, Naomi did something completely unexpected. Closing her eyes, she reached for Ruth's hand and gripped it tightly between her own. Rocking slowly back and forth, she began to recite words – precious words, beloved words – from memory. Words that were so familiar and so very dear to Ruth's heart, words laden with strength and hope...

"And when Pharaoh drew near, the children of Israel lifted their eyes, and behold, the Egyptians marched after them. So they were very afraid, and the children of Israel cried out to the Lord. Then they said to Moses, 'Because there were no graves in Egypt, have you taken us away to die in the wilderness? Why have you so dealt with us, to bring us up out of Egypt? Is this not the word that we told you in Egypt, saying, "Let us alone that we may serve the Egyptians"? For it would have been better for us to serve the Egyptians than that we should die in the wilderness.'"

The words were powerful, all-encompassing, burning like fire within Ruth's troubled heart. Sobs wracked her entire body, and with every tear shed, she felt measures of fear leaving her as well. The Israelites had feared for their very lives in the face of distress. They had not trusted their Lord in the critical moment that mattered the most. *Oh, Lord God,* she silently pled, *strengthen my heart. Do not allow me to follow in their shame. Rather, use me in this situation to glorify Your great name...*

Naomi continued to speak, her voice soft and lilting, yet powerful. Her voice rose passionately as she spoke out the timeless promises of their God. "*And Moses said to the people,* ***'Do not be afraid. Stand still, and see the salvation of the Lord, which He will accomplish for you today.*** *For the Egyptians whom you see today, you shall see again no more forever.* ***The Lord will fight for you, and you shall hold your peace.'"***

This time, it was Ruth who flung her arms about Naomi. "Oh, Naomi, thank you! Our God is indeed mighty, and He will deliver me just as He delivered your people so long ago."

Naomi returned the embrace, her cheek pressed firmly

against Ruth, their tears mingling. "*Our* people," she whispered forcefully. "Our people."

Ruth smiled through her tears. "Yes. Our people."

Naomi's eyes grew very serious, and she did not release her grip on Ruth's hand as her penetrating eyes searched Ruth's. "My daughter, something I long for you to understand above all else – "

"Yes, Naomi?"

"I trust our Lord to work miracles. He has already worked so many – what is one more?" Here, her eyes sparkled playfully. "But this I know: Even if the Almighty sees fit to work this in a way other than what we ask, even if Boaz cannot redeem you, you have another Redeemer – One who loves you more than even Boaz could."

Ruth could feel the hot tears stinging her eyelids, but this time, she was determined not to let them fall.

"You have already been redeemed, my daughter. You are a child of the King – the Creator of all things. You are safe in the palm of His hand. Never forget that."

"I will remember, Naomi," Ruth breathed shakily. "Always."

Naomi gave her hand a gentle squeeze. "Good! You must *be still*, Ruth. Be still, and see the salvation of the Lord."

Ruth nodded, gathering the strength to rise to her feet. "Be still."

Naomi smiled. "Yes, be still."

Chapter 30

THE APPEAL

The city square was bustling as usual. The clamorous village activity seemed to awaken with the sun. Eager merchants shouted out to passers-by, eager to sell their wares. Women bargained for goods and groceries in shrill tones. Cattle lowed mournfully while donkeys brayed noisily. Wagon wheels clattered and clanged metallically upon the cobblestoned pavement.

Boaz did not hesitate. He appreciated Kemuel's purposeful resolve as the young man strode alongside him, straight to the elders sitting in a long, imposing line at the city gates.

Boaz offered one last, silent prayer as he made eye contact with the head elder. *Lord God, I submit myself to Your perfect will. Do as you see fit, Lord.*

Ezra's sharp eyes had spotted the two determined men long before they had reached the gate. Immediately he drew closer to the elders surrounding him and began to whisper in facetious tones. Boaz had no desire to be privy to their conversation.

"Good morning, men," Boaz called cheerfully, surprising

even himself by the steadiness of his own voice. "The Lord be with you!"

There was a moment of frenzied confusion as the elders eyed each other questioningly. Boaz's enthusiastic greeting was therefore met by a broken string of a few less-enthusiastic *The Lord bless you*'s.

Ezra appeared to be seething like an agitated viper, yet he did not dare speak out after encountering Boaz at Kemuel's home several nights before.

Zakai, an elderly man with deep, creased features and a graying beard that hung past his chest, raised a fist in greeting. "Boaz. What brings you to our gates this fine day?"

Boaz responded with a confident smile. "I have business to attend to, my fine sir." Purposefully, he ignored Ezra's gaze. The silver-haired man appeared to be strangling.

Zakai, on the other heand, studied Boaz with clear, kind eyes. He nodded. "Waiting for someone particular, I expect?"

"Yes, indeed."

Zakai responded with a firm shake of the head. "Take a seat then, my man. Wait as long as you must."

"Thank you for your kindness, sir." Boaz settled himself as comfortably as possible a safe distance from the elders and their stony gazes. Kemuel appeared ready to strike at the slightest grievance as he remained standing at Boaz's shoulder.

"You look ready to take on an army, my friend," Boaz commented playfully.

"If need be," was the sober response.

Boaz grinned. "No such measures will be necessary today, brother."

Warily, Kemuel's eyes scanned the crowd. "We shall see," he muttered. "We shall see."

~

Boaz did not need to wait long. Half an hour later, Yigal strolled carelessly into market. Boaz winced at the sight of him. The man appeared reptilian rather than human with his predatory movements and leering, jagged-tooth grin.

Boaz allowed his gaze to sweep cautiously over the hustle and bustle of the square. Had his womenfolk found their way to the square yet?

"There." Kemuel was one step ahead of him.

Boaz followed the younger man's gaze and saw four women huddled against a nearby wall, their veiled faces unrecognizable and their plain dress inconspicuous enough. Boaz offered the slightest nod in their direction to indicate that he was aware of their presence – as well as their prayers.

He then directed his attention to the gangly, awkwardly proportioned man that appeared to be carefully observing every female form that happened to cross his path. Boaz felt his gut tighten. *Lord God, protect Ruth from this scoundrel.*

Drawing himself up to his full, imposing height, Boaz strolled casually towards the boorish young man. Kemuel followed closely behind, his eyes steeled.

Yigal noticed Boaz's approach immediately, and his beady little eyes widened to an astonishing size. For a moment, he appeared to be considering whether or not he should stick around or flee for the safety of the jostling crowd. But something in Boaz's expression must have commanded him to remain right where he was.

"Yigal, good day to you, sir! The Lord bless you!" Boaz clamped down hard upon Yigal's slight shoulder.

The man swallowed hard, his Adam's apple bobbing grotesquely. "Sir?" he nearly choked.

"Boaz, it is. And this here is my good friend, Kemuel. We have a pressing matter to discuss with you."

The man's expression bordered that of hysteria. He gulped noisily. "A pressing matter?"

Boaz must have filled the man's entire frame of vision. "A very pressing matter, indeed."

Huddled closely together, the four women watched Boaz's somber proceedings with bated breath.

Ruth could see that Boaz had addressed someone. However, the man with which her beloved conversed was a good head shorter than Boaz, and the frenzied crowd of bustling humanity made it maddeningly difficult to see the recipient of Boaz's conversation. The elders had also closed in about the trio, forming a human shield that seemed nearly impossible to penetrate.

Adara's curiosity had gotten the best of her. "Who is he talking to?" she demanded insistently, standing on her tip toes.

"Hush, child!" Ada hissed. "We are to remain inconspicuous."

"To blend in," Naomi reminded her calmly.

Ruth reached for Adara's hand and the two exchanged knowing looks. "Perhaps it is best we do not know," Ruth offered sagely, though her every thought screamed with suppressed curiosity.

Though the lower portion of Adara's face was veiled, Ruth could tell by the delightful crinkles about the corners of her friend's eyes that she was smiling broadly. "He must be small, whoever he is," she whispered naughtily. "I believe the four of us could take him, Ruth."

"Shah, child!" This time, it was more than a hiss. "Patience," Ada chided hotly. "Patience, as well as *silence*."

Adara quieted down but Ruth noticed that she still seemed to be sizing up the narrow form that quaked anxiously before Boaz and her imposing husband.

Curious though she was, Ruth preferred to look away rather than observe the formal proceedings. She was still not familiar with the customs of this new land, and she feared that even if she could witness the event, she would be utterly unable to follow along with the proceedings, much less understand them.

Ruth willed her eyes to travel in Boaz's direction. She saw that he was directing a handful of the elders – she counted ten of them – to their proper seats. She also noticed that Ezra was not one of the ten chosen. The man's face reddened in ire and protest, but he remained silent. Ruth was grateful.

A short gasp escaped from Adara's lips.

Ruth glanced sideways to see that Adara had cleverly used the ancient wall as a stepping stone to gain a better view of their two men. She had placed one foot on a stone that jutted conveniently from the bottom of the wall, and pulled herself up momentarily for a better look. Now she remained poised where she was, one foot on the crumbling rock ledge and the other dangling in mid-air. She gripped the wall clumsily, the color completely drained from her face.

Ruth reached for the young woman and pulled her back in place. "Adara, whatever were you thinking?" she gasped. "What is it?"

But Adara remained ghostly pale, unable to bring herself to meet Ruth's scrutinizing gaze.

"What is it?"

Still, no response.

"Adara?"

When Ruth saw the tears forming in Adara's lustrous dark eyes, she felt an unwelcome knot tightening with violent force within her chest. She gripped her friend's small shoulders. "Adara, answer me!"

But Ada had pulled both women in close, the way a mother hen might correct two wayward chicks. "That's quite enough from both of you," she harrumphed, keeping one hand anchored to either girl.

Adara said nothing. She simply reached in front of Ada and gripped Ruth's hand. Ruth could tell by the fervent set of the young woman's eyes that she was praying silently – fervently.

Rocked with confusion, Ruth strained her eyes and focused with all her might on the scene before her. Even as pedestrians passed to and fro, Ruth kept her eyes glued to the scene, trying to determine what had upset Adara so violently.

That's when the shorter man conversing with Boaz planted both hands on hips and turned so that he was nearly facing the crowd.

A nauseating wave of sickness washed over Ruth – deep, pungent, and overwhelming. Suddenly, she was brought back to that day when she and Adara had visited the marketplace... the day when the stone had been hurtled viciously through the air, striking her squarely in the face... Mechanically, she reached up with her free hand and touched her own rosy cheek, as if expecting to find the tender bruising still there.

Her entire world was spinning, and desperately, Ruth fought to maintain control as the sickening waves threatened to claim her. She could scarcely believe her own eyes...

Her kinsman redeemer was that despicable, leery snake of a man from the marketplace!

~

Boaz found himself astounded by the overwhelming sense of calm that had engulfed him the moment he had set foot in the city square. He knew he owed it all to His Lord, and he uttered a silent prayer of thanks even as he turned to squarely face the ten elders.

Zakai, naturally a leader of men, assumed command of the ten. "We are assembled together today in the presence of Almighty God and these many witnesses..." Though his voice had grown thinner with age, it still held an authoritative quality that would have been quite difficult to defy or ignore.

Boaz waited patiently until Zakai had made the proper introductions according to custom and protocol, then resumed his business there. "Yigal," he declared, his voice strong, "You have heard of Naomi, the widow of one of our own – Elimelech – who has returned to our beloved homeland after many long years living as a foreigner in the land of Moab?"

The man crossed his arms and grinned smugly. "Who hasn't heard of such?"

"Clearly you have failed to remember that you, sir, are the closest living relative of Naomi's deceased husband."

This bit of news nearly sent the spindly man into a frenzy. His eyes bulged once more, and he appeared to be battling several conflicting emotions. After taking a moment to recover himself, he pasted on the same smug grin and attempted to appear in control. "You don't say?"

"I do, indeed. There is a tract of land in question that

once belonged to Elimelech. If you intend to redeem it, buy it back this very day in the presence of all these witnesses."

"A tract of land? How large is this piece of land which you offer me?" The man rubbed his hands together greedily.

"A decent size, I suppose. I have heard that it is no longer in the best of shape, but amends can certainly be made. Will you redeem it, sir?"

Slapping his hands together loudly, the man resumed rubbing his hands together noisily and grinned. "I will do it!" he declared, without a moment's hesitation.

Boaz felt Kemuel stiffen beside him, and he turned and cast him a warning glance. He had expected as much. It was time to drive the nail into the coffin. He smiled. "There is just one thing..." he added, with an easy shrug of his broad shoulders.

Yigal's eyes narrowed in suspicion as he allowed a low hiss to escape his nostrils. "Yes?"

Ruth could bear the tension no longer. Breaking free from Ada's firm grip, she pushed her way through the thick mass of people that had already gathered to observe the transaction that was about to take place between two very unlikely candidates – a highly respected landowner and the local village creep.

"Ruth! What on earth are you thinking, child?"

Ruth could hear Ada's cry of alarm, as well as a gasp of displeasure that had escaped from Naomi's pale lips. But she did not look back. She couldn't. She had to know what was being discussed on her behalf. She could no longer contain herself. She felt as though she would burst.

She received angry glares from both men and women

alike as she continued to struggle her way forward through the crowd. She paused only when she was within hearing range of the men's conversation.

She felt an angry tug on her sleeve and gasped in fear. But when she turned, she found herself face-to-face with a very addled Ada. Naomi and Adara had also followed, and now stood breathless after a harried attempt to keep up with the spritely housekeeper who had so easily pushed her way through the throng.

"I don't know what has gotten into you," Ada rebuked sternly, "but even if you insist on giving yourself away, we must remain together. Understood?"

Ruth felt ashamed to meet the blunt woman's gaze. Her cheeks aglow, she said quietly, "It was foolish of me. Forgive me, Ada."

Ada's staunch features softened. "Of course, my child. I can't imagine what you must be going through. Still, no more funny business."

Ruth smiled in spite of herself. "Yes, ma'am." She could now clearly hear the dialogue carried on between Boaz and the kinsman redeemer. *Her* kinsman redeemer. She shuddered, and, swallowing hard, turned to observe the fearful scene before her, steeling herself for what was surely to come.

All of the elders – even those who had not been chosen to preside over the ceremony – appeared to be waiting with baited breath. In fact, the entire crowd remained strangely, eerily silent. What was it about this moment that had so attracted the attention of the passers-by and completely stilled the hectic commotion of the market square?

Boaz remained steady, his eyes fixed upon the man before him. "You may recall that Elimelech had a son. This son also died, leaving a widow behind. In order to redeem the land, you must agree to redeem his widow as well."

An eagerness sprang into the young man's eyes that turned Boaz's stomach. "A widow, eh?"

"Yes, indeed."

The man appeared to be searching his mind for some recollection of the woman mentioned. In an instant, his eyes shone with predatory recognition. The jagged-toothed grin returned. "Yes, yes, of course! I remember her well…"

Boaz fought the urge to strangle the man. He turned to look at Zakai, the elder. The wizened old man gazed upon him with a look of utter regret. He, no doubt, shared Boaz's disdain for this depraved young man.

"Name the price," Yigal boasted loudly. "I will take the land and the girl."

He had spoken as if he merely planned to purchase a few paltry vegetables from the market. Instinctively, Kemuel began to close in. Boaz held up a hand and cast another warning glance in his direction. Kemuel stiffened, clearly infuriated by the callousness with which the kinsman regarded his wife's dearest friend.

Ruth nearly collapsed. "No…" never before had she felt so weak. Both Ada and Naomi reached for her, supporting her by the elbows.

Adara, too, looked sick. Any and all natural color had drained from her face. She clutched her belly with one hand, looking genuinely distressed. "I fear I am going to be sick…" she breathed.

Ruth reached for her hand.

"Oh, no..." the young woman turned and pushed her way backwards through the crowd. Ruth watched in both horror and amusement as her friend doubled over and lost her lunch on a furious onlooker's leather sandals...

Boaz took a step closer to Yigal, his jaw set grimly, his eyes ablaze with determination. "There is still one more thing to consider," Boaz continued, his voice low and even.

"What is it?" the man whined.

Boaz looked once more to Zakai, and the kindly old man offered him strength as well as silent encouragement. Squaring his shoulders, Boaz went on. "If you take the young woman as a bride, then the land as well as the resulting offspring will rightfully belong to the family of her deceased husband. This would be, after all, a Levirate marriage. You fully understand the terms."

At this, the man's brows furrowed with indignation.

Boaz resisted the urge to smile. He knew of very few men who had any desire to purchase land with his own hard-earned wages, only to labor and sweat over a crop that would never belong to him – of which he was never to reap the benefits. He knew even fewer men who desired to wed a woman – especially a *foreign* woman of ill-repute – in order to produce an heir for *another* man, an heir who could very easily rise up against his own sons and steal away any legacy that his own flesh and blood might one day hope to possess.

This was it – the moment of truth, the moment of reckoning. Ruth's fate was about to be sealed, as well as his own. This one moment would change both of their lives forever – and, yet, it was completely out of their hands!

But it is *in* Your *hands, Lord. My life is in Your hands, as well as hers. Thy will be done, Lord.*

Ruth bit down upon her lip so hard that she was certain it was bleeding. Her fists clenched, her breath broken and unsteady. She prayed more fiercely than she ever had in her life.

Adara had rejoined them, looking a bit better in spite of her humiliation. The color was slowly returning to her cheeks as her horror had given way to embarrassment. Fortunately, the onlooker with the soiled sandals had merely shaken an angry fist and hissed a few crude threats before taking flight, addled and barefoot. Ruth couldn't help but wish it had been Yigal standing in Adara's way.

But now Adara seemed to have regained possession of herself, the color returning to her pallid face. Her slender brows knit in suppressed indignation. How dare that slimy, little man cause her dear friend such pain! Why, she had a mind to march right up there and teach him a thing or two herself!

But now was no time for such wistful reveries. Ruth needed her desperately. She needed her *prayers*. She needed her *support*. And despite her own discomfort, Adara was determined to give both.

Grasping Ruth's hand tightly with her own slender fingers, Adara whispered her prayers with such purpose that Ruth nearly wept. "Father God, protect this precious daughter of Yours. Your will be done in her life, Lord. Protect her, Father. Hide her in the shelter of Your mighty wings..."

"Surely you needn't even consider such a bargain, young man! Just what are you waiting for?"

Boaz snapped to full attention. Who had spoken such rash encouragement to this irresponsible leech of society?

Boaz's eyes flashed when he saw that Ezra had finally found his tongue and was indeed speaking with Yigal. The gaunt elder leaned forward in his chair in an attempt to gain Yigal's attention. "The land is good and the girl is lovely. The decision is yours!"

Kemuel looked as though he would self-destruct. He turned to look Ezra squarely in the face, his flashing eyes daring the old man to speak another word. But the elder carefully avoided Kemuel's gaze, his own eyes remaining fixed on the torn young man standing before Boaz.

"On the contrary," the voice that broke through was not to be argued with, and Boaz raised thankful eyes toward Zakai – a man he resolved that he would never again take for granted. "This is a life-changing decision. Consideration is not only wise, it is crucial." With that, he perched his elbow on his knee and leaned in closer toward Yigal. "Young man, do you fully understand the responsibilities that such a decision would present?"

Ezra's veins bulged red and angry as he propelled himself to his feet. "You are trying to persuade this man!"

"To make wise decisions? Yes. And you would be well-advised to do the same."

There was a collective gasp of pleasure from the gathering crowd, and Boaz suspected that there were many among them who had long desired to put the pompous, silver-bearded elder back in his place.

"This is a mockery!"

"Sit down, sir. That is quite enough."

Seething, Ezra adjusted his robe and took his seat.

With kind, understanding eyes, Zakai turned his attention back to the lean figure standing before the council of elders. "Young man?"

Shockingly, Yigal had undergone a surprising transformation in the moments the elders had disputed. He gazed upon Zakai with a look of admiration and even regret. His mouth formed one long, grim line. Without a word, he stooped and began to untie his sandal.

Chapter 31

BETROTHED

"What is he doing?" Adara demanded, unwilling to believe her own eyes lest her heart be deceived by any false hope.

"His sandal!" Naomi cried out, as she and Ada gripped each other's arms with a zeal that was delightful to behold. "He is removing his sandal!"

"Dare we believe he shall give it to the good master?" Ada breathed, her ruddy cheeks aflame with hopeful color.

Ruth wondered if she had suffered a nervous breakdown. Was she hallucinating? Surely Naomi and Ada were not discussing the man's choice in footwear at a time like this! It was all too strange and very disconcerting. "What of it?" she floundered, her thoughts racing. "Why is the man concerned about his sandal when so much is at stake?" she wondered if her words sounded as strangled and panicked to the others as they did to her own pounding ears.

Both Ada and Naomi exploded in giddy laughter at Ruth's childlike innocence and naiveté.

"Why, of course the poor girl wouldn't understand such

a custom," Ada declared, finding it all a little too humorous for Ruth's frazzled nerves.

"My dear, sweet child," Naomi exclaimed, taking Ruth by the arms. "In a case legal and binding such as the redemption of property and Levirate marriage, it is customary for the man forfeiting his claim to remove his sandal and offer it up to the man who intends to do the redeeming!"

Ruth was certain her stomach turned. Her eyes glued to the scene before her, she watched with unbroken attention as Yigal straightened himself to his full, unimpressive height. Slowly, purposefully, Yigal extended his hand, offering Boaz a worn, leather sandal...

Boaz fought the urge to blink in order to clear his vision. Did his eyes deceive him? Had Yigal truly surrendered his rights as kinsman redeemer so quickly, so readily? He cast a quick glance at the serious Zakai, intentionally avoiding the gaze of a huffing, red-faced Ezra. Could they possibly be seeing what he himself was seeing?

Then Boaz felt rather than saw Kemuel clamp an affirming hand upon his shoulder. Boaz accepted the sandal before the man could blink, much less reconsider.

"Congratulations, brother!" The joy in his foreman's tone was touching. Boaz accepted his congratulatory handshake, then turned to face the elders. Raising the sandal for all to see, Boaz firmly concluded to the elders as well as the gathered crowd, "You have become witnesses this day that I have purchased all that was once Elimelech's, as well as everything belonging to his sons."

The eager onlookers erupted into joyful cheers. Many of them had experienced Boaz's wisdom as well as his kindness at some point or another, and all seemed truly glad to see the man successful in his pursuit.

Boaz raised a commanding hand to silence the friendly uproar. "Even more so, this day I choose Ruth – the widow of the son of Elimelech – to take for myself as my wife. In this way, the name of the dead may not be cut off from among his brethren. I say again – you are all witnesses this day!"

Again, the bystanders exploded with joyous shouts and cheers.

Zakai smiled faintly for the first time that morning. Rising to his feet, he placed a leathery hand upon Boaz's shoulder and beamed upon the surrounding witnesses. "We are indeed witnesses, sir. May the Lord make the woman who is coming to your house like Rachel and Leah, the two who built the house of Israel; and may you prosper and be famous in Bethlehem."

Boaz smiled broadly, basking in the warmth and promise of Zakai's blessing. How often had he heard the familiar words recited before the guests at a wedding feast? And had he ever dreamed that such words would ever be spoken to him at such a time and in such a place, under such extraordinary circumstances?

Offering up a silent prayer of jubilant thanksgiving to the God who had worked mightily on his behalf, Boaz turned to survey the crowd. The young woman he loved was his to claim. And he could not imagine a better time or place to do so than at that very moment.

Ruth welcomed the warm embraces of the three women who had stood beside her through her most uncertain moments. They laughed and wept and continued to embrace, knowing that they must look very silly but not caring one bit.

Ruth pulled gently away when she saw him. He stole confidently through the sea of people, his shoulders thrown back, his steps sure, his features aglow with the deepest kind of love.

Respectfully, Naomi, Adara, and Ada stepped aside, still aflutter with giggles and happy tears.

Boaz did not even appear to see them. His eyes were fastened upon the beautiful young foreigner who had stolen his heart from that very first meeting, when her humility and sacrificial heart had been so clearly demonstrated as she labored in the sweltering fields to provide for an aging, grief-stricken mother-in-law.

Ruth lowered her veil, not completely, but enough to allow her beloved to glimpse the shining happiness upon her face. She smiled even as tears streamed down her cheeks.

When Boaz finally reached her, he took both of her delicate hands gently in his own strong ones. Ruth closed her eyes and willed herself to still her pounding heart. This was it – the moment she had longed for, prayed for. Her God was so faithful. He had come through for her, for Boaz, for Naomi… for all of them.

"Ruth," Boaz's voice possessed a tenderness that touched her to the very core. "Do you trust our God?"

Ruth was carried away to the previous night, when Boaz had asked her the very same question. In that moment, their future had seemed so impossible, so bleak, and yet she had answered him with conviction. "I shall always trust Him," she whispered. "As long as I live."

"He is good, isn't He?"

Ruth laughed through her tears. “He is, my love.” *My love!* How naturally the words came! And how sweet they sounded when spoken to the man the Lord Himself had chosen for her.

Boaz gripped her hands a bit tighter, then gazed directly into her eyes. His own held such promise that Ruth could not look away, despite the crowd of nosy onlookers that pressed in from all sides, eager to witness the conclusion of the morning’s unusual attraction.

“Ruth, will you give me the great honor of becoming my wife?”

Gently taking his face in her hand, she smiled up at him with all the love and trust in the world. “I will. With all of my heart.”

Chapter 32

THE WEDDING

There was no wedding procession to twist and wind about the village streets as the bridegroom eagerly drew forth to claim his glowing bride. There was no wedding feast filled with happy onlookers and well-wishers. There was no jubilant dancing nor the merry jingle of the women's tambourines as their hands attempted to keep up with their galloping feet. There was no tantalizing spread of savory meat, freshly baked bread, and mouth-watering sweetmeats to beckon and call to all who had gathered to witness the sacred union of man and wife.

But Ruth didn't mind a bit. She had everything that she could possibly need – a mighty God who had fought powerfully on her behalf, and a strong husband-to-be who treasured her more than life itself. She had a mother-in-law whom she loved as if she were her very own flesh and blood. She had dear friends who loved the Lord and provided sweet, like-minded fellowship. What more could she possibly desire?

Though it was not customary to host an extravagant wedding feast in the case of Levirate marriage, Boaz had insisted that Naomi, Kemuel, Adara, and Ada – as well as his hired hands – attend the blessed occasion at his home.

Zakai's services were requested to pronounce Boaz and Ruth man and wife. The aging elder was delighted to oblige, and arrived at Boaz's estate the morning following Boaz's meeting with Yigal, as they had previously arranged.

Ruth and Naomi had spent the previous evening packing their few meager belongings, loading them upon their creaky, old wagon, and wondering what it might possibly be like to live in a large, stately home unlike any they had formerly set eyes upon. Boaz had insisted that Naomi come to stay with them as well, and he had refused to take *no* for an answer. "The Lord has blessed me with the family I have been longing for, after all these years!" he had laughingly explained, pulling the two women close. "Now I may finally put all these empty rooms to good use!"

Ruth had nearly wept with joy. What a blessing to Naomi! Imagine – having lost everything, yet to be blessed in such magnificent ways so much later in life! Why, it was rather like the story of Job. Naomi had shared the tragic tale with Ruth one night before their campfire. The man had lost absolutely everything – his wife, his children, his animals, his home and possessions...yet he remained faithful to his God, and the Lord had blessed him a hundred times over by the end of his life. Ruth couldn't help but smile. Yes, the Lord had truly blessed them – just as He had blessed His faithful servant Job.

Though Naomi was excited about the prospect of living on Boaz's breath-taking estate, Ruth knew that living across the hall from her dear friend Ada held even more appeal to Naomi than the countless charms of the impressive stone house.

When the blessed moment finally arrived, Ruth felt

nearly dizzy with happiness and wonder. In fact, when the time came, she barely remembered the ceremony, though Ada, Amal, and Samuel had spent the wee morning hours frantically throwing together an impromptu spread of delightful treats for the few guests who would be present. Both Naomi and Adara had assisted Ruth as she prepared herself for her new husband – dressing in fine silken linens, combing her hair until it shone, and anointing herself with perfumes – and they had both *oohed* and *ahhed* over the final result. "You look stunning, my dear," Naomi had proudly proclaimed, carefully arranging the flowing cream-colored veil draped carefully about Ruth's graceful shoulders.

On wobbly legs, Ruth had allowed Naomi and Adara to lead her down a long, tiled corridor and into the lush garden courtyard, glowing in the rich golden hues of the early morning sunlight. Ruth had never seen such splendor, and she could scarcely believe that in a few very short moments, this would be her home.

Yet even the dazzling splendor of the lovely estate dramatically paled when Ruth was led to her husband-to-be. The moment their eyes had met, everything else had faded into the background.

Boaz had stood across from her dressed in his finest attire, clasping her hands tightly in his own, his eyes glowing with love and tenderness.

Lord, I am so happy! Ruth's heart had silently cried. *So happy!*

The ceremony was short. Zakai pronounced them man and wife, his deep-set gray eyes crinkling with delight as he did so.

The courtyard erupted with shouts and cheers as Naomi and Ada, Adara and Kemuel, and both of Boaz's hired hands broke into heartfelt applause.

And then Boaz was taking Ruth's hand and leading her away, back down the long, tiled corridor from which she had come.

Ruth barely noticed the cool, smooth tiles beneath her feet or the dizzying swirl of mosaic images on the walls. On either side of the narrow corridor, torches burned steadily from their wrought iron mounts upon the wall.

"You look beautiful," Boaz whispered gently as he took an unexpected right turn and led her up a steep flight of massive stone stairs.

Ruth felt her cheeks flush with pleasure at his compliment, and she lowered her eyes humbly. "And you..." she managed softly, "...you look very handsome, my husband." Her *husband*! She could scarcely believe her own words! How the Lord had provided!

At the top of the stairs, a large marble archway arced gracefully above their heads, leading into a spacious, well-kept chamber. Light poured into the room from several arched, tile-lined windows. Ruth gasped in delight and held herself in check before she could race to the window and lean out into the fresh morning air. The massive arched windows framed the gently rolling green hills of Bethlehem – a beautiful land that Ruth had grown to love.

Before she could speak, Boaz reached for her arms and turned her toward him. She gazed up into his hazel-colored eyes and smiled gently, sincerely. She hoped to communicate her every ounce of happiness with that smile.

Boaz looked deeply into her eyes, his expression that of wonder. He held her arms tightly and smiled down upon her. "Do you like it?"

Ruth was touched by the nervousness she detected in his otherwise strong voice. She smiled again. "I love everything," she answered readily. Then, reaching up and clasping her hands gently behind his neck, she added softly, "But not nearly as much as I love *you*, my husband. You have brought such joy to my heart. I am so happy, Boaz. And I thank you."

Boaz shook his head in amazement. "*You* thank *me*? No, it is *you* I have to thank, my dear. You have made this house a home. You are everything I have prayed for, Ruth, and so much more."

Ruth lowered her eyes, unable to speak for the moment. Eventually, she found her voice. "Boaz, may I share something with you?"

"Anything, my love. Always."

"I never had the chance to tell you... I gave my life to the Lord a very long time ago. Well, at least, it feels as if it were a very long time ago."

Boaz smiled his patient understanding.

"I had seen Naomi's great faith and heard the stories of her God, and I longed to serve Him, to know Him. But I was afraid. I feared that He would not accept a... a Gentile."

Boaz's eyes softened, and he pulled his young wife a bit closer.

"However, one night, as Naomi and I sat before the fire, she shared with me a story. It was the story of a young Gentile woman who put her trust in Naomi's God. When the mighty warrior Joshua sent spies to Jericho, the Gentile woman was there. She sheltered the spies from evil men. The men repaid her for her kindness, and her life was spared when Jericho was destroyed."

Boaz's eyes had lit up with recognition and a slight trace of alarm. "Naomi knew this woman?" he managed after a long pause, his voice slightly choked.

Ruth smiled understandingly. "She knew of her. Well, the Gentile woman put her trust in the God of the

Hebrews, and He accepted her. She became one of His own people."

"Ruth," Boaz's voice trembled ever so slightly. "That Gentile woman of which you speak... she was my mother."

Ruth had already known this. She remembered that night when the men and women of the village had come for her, torches in hand and anger in their hearts. She remembered Boaz's stoic defense of her. He had referred to his noble mother as an example. How many nights had she longed to share this with him? Leaning in as closely as she dared, she whispered quietly, "Boaz, your mother is the reason I came to know the Lord. She gave me the confidence, Boaz. The courage. She gave me hope."

Boaz leaned forward, resting his forehead against her own veiled head. He said nothing for several minutes, breathing somewhat unevenly. When he had finally gained his composure, he lifted his head and met her gaze squarely, evenly. "Thank you for sharing that with me, Ruth. It is truly incomprehensible. The Lord God truly does work in mysterious ways. Do you know that my mother prayed for you every single day?"

Ruth tilted her head to one side, confused. "How could she?" she asked honestly.

"She did not know you, of course, but she knew that one day her son would take a bride. Each day she prayed for the woman I would marry. And, Ruth, that woman was *you*. What a miracle. What a remarkable story indeed!"

Ruth shook her head, amazed. God's mercies never did cease.

With one hand, Boaz reached forward and drew aside Ruth's veil. He gazed tenderly upon her and gently caressed her cheek. "There is something we must discuss, my love, now that we are husband and wife."

His tone was serious. Much too serious. Ruth gazed trustingly up at him, her clear dark eyes clouded with concern.

"Do you understand the conditions of a Levirate marriage, Ruth?"

The conditions? Ruth shook her head slowly, uncertain that she would like these conditions, whatever they were.

Boaz's hands traveled from her arms to her hands, and he clasped her fingers tightly. "We are husband and wife, and we will enjoy all the privileges of marriage together. We will share a home. We will share a family. Our two separate lives shall become one. However..."

Ruth held her breath, fearful of what might proceed from the mouth of her husband next.

"...The very first child borne of a Levirate marriage legally bears the name and heritage of your former husband. He will carry on your dead husband's family line. By such provisions, the name of the dead shall not be cut off forever."

Ruth gazed up at her husband imploringly. Though it was the very first day of their marriage and she couldn't yet fathom the prospect of children, she balked at the idea of honoring an abusive, deceased man in such a way. "Oh, Boaz, please don't."

"It is not for me to decide, my dear. It is the Law."

"But why? Mahlon was not a good man. I cannot look a child – *our* child – in his innocent eyes and call him by such a hateful name!"

"It doesn't have to be Mahlon's given name. It must be a name in his family – the name of his fathers."

"Oh, Boaz. I can't."

"But you must."

"I can't."

Ruth was stunned to see a playful twinkle in her new husband's eyes. "My dear," he ventured good-naturedly, "we haven't even borne the child yet. Perhaps it is too early to be concerning ourselves with such things!"

Ruth felt her cheeks burning crimson and she lowered her head in embarrassment. This was all new to her – talking in such a frank manner to a man. *But,* she reminded herself, *this is not just any man. This is my beloved husband.*

Chuckling softly, Boaz tipped her chin upward and smiled kindly upon his new, young wife. "Any children the Lord may choose to bless us with after the first child will be our own, though the firstborn will still be ours to raise, to love. He will belong to another in name only, my dear."

Ruth managed to nod her head in understanding. She had never taken the time to consider herself a mother. She had never particularly desired to be one. But the thought of raising a family with this man she loved so fiercely was nearly too joyous to comprehend. She smiled and tightened her grip about his neck. "Regardless of what the Lord may have in store for our future, Boaz, God has given us this: *now*. I have this moment. I have *you*, my husband. I could not ask for anything more."

Pulling her close to him, Boaz leaned forward to kiss his new bride.

Chapter 33

JOYFUL DISCOVERIES

Adara's every nerve was alive, tingling, afire with anticipation and excitement. She paced nervously back and forth, back and forth, back and forth.

She had never known that so much joy could be crammed into such a small amount of time. So much had happened over the last month! Her dear friend Ruth had married Boaz – the faithful friend of her husband and their fellow brother in the Lord. Her heart had soared with happiness as she had watched them exchange marriage vows, their faces bright and beaming.

Then, of course, Naomi had also joined Boaz's household. She had been informed that Naomi and Ada worked busily in the kitchen together – laughing, talking, and sharing their hearts in a way that only true sisters in the Lord really could. Adara was thrilled that the two older women had been granted such joy and peace in their later years – years that were not often pleasant for others.

Not only that, but Kemuel's mother had offered her a somewhat flimsy apology regarding her attitude toward her in months past. She had not outright apologized, but she had stammered out a few weak excuses and attempted to pay her a few visits without a display of obvious resentment or hostility.

But as for the crowning joy of all joys... Well, Adara had just recently discovered it. That very morning, in fact. She wondered how such anxiety could so quickly be transformed into sheer ecstasy!

She had been fearful at first. She hadn't been feeling well lately. In fact, she hadn't felt at all like herself in *weeks*. The nausea was becoming unbearable, and she was having a great deal of difficulty keeping down her meals. She was beginning to wonder if she should be concerned. Was something wrong with her? Was she ill? Would she ever recover?

That's when Naomi and Ada had shown up at her doorstep, each toting a basket brimming with golden loaves of freshly baked bread. Kemuel had been away at work at the time, and Adara, nearly beside herself, had poured out her woes to her two dear friends.

Neither older woman spoke for a time, then, after exchanging one long, knowing gaze, they had both erupted in a fit of laughter.

Adara had felt a bit miffed, especially since they found her discomfort mirthful. However, she had held her peace and simply stated matter-of-factly, "Well, I don't see what is so funny about the situation..."

That's when Naomi had spoken up, her eyes gleaming with merriment. "My dear girl! You have been praying so long and hard that you seem to have forgotten what it is that you are praying for!"

Adara had not followed.

"My child," Ada had cut in, her cheeks rosy with color. "Have you considered your symptoms at all?"

"My symptoms?"

"What is it that you and your husband have been praying for?"

The verdict had hit poor Adara like a ton of bricks. Mentally, she reviewed the past few months and wondered if it could be possible. Dare she even hope such a thing?

The color had left her face, and Naomi had reached for her arm to steady her. "There, child! You're white as a sheet!"

"Don't forget to breathe, now!" Ada had cautioned in good humor.

"But... but, Ada, Naomi... do you possibly think...?"

"Of course we do," Ada had put in promptly, as if that settled the entire matter.

"But... but how can I be sure?"

"Have you seen the village physician?" Naomi had asked calmly.

"Why, no, but – "

Ada had set aside her basket and reached for Adara's arm. "Then you're coming with us, and don't protest because it won't do you a bit of good! We'll go with you, for support, you know. You may need it. Come! Let's not wait another second. Precious time is a-wasting!"

And with that, the two older women had dragged the much younger woman down the winding village pathway to meet with the physician.

Now, several hours later, Adara smiled to herself as she thought about how she would remember those moments with Ada and Naomi for the rest of her life. The physician had confirmed it: they had indeed been correct in their motherly assessments, and now Adara could barely contain herself as she waited for her husband to arrive home.

How shall I tell him? What should I say? Adara realized that she had been praying for this moment for nearly a decade, and now that the wondrous moment had finally arrived, she had absolutely no idea what to do. The only thing she truly knew was that she was beside herself with joy!

Folding her arms before her chest, Adara did one last inventory of the small, homey cottage. Every inch of the place was swept clean and spotless. The room still smelled of the freshly baked loaves that Ada and Naomi had brought for her table. Kemuel's supper was prepared and waiting for him. The lamps were all lit, glowing softly in the faint light that arrived just before dusk. The sun was setting in its graceful manner beyond the western hills. She knew that she could expect her husband's arrival at any moment.

Her heart leapt when she finally heard her husband fumbling with the latch outside the door. She had planned to be there, to swing it open easily upon his arrival and to greet him with a disarming smile. But now she found that she could not move. The moment had arrived – the moment she had longed for, waited for, prayed for, wept for. It was here – truly here! And – much to her dismay – she found that she was so overwhelmed, so filled with hope and peace and longing, that she could not move. She could not speak. She could not even bring herself to place one foot in front of the other.

Her husband's tall frame emerged through the narrow doorway, then momentarily turned to latch the door in place.

Adara tried to muster up a cheerful greeting, but no sound would come. She simply stood rooted where she was.

Kemuel looked weary – exhausted, even. He turned to look at her, and her heart ached at the weariness in his eyes. It was obvious that he had suffered through a very long day's work.

No! Her heart cried. *It wasn't supposed to be like this!*

Everything was supposed to be perfect! This moment was supposed to be perfect! She felt the hot tears begin to sting her eyelids.

Then, something completely unexpected happened. Kemuel stopped in his tracks, and he, too, appeared firmly rooted where he stood. His copper-colored eyes sought out his wife's, still wet with tears of both joy and sadness.

See, I AM faithful. I AM good. I can be trusted. I will always come through for you... Adara's entire body trembled as an overwhelming flood of peace washed over her soul. She had never in her entire life heard the Lord speak so clearly to her heart, and she was truly overwhelmed. The tears flowed unbidden down her cheeks, and she could not look away from her husband's intense gaze.

Kemuel looked to her, a question upon his face. He did not ask. He did not speak. He only looked.

And Adara knew exactly what question was upon his lips. She did not say a word. She simply raised her head, and slowly, surely, she nodded an answer to his question: *Yes.*

The next few moments were a whirlwind of furious reaction. She heard Kemuel shout her name, and then she was swept up in his arms as he cried out to the Lord and thanked Him for His goodness and His mercies.

"Thank You, Lord," her husband wept. He repeated his prayer over and over and over again. "Thank You, Lord. We thank You. We thank You..."

Adara simply clung to her husband and silently uttered her own prayers of thanksgiving, her heart far, far too full to allow her to speak. Yes, indeed, there was much to talk about, much to discuss. But the proper time for such talk would come later. For now, it was simply enough to be held and to thank the Lord for His goodness and for His awesome power.

The sun was just beginning to peak around the graceful hillside, eager to announce the dawn of a new day as well as the tender mercies of the Redeemer who fashioned it.

Ruth lay on her side, propped up on one elbow, watching her husband sleep. She knew that he would be stirring very soon. For now, she would simply enjoy this quiet time to thank the Lord for this good man who lay beside her – a man who had so willingly redeemed her from her pain and her troubles, a man who had fully given her his heart and his life, a man who had held nothing back. Smiling softly, she admired his sharp, chiseled features, the firm set of his jaw, the strength of his broad shoulders. What burdens those dependable shoulders had carried! She praised God for bringing him into her life. She prayed that she would be a worthy helpmeet for this man who had spent his entire life serving others.

They had been married for a little less than two months, but already she was learning things about her husband that she had never known...

The way he praised as well as instructed the young boy Samuel, who had come to live under his roof after losing his own parents. The boy gazed upon Boaz with both admiration and respect.

The way he ministered to Amal – the quiet man under his employ who rarely spoke, rarely smiled, rarely demonstrated any type of emotion whatsoever. Ruth wondered what could have possibly happened in the servant's past to so shut him off from the rest of the world, but Boaz seemed intent upon slowly, surely, drawing him out of his morose, solitary state. Several times now, Ruth had witnessed the care-hardened man offer her husband the slightest trace of a smile. She knew that Master Boaz was indeed making progress with him.

The way Boaz respected and looked after both Naomi and Ada. Already, Ruth had learned that Ada had stepped in to fill the gap left behind when Boaz's own mother had passed away. The woman had been looking after him for countless years, and had even served his own mother, Rahab. Ada was just a young girl then, and Ruth had hungrily questioned her about the courageous woman of Jericho – a woman she had never met, but still a woman who had affected her life profoundly.

Ruth sighed contentedly as she leaned forward to stroke her husband's face. His beard was neatly trimmed as usual, and slowly, she traced the smart line with one delicate finger.

What might I do to bring a smile to his face today? With a mischievous smile, Ruth carefully slipped out from beneath the soft linen blankets and tiptoed from the room, down the long stone staircase, through the seemingly endless corridor, and towards the spacious kitchen.

I shall help Ada and Naomi prepare the morning meal, she had decided, determined to be of some use. The older women always insisted on preparing the meals, which often left Ruth feeling useless during mealtimes. She knew that it brought the women great joy to work in the kitchen together, and she certainly appreciated their help – after all, Boaz's home was a large affair and there were plenty of chores to keep her hands very, very busy. But she often found excuses to assist the older women anyway – mostly because it brought her great satisfaction to prepare pleasing meals for her new husband.

Perhaps this morning, I will arrive early enough to prepare a meal for Ada and Naomi! It was an exciting thought, though she doubted she would be so fortunate.

As she entered the large, open kitchen, Ruth found Ada and Naomi already chatting busily, their hands moving nearly as quickly as their wagging tongues. Delicious aromas wafted through the air, promising a satisfying morning meal.

"Ruth! Good morning, my daughter!" Naomi's voice was cheerful, melodious.

"Don't tell me you are about to attempt to shoo us from the kitchen again!" Ada griped teasingly. "You can try, dearie, but it won't do you a bit of good!"

Ruth laughed, her heart warmed by the two women. "I wouldn't dare! But I would certainly like to lend a hand." She grinned playfully, holding her hands up for both women to see. "Two, in fact!"

Ada arched a skeptical brow. "Now you get yourself back to bed, missy. You know what Master Boaz would say!"

Ruth dropped lightly to a stool before the massive work-table and leaned forward eagerly. "And just what do you believe he would say?"

"Well," Ada stated coolly, her hands skillfully pounding out dough with a rolling pin, "being the wise husband that he is, I'm sure he'd say that a woman in your condition has no business slaving over a hot stove!"

Ruth blushed slightly at the mention of her "condition." She had recently made a very shocking and yet, very heart-warming, discovery. She and Boaz were expecting their first child. She would never forget the love and the longing and the sheer joy that had transformed her husband's features that sacred night when she had shared her joyous news with him. Nor would she forget the laughter, the happy tears, the hours of intimate conversation within each other's arms, that had followed.

"Now get yourself back to bed!" Ada repeated, drawing Ruth from her silent reverie. "If not for yourself, for the child at least!"

Ruth smiled contentedly. "I rested well. I couldn't feel any better than I do now."

"Then why don't you get yourself over to that lovely lady's house and tell her your news?" Ada's hands were planted firmly on her hips now, and she leaned forward impatiently. "She'll never forgive you if you keep your little secret from her. She would want to know, Ruth!"

Ruth forced an uncomfortable chuckle. "Well, aren't we full of suggestions this morning!" She was stalling, and both Ada and Naomi probably knew it.

Naomi smiled warmly. "Truly, Ruth. Adara is your closest friend. She would be hurt if you kept such wonderful news to yourself. It's a beautiful day – why don't you take a quick walk to see her and tell her the news?"

Ruth studied her own fingernails for no particular reason, uncomfortable. The truth was, she knew how desperately Adara longed for a child. The lovely young woman and her husband had been trying to have children for nearly a decade – unsuccessfully. Now, Ruth feared to take her own special news to her dear friend. Would such an announcement drive an unnecessary wedge between herself and her dearest friend? Would Adara feel hurt? Jealous? Resentful? Certainly not intentionally – Adara was the kindest, sweetest person Ruth had ever met. But Ruth couldn't help but think how she herself would feel if the roles were reversed. If *she* had been unable to have children for years, and then her newlywed friend conceived within the first few days of her marriage... Ruth sighed shakily. Sometimes, life didn't seem fair. That was all.

"Ruth?"

Ruth glanced up and saw both women eyeing her with concern. Again, Ruth sighed. "It's just that – well, I'm not... um, I'm not – "

"You're not sure how Adara will receive such news?" Ada finished for her.

Ruth simply nodded, hot tears stinging her eyelids. "I don't want to hurt her," she whispered.

Naomi and Ada exchanged knowing looks, but Ruth's eyes were too tear-filled to notice.

"Well," Ada ventured slowly, rolling pin in hand. "How long do you plan on keeping it a secret? Eventually, she's bound to notice *something.* Especially when you are out to *here* and about to burst..." Ada used her hands to indicate an imaginary, round belly.

Ruth glanced up again, somewhat perturbed. Naomi and Ada just seemed to be acting so... insensitive.

Before Ruth could respond, young Samuel appeared in one of the arched entryways. A smaller figure stood near his elbow. "Good morning, my ladies," Samuel announced cheerily, his boyish features bright and ruddy. "You have a guest!" With that, he gave a slight bow and disappeared into the shadows.

Ruth nearly gasped when Adara stepped into the kitchen. "Adara?"

"Ruth!" The young woman ran to her friend and threw her arms about her neck. Drawing back, she took both of Ruth's hands in her own and offered a beaming smile. "How I have missed you! Have you been well?"

Ruth attempted to swallow the lump forming in her throat. "I have."

"Oh, good! I was beginning to worry!"

"There is no need to worry, my friend," Ruth managed, mustering up as much cheerfulness as possible. "I'm fine."

Adara flashed her winning smile again. "Then why have you stayed away?"

"Stayed away?" Ruth stammered, the tears returning.

"We'll leave you two alone to catch up a bit!" Ada announced rather abruptly, setting aside her rolling pin and disappearing around the corner with Naomi.

Ruth glared after them. How could they possibly desert her at a time like this?

That's when Adara did something completely unexpected. Reaching for Ruth's hand, she seated herself at one of the stools and motioned for Ruth to do the same. Obediently, Ruth seated herself and braced herself for the worst.

"I think," Adara began, very slowly and very purposefully, "that perhaps you have stayed away for some time now because... because you are afraid to tell me something. Is that true, Ruth?"

Ruth bit her lower lip. She could not lie to Adara. That would be breaking one of God's commandments. And yet, she just couldn't bring herself to hurt her friend in such a way. Rather than answering Adara's pointed question, Ruth looked away.

Adara continued to smile, her eyes aglow. "Ruth, look at me."

Painstakingly, Ruth did.

"Ruth, I am so happy for you! And so happy for Boaz! You are expecting a child, are you not?"

Ruth broke down. Dropping her head in her hands, she sobbed and rasped out in the most pathetic manner, "Yes!"

Much to her surprise, Adara burst out laughing and

threw her arms about Ruth's trembling shoulders. "Oh, Ruth! I am just so happy! So happy!"

Ruth drew back and gazed at her, her eyes wide. "You are?"

"Yes! What a blessing! A child for you and Boaz! How good the Lord is!"

Ruth swiped at her tears and attempted to smile. "He is, indeed. But how did you know?"

This time, Adara's eyes filled with tears. "I knew there must be some reason you had not come to see me, Ruth. And when I thought about your kindness and that compassionate heart of yours, I put the pieces together. I knew there must be some reason you were afraid to come see me. And then I realized that you were afraid to come see me because you didn't want to hurt me. Oh, Ruth, you are such a good friend, and your kindness touches my heart to the very core!"

Ruth's smile was more genuine this time. "You are a wonderful person, Adara. Thank you for sharing my joy."

Adara grinned mischievously. "I will always share your joy, Ruth, under one condition."

Ruth delicate brows lifted curiously. "And what condition is that?"

Playfully, Adara replied, "If you will also share *my* joy with me..."

Ruth looked to Adara, and suddenly she wondered why she had not noticed that Adara's every feature was alive and shining with happiness, with pride, with joy. Ruth's eyes widened, her jaw dropped, and she cried out in a voice that she was sure must have awakened her sleeping husband upstairs, "Are you saying – "

"I'm saying that Kemuel and I are expecting a child!"

Ruth gasped and threw her arms around Adara's slight

form, sobs wracking her body. "I'm so happy for you!" she gasped. "Oh, Adara, I'm just so happy for you both!" And she meant it with all her heart.

The two women remained where they were for a long moment, seated on the tall stools, their arms about each other's shoulders, happy tears mingling upon their cheeks. When they finally pulled away, Ruth's eyes widened in recognition. "Adara," she started slowly, "did Ada and Naomi know about this?"

"Of course they did. They were with me when I saw the physician."

Ruth laughed aloud. No wonder they had been so eager for Ruth to visit Adara. The sly rascals! They had kept Adara's secret, and though Ruth felt slightly chagrined, she *was* glad that Adara herself had been the one to share the remarkable news.

"I have been praising our God with every breath that I have," Adara explained, leaning forward on her stool. "It is almost unreal. After all these years, to see our prayers answered so mightily, and when we least expected it..."

"There is no end to His miracles," Ruth agreed, her heart nearly bursting with thanksgiving.

"And His timing is perfect. Though I longed for a child for years, the Lord knew when the time was right."

"He did."

Adara shook her head in wonder. "Just think, Ruth – our babies will grow up together! What a support they will be to one another! In a world where there is so little truth, so few followers of what is good, they will have their God and each other to cling to. It is truly a blessing."

Ruth had never known such contentment, such peace. "Yes," she replied wholeheartedly. "It is a blessing indeed."

Chapter 34

REDEEMED

Two beautiful, healthy babies were born in Bethlehem the following spring – a boy and a girl.

Ruth swayed gracefully as she stood on their sprawling patio, a small, precious bundle tucked within her arms. A strong little boy gazed up at her with milky infant eyes, and she found herself marveling at the immense, immeasurable love that a mother's heart could hold.

Boaz stood behind her, one arm about her waist and the other cradling their little son.

"Does God love us this much?" Ruth whispered in awe as she rocked the little bundle in her arms. "The way we love our little son?"

Boaz leaned in close and whispered, "No, my dear. He loves us even more."

Across the patio, Adara held her own little girl in her arms. Kemuel smiled proudly upon the pink pixie face. "She has your eyes, my love – big and bright and beautiful."

Adara smiled graciously as she freed one hand to lightly brush her husband's rough cheek. "I pray that she also has her father's heart. Nothing would bring me greater joy."

The two couples met in the center of the patio, enjoying each other's quiet company and basking in the rich blessings that the Lord God of Heaven had so generously showered upon them. Stretched out before them were the gently rolling hills of Bethlehem, a dazzling sea of emerald green beneath the warm spring sun.

Their silent reveries were interrupted by delightful chatter as Ada and Naomi returned from the marketplace, baskets of produce draped over their arms.

"Where is my darling?" Naomi cried, hurrying to Ruth's side and snatching the sleeping little infant from Ruth's arms.

Both couples laughed as Naomi cradled the baby in her arms and cuddled him close to her breast. "Ah, at long last, I have a little grandson of my own!" Naomi exulted, a tear trickling down her cheek.

Ruth laughed lightly. "Was he worth the wait, Naomi?"

"He was, indeed!"

Ada, who had relieved Adara of her own little bundle, rocked baby Ruthie in her arms as she glanced over at Naomi. "You must tell them what the women were saying at the marketplace!"

Naomi threw her head back and had a good, long laugh. "You would never believe it," she informed the small group, her gray eyes dancing.

"Well, try us and see!" Boaz urged her playfully as he held the hand of his pretty, young wife.

Naomi smiled proudly. "Well, we may not have received a warm reception upon our arrival in Bethlehem," she began teasingly, and everyone on the patio chuckled merrily. "But the women of the town are now saying that I am indeed very blessed! And I must say that I agree with them!"

"And how could we not agree?" Adara declared meaningfully.

"Not only do they say that *I* am blessed, but they also bless my dear, sweet daughter-in-law, who has given me yet another reason to bless my God and enjoy the years remaining for me on this earth." At this, Naomi gazed lovingly upon the sleeping child in her arms and tenderly caressed his ruddy cheek.

"I would like to point out that I was a crucial part of that process," Boaz reminded her, and they shared yet another laugh.

"But what did they say?" Adara urged, eager to hear the rest of the story.

"They gave her a compliment of the highest honor by saying that Ruth – my daughter-in-law by marriage – is an even greater blessing than seven sons of my own flesh and blood! What a compliment! And how true it is!"

"It is good to finally hear them speaking truth," Boaz replied, winking at Ruth as she flushed at Naomi's praise.

"I must agree with them as well," Ada asserted, gingerly offering baby Ruthie to her mother. The baby girl had awakened from her nap and began to whimper and protest as she changed hands again.

Naomi smiled down upon the baby boy in her arms, stroking the soft fuzz that covered his head. "My sweet little baby Obed."

"Ruth, I have been meaning to ask you something," Adara asserted brightly as she rocked her fussing baby in an attempt to pacify the little girl. "You know, of course, why we decided to call our baby *Ruth*. But how did you come to name your sweet child?"

Ruth and Boaz exchanged knowing looks. "Even more so than the fact that we chose a family name," Boaz explained in his deep, strong voice, "the name Obed means *servant.* Ruth and I have learned that we are all given a purpose on this earth, and that is to love the Lord by serving others. We pray that Obed will grow up to fully understand the importance of that calling."

"Obed – what a fitting name for the child of two people so completely committed to serving others!" Naomi exclaimed, teary-eyed as she remembered the way Ruth had dedicated her young life to serving an aging mother-in-law. "It is perfect."

Lovingly, Naomi transferred the sleeping child into his mother's waiting arms.

"Perhaps it is simply because I am his mother," Ruth said softly, her eyes distant, "but I can't help but feel that the Lord has a very special plan in mind for our son. I have no doubt that he will grow into a strong man of God, just like his father." She smiled up at her husband and he squeezed her hand in loving affirmation.

"I wouldn't be surprised," Kemuel spoke up for the first time. "We have seen the Lord work in mighty ways. He has shown us that nothing is too hard for Him."

"Nothing," Adara repeated gently.

"I suppose we should be off," Kemuel stated thoughtfully, guiding Adara in the right direction. "Thank you for your hospitality this fine evening, my brother."

The two men clamped hands briefly and the women exchanged loving embraces before Kemuel and Adara started down the winding path that would lead them home.

Still laughing and chattering enthusiastically, Ada and Naomi made their way back to the kitchen, leaving Ruth and Boaz alone on the patio to enjoy the early evening hours together.

"*Soon,*" Boaz remarked, his eyes upon the vast golden horizon. Before long, the sun would be setting behind those familiar hills.

Ruth looked questioningly up to her husband. "Soon?"

"I felt the Lord impressing that one word upon my heart, just before He brought you to me, Ruth. Kemuel felt the same, and the Lord has blessed him with the child he longed for."

With one arm carefully supporting their sleeping son, Ruth wrapped her other arm around her husband's waist and followed his gaze out into the distant horizon. "He has blessed us so much, hasn't He?"

"He certainly has. See how far He has taken us – from that first day when I found you gathering wheat in the fields?"

Ruth smiled easily. "How could I have known that I would be granted the honor of marrying the handsome owner of that field?"

"And how could I know that I would be given the honor of taking that gorgeous young woman to be my bride? Never in my wildest dreams would I have imagined myself here today, Ruth."

"I was so afraid, Boaz. Kneeling in that field, praying to God that I would find enough wheat the keep Naomi alive and healthy and strong, fearful for my very life in a land full of hostile strangers..."

"The Lord has truly fought for us, Ruth. I have no doubt that He always will."

"The Lord will fight for you..." Ruth mused, repeating the sacred words that had become so dear to her heart.

"Amen."

"Not only has He fought for us, Boaz. He has *redeemed* us. He has redeemed *me.* He knew that I was drowning. He knew that I needed saving. So He sent *you* to me."

Boaz chuckled. "And what if I was the one in need of the saving?"

"*You* are my kinsman redeemer, Boaz. It is not the other way around!"

"Or is it?"

They shared another laugh as the sleeping Baby Obed gurgled his agreement.

Ruth smiled, savoring the sound of her husband's hearty laughter. "My kinsman redeemer. I will always remember the moment you claimed me. The moment our God sent you to save me. God used you, Boaz. I will never have to be afraid again. I have been redeemed."

Boaz drew his wife even closer. "Redeemed?"

"Yes," Ruth drew herself up a bit taller to plant a kiss upon her husband's cheek. "Redeemed."

Those who sow in tears shall reap in joy.
He who continually goes forth weeping,
Bearing seed for sowing,
Shall doubtless come again with rejoicing,
Bringing his sheaves with him.
Psalm 126:5-6

ABOUT THE AUTHOR

Rachael Duncan is a passionate follower of Christ. Her goal is to reach as many people as possible for the sake of Christ and His kingdom. She believes that God has gifted each of His children with different gifts to be used to strengthen the body of Christ and fulfill the Great Commission. (Matt. 28:19-20; 1 Cor. 12)

Rachael was blessed to be raised in a strong Christian home, and she accepted Jesus Christ as her Lord and Savior at a very early age. Since then, she has determined to live her life in accordance to His Word and to share the love of Christ through the gift of writing.

Rachael has been passionate about writing since she was a small child. She especially loved writing plays and short stories. At the age of fourteen, she wrote her first play, which was performed as a dinner theatre production by a local school.

She has been actively involved in both women's and children's ministries for over a decade. Currently, she enjoys teaching a weekly girls' Bible study, writing plays for a local homeschool group, and participating in local ministry outreaches for women and children.

Rachael currently resides in Texas with her husband and their first "child" – a playful rescue puppy named Riley! In addition to her writing, she is an enthusiastic "keeper of the home" and "helpmeet", as well as being actively involved in ministering to the women and children God has placed in her life. (Titus 2:3-5; Gen. 2:20-23)

Find Rachael Duncan at: http://christiankindlenews.com/our-authors/rachael-duncan/

Made in the USA
San Bernardino, CA
19 February 2019